Th   ·

The End
of the
Yellow House

Alan Bilton

W Watermark
Press

Also by Alan Bilton

The Sleepwalkers' Ball
The Known and Unknown Sea
Anywhere Out of the World

For Pamela

Published in UK by Watermark Press 2020

© Alan Bilton 2020

The moral right of Alan Bilton to be identified as the author of
this work has been asserted by her in accordance with the Copyright,
Designs and Patents Act, 1988

A CIP catalogue record for this book is available from the British Library

ISBN: 978-1-8380043-0-9

Typeset in Book Antigua

Cover design by nb-design.com

Printed by Imprint Digital

Watermark Press
Unit 77 Penn Street, Duo Tower, London, England, N1 5FF
www.watermarkpress.co.uk

"I am obliged to report that at the present
moment the Russian Empire is run by lunatics"
– MAURICE PALÉOLOGUE, *French Ambassador
to Russia, 1916*

"The rye's on fire, the seed's all dead,
But who will save it and risk his head?
… An army of madmen has broken loose,
And like Mamai, they'll scourge all Rus"
– IVAN BUNIN, '*The Vigil*'

one
1

When Nikolai found the body, Chief Superintendent Lepinov had been missing for two days. Nikolai – who'd spent most of this time drinking heavily, chasing after Alyona, and quarrelling with Shiskin the cook – had been despatched by Starchenko to fetch a bottle of Holy Water for the Tsar – the usual nonsense about his sickly son, no doubt. Alas, the inebriated Nikolai was a poor choice for such a task; by the time he reached the monastery, he'd lost his bucket, his hat, and – somewhat inexplicably – both boots. Cursing his luck, the old yardman tied the bottle to a long pole and lowered it into the gloom, all the time struggling not to lose his grip and topple in beside it. After a minute or two of effort, the rough pole bumped against something large and round: the Chief Superintendent's arse. Nikolai lit the Icon lamp and spat. No, Chief Superintendent Lepinov was not looking well. Twisted limbs, bloated torso, broken back – and on his head resided a stout padded box, odd bits of tubing sprouting from the top. Removing it, the yardman could see where the Superintendent's skull had been folded in like dough, his eyes seeming to say 'What counter revolutionary force has robbed me of my role in the world struggle?' Nikolai stared at Lepinov with some degree of bitterness. He had lost his good winter boots for this?

By the time the yardman had lolloped barefoot to the Yellow House, it was already time for supper, so the old man sat straight down to eat, fearing that if he announced the Chief Superintendent's death, his belly would remain empty for hours. A sign above his head read 'Comrades! For the sake of your health, preserve cleanliness!', though the place smelt of cabbage, disinfectant and piss.

Ignoring the ceaseless prattling of Zvonkov and Shiskin, Nikolai spooned in his gruel, vague thoughts of the dead man buzzing around his head. Once Lepinov had been here, and leant him a few kopecks to buy a bottle on his name day – well, all and good. But now Lepinov was gone and that was no shame either. No doubt somebody else would come along to bark orders and pull the old man's beard: such was the way of the world. Whether Lepinov, Lenin or Tsar Nicholas himself, there would always be somebody demanding the yard be swept, the coalscuttle emptied, or the shutters fixed. Why work up a sweat digging your own grave? As long as there was bread on the table and something to drink, give thanks to God and go find your place on the stove. Meanwhile the kasha warmed the old man's innards and after a while, the feeling started to come back to his toes.

"Nikolai!" yelled Zvonkov, his nose red with catarrh. "You were barking last night, you old dog! Out on another spree, eh, you rascal…"

"Not I," said Nikolai, mechanically shovelling food between his greasy lips.

"Not you? Foo – supping from Alexander's cup."

"It must have been the nutters," muttered Nikolai, sadly. His sadness was deep and genuine. As soon as he finished his bowl he would have to tell one of the doctors about the superintendent and then the cock would begin to crow. Poor Nikolai! Already his head throbbed and the smell of the corpse hid up his nose.

"The nutters? Not outside my window, Uncle." Zvonkov had a deeply irritating voice, hoarse and whiny at the same time. The orderly stared at Nikolai's feet. "Lost your boots, eh? Dancing

2

with the devil no doubt…"

Had Nikolai lost his boots while in his cups, on the way to the monastery, or later, down the well? In his befuddled state, it was hard to remember. Oh, what did it matter? All he wanted was for the orderly to shut his trap.

After scraping the bottom of his bowl, the yardman reluctantly made his way to the doctor's table where Zinaida Yevgrafovna was conducting yet another furious argument with her fellow physicians.

"All this talk of the mind is as bad as theologians pulling their beards out over the existence of the soul," yelled the doctor, her hands dancing up and down the table. "There is the brain, there is the nervous system, and there is the spinal chord. Everything else is simple superstition."

"Superstition?" Aleshin banged on the table with his spoon. "Are you denying that class and social factors play no role? Psychosis conforms to the laws of historical determinism like everything else."

"We are speaking of tissues, colleague doctor!" The dark rings under Yevgrafovna's eyes and her sharp and pointed nose gave her the expression of a bird of prey, though by the look of her, she hadn't eaten a mouse in quite some time. "What counts is the movement of proteins along an infinitely delicate network of tubes and fibres."

"Such talk is non-progressive and undialectic."

"All mental illnesses are brain diseases," countered Yevgrafovna, speaking as if delivering a lecture to a packed hall. "As a doctor there can be no other point of view. Frumkin?"

Frumkin's curly beard looked up from its bowl. "Me? I pat their heads and try not to let them bite." The *feldsher*, or doctor's assistant, pulled a smile out of his bag and gestured with his spoon at Zinaida. "To reason with a lunatic is folly…"

"You can dress it up however you like Comrade Yevgrafovna, but this talk of fibres and tubes is just another name for the humours. Why…" With a start, Aleshin suddenly noticed Nikolai standing there, the old yardman blinking at them like a simpleton. "Yes, well, what is it?"

"Superintendent Lepinov, your majesty, he…"

Aleshin snorted. "Dragged himself out of his ditch has he? Well…"

"No sir, Master Lepinov, he, ah…"

Nikolai's eyes seemed to roll backwards as if someone were holding him by the scruff of his neck. His hands trembled and his throat turned dry.

"What? Well? I hope that Comrade Lepinov realises that I will have to report any unauthorised absence to the Red Authorities."

"I found him with my pole, sir. Down the well, he was, curse him. With his head in a box."

Aleshin stared at Nikolai as if he were a goose who had just wandered into his study.

"A box?"

"A box, the devil take him. With horns coming out of the top." Nikolai wrung his cap's neck like a rabbit, shifting uncomfortably from foot to foot.

Aleshin, Yevgrafovna and Frumkin all stopped eating. What was the yardman saying? As if seeing Nikolai for the first time, they took in the stains on his uniform, the mud on his bare feet.

"Lepinov? Lepinov's dead?"

The three doctors exchanged glances.

"But, I saw comrade Lepinov only…" Aleshin paused. "A box, you say?"

The yardman looked at them craftily and out of nowhere began to growl.

2

Of course, in many ways the news of Chief Superintendent Lepinov's demise was no great surprise. Lepinov was an incorrigible melancholic, a chronic hypochondriac, and, despite his advanced medical training, a devoted spiritualist. He spoke of himself as "a mere visitor to this pale world" (he'd been twice arrested for tax evasion) and described Death as "his one true wife". Typically, his sentences began as a whisper and ended as a shout – almost as if he were picking up messages from the other side. The guests in the Yellow House both feared and despised him. Lepinov would inspect their tired bodies, sigh deeply, and conclude his diagnoses with the doleful conclusion that "from dust we came and to dust we shall return." "We are all but temporary guests here," he averred, "awaiting that invitation that we cannot refuse". As a scientist, he had his eccentricities. The Superintendent refused to wear a pocket watch, because there was no such thing as time. He wouldn't allow his apartment to be cleaned because the souls of the departed lived on as dust. He clapped his hands twice upon entering a room. "I'm not long for this world," Lepinov would say at meal times – "why not add a little sugar to the kasha?"

He was also (and this despite the chronic food shortages plaguing the yellow house) enormously fat. Whilst other doctors and guests wasted away, Lepinov ballooned like a pregnant sow. No one knew from whence he received such calories. It was well known that he did secret deals with Shemiakin the Bagman, exchanging morphine for goods from the city, or (malicious tongues whispered) stealing the guests' possessions and selling them on for drugs. Despite the presence of bandits, deserters and anarchists, Lepinov was in the habit of taking long walks in the woods, returning without mushrooms or berries or roots of any kind. At night, he received unknown visitors, admitted by Nikolai, but unseen by anybody else. Yes, everything about him was odd. Urodlivy, the peasant, had cursed him. He had enormous green bags under his eyes. One of his fingernails was so long it had started to curl.

And besides – why not Lepinov? Since the war had started, Death was as likely to snatch the Chief Superintendent as any other. Typhoid was rife amongst the guests in blocks three and four. Lice, bedbugs and excrement were ubiquitous, and the Yellow House was desperately short of heat, soap and water, never mind actual medicine. Robbers, feral children and the starving often broke into the estate's outhouses, and it was a rare day in which the echo of gunfire could not be heard somewhere. If Lepinov had not taken his own life, then there was no shortage of others willing to lend a hand. Indeed, if not for the matter of the strange box – and the fact that Lepinov, for all his faults, was still Chief Superintendent, and something of the old table of ranks still persisted – a soft bed would have been quietly provided for Lepinov's bones around the back of the dispensary along with everybody else.

As it was, however, Aleshin insisted on a thorough investigation. With a barked order, Zvonkov and his son were dispatched to the old monastery to retrieve Lepinov's body from the miracle-working waters, the Chief Superintendent brought back to the house on a two wheeled cart packed in straw.

It was a melancholy journey. Nettles whipped the orderlies' legs and briars pulled at their aprons, while all the time the lantern sputtered like a fat man on the stairs.

Laid out on a slab in the old dairy, the two doctors and Frumkin the *feldsher* examined the Superintendent's corpse, poking at the dead man's lump with their scalpels. The level of decomposition suggested that he had been at the bottom of the well for some time, his hue somewhere between crayfish pink and cucumber green. Lepinov's head had been bashed in with a blunt object, his body vigorously assaulted, hairs plucked from his beard. And his soul? Heaven alone knew: only Lepinov's shade could say for sure...

The makeshift autopsy immediately threw up a series of problems. If Lepinov had died elsewhere then how did his corpse make its way to the well? Why were there no other footprints but Nikolai's amongst the mire at the old monastery gate? And given the fact that he had last been seen only the day before, why did he resemble a shank of rancid meat?

"Well, so much for the holy water," noted Frumkin, tapping Lepinov's skull.

And then there was the factor of the Superintendent's strange head-gear – a peculiar set of padded blinkers, with a small opening for the mouth and a complicated set of tubes emerging from the top.

"I'm sure I've seen something like this before," said Frumkin. "In some old medical brochure maybe... Zinaida?"

"Why would I know?" she snapped, staring hard at the box. Her normally pale cheeks turned red and then she stiffened and looked away. "The thing is an antique ... who would use such a device today?"

"Completely reactionary" sniffed Aleshin. "But how did it wind up between Lepinov's ears?"

"Lepinov squirreled away all kinds of strange junk," said

Frumkin examining the tubing. "Kinky stuff, too. But I think we can rule out suicide. Not even our glorious Superintendent could strangle himself and drown at the same time."

Aleshin fastidiously wiped his gold-rimmed spectacles with a cloth. "A conspiracy … some kind of seditious scheme…"

A name popped into Frumkin's mind: *The Tranquilizer*, was that it? Lepinov was certainly tranquilized now. His tongue stuck out of the box like a cuckoo from a clock.

After the preliminary autopsy, the members of the medical team retired to the consultation room and began to smoke. It was nearly dawn by now and all present felt a little giddy and a little sick.

"Okay," said Frumkin. "What now?"

Aleshin argued that the Chief Superintendent's demise was a clear case of counter revolutionary activity, and that the matter should be reported to the Red Guard without delay. Zinaida Yevgrafovna countered that the Bolshevik authorities lacked uniforms, ammunition or footwear, and were consequently consigned to their barracks at Chermavka: better to send someone to the railroad at Yamskai, where at least some kind of police officer might be found.

Aleshin made a swift, obscene gesture. "The police are no more than relics of the old bourgeois regime. Why bother? The dictatorship of the proletariat requires a revolutionary form of justice."

Yevgrafovna and Frumkin could not agree – murder was murder, even in wartime. Eventually it was agreed that Petr, Zvonkov's son, should take the last remaining horse and try to make contact with some kind of revolutionary authority. Given the circumstances, this was by no means a straightforward plan. Chermavka was nearly twenty miles away, and with the October rains, the roads were swiftly turning into thick rivers of mud.

There were other dangers too. Ryabovsky's estate had been ransacked and abandoned. The nearest village, Chulm, was without any adult males since the Red Army conscripted the peasants, taking deserters' families hostage. Davydovka was some twenty versts in the opposite direction, Voronezh beyond that–that is, if Denikin and the Volunteer Army hadn't already overrun it. Yes, the Yellow House was but a tiny island in a great sea of blood; it was only a matter of time before the tide broke angrily o'er it.

Aleshin loosened his necktie and checked his watch: nearly six. If Zvonkov's son left at dawn, he might reach the Red Army before nightfall. Despite Yevgrafovna's protestations, there was no point in heading toward the railway: the lines would inevitably be sabotaged, telegraph wires cut.

Petr was sent for and arrived looking sleepy and scared. Tufts of his hair pointed in all directions like a way sign.

"Comrade Zvonkov Junior," began Aleshin, clicking his heels together. "It is the people's will that you should go from this place and make contact with the larger Red forces of progression."

Petr blanched and immediately began to cough, his chest as clogged as a peasant's chimney.

"Tell them Chief Superintendent Lepinov has been murdered and we require assistance," said Yevgrafovna. "Also, some bandages, and a little sausage..."

The boy looked at them blankly. "The chief?"

Aleshin stepped forward in a military manner. "Proceed South East toward the Red encampment at Chermavka. Avoid peasants, Greens, and Counter-Revolutionary forces. Maintain iron discipline at all times."

The boy's eyes widened. "The chief is dead?"

Yevgrafovna stepped forward and stared intently at Aleshin. "Chermavka? No, no, the station at Yamskai. The station master,

Kukushkin will…"

"Kukushkin? That fool couldn't pluck a goose. No, no, report to Comrade Ablemov and…"

"This is a matter for the police not the military…"

Aleshin slapped his sides in exasperation. "Comrade Yevgrafovna, there are no police. Revolutionary justice is the prerogative of…"

"Justice? And what is this Red Justice? When soldiers last came, the nurses all had to hide."

Petr stared at the various pale and angry doctors and began to cough. The truth was, he had no idea of the way to Chermavka, or the railway line either.

"So," said Frumkin, "do we give the pup a gun?"

The group fell silent.

"No, no, the lad will be fine," said Aleshin. "Eh, boy? Mm, what do you say?"

The doctor patted his head and Zvonkov arrived with his good winter coat. "Don't get mud on it," he said. "And don't put anything heavy in the pockets."

Outside rain had started to fall in crude, thick strokes. The avenue of birch trees lined up as if before a firing squad. It was just about dawn.

"God speed son," said Zvonkov, with some emotion. "The Lord protect you and bring you home."

Petr nodded. Beyond the fence with the rusty nails lay the outside world, open like a door.

"Stick to the roads. Watch out for wolves. Don't let anyone steal your coat."

The lad coughed like a steam train.

"Here, take this. 'Tis a protrective charm, belonging to your late mother. Of course it did her no good, but still…"

Petr wiped his nose and placed the charm around his neck and a small crust of bread in a bag. Yana the horse whinnied and looked back at him. Her eyes were large and black and stared at the boy as if she knew exactly how all this was going to pan out.

3

Exhausted by events, Gregory Aleshin retired to his apartment and lay down on his bed. So: historical determinism had decided that he should succeed Lepinov as Chief Superintendent. Well, politically, who else was appropriate? Yevgrafovna was a crude materialist and Frumkin a fraud. Yes, the responsibility for the Yellow House now fell entirely and irrevocably upon his head – a not entirely comfortable position given the proximity of the White Army and the bands of outlying Cossacks. Still, the good doctor knew that, ideologically speaking, he was the only one up to the task.

Aleshin was the youngest of the three doctors, but compensated for this by adopting a mature, military manner entirely in keeping with the seriousness of the situation. In this his long, fair hair, smooth chin and gold-rimmed spectacles (he was extremely shortsighted) clashed unavoidably with the Red Army uniform he wore beneath his doctor's smock, but there was little he could do about that. His features were pretty and his watery eyes a little dreamy. He countered this by speaking as harshly as possible, barking at nurses, orderlies and colleagues in a strident voice borrowed from one of Tolstoy's generals.

His favourite book was Chernyshevsky's *What is to be Done?*, and he modelled himself on its hero, Rakhmetev. Stern, ascetic, and unemotional, Chernyshevsky's protagonist exercised daily, ate only meat, and slept on a bed of nails to curb sexual desires.

Like Aleshin, Rakhmetev had no time for the inessential: only politics and science were real, everything else an effeminate distraction ('Yes, yes,' thought the doctor, underlining his favourite passages in red.) From Chernyshevsky's tome, Aleshin imbibed the need for rigorous personal discipline, sexual abstinence, and the strict renunciation of any personal feelings or thoughts. All that was soft and tender had to be strangled, he averred; the New Man must be single minded in the cold pursuit of the future. And what future was this to be? Why, a future of timetables, efficiency and maximum productivity. In a black notebook, Alshin recorded his meals, reading list and exercise regime. The figures were exact and the handwriting neat. Sometimes Aleshin's record keeping took up so of his evening that he didn't have time to sleep.

This morning though, which is to say, the morning after Lepinov's demise, he permitted himself a moment to rest and reflect. So: Lepinov's wish had finally been granted – he had gone to lie with his bride. Yes, well, all well and good: a flabby recidivist like Lepinov had no place within the ruthless organization of the revolutionary vanguard. As for his murderer, nu, the Red Guard would deal with that: take the dog out and put him up against a wall.

In truth, of course, Aleshin was well aware of the shortcomings of the armed representatives of the People's Will. The Red soldiers who had turned up at the house over a month ago had been dirty, drunk and insolent: they had attempted to rape Alyona, and the Three Graces (as the nurses were called) had been forced to take refuge inside Lepinov's private chambers. The purpose of the soldiers' visit, as far as Aleshin could judge, had been theft, extortion and intimidation, and they had gone about this in a completely undirected manner. They demonstrated none of the iron will, which Trotsky, as Commissar for War, had asserted, was the prime asset of the Red Soldier; rather, they had shot at the windows of the bathhouse and taken away as many vegetables as they could drunkenly stack on their cart.

Aleshin rubbed his sore eyes and tried to sleep. Taking over the running of the Yellow House, countering the rampant waste and inefficiency of Lepinov's reign, defending the estate against the threat of Denikin's Whites: all this required pure, hard determination and absolute dedication to the cause. Socialist citizens were responsible not only for their actions, but also for their thoughts – like the mad, in a way. Aleshin elected to sleep for precisely twenty minutes and then awake refreshed.

Alas no sooner had he decided this then he was disturbed by a frantic rapping at his door. It was Old Man Starchenko, the Yellow House's ancient *Prizhivalschik* or Estate Manager. The old man's features resembled a candle that had been allowed to burn down; at any moment, his eyes seemed ready to dribble down past his nose.

"Your excellency… I am most sorry to disturb you, sir, but, well…"

Aleshin stared at the old retainer through his gold-rimmed spectacles.

"Yes? Yes, well, spit it out…"

"Doom sir! Destruction! The whole globe is spinning from its axis and will dash itself to bits."

Aleshin rubbed his forehead and waited for the ancient servant, dressed as if still living in Catherine's day, to calm down. Starchenko was as giddy as a schoolgirl, but nobody knew his way round the estate like he.

"Well?"

"Churkin, sir… he's dead too."

The doctor leapt from his bed.

"Dead? How so?"

"Hung sir. By his very own neck."

"Hung? Nonsense, nonsense … well, let me see".

Blinking in the insipid light Aleshin followed the old man's back to the servant's quarters, the part of the estate that had changed least since the days of the Old Count. Churkin was permitted to sleep in a small room there, though nobody could quite remember whether he was a servant, patient or guest. Tirelessly enthusiastic and hard working, Churkin was happy to chop wood, wash clothes, sweep floors – everything which Nikolai and Alyona were supposed to do, but about which they complained so bitterly. True, Churkin was a little touched, and babbled all sorts of religious nonsense if you let him, but he rarely complained, never shirked, and invariably carried out all orders to the letter.

And there he was, his feet hanging twelve inches above the floor, a noose of coarse binding twine around his neck. Aleshin noticed with distaste the spread of brown on his leggings, the pool of urine beneath his toes. With Churkin gone, who would clean up now?

Starchenko leaned in with his lamp. Churkin looked very much surprised and more than a little confused.

"He must have heard of the Chief Superintendent's death and … oh heaven preserve us, sir!"

"Suicide? Nonsense – suicide is impossible in revolutionary conditions."

In truth, the room was so small, to hang one's self would indeed require great presence of mind. It looked as if with one small step Churkin could hop down and recommence his duties.

"A great darkness," whispered Starchenko. "The opening of a vast and terrible void…"

Aleshin stood on tiptoes and examined Churkin's dirty, purplish neck. "This is intolerable. Get him down man, get him down."

"Me sir? Oh dear, well…"

Starchenko made such a hash of it that Aleshin was forced to try to undo the bindings himself. Unfortunately, he couldn't cut the twine either.

"Damn and blast it, you dog…"

Churkin swung between them like a pendulum, whilst outside Ilya the cock began to crow – a full hour late, reflected Aleshin, scratching his nose.

"Go and get Nikolai – or Zvonkov, at least. There must be some kind of blade in the house."

Starchenko shuffled out, leaving Aleshin alone with the corpse. The body hung there, heavy and awkward, filling the room entirely.

'A shame about the simpleton,' thought the doctor. 'The revolution requires broad backs.'

Glancing around, he patted down Churkin's jerkin, something long and heavy weighing down one pocket. What was that thing? The object was so heavy that the fabric was torn, a dirty strip of rag hanging down from the side. The doctor removed the offending item and then gazed back at the corpse. What a fool, what a goose! Churkin's tongue stuck out like a child trying to taste snow.

By the time Starchenko returned with Zvonkov, the object was gone, Churkin's box and satchel emptied entirely.

In his large, well-appointed room above the gymnasium, the Tsar impatiently awaited Starchenko and the vial of Holy Water from Saint Leonilla's well. Ho, what was keeping the doddery fool now? Things were going from bad to worse all over the estate. The soup was awful, the bread mixed with straw, the plates badly washed: yes, the forces of chaos were squatting at the very gates. How the Tsarina put up with this was quite beyond him: she could not abide dirt, sloth or unsatisfactory service of any kind, and flew in to a rage if so much as a hair were found in her *kvass*. One could only imagine that she was distracted from the times they were living in by her ceaseless maternal concern for Alexei – the child for whom the life-giving waters of Saint Leonilla were required. Poor Alexei; at the thought of his son, the Imperial Autocrat's eyes turned damp and pale. Fishing in his mouth, another tooth plopped out: soon his mouth would be as soft as a carp's. Yes, tooth by tooth, brick by brick, the old world was crumbling. He was no longer permitted to tour the Imperial garden, his Royal couch had been impounded, he hadn't had a proper bowel movement for weeks. While he remained cooped up in this room all of Rus was ablaze.

Finally, a soft knock was heard and his Imperial Majesty called "Come."

Starchenko arrived looking terribly distracted, his frock coat stained, and wig skew-whiff. His whole body looked as if he had been placed in an apple press, his nose bending over to sniff his toes.

"The water?"

"Here, your majesty."

In reality, Starchenko had swiftly filled an old bottle with water from the communal butt: what did it truly matter? At least he'd remembered to top it with the requisite cloth.

"Yes, yes, very good…" said the Tsar, moving his hand across the stopper whilst mumbling something vaguely resembling a prayer. Then the Tsar paused and stared at Starchenko intently. "Last night I dreamed that you were a pickle. What do you suppose this means?"

"I have no idea your majesty."

"Further misfortune, no doubt."

With this, the Tsar seemed to grow distracted, and he absent-mindedly sipped from the bottle himself.

"Yes, we have been born into dark times…"

"Indeed your majesty."

"At night, sparrows fly in and pluck at my beard with their tiny little beaks. Peck, peck, peck! And when they sing they sound just like a speech by that Jew, Kerensky. How can this be?"

"I don't know your majesty."

"Well – there it is. Take this cup to my boy. Tell Alexandra that I love her and long to caress her hand once more."

"Of course, your majesty."

The Tsar was naked below his shirt and strained fearfully upon his commode – alas, to no avail. All that was released was a silent, sulphurous blast of air.

4

Before her expulsion from the Advanced Psychiatric Institute in Moscow, Zinaida Yevgrafovna had felt herself to be teetering on the edge of a great intellectual discovery. That madness was a degenerate condition, handed on from generation to generation was well understood. Alcoholism, idiocy, sterility – all these were passed between parties via some kind of defective germ plasm, as the case of congenital syphilis plainly showed. But what was the exact nature of the vessel in which this tainted cargo set sail? For Hippocrates, the answer to the mysteries of wellbeing lay in the humours: phlegm, bile, gastric juices, all the fluid substances of man. Hence the physician's desire to purge the individual, whether by vomiting, sweating or the extraction of blood, rebalancing the elements, thereby draining the excess. Though the notion of humours had since been supplanted by an understanding of the nervous system, something of the sense of the body's internal sea remained. Man was nearly all liquid, biology taught, his mind prone to spring tides and autumn floods. In a way, the discovery of an intimate waterway of fibres and tubes only served to strengthen the suspicion that somewhere in the viscous tunnels of the body lay the source of all of mankind's unhappiness.

Zinaida had been expelled from the Institute after the revelation she'd been caught secretly infecting her patients with Rat Bite Fever, a febrile agent intended to cleanse the brain. Although cleared of any criminal intents (her subjects were drawn from the ranks of the very lowest kind of lunatic) Yevgrafovna had nevertheless been quietly farmed out to the provinces – to the Yellow House at Bezumiye more precisely, where her once glittering intellectual career seemed destined to sink beneath provincial mud.

When she'd arrived, some fifteen years ago, the sanatorium still functioned primarily as a spa, its 'cure' dependent upon the so-called *Christy* waters of Saint Leonilla's well. That this Miracle Making elixir was pure superstition was clear to all. That the whole set up was essentially a moneymaking racket for the Sanatorium's Chief Superintendent – first Bezenchuk and then Lepinov – was also beyond doubt. And yet, slowly, somewhat reluctantly, Yevgrafovna had made her home here. This had little to do with her patients; the wealthy, aristocratic clientele who came to take the waters were of no concern to her. They were depressed and unhappy, somewhat in the manner of Chekhov's minor players, but they were not, to Yevgrafovna's mind, demonstrably ill: their ineffectual melancholy was a result of their own passivity rather than degenerate tissues. Hence, Yevgrafovna was left alone to pursue her own scientific investigations in her laboratory. Samples were taken, chemicals analysed, new elements introduced. And when the prosperous and upscale patients began to drift away, replaced by the chronic patients shipped in from Davydovka and elsewhere – well, this simply afforded Yevgrafovna the opportunity to begin to put her various medical theories into practice.

Unlike the morbid and ghoulish Lepinov, the guests admired and believed in Dr Yevgrafovna. She had no favourites and demonstrated no prejudice. Her physical examinations were flawlessly thorough, every nook and cranny professionally swabbed. The guests had no doubt that whatever the doctor removed or inserted into them was for their own good: besides, she never smelt of alcohol and her smock was as clean as November snow.

When the war with Germany began, Yevgrafovna's gender saved her from being posted to the front along with the other doctors. Instead, she was joined by lickspittle Reds (Aleshin), dubious con men (Frumkin) and peasant nurses she could easily bend to her will. But now Lepinov seemed more interested in the spirit world than profits – foo, everyone knew that without Zinaida Yevgrafovna the whole place would have gone to seed. Instead it took in wounded soldiers from the front, admitted inmates from a nearby, all but bankrupt asylum, and did its best to treat typhoid patients from both neighbouring villages and even Voronezh itself. Only when the revolution came did the Yellow House start to drift away from any earthly realm…

The day after Lepinov's death, Yevgrafovna went about her rounds in her usual energetic and efficient manner. She checked that the bedding had been boiled, the dispensary hadn't been broken into, there were no animals in the consulting room. Afterwards she toured the typhus wards (wards that, characteristically, both Aleshin and Frumkin tended to shy away from), encouraged the guests in ward five to exercise, and made sure that the chronics in ward three were vigorously washed and scrubbed.

The first Yevgrafovna heard about Churkin was whilst she was bleeding the guests there: milking time on the farm, as Frumkin put it. Nadya, the youngest, darkest and shortest of the Three Graces, arrived to assist, her eyes already puffy from crying.

"Colleague Nadya," said Yevgrafovna, appraising her depressive condition and sore lids. "What is wrong? Are you upset about Chief Superintendent Lepinov?"

"Lepinov? That creep?" Nadya dabbed here eyes. "No, no – it's Ivan – the sweet soul."

Yevgrafovna started. "Ivan? Ivan Churkin? Why, whatever do you mean?"

"Zvonkov told us. Strung up his was – by his neck. The little dove! And such a kind, Christian boy."

Yevgrafovna couldn't believe it. Churkin gone, and she the last to know? In a fury, she marched over to Aleshin's office and knocked twice on the young doctor's head.

Aleshin regarded her with weary indulgence.

"Comrade Churkin has been assassinated by unknown class elements. I conducted a comprehensive investigation and concluded that the cause of death was asphyxiation by means of twine. I then gave leave to Nikolai to bury him in the small field behind the dispensary."

"Buried?" Yevgrafovna could not believe her ears. "Do you mean to say you've already inhumed the remains?"

"Indeed. What with the level of disease present and the severe shortage of soap, such a decision was the only progressive course of action. This is no time for female sentiment, Comrade Yevgrafovna! During wartime communism, it is imperative that..."

Yevgrafovna stared at Aleshin's boyish face and gold rimmed spectacles and felt an intense desire to smash both. "This is an outrage. How dare you presume to dispose of the evidence?"

"Evidence? Comrade Yevgrafovna, my first duty is to the maintenance of order and political morale. As the new Chief Superintendent, I simply could not allow..."

Yevgrafovna's cheeks twitched. "You? I need hardly remind you that I am the senior doctor at this institution and that as such..."

"Longest standing, perhaps ... but may I remind *you* that as the highest ranking Party member it is my responsibility to undertake complete ideological control during these revolutionary times."

Yevgrafovna looked as if one of the Typhoid patients had suddenly sneezed in her face.

"These are meaningless terms. I am the senior medical practitioner at the Yellow House and therefore…"

"Comrade Yevgrafovna," said Aleshin, coldly. "Superintendent Lepinov may have cast a blind eye at your illegal and unsanctioned experiments, but I have no intention of such leniency. Unless you wish your activities to be reported immediately to the representative of the people's army I suggest that you…"

"This is completely unacceptable," said Yevgrafovna, shaking like a leaf. "In this matter, you have no legitimacy and no jurisdiction. Your order to bury Churkin is both gratuitous and, in the circumstances, highly suspicious. When Petr returns with the police then…"

"What times do you think you are living in – those of Alexander the First? There is no law outside of Revolutionary Justice, and there is no authority except that of the party. The White dogs are sniffing at the post, Comrade Yevgrafovna – if you choose to contradict the will of the proletariat, then I cannot be held responsible for the consequences."

Yevgrafovna wanted to strangle the young pup, but what else could she do? Instead of snapping Aleshin's glasses, she angrily took her leave, the black bile in her spleen bubbling away inside her.

Despite her misgivings, there was nowhere else to go but Frumkin's. The *feldsher* was strolling near the old orangery with one of the newly arrived guests from Davydovka: Martynov, or something. For some reason Frumkin kept the new arrivals as far away from Yevgrafovna and Aleshin as possible – to try out his so-called 'talking cure', she surmised. Frumkin was chatting away with Martynov like Dr Ragin in Chekhov's famous story. The two of them seemed to be sharing some kind of a joke and Zinaida watched Frumkin's shoulders fairly shake with mirth.

"Colleague Frumkin? Colleague Frumkin, a word if you please…"

"What? Oh, sure, sure." He turned back to the tall, bearded inmate and patted him on the back. "Um, you know your way back to your room don't you? Oh, right, off you go."

Playing with his curly hair, Frumkin wandered over. The *feldsher* was short, jumpy and fuzzy, like a recently escaped sheep. His lively eyes glittered with a sceptical amusement.

"Zinaida! You're looking as fetching as ever. Have you boiled that smock? No? Your hair?"

Scowling, Yevgrafovna set out the details of Churkin's burial and Aleshin's ascendance to the throne. Frumkin shrugged.

"Hey, if he wants to put his neck in the noose, that's his business. We have a saying amongst our people: get yourself noticed, get yourself problems. Come on – let's walk."

So saying, Frumkin took Yevgrafovna's arm and promenaded with her toward the dispensary.

"We both know Aleshin is an idiot. Revolutionary this and ideological that – it's like he's cramming for some test. None of it means anything, probably even less." Frumkin tickled his curls. "The thing is to keep our heads down and see who turns up at our door first. If it's the Reds, then 'Hello Comrade, welcome to the proletariat struggle.' If it's the Whites, then 'Down with Red Terror.' And if it's the Cossacks then I'll be hiding under Alyona in the pantry."

"Aleshin's claim to promotion lacks all legitimacy. The pup is barely out of short trousers. What gives him any right to…"

"Well, he's a party member, not a woman or a *zhid*. But if he wants to play at being Lenin, let him shave his head and grow a beard. Why worry? If there's a search, rustle and tell them you're paper."

"And Churkin?"

"Churkin was a sweet kid but no brain. Maybe he saw something, or maybe he got in the way. Who knows? Aleshin may talk of throttling the bourgeoisie but I don't see him as the strangling kind. Death by a thousand memos, maybe…"

Yevgrafovna shook her head as if trying to clear it. What was that just above her hair-line? Dried blood? "And Lepinov? Perhaps Aleshin saw only one way to create a vacancy."

"It had to be somebody strong enough to drag Lepinov's belly over to the well, and trust me, that's no small undertaking. Aleshin? He stores weights under his bed but still breaks into a sweat trying to pick up his dictionary. Look, I'm no great fan of revolutionary discipline either, but let Aleshin wear out his jack boots for a while. When the Whites come they'll be kicking the air like Churkin's."

Was Frumkin right? And yet his flippancy irritated Yevgrafovna and seemed to mask some deeper purpose.

"I'm not sure that you grasp the serious nature of the situation," she growled. "There is a murderer at large in the Yellow House and we have no idea as to their reason or purpose."

"My dear Zinadia," said Frumkin, opening his palms. "There are hundreds of murderers out there, just waiting to do us in. What do you want us to do? Night has fallen over Russia. Wake me up when the cock crows."

And with that he kissed Yevgrafovna on the hand, and strolled back to the orangery like a holiday maker taking in the air. All around him, the rain fell like curses.

two
1

From the Yellow House, Petr had headed north toward the railroad; of Red soldiers, he had seen enough, may they be covered up to their heads. Besides, he had never seen a train and had only the vaguest notion of what one might be: like a great stove on wheels, according to Old Nikolai. At first, the rain didn't bother him; in this part of Russia, who didn't know rain? Nor did the size of the outside world frighten or appal. He was a man now, a grown up, the first shoots of wheat growing on the fields of his face. What kind of bird takes fright at the first sight of the sky? No, Petr felt proud to be outside the estate gates on his own, entrusted with a matter of great importance. If only his wretched coughing would stop…

Before today, the estate had been his entire life. True, he had been out hunting with his father, and as a child had been allowed to roam freely betwixt the woods and the monastery, but that was before the coming of war and war's best friend. Since then Petr had been no further than the elms malingering outside the gates like beggars. 'Don't even think about it,' hissed his father. 'If the Reds see you, you'll be shining Lenin's shoes before sundown.' Spittle formed beneath his father's moustache, and his yellow eyes glowed intensely. 'You can't see the world from inside a box'.

So it felt doubly strange to be wearing his father's astrakhan coat, riding Yana (more of a pony than a horse, but still) and whittling a rough riding crop from the grass. The meadows were untended, the rye gone to seed. Every once in a while a grey rabbit darted out, while a keen-eyed kite circled overhead. Yes, the world turned like a mill; even in the rain, finches quarrelled ceaselessly over the berries in the hedgerows and jackdaws hopped from tree to tree. Yana flicked her tail and swayed from side to side like an old woman praying at church. One of her legs was lame and she always tended toward the left.

A feeling of intense freedom occupied Petr for most of the morning: after that, he simply felt bored. The mud clung to Yana's hooves and rain trickled down the back of Petr's collar. The sky looked like black rye dipped in milk. Horse and rider passed green and yellow huts, broken fence posts, odd bits of corrugated iron. The tall white cross marking the staging post had vanished, most likely dug up and carted away. There were no wheel tracks, no footprints. It felt as if all of humanity had fled this place. The kite was still following him, turning in slow, silent circles. The sound of the rain on Petr's hat was like a gloved fist on a door.

To evade the mud Petr drove Yana away from the path and into the trees, but even here the ground was boggy and treacherous, the roots grabbing at Petr's feet and briars catching on Yana's mane. Beneath the canopy, it was as dark as the hour before the lamps are lit. Cruel mouths sneered from the tree trunks and branches grabbed for Petr's hat. If only he were back by the stove, eating pancakes with Alyona and Churkin! Instead, his boots were caked in mud, his coat as wet and heavy as a bear. Every step seemed to take him into another hole. 'Foolish cub,' jeered the crows. 'Don't you know where all this will end?'

Still, at least the impenetrable green of the birch-wood provided some cover, as well as a little respite from the rain. The boy swallowed sour black chunks of bread and Yana chewed on some bracken. Had he been this way before? He remembered his father throwing a stone at a snake, the taste of dill pickles, an old peasant selling bait. Yes, this was the way to Chulm – the village of women. Petr's heart began to thump. His father had not ventured to Chulm since the Reds had come to take away their men. The word was that their women still waited for them, bringing in the autumn harvest and protecting their village as best they could. Old Nikolai swore that the women were even more savage than the Reds: "Don't let your balls fall into their hands!" he whispered, his beard full of food.

And yet despite such warnings, Petr faltered. Did Dusya still live at Chulm? Petr pictured her large black eyes and bluish lips, like an infant struggling to be born. What could he say? Dusya had bewitched him. On her *sarafan* she had drawn circles with eyes, flowers with mouths, fish with human legs. She wore a magic amulet and possessed the ability to cast the evil eye. Once she had shown Petr her bare behind and made her moon-like buttocks speak.

O Dusya! For a time she had come to the Yellow House almost every week, arriving with cucumber, juniper berries and mushrooms, and returning home laden down with pots, pans and bedding of all kinds. She was no older than Petr but carried herself like a grown up matron, driving a hard bargain and slapping Nikolai when he got too close. Alyona, who was terribly jealous, had claimed that Dusya was a dark spirit, and afterwards the servant girl had become terribly sick, throwing up outside the fruit cellar all night, her hair mysteriously green. Was Dusya a witch? Petr dreamt about her at night and in the morning, his bed was wet with dew. She smelt of bonfires and pine needles. Nikolai said that to touch her was like grasping a nettle. Her bare feet seemed to end in claws, like a chicken.

What had they exchanged? Gifts, kisses, caresses. She gave him a carved figure whilst he brought her poisons from the infirmary. When he touched her almost perfectly flat chest she answered him with riddles.

"Who do the dead marry? Where do they hold the bridal feast?"

"Marry?" said Petr, his hand seeking out a hard, dark nipple.

"A coffin's too small for a marital bed. No, the dead seek other chambers, other doors. And in the morning the groom's beard is as white as frost."

Petr withdrew his hand and nodded. The girl's eyes were as dark as the black earth.

And then, just when Petr had prepared his heart to speak, Dusya had vanished. In her place, a spotty young lad arrived, wide and dull as a dung cart. Where was Dusya? The lad didn't know. Visitors to Chulm never mentioned her, and her silhouette could no longer be seen working in the fields. Then the Reds had come and contact with Chulm snapped like a branch

Petr caressed his horse sadly. 'Yes', Yana's eyes seemed to say. 'Finding happiness is like catching sunlight in one's hat.' Petr patted Yana's mane and ran his fingers along her neck. No, better not go to Chulm: he had been ordered to stay away from the villages, and feared his father's stick. Besides, even if he did find Dusya, what would he say? Fingers of rain slid between the trees and thence inside his coat. Frogs croaked. Leaves stuck to Yana's hooves. In such a place, why linger? Petr's cough rattled like stones in a pipe.

Instead of heading straight back to the road, Petr followed a rough hunting track through the wood, the flattened earth coming and going between the trees. He passed the rusty stain of a peat marsh, the blood red berries of dog rose. The silence grew deeper, as if they were heading not into the woods, but rather down a deep, dark hole. In places, spectral patches of mist hid the ground; at the base of tall trees, Petr could make out strange pale mushrooms, the colour of bone. A fallen larch made him think of the lost tombs of the Bogatyrs, the branches gathered around its torso like mourners, oil-cloth leaves and leathery bark. Everything here was old and broken and brown. It was hard to imagine that anything living had ever been in such a place before.

The track seemed to be taking Yana further and further from the main road, and Petr began to fear that he would be unable to find the way back. Branches stooped low and twigs tickled his nose. Walking alongside Yana, Petr whispered 'Good girl, little mother, little goose.' Yana's eyes were two great saucers, ringed with sticky tears, and Petr's heart gave a lurch of love. 'Yes,' he thought, 'put everything you have on the little horse, she can bear it all…'

Eventually boy and horse emerged atop a high bank, the post road just a few feet below them. The mud was as high as a carriage wheel and the way stones barely visible, but for the first time Petr could make out deep ruts through the mire – some carriage had come this way before him. What did they bring: a snare or an egg?

He heard the first shot – a feint, high pop, somewhere up the road – without quite realising what it was. But then a second shot rang out much closer – someplace behind his ear, it felt. Petr toppled from Yana's back and hid himself amongst the nettles and leaves. More thin, high bursts could be heard ahead. Yana seemed not to notice and regarded Petr curiously. The boy's face was pale, his throat trembling as if trying not to bark.

The shooting went on for a few more rounds, but more distant now, a vague buzzing somewhere between his ears. Petr took hold of Yana's reins and led her back amongst the trees. He still felt the need to cough but struggled to contain it. Yana wanted to stop and eat bracken but Petr pulled her on. Where could they hide? A forlorn looking path led from the trees across an untended meadow. Rotting hayricks, now empty, hunched in the rain like rabbits. A little further along was a half-collapsed barn and some kind of green latticework. Beyond that could be glimpsed the squat shape of a stone bathhouse, the walls stained green and black.

Petr crouched beside Yana and waited to see whether the lazy gunfire would stop. Outside the *banya* cut grass had been heaped in great shaggy mounds, but otherwise there were few signs of human agency. Petr guessed that he had reached the outskirts of the old Ryabovsky estate, destroyed by peasants during the first days of the Revolution. The family had fled, and Petr had heard tell from Nikolai how the raiders had over-turned furniture, smashed family heirlooms, and torn up rugs and furnishings. Paintings had been ripped from their frames and libraries burnt down: looting the looters, the Reds called it. Tools, farm machinery and food were taken back to nearby villages, everything else broken beyond recognition.

Tethering Yana, Petr cautiously peered into the *banya's* mouth. Instead of the scent of birch leaves and fragrant grasses, the bathhouse smelt powerfully of sweat and piss. The tubs were full of foul, bespattered straw, the marble slabs coated in a fine layer of dirt. It was hard to imagine what this place would have been like back in the days of the Ryabovskys: the slap of cold water hitting the stone, the hiss of steam, the swish of the swollen switch of leaves. The place smelt of pigs, but the pigs had departed too.

Keeping one eye on the door, Petr advanced a little further. The washroom was cracked and flaking, the white walls covered in spots, like the bodies of the old. On one side was the chain one pulled to release a wooden cask suspended just above it; on the other a wooden platform where linen winding sheets had once been kept. Mice had made a nest in one of the old boxes, and there were tiny beetles everywhere. For Starchenko, such desecration would have marked the absolute desolation of Russia itself; for Petr, who had only the vaguest memory of when the bathhouse at the House still functioned, it seemed no more than a convenient place to hide.

Stumbling about in the gloom, Petr heard Yana whinnying outside. Had she heard something? He was about to turn back, when he sensed a deeper patch of darkness ahead of him, some sort of perfect square, like a hole cut out of the world. What was it – an opening, some strange pocket of space? Petr wanted to investigate further, but had neither lamp nor torch – and besides, Yana was making a terrible fuss outside, and he needed to go and calm her. Shaking his head, Petr turned and saw something round and black right in front of him. For a moment, the shape seemed confused with the tunnel into which he'd just been staring, and it took him a few seconds to identify it as a barrel of a gun.

Petr's hand tightened around his protective charm.

"Oh," he said, and then everything fell into place.

2

Zvonkov had been attempting to seduce Alyona by reading salacious passages from *The Night Orgies of Rasputin* to her, late at night. Alyona's cheeks were as red as a beetroot, a faint shimmer on her upper lip. "Disgusting!" she whispered. "Terrible. Oh, read on…" Alyona was sitting by the stove with her apron balled up and her hands between her legs, a tall, thin girl, her shoulder blades as pointed as knitting needles. Zvonkov was as close as he dared, careful not to upend the lard. Nikolai the yardman pretended to sleep, occasionally letting out a snort of derision or loud sniff, while Shiskin the cook limped in from time to time, usually with a pint pot and a brush. The Tsarina was tied up in Rasputin's bedchamber. Rasputin busy with a lady in waiting whilst the Tsarina looked on. It was very, very late.

"'Tis because she's a German," announced Shiskin, sniffing suspiciously at a pail. "Germans eat all sorts of things: crows, leaves, mice. They even add milk to their sausages, though the Bible proscribes it."

Lean and toothless, it was impossible to guess Shiskin's age or place of origin: Tatar, some whispered. Rogue hairs sprouted from both chin and skull, like weeds trying to find vague purchase.

"If I were the Tsar," mumbled Nikolai, speaking as if in his sleep. "If I were Nicholas, well, by God…"

"Germans are as they are because of their digestion. They can't help it. Too many beans leads to war."

The kitchen smelt of a mixture of warm milk, bacon fat and vegetables. Strings of onions dangled from the smoke-blackened roof, mice rustling amongst them.

"The Tsarina's face was distorted by fear and desire," recited Zvonkov. "As she struggled in her bounds the ropes pulled tighter around her chest and her breath came in urgent gasps…"

"The Tsar's too soft with her," spat Nikolai, rolling over to one side. "Everyone knows – the more you beat your woman, the tastier the soup."

"Shut up you old goat," cried Alyona, swiping at him with a frying pan. "Zvonkov is reading… and such a nice voice too…"

Zvonkov bowed and continued with his book. In truth, the dog-eared copy (procured from Shemiakin the Bagman) continued many words he could not understand, but he had wit enough to invent things, as well as a boundlessly scurrilous imagination. "Rasputin's eyes glowed with an unearthly fervour," he read in that strange breathless voice of his, "eyes which had gazed upon Woman's most intimate treasures…"

"Even German soup is odd," said Shiskin, mopping the top of his head with a rag. "They add moss and pond water to it, as well as cold lumps of lard. And as for the seasoning … well, I'd rather eat with the pigs."

"All Germans are dogs," spat Nikolai. "And the Tsarina filled the court with them. Traitors, swine, scum! Nikolai should have had about her with a stick."

Varva the cat strolled over to see what was going on, rubbing up against Zvonkov intently. She was a small, grey smudge, skinny as a wishbone, with a flattened tail where a cart had rolled over it. She now spent all of her time begging for food in Shiskin's kitchen, no longer deigning to go outside and hunt for mice. If you stroked her side, her ribs felt like a comb.

"The Black Monk no longer had any use for Nina the serving

girl," read Zvonkov in his hoarse voice, one hand reaching out toward Alyona, the other cradling his book. Although schooled in both numeracy and book learning, the orderly still dressed like a peasant, his long black moustache no neater than his smock. Like Alyona, his face was flushed and ruddy.

"Serving girl?"

"I mean, lady in waiting, princess, my mistake... my finger, ah, it slipped..."

Varva rubbed herself against Zvonkov's chin and seemed to put him off his stride. "Ra, Ra, Rasputin..." he stuttered, still making cow's eyes at Alyona. His moustache quivered like a bird.

"A German will drink only beer or milk," lectured Shiskin, cradling his pan like a newborn. "A drop of good Russian vodka is like poison to them... they shrivel up and die, like a slug."

"Vodka?" said Nikolai, coming round. "If only I had a nip to get me through the night."

Zvonkov's smooth chin was now very close to Alyona's cheek, even though the cat kept getting in the way.

"Rasputin eased his powerful, masculine body alongside the Empress, a musky smell overwhelming her, his eyes seeming to penetrate to her very soul. She turned her head yet angled her body toward him, her chest pointing straight at him, as if with two daggers drawn. With a snarl he tore her night gown from her, and in an instant Alyona's bosom was exposed, her..."

"Alyona? Why you cheeky ram." And with that Alyona leapt from the stove and swung the frying pan at his head.

"I mean Alexandra..."

"I know your game, you letch..."

"Alenka, listen..."

Varva jumped from Zvonkov to Shiskin, rubbing her scrawny back against him "And yet the Germans can make magnificent cakes – I give them that..." said the cook, idling picking one nostril. "A genius for strudel."

Alyona glared at Zvonkov, one hand on the pan, the other balled up into a fist.

"Reading such filth…"

"Alenka, my kitten…"

"Filling my head with such things…"

"But…"

"Oh forget him," said old Nikolai, finally struggling to his feet. "Let's find a bottle and warm ourselves up, eh? He's a cock that can only crow."

Alyona pulled a face. "Unlike you, eh? Get away with you uncle. I'll have no grey hairs in my cup…"

The only window in the kitchen looked out onto the eternal night. The autumn wind blew at a shutter and the floorboards creaked. The night felt like a bag into which the whole world could be placed.

"Oh, come on girl – come and keep me warm on my rounds. I've a bottle stashed away and we can talk about sweet things."

Alyona placed her hands on her hips and scornfully sized up the yardman.

"A bottle? Pish, you haven't even got a pair of boots. What are those things made of – bark?"

"Don't mock me woman," he growled.

"What happened to your boots anyway?" asked Alyona, warming to her theme. "Dropped them down the well with the superintendent did you?"

"That's a filthy lie," said Nikolai, picking up his coat and looking for the lamp. "If I were a few years younger I'd take my belt to you."

"Hold now Uncle – what were you doing that night?" asked Zvonkov, inching his way back to Alyona and the stove again. "I heard you prowling around, howling like a she-wolf…"

"Rubbish."

"More like a beast than a man. What had you been supping Uncle – kerosene straight from the lamp?"

Nikolai's jaws clamped shut as if a trap and he busied himself with his lamp.

"I heard those boots of yours – dancing on Lepinov's head."

Nikolai scowled darkly.

"A man in his cups, he doesn't know what he's up to."

"Lads, lads," said Shiskin, stepping between them, still cradling the cat. "A man is dead: it does no good to talk this way."

Zvonkov raised a quizzical brow. "Aye, it was probably your meat that poisoned him."

"Meat?" said the cook. "No, Master Lepinov would not take any meat – not rabbit nor woodcock nor pork. Said that no good could come of partaking of the flesh of dead things, with their souls still swimming just above 'em. He had to have a special diet, the Superintendent, specially prepared."

"I bet he did," smirked Zvonkov. "Did him in yourself did you? What was it – mushrooms from the forest or herbs from the swamp? When the lad and I pulled him out of the well, he was the colour of a toad. Now don't tell me the sacred waters did that."

Now it was the cook's turn to glower at Zvonkov. "I didn't murder anyone," he muttered, rubbing Varva's ears. "It does no good to make jokes about the dead, the Lord take his soul."

With this all three fell silent, the only sound being the banging of the shutter and the purring of the cat. For some reason Nikolai took off his coat again and laid down his lamp. Alyona lay down sleepily by the stove. Shiskin went back to his pans.

"'Tis a shame about poor Ivan," said Alyona sleepily. "Lovely little fella, always smiling, never an unkind word."

"That's true," said Zvonkov. "He'd empty the troughs for me, and never a word of complaint."

"Aye, a good lad," said Nikolai, softly. "A good lad."

All three thought of Churkin, his crooked face, bandy legs, kind eyes. His features were a little lopsided, but when he grinned, they all seemed to fall back in to place.

"Is it true, what they say?" said Alyona to Zvonkov. "Did he do away with himself?"

"Swinging like a bell rope. But I can't believe he tied that knot himself. Why would he? Always singing about the Lord and his soul's salvation."

"An angel," whispered Alyona, sadly. "A little lamb…"

At this Zvonkov's own son came to his mind, and in that moment he felt as if his boy were in mortal danger, as if Petr were there before him, crying out in pain.

"God keep him," said Zvonkov, shutting his eyes. "The Lord keep him close."

Had he been right in letting Petr go? But what else should he do – the doctors were insistent and no one else could be spared. Still, as long as he stayed away from the woods and didn't get picked up by the Greens, the lad would be fine. Besides, he had his mother's charm and was riding Yana – a horse's head is bigger than a man's, wiser too. Zvonkov looked at Alyona's sleepy shape and felt an urgent need to caress it, a little pleasure to take away bad thoughts. Unfortunately, Alyona was crying so instead he just sat there, listening to the mice nibbling away in the gloom.

Zvonkov's wife had died nearly five years ago of women's problems, something eating away in her womb. On the night she passed, all the cupboards in their hut had blown open, the contents tumbling out as if thrown by a demon. Zvonkov and his mother in law ran to investigate, and when they came back, Mashenka's bed was pointing in the opposite direction, the dead woman face down on the pillows.

Looking back, it was as if she had called out to him one last time.

Now Zvonkov again turned his head to the darkness, straining to hear if Petr too had met some final, terrible fate. No, no, nothing: all he could hear was Shiskin banging around in the washroom and Old Nikolai hawking and coughing. Where was his son? Would the Reds help him or take him away? And how far away were Denikin and the Whites?

Nikolai seemed to have abandoned any thought of doing his rounds and lay on his coat like a dog. Shiskin finished with his chores and pulled off his apron. Varva had disappeared.

"No, t'aint right to accuse a good Christian man of acting like a German," Shiskin muttered, petulantly. "Was it my fault that the Superintendent would no longer take his meals with everyone else? Or refused to let a scrap of flesh pass his lips?"

Shiskin stared accusingly at the three figures but nobody moved.

"If he wants to eat roots and berries from the woods, then let him – learned gentleman that he is. If it pickles his insides, then good luck to him. Not my fault if his nails start to curl."

Shiskin found a spot by the stove by Nikolai, bestowing on the yardman the blackest of looks.

"Besides – who did you let in to see the superintendent every night, eh? Doors creaking past midnight, strange visitors, furtive steps…"

Nikolai was either asleep or ignoring him. After a while, Shiskin's complaints started to turn from words to mutters and growls.

"Roots and herbs… long white mushrooms … berries even the birds wouldn't eat."

The cook smacked his lips and finally fell asleep. Nikolai breathed out noisily. Only Alyona and Zvonkov remained awake.

"It's no good," murmured Alyona, "I can't stop thinking of Ivan. What harm did he do anyone that folk should string him up?"

"Shh, shh princess," said Zvonkov, still dreaming of his wife.

and son.

"He'd do whatever you asked him, little Ivan – and never a word of complaint either."

"It's all in God's hands," said Zvonkov, moving closer.

"Do anything for you, anything you asked..."

The night felt endless, a hole without end. There was a muffled crack, like a branch breaking somewhere, or a shot far away. No, thought Zvonkov, a grave can never be filled...

"Read to me Mitka," breathed Alyona. "There's still a little candle left. Read to me 'till I fall asleep..."

Zvonkov smiled and retrieved his book. "Rasputin's caresses grew more violent," he read, "the Tsarina struggling in her ecstasy and her shame. Finally, when neither body nor soul could resist any longer, she untied her knees and sweepingly succumbed. The monk fell upon her like the night. 'My darling!' she cried out, holding on to his beard, his twin burning orbs floating just above her. 'My dark priest!'"

"Just awful," mumbled Alyona, smiling. "Mitka, keep going..."

Aside from Zvonkov's voice, the kitchen was perfectly silent, the kingdom of day still many versts away. A tiny grey mouse scuttled out and looked Nikolai in the eye. Of Varva the cat, there wasn't the slightest sign, her dark smudge merged in with the night. No paws, no whiskers, no tail. Cat? There was no cat. There was a cat that really was gone.

3

Two days had passed and there was still no sign of Petr. Not that it was time to unfurl the winding sheet just yet: the roads were awful, Yana slow, and both the Red camp and the railway line very far away. Besides, the land around Bezumiye was a mess. The fields were neglected and filled with weeds, the autumn ploughing abandoned, Ryabovsky's automatic baler lying rusting in a ditch. And all the while, the mud took everything, like death.

That morning, Nadya, the youngest of the three graces, was helping Moises Frumkin with the guests in the *flügel* on the edge of the old count's estate. The guests had arrived from Davydovka some three weeks ago, but remained hidden away from the main complex to prevent the spread of typhus – though in truth, typhus was rife in the other wards, whilst the newcomers remained (thus far) mercifully exempt. Aside from one well-dressed old man who had obviously been savagely beaten, few of the guests seemed to suffer from recognisable ailments; indeed, many of them looked somewhat healthier than the doctors. Fashionably dressed, well to do, and possessing an inescapable air of urban sophistication, they seemed more at home in a literary salon than some Yellow House for the ill. Yet they too suffered from a strange malady. Upon seeing Nadya the guests would start to yell and dance and call out in strange tongues, whilst Frumkin's presence seemed to have the opposite effect: around him they acted just like ordinary folk, their peculiar symptoms appearing only upon the nurse's arrival.

"I wouldn't take it personally," said Frumkin. "Just try not to flap your arms."

Nadya didn't know quite what to make of the *feldsher* with his mop of untamed hair, large brown eyes and hooked nose – a Jew's nose, said Marya.

"Frumkin's a Jew?"

"Of course he is."

"But I thought a Jew had horns…"

"What do you think those are under his curls?"

And yet for all this, Nadya much preferred working alongside Frumkin to emptying bedpans for the others. Aleshin had beautiful hair but barked like an old man, whilst Dr Yevgrafovna treated the nurses harshly, slapping them from time to time with a small wooden bat. As for Lepinov – well, Nadya would quite happily dance on his grave.

Frumkin though, was different. He joked, whistled and didn't yell if there was too much salt in his soup. Was a *feldsher* different from a doctor? After a year at the Yellow House, Nadya still couldn't tell. All she knew was Frumkin didn't check her nails or go on about the workers' struggle with spittle on his lips.

When she brought the change of bedding, Frumkin and the guests were talking politics in the day room. The word from Davydovka was that the Sixth Army had been almost totally destroyed, the Cossacks retaking Tambov, looting and raping as they went. Artillery units had refused to join the Bolsheviks, choosing to sell their weaponry on the black market instead – an anti-tank gun had been seen for sale in the town square. Other rumours sounded more fantastical: Lenin and Trotsky had raided the National Treasury in Moscow and fled to parts unknown. Clergymen in white robes, carrying banners for 'The Salvation of

Russia', had caused the Soviet building in Bobruv to fall to the ground. The late Tsar's image had appeared above St. Isaac's Cathedral in Petrograd accompanied by a shower of feathers. To some, these were signs that the end of the Bolsheviks was nigh; others weren't quite so sure. Businessmen had been arrested and their assets confiscated. The University had been burnt down. Zhmukin, the Menshevik head of the local Soviet had been executed, his body dumped with unknown others in a quarry out of town. And all the time the food situation went from bad to worse, butter selling at forty five roubles a pound, cocoa at twenty.

"You know what the Reds are saying?" said one fellow. "'We have put you bourgeois in a bag – now we shall tie the string'."

A genteel looking woman was just launching into a diatribe on the taste of barley coffee when she noticed Nadya standing to one side with an armful of blankets; the instant she spotted the girl, she immediately began to bray like a donkey, half singing and half yelling a kind of tuneless dirge. Others around her also began to spin and hop, one elderly lady throwing herself on the floor and kicking out her legs like a fly.

"Nadya!" cried Frumkin. "Leave those here, you can change the sheets soon enough..."

Nadya nodded and slowly backed out of the room. One guest with a pince-nez was speaking in Greek, another howling. The overall effect was of a hastily choreographed pantomime, amateur hour in Bedlam.

As soon as Nadya left, the day room quietened down. A few minutes later Frumkin rejoined her, tugging on his waistcoat like some famous conductor.

"Okay," he said. "We'll give them a little more playtime and start the interviews after lunch. What do you think: Shiskin found a carp in his bath?"

Unlike the other doctors Frumkin neither prescribed medicine or physical activity. "Pills we don't have and exercise we don't need. If a Cossack is there, then run: otherwise, pull up a chair. What is there that's more fun to do standing up than sitting down?"

Instead Frumkin's therapeutic methods revolved around something he called 'the talking cure' – leisurely chats, as far as Nadya could tell. The interview sessions were invariably scheduled after meals and seemed to revolve around gossip and the meaning of dreams: ill omens, usually.

"Shouldn't we bleed them?"

"Are you crazy? Blood should be on the inside."

"But Comrade doctor Yevgrafovna…"

"I know, I know – she's bathes in the stuff. Listen, here we do things different. No sedatives, no bleeding, no purging. They talk, I write. It works for us all…"

Nadya smiled and playfully picked a long hair from his smock. "Aleshin says that you're a swindler and a bilk."

"Well, cold baths and sit-ups aren't the answer to everything, believe me. Let him worry about his guests' ideological health: if anyone asks, I'm not me, and the horse isn't mine."

Nadya rarely understood his talk of transference and sublimation, but at least with Frumkin's methods she didn't need a mop. Besides, Frumkin had a pleasant voice and lovely soft hands. Was it true that the Jews had killed Our Lord? It was hard to imagine Frumkin harming anyone.

With no opportunity to leave the Yellow House and return to their villages, the world of the nurses had shrunk to the size of the estate. Lacking any other outlet, the compass of the graces' thoughts turned inward, the nurses endlessly gossiping about the doctors and their habits: Aleshin's weight lifting, Frumkin's card playing, Zinaida's wandering hands. Naturally, now that he was dead, all talk turned to Lepinov.

"Even before he died he was cold as a fish and smelt like a corpse," snapped Nadya. "Throwing him down the well just finished the job."

Marya, the pale, blonde middle grace, nodded vigorously as she sterilised the bottles.

"'Twas some kind of evil spirit, summoned up by Lepinov himself. Remember that corridor behind his chambers? Full of all kinds of strange symbols and shapes it was. You ask me, he called up a demon and it slew him…"

"Oh, away with you," said Polina, the eldest grace. "I've been here the longest and let me tell you – that man was more interested in earthly treasures than goblins and sprites. One deal with the Reds, another with the Greens, and a third with the bandits: he'd buy coal from the devil, that fellow. His murder's no great mystery. Just days before it happened I heard him arguing with Shemiakin the bagman: now there is a man you do not cross." Polina regarded her sisters-in-mercy patronisingly. "Spirits, ghosts, fee – you don't need a demon to drag you down to Hell."

"I tell you: whatever took his breath was no earthly agent," argued Marya, her eyes wide open as if staring at the devil right now. "Told me so with his own lips: 'I've opened up the door' he said, 'and dragged the barred gate open.'"

"Makes me shiver, just to think about him," said Nadya. "When they found him, his head was turned to metal with great horns growing out of the top…" She mimed the shape with her hands. "His tongue, they say, was the shape of a snake's."

"Nu, don't you go listening to that Nikolai," said Polina, who knew full well what that box was. "When he's had a skin-full he's nuttier than all the guests in a row."

Polina had come to work at the Yellow House some nine years ago, after her husband had been killed by a bull. Villagers whispered that she'd been cursed with the evil eye: she had no children, a pock-marked face, and now a husband crushed beyond recognition. Perhaps because of this she had no time for superstition. 'We're all just flesh and bone' she liked to say. 'Life is like the rain, it comes, it goes. One day there'll be thistles growing on my head and on yours too…' She deeply admired Zinaida, whose brisk efficiency and lack of sentimentality spoke to something deep within her. There were no such things as curses, spells, sins: when a tree died, it was because bugs were eating it or a storm had upended its roots.

"I'll tell you this for free," said Polina, with the air of one conveying a great secret to the masses. "The night I overheard Lepinov arguing with Shemiakin the bagman, Comrade Doctor Yevgrafovna had sent me for some kind of pump from Lepinov's quarters. When I got there, Lepinov and Shemiakin were going at it like stags, each yelling that the other was a crook. After much cursing Shemiakin leaves with two big bags and the Chief calls for Churkin. 'Fetch the steamer trunk' he says. 'And the other cases too.'

"Cases?" Nadya blushed and looked down while Marya pulled a face. "And where would he go with this steamer trunk? Carry it on his back through the mud? Poor Yana wouldn't even make it to the Post Road. And then where? The woods are full of bandits and deserters: I'd like to see how long you'd last with a box full of treasure on your hump."

"Oh, he was a shrewd one that Lepinov – while our bellies were full of oak leaves his got bigger and bigger."

"He still wound up on his back though," said Nadya, her cheeks strangely flushed. "And I'll shed no tears for that. But what about poor Ivan? Who do you think…?"

"Seems to me he saw something in Lepinov's bags – or else Lepinov let slip where he was going. And for such a crime, the poor lamb was hung."

"Aye, hung" nodded Marya. "But who tied the knot?"

The three graces shuddered and moved a little closer. Outside the nurse's station, Zvonkov was chopping wood. From time to time, he'd stop in his toil and stare out at the horizon: seraching for Petr, they guessed.

"You mean somebody from the Yellow House?"

"Who else? We're cut off on all sides. The men from Chulm have been taken and the Reds do nothing quietly."

Nadya looked close to tears. "But didn't you say that Shemiakin…"

"Who let him in and out? And who was Nikolai opening the door for, two strokes after midnight? It seems to me that the yardman knows a lot more than he's letting on. Found the body, eh? Or did he drop him in?"

Once again, the three graces felt an urgent need to hold on to one another, as if some awful wind was trying to blow them away.

"But the doctors," said Marya, hesitantly. "I'm sure that they'll …"

"The doctors? Ha!"

"Dr Aleshin, he…"

"That pup? 'The bourgeoisie should be strangled with both hands' … and his hands haven't done a stroke of work in their life!"

For Polina, Aleshin's long blonde hair, dim eyes and gentle lashes were a source of derision; it was only Marya, the middle grace, who considered him the most beautiful creature she had ever seen. Behind those gold rimmed glasses were the sensitive eyes of a young fawn – a kitten, maybe.

Three months ago, on some chore or another, Marya had found herself outside of Aleshin's quarters, late at night. The door was open, just a crack, and Marya could hear a stifled sobbing, as if something inside was struggling to breathe. Peeking through, she saw Aleshin at his desk, his fine features illuminated by the soft light of a lamp, his face more like an angel than ever. But what was he doing: reading, writing, inscribing something in his ledger? Marya's breath quickened. No: he was cradling a picture of a woman, a woman almost as beautiful as he was, her long blonde hair combed out like sunshine. Was this his sweetheart, some lady from Voronezh? Aleshin stared at her as if at an icon. O, how refined she looked, how accomplished! Standing there in the doorway, Marya felt her own heart start to break. Was the good doctor crying? His whole body contracted as if trying to choke back a howl, his hands balled up into fists. And yet, for all his red eyes and runny nose, he seemed more fine than ever, the doctor somehow hallowed by his grief.

"Dr Aleshin?" she whispered. "Gregory?"

Aleshin gazed at her through his eyelashes as if inside a cage.

"*Mamochka*..." he murmured.

"Mother?"

"*Mamochka*, I'm lost..."

That was the first night in which they made love. After that, she came to his bedroom every few days. After the act, he would cry and talk about the glorious future awaiting humanity just over the horizon, a socialist society in which a man and a woman would be able to express their feelings free from the stifling sentimentality of bourgeois mores. After this, he would grow angry and speak of the necessity of class judgement. Only then could he sleep.

Staring at his radiant features, Marya was deeply moved. His lips were as red as if he'd just been feasting on strawberries, his hair as soft as goose down. Asleep, he looked even younger than when on his rounds: a child, almost. Only by a supreme act of will could Marya manage to pull herself from him and return to the room she shared with the other graces. Did they know by whose side she spent the night? If so, no one spoke of it. In the morning, Aleshin's voice would be harsh and irritable. Holding down the tongue depressor on another guest, Marya would bow her head and pray for the salvation of the doctor's soul.

three
1

Although Nikolai was supposed to be on guard, it was Alyona who first saw him, a lone man on horseback, picking his way carefully amongst the ruts and the hollows. It was a late afternoon, five days after Petr's departure, the sky, clouds and dusk merging to form one solid mass. Alyona had been out collecting eggs and avoiding Zvonkov, who was still pestering her with his Rasputin. She crouched by the hen house, her basket full of rain. It was only when the stranger stopped outside the fence that she realised he was riding Yana.

Alyona fled inside and went to find Aleshin.

"It's Yana," she breathed, "he, ah…"

"Yana? Do you mean Petr?"

"No, no – someone else".

Aleshin hurried to disguise his doctor's smock inside a military coat. When he arrived at the entrance, a stranger stood passively by the fence, holding Yana by the reins.

"Inspector Tutyshkin," said the stranger, waggling his fingers through the bars. "I believe you requested my assistance."

Aleshin slipped awkwardly in the mud. "Requested? Well, that is to say…"

"Your young man told me how to find you – and this fine horse led me the rest of the way. Now comrade, where is the door?"

The rain fell on Aleshin's spectacles, making it hard for him to see. For some reason the stranger's voice made him think of his father.

"The door? Well…"

"There's a good fellow. And perhaps a little kasha with some milk? The horse is in need of a snack too…"

Tutyshkin was tall and gaunt with a strikingly pointed chin and a shaved, distended head. He was wearing the uniform not of an inspector, but a common rural policeman: pre-revolutionary garb, though that was nothing out of the ordinary. Aleshin couldn't help noticing that the uniform was rather short and rather tight. It was also coated in mud, in places little more than a strip of rags.

"So – you've spoken with our Petr?" said Yevgrafovna, watching the inspector at work in his bowl. Although ravenous, he ate like a gentleman: a sure sign of his class origins, as Aleshin would say.

"Indeed," said Tutyshkin, examining himself in his spoon. "A strong lad and a brave one too. Without him, I would have been supper for the wolves… He told me all about the Inspector and the goings on at the Yellow House. Your Lepinov dead? A damned shame. I'm sure you all must be terribly upset."

Frumkin coughed and Yevgrafovna knocked over the salt.

"Yes, yes, your Petr told me all about it – 'Come quick,' he said, 'for our Inspector is murdered and the House in peril.'"

"Petr said that?"

"Mm, mm," said the Inspector, his spoon rowing across his soup. "The yellow house at Bezumiye. A house of refuge and sanctuary."

The doctors exchanged glances.

"But the really funny thing," said Tutyshkin with a little laugh, "is that this place" – and here he gestured vaguely at the peeling walls of the canteen – "was my destination all along…"

"Here?" snapped Yevgrafovna.

"I know, I know," said Tutyshkin with a chuckle. "Isn't it most deliciously absurd?"

Aleshin coughed angrily. The more the Inspector's voice reminded him of his father, the more irritated he became.

"Yes, yes." Tutyshkin brought his napkin to his lips as if suddenly called to give an after dinner speech. "Well, it's the most remarkable thing really…"

The doctors stared at him intently.

"I mean, it's actually quite difficult to believe…"

"We're tremendously open-minded here," said Frumkin.

Tutyshkin's hands flapped like a bird. "Along with several of my best officers I was entrusted with the transport of a guest to your facility … a rather famous one by the name of Sikorsky."

Tutyshkin stared at his audience expectantly, but the name failed to inspire even a flicker of recognition.

"Ah, but perhaps news of his crimes has yet to reach your enlightened institution."

"Crimes?" asked Yevgrafovna.

"Just so, my dear doctor. Unfortunately, on the way here our carriage was set about … bandits I imagine, or anarchists of some stripe. My officers were shot dead and Sikorsky escaped. Awful. My dear doctor, please don't fuss about the salt."

"And where did this shoot-out take place?" said Frumkin quizzically. "In the deep dark woods?"

"Near an old manor house some distance from here – though only the walls are left standing."

Yevgrafovna glanced at Frumkin. "Ryabovsky's?"

"Ah, that I cannot say sweet lady."

"And your assailants?"

"Melted back into the gloom." Tutyshkin smiled agreeably, though he had truly terrible teeth. "More like spirits than men…" And then he laughed.

"And this is where you met Comrade Zvonkov?"

"Mmm – he heard the shooting and raced to my assistance, the sweet lad..."

Yevgrafovna regarded him icily. "So where is Petr now?"

"Well, that's another funny thing..."

"Funny?"

"After telling me of your... difficulties, he announced that he still had to find the railway line. Quite insistent, he was." Tutyshkin showed his empty bowl to his audience. "You know boys and trains."

"And yet you're riding his horse." said Frumkin.

"Indeed. He demanded that I take it. I was a little out of breath after the gunfight, and the lad said he'd cover the boggy ground just as fast on his own two feet."

"But why would he go on to the railway line?"

Tutyshkin shrugged. "Is that the samovar I hear a'bubbling?"

"Petr was under strict orders to return here. For what reason would he go and..."

"Ah, that I cannot say. He was certainly in a hurry though."

Aleshin narrowed his eyes. "I see. And this prisoner of yours – you say he escaped?"

"I know – awful. But I don't imagine he'll get far. He had no weapon or shoes and was dressed in prison rags – and a man like Sikorsky isn't used to the wilds."

"I haven't heard anything of any Sikorsky," said Aleshin, struggling to make his voice as gruff as possible. "Do you have the correct documentation regarding this transfer, Comrade Inspector?"

"Oh indeed, Comrade Doctor. You'll find all the certificates in your horse's saddlebag – fully stamped and authenticated. A Russian must always be correctly stamped, don't you think? A man without papers is less than a ghost."

Starchenko served the tea, the Inspector taking his with four spoons of sugar as if sitting in Sapezhnikov's tearooms. Aleshin watched him play with his silver spoon, sipping from his cup like a countess.

"And what of your authority, Inspector? I mean, in an ideological sense."

"Mm, dear chap?"

"Your class origins, Inspector. I'm sure you agree that the former constabulary was a counter-revolutionary force opposed to the creation of a proletarian state." Aleshin stared at the Inspector's bald head significantly. "By what right do you claim jurisdiction, Comrade Tutyshkin? This institution does not recognise…"

Tutyshkin made a dismissive gesture. "I'm not sure that this institution is in any position to…"

"Position? I am speaking of the worker's struggle comrade." Infuriated, Aleshin turned to Yevgrafovna. "This is a matter for the All Russian Extraordinary Commission for Struggle against Counter Revolution and Sabotage – not for some bourgeois…"

Yevgrafovna scratched the scar at the top of her scalp. "Aleshin, listen to what the Inspector has to…"

"Dr Aleshin?" said Tutyshkin quietly. "I believe I had dealings with your father in Voronzeh – in connection with his banking firm, if I'm not mistaken."

"My father?"

"Yes, yes, it comes back to me now – some matter of financial irregularity, if I recall. Not that I am impugning your perfectly respectable father of course… And your beautiful mother, how is she?" Tutyshkin's napkin touched his lips like a butterfly.

"My mother is of no concern to the world revolution."

"Indeed," said Tutyshkin, "I'm quite sure of that."

"If we could see the papers regarding this Sikorsky, Inspector," said Yevgrafovna, scraping her chair. "Do you think he might have followed you toward the Yellow House?"

"Barefoot and without horse? No, no – I'm sure that you can sleep safely in your bed, my dear doctor. If a doctor does sleep, of course. What is it Korsakov said? 'A doctor is like a candle – he sheds light while burning himself out'."

"The papers, Inspector."

"Oh, I'm sure there's plenty of time," said Frumkin, stroking Yevgrafovna's hand. "After all, it took the Inspector three days to ride from Ryabovsky's. Where should we put him up Starchenko – in Lepinov's old digs?"

The old retainer wobbled on his pins. "If you consider that appropriate sir."

Tutyshkin held up his hands in mock horror. "No, no, don't worry old man – best not contaminate the evidence, eh? After days on the road I'm happy to bunk wherever you think is best."

"With the servants?"

"We're all servants here," said Tutyshkin. "Of the proletarian revolution, I mean." He winked at Frumkin and stretched out on his chair like some pasha in his pleasure dome. "Now perhaps I could rest for a while before commencing my inquiry. Your poor Dr Lepinov must be rolling in his grave..."

Aleshin took his meal in his quarters that night, pouring over the paperwork regarding the escaped detainee and mulling over the events of the past few days. That left Yevgrafovna and Frumkin to sit at the doctor's table and discuss the strange case of the inspector and the odd state of his head.

"Shaven not bald," said Yevgrafovna, scowling. "A peculiar affectation for a police officer. Lice?"

Frumkin pulled a face. "That uniform fits him like breeches fit a snake. But what can we do? We ask for help and Tutyshkin comes wrapped up like a gift. And yet I'm sure I've heard that name before: some famous case in Voronezh... Anyway, he's got all the right forms and stamped in all the right places. Who are we to argue with paperwork?"

Yevgrafovna, skinny as a Cracow sausage, placed her eggy spoon in her hair. "And Petr? Why would he take off like that? And without Yana too."

"Well, there's little enough for him here. Maybe the propaganda train pulled in and the kid got converted, or maybe he got sick of his dad beating him with a mop. But you're right – something doesn't add up. Ryabovsky's place isn't so far from here. If the carriage is still there, somebody should go and take a look."

Yevgrafovna looked at him searchingly.

"Hey, not me" said Frumkin. "Did you hear those shots? I'm allergic to lead poisoning. Let Zvonkov find his kid – or Aleshin help the workers. In the meantime you try and get those papers from the people's representative and I'll keep an eye on our inspector. Something about him stinks worse than Nikolai's toes."

While the doctors chatted, Zvonkov led Yana back to the stables, gently stroking her neck and mane. Alyona had told him the news about his son. Had Petr really fled, abandoning his father and the House to take off like a thief? It was hard to imagine the boy could be so foolish. Was it something to do with that girl he was mooning about? Or was he dumb enough to run off and join one side or the other, believing he was fighting for Mother Russia?

Yana's rear leg was very lame and she tottered into her stall as if walking across a frozen pond. Her hair was matted with mud and filth and the unfamiliar saddle rubbed up against her back.

"Eh, what did you see out there, old girl?" said Zvonkov. "What happened, eh?"

Yana looked back at him with eyes full of sorrow, like something painted by Rubelev in his prime.

"Where's my boy, eh? What trouble has he got himself into

now?"

Yana shifted awkwardly and flicked her ears. She moved her muzzle as if to speak, but then thought better of it. Instead, she licked the orderly's hand and swayed from side to side as if grieving. Eventually the little lamp went out.

2

It goes without saying that the Yellow House wasn't really yellow. Rather the manor house was a pale shade of pink, the top storey sagging a little, the plaster weathered and faded, like a princess after a ball. The *flügel* was a dull ochre, the wooden outhouses green and black. Under a heavy Russian sky, everything turned to the colour of rain. Even the jackdaws seemed washed-out.

Bent as a starting handle, Starchenko led the inspector across the yard from the house, struggling to hold a torn summer parasol above his head. The fabric flapped crazily and the rain fell like knives.

"There's really no need, my dear fellow," said Tutyshkin, hit once again by the parasol's shaft. "I can manage perfectly well, I assure you."

Strachenko gravely shook his head and whacked the inspector on the nose. The old retainer was soaked to the bone but stuck to Tutyshkin like his shadow.

"This way, sir. Please mind the mud."

Starchenko had been instructed to take Tutyshkin on a tour of the estate, the doctors believing that it would be beneficial if the inspector familiarised himself with the locale.

"Charming place you have here," said Tutyshkin. "I'm sure Repin must have painted it once or twice."

Beyond the yard at the rear of the manor house was an untidy jumble of barns, storehouses, stables and huts, seemingly scattered at will. There were also two wells – one in the yard and one further out by the allotment – though these were filled with ordinary water rather than the holy *aqua* from the monastery. The soggy quagmire of vegetable plots ran down to the old *banya*, now filled with firewood. From a wooden pen, three brown pigs surveyed the wreck of the estate with ironic eyes. Next to them, a few hardy sheep nibbled at the weeds uncomplainingly, their wool filthy and matted, their yellow eyes blank. Facing the pens, an untended meadow, clogged with burdock, nettle and hemp, seemed to be used mainly as a rubbish dump, odd bits of furniture, masonry and rusted machine parts abandoned alongside vegetable peelings and household waste. For some reason Lepinov's automobile – the only one of its kind in the immediate area – had been left to decay amongst the refuse and the mire. One fender had fallen off, its paintwork had turned green, and goats had eaten the tyres. Why Lepinov hadn't arranged for it to be kept inside one of the many barns, or at least under some kind of awning was a mystery; he had driven the car to the meadow one spring morning and in the meadow it had remained – though of course the roads were too rutted and muddy for most of the year anyway. At the far end of the meadow could be found a ditch of brackish water, one more half-collapsed out house, and the sharp nails of the estate's outer fence. Beyond that was the old orchard from whence the shots had been fired. A string of crows lined up along a branch as if queuing for kerosene. Yellowing leaves jumped from the branches. The rain went on forever, like debt.

"And beyond the trees?" asked Tutyshkin.

"Beyond sir?"

"If I were to make my way from the rear of the estate where would I be?"

The old retainer looked at the inspector in some degree of confusion.

"Why, nowhere sir."

"Nowhere?"

"Yes sir. This is where the Yellow House ends."

"Of course," said the inspector, after a few seconds delay. "Good fellow."

From the neglected meadow, a ghost of a path led alongside the west wall of the manor house to the graves at the rear of the dispensary, each marked by a simple wooden cross.

"Your grave digger must be weary," said Tutyshkin.

"Oh – Old Nikolai does that sir. And dear Ivan, before he made his bed here too."

"But why so many? Are there really…"

"Typhus, influenza, cholera. And the war, of course. For a time we admitted many wounded soldiers and several decided to stay on."

"Well, who wouldn't?" said Tutyshkin, dodging the parasol's wooden spike. "And are there any representatives of the People's army posted here now?"

"Oh no sir. The front moved on and the field hospital was closed down. Over a year ago sir…"

Tutyshkin regarded the graves and nodded. "And yet your doctors were given leave to remain?"

"Sir?"

"Your doctors. Why weren't they ordered to accompany the Reds to the front?"

Starchenko's lips puckered as if expecting a kiss. "Oh sir – there have always been doctors at the Yellow House. What kind of a house would it be without them?"

From the dispensary, one made one's way to the various wards, positioned at the corners of a once-formal garden like dials on a timepiece. At the centre of the garden, a naked goddess looked forlornly at a foul pond and the swamp of her flowerbeds.

"A most charming spot," said Tutyshkin. "Shall we shelter for a moment in one of those romantic arbours?"

"If you will, sir."

"Ah, there we are: sit, sit! What a simply delightful place. If only these blooms could speak eh? Of what moonlight assignations they would tell. I'll squidge up: no need to stand there like a conductor. Now tell me all about this place."

"Sir?" Water dripped from the retainer's soggy wig, which resembled a place mat much more than a hairpiece. The old man's rouge had run a little too.

"Well – how long have you been at the Yellow House Uncle? A learned fellow like you … why you must be a walking library by now."

Starchenko's face betrayed no emotion, his voice like the slow creaking of a heavy wooden door.

"My father was employed here as a footman back when it was the old Count's estate. But he was a true gentleman sir, with his mind on higher things, and after he lost his serfs he had to mortgage off the land piece by piece. By the time I was old enough to take his place the land was gone and the manor house sold to a Dr Sapezhnikov as a sanatorium, a place of rest and recuperation for gentle folk. In the early days guests stayed either on the first floor of the house or else out in the *flügel*, God-fearing Christians, sir, come to take the *Christy* waters."

"The waters?"

"From the monastery sir: Saint Leonilla's, up on the hill. There were still holy men there until the start of the war. Then the Reds drove them out like crows.

"I see. And guests would walk from here to…"

"Along that yonder path, penitents all sir, to take the waters for the salvation of body and soul."

"And that's where your dear Lepinov was discovered? Down

the well?"

"It's a bad business, sir."

"Indeed. And that path along the crag is the only way from the house?"

"Why, yes sir. Now back in the day there were all sorts of tunnels leading from under the manor house to the monastery – not all the guests fancied the stroll and there were even pipes leading directly to a fountain in the great hall. But the tunnels proved unsafe and the pipes broke long before the Chief Superintendent arrived."

"And could I see these tunnels?"

"Oh, they're all blocked up, sir. Subsidence. Nobody has been down there for years. Apart from myself I doubt whether anyone else even knows of their existence."

"Well – there's a blow." Tutyshkin winked and pulled a face.

"Oh, these old houses are full of hidden passages. Intended for the servants to move about without inconveniencing the gentlefolk with their presence. Sliding doors, spiral staircases, wall cupboards, cellars…"

"How frightfully literary! But back to our dearly missed friend, Superintendent Lepinov. When did he take over from Sapezhnikov?"

"You're missing out Dr Bezenchuk sir."

"Is he relevant to the plot?"

The old retainer paused. "I wouldn't think so, sir."

"Just so: Lepinov then. Stout fellow eh?"

"'Tis a sin to speak ill of the dead."

"But of course. And did the house thrive under our Lepinov's wise stewardship?"

"Well, I wouldn't like to criticise sir, but the rank of guest did start to fall rather. Businessmen, lawyers, administrators and the like. He even accepted Jews, and on one occasion a Turk."

Strachenko's expression was that of a princess who had forgotten to sugar her grapefruit.

"And many of these guests, sir – well, they were a little odd. Funny habits and strange ways, if I may be so bold."

"In what sense?"

"Fitting during meal times. Crying, laughing, singing. Barking like a dog: that kind of thing."

"Most alarming, I concur."

"Of course by this time the guests had been moved out to the summer houses. And then we had to put bars on all the windows."

Nodding, Tutyshkin gazed past the petrified nymph toward the once elegant single storey buildings, their pale green or mustard walls turning inexorably to a dirty white.

"To be fair to Master Lepinov, even under the former Superintendent, things had begun to slide. There was one fellow, Orlov – a real devil he was, sir. Broke out and bashed Dr Yevgrafovna on the head. After that we had to start locking the guests in."

"And Orlov?"

"Oh, he was too dangerous to remain here, your Excellency. Someone came in a cart one night and took Orlov away. Howling like a wolf he was, and naked as a newborn. Heaven knows what the other guests must have thought."

Tutyshkin and Starchenko advanced toward the closest of the summerhouses, a lopsided wooden structure, its roof jutting out at odd angles and chimney half collapsed. Great stacks of old mattresses were dumped in the lobby, the pile giving off a strong acrid smell. At the other end, a locked and barred door looked onto a capacious room daubed with dirty-green paint, the foul smell of chemicals burning the inspector's nose. A series of beds were screwed onto the floor, illuminated by a four long windows, all securely barred. If one squinted one could almost imagine the pleasant reception room this might once have been, though the sky-blue ceiling was now disfigured by soot, and the red and green morocco armchair had seen better days. In the room's red corner, an icon lamp and portrait of Saint Sergius of Radonezh had been permitted to remain; next to it could be found a mop, a bucket, and a brass and mahogany commode.

There were five guests in here, either lying on their cots, sitting bolt upright or standing by one of the windows: the old Moroccan armchair was unoccupied. Each wore navy-blue hospital smocks and old-fashioned nightcaps, all men, their ages difficult to determine. The one closest to Tutyshkin was tall and bony, and his pale face focused on the inspector with a bitter smile. When Tutyshkin moved to one side, the eyes did not follow: the fellow seemed lost in a different world, his expression dignified, thoughtful and sad.

"And there are other rooms beyond this?" asked Tutyshkin.

"Two more sir: thirteen guests in total. These gentlemen were admitted when the asylum at Davydovka was forced to close. Very quiet and respectful gentlemen, sir. No bother at all."

Tutyshkin watched one of the patients rock gently from side to side. "And are they ever allowed out?"

"But of course, sir. In better weather, they're given the free run of the garden. But on days like today – better off in the dry, your Excellency. Don't want to get any more ill."

Indeed several of the guests coughed unceasingly, their emaciated cheeks coloured by bright red spots.

"And are they always this … reserved?"

"Very gentle souls, sir, never any trouble. It's like they're all half asleep – though they eat readily enough. You ask me, they think all this is a dream sir. Inside, they're still sitting on their sedans back home, all this but a passing fancy."

"I see, I see…"

At this, the police inspector seemed to lose himself for a moment and when he came to the old retainer was already on his way.

"This way your Excellency, if you please."

From the first summerhouse, Starchenko led the inspector along a diagonal path toward the next wooden dwelling. To Tutyshkin the careful arrangement of buildings – so different to the haphazard jumble of shacks at the rear of the estate – again seemed to resemble some kind of enormous architectural compass or clock face. The paths, the gazebos, the lines of hedges: everything implied the movement of hands across a face. But what was the purpose and whither the hour? Rain slid down Tutyshkin's nose, Starchenko's breeches sticking to him like wallpaper.

During the summer, a stroll along the trellised walkways, crowned with octagonal latticework, would no doubt be most pleasant; today however, the patterned shapes gave no shelter and the path was treacherous and muddy.

The second summerhouse was a mottled pinky yellow, not unlike the lichened bark of birch trees. Tall weeds grew from the thatched roof, but otherwise the wooden building seemed in a better state of repair than the first. Pots of geraniums were set out by the lobby and the entrance was tiled rather than wooden. Unfortunately, the same stringent smell of chemicals persisted here too.

"This is for the ladies," said Starchenko, his sodden wig covering one eye like a patch. "Although in my experience ladies are more prone to upsets of both womb and mind, we have very few ladies in residence here, illness and privation being particularly vexing to the delicate sex."

Despite the geraniums and a cheerful mural depicting Ivan the Terrible, this second *dacha* was unquestionably more chaotic than the first. In what must once have been a pleasant drawing room, one elderly woman was squatting hunched behind some curtains, a younger guest moaned and pulled at her night gown, while a third played a game of hide and seek all on her own.

"We should not linger here for long," said Starchenko. "Several of the ladies are prone to disrobe without ever giving notice."

"Really?" said Tutyshkin, "well…"

Starchenko advised against visiting the next ward; the guests there were very sick and not long for this world. Although Dr Yevgrafovna still tended to them, their souls already trembled at the gate. Nor were the guests in Ward Four much better: through the bars Tutyshkin could see them either shaking uncontrollably, coughing, or lying prone. The smell of disinfectant was so strong here the inspector could feel his nose hairs burn.

"I wouldn't get too close," said Starchenko. "I believe that the illness travels in spores."

"And did the superintendent ever visit these wards?"

"For some reason his duties tended to engage him elsewhere, sir."

"I see."

A thin grey cat – Varva – was curled up under the rough wooden awning, one eye open for mice, the other for passing souls.

"Yes, this place must be a trial, even for a skilled physician. Tell me, did Lepinov ever speak of leaving here, perhaps moving closer to town?"

"Oh no, sir. Even before the war, the Superintendent rarely went far from the estate. You have seen for yourself sir, the state of his automobile. He would take strolls in to the wood, perhaps to the village at Chulm, but as for Yamskai or Davydovka – never. And I cannot remember him travelling to Voronezh as long as he was engaged here."

"And did anyone come from the outside to visit him here?"

"Oh – various traders in a professional capacity." Starchenko stopped in his tracks. "Obviously not in terms of illegal or illicit marketeering, Inspector..."

"Obviously not."

"But since the outbreak of the war we have had to fend for ourselves sir, without funds or supplies or aid."

"Simply awful."

"And when the authorities requisitioned the house as a field hospital, they took everything from us sir, saying it was needed for the front."

The rain fell unceasingly, tapping on the parasol like a beggar shaking his tin. In places, the two men had no choice but to jump across wide puddles, Starchenko hopping like a small tin frog.

Eventually the pair reached the next ward, a mustard coloured building with a wide ground floor and a small floor above. Back in the days of Sapezhnikov's sanatorium the building must have housed some kind of gymnasium or treatment centre; the dormitories were grouped around a large indoor yard, the floor-boarded yard filled with rickety wooden chairs and equally rickety guests. Polina was busy coaxing the elderly clientele from their beds, encouraging the more active ones to toss a rubber ball to one another, the more infirm to move their arms and legs in a semi-circular motion. The nurse sneered at the approaching inspector with a mixture of scorn and trepidation.

"Ah, Nurse Polina," said Starchenko. "This is Inspector Tutyshkin – here to help with the superintendent."

"I would have thought him beyond help," said Polina, measuring up the inspector. Like most Russians, she knew that the police worked for 'them' – whoever historical circumstance determined 'them' to be.

"Oh carry on, don't mind me," said Tutyshkin, mildly. "Pretend I'm not here."

A few guests wobbled on their chairs while others had been placed on a kind of commode on wheels. One old man tossed a beanbag to his neighbour with childish enthusiasm, but most looked on in a state of bemusement. A tall, skeletal guest jogged slowly, endlessly, around the perimeter, the fellow dating from ancient Greece itself.

"Yes, many of our guests have been with us an awful long time – even from the days of the *Christy* water. Noble folk, gentlemen, once prosperous entrepreneurs – heaven alone knows what they make of the current circumstances. Of course most are simply unaware of the disaster which has befallen us."

Tutyshkin stared inquisitively at the ancient yellowed skulls of the withered guests, stray hairs sticking to the bone like wild grass on the steppe. Few souls still emanated any kind of spark; instead, the guests appeared fossilised, noses turned to stalactites, their lips petrified and cracked.

"Yes, yes," said Tutyshkin, "the light has departed…"

One soul however seemed uncommonly animate, tossing his beanbag with a sense of sporting relish and devil-may-care abandon. His eyes were as small and dark as a squirrel.

"Yours!" he yelled, and with that, he flung the bag into the face of a sour faced man peeking out from under a black cap. "The devil take you!" snapped the man, who resumed scowling into dead space.

"Well, at least there's one jolly soul," said Tutyshkin, clapping his hands dramatically.

"Yes sir. You may remember that I made reference to the gentleman before. That's Dr Bezenchuk sir – the Chief Superintendent before Lepinov."

Tutyshkin paused and regarded Starchenko curiously. "The old Superintendent?"

"Yes sir."

"But why would he remain here?"

"It was felt best, after he fell ill, sir – where else was he to go?

After all those years spent granting aid and succour to the afflicted, 'tis only right that the same privilege should in turn be extended to him. And look how happy he is! Here in familiar surroundings, surrounded by those he gave his life force to heal."

"Mm," said Tutyshkin. Bezenchuk's eyes sparkled with malice and mischief. The beanbag once again bounced off the bonce of the fellow in the black cap.

"Leave me alone you swine," cursed the grimacing invalid. Bezenchuk snickered and Polina retrieved the beanbag, passing it to another a different antique.

"And him?" asked Tutyshkin, speaking as if the fellow were elsewhere.

"Why, that's Turkin – one of the fellows sent here for re-education under orders from the state. Some kind of red or rabble-rouser – I forget. Yes, Turkin has been here even longer than Bezenchuk. A dissenter, sir. We had an awful lot of them here once upon a time."

"Really? But I thought that the Yellow House was..."

Starchenko smiled slyly. "Well, what is political subversion but a kind of illness, sir? How did Bezenchuk put it – 'crime is a deviation from generally recognised standards of behaviour, frequently caused by mental disorder'? And in its own small way the Yellow House has done its best to help."

Tutyshkin watched Turkin scowl at his old jailer, his features petrified by loathing. "And our dear Mr Turkin – is he aware of events in the outside world? Does he know that his beloved revolution has already taken place?"

"Oh no sir," said Starchenko. "Wouldn't be good for him, your Excellency. Too much disruption. No, he's better off looked after here, than left to the wolves outside."

The exercise hour was now nearing its end, Polinaa leading some of the more doddery guests back to their beds. The emaciated figure was still running. The old Superintendent tried to kick a guest's stick away as he passed.

"And Bezenchuk" said Tutyshkin gently. "What happened to him? In what way did he become, ah, blessed?"

"O, it was just after Orlov was taken away. He suddenly started raving and yelling that Orlov was still among us, hidden in the Yellow House." Starchenko paused. "To be a physician of the soul is no light undertaking," he said in a low whisper. "It is a doughty worker who can stay within these four walls for any time and not be affected."

"And what of you my dear fellow?" asked Tutyskin, smiling. "Why, you've been here longer than anyone!"

Strachenko bowed as stiffly as a rusted automaton; Tutyshkin could almost see the cogs and gears moving inside him. "I serve as best I can, sir. But perhaps we should move on..." Unfortunately, after bowing the *prizhivalschik* found he could no longer rise.

"Is there more to see?" asked the inspector, flicking the rain from his eyes. "I was thinking that perhaps we might sample a spot of lunch..."

Polina, busy steering some of the more mobile occupants toward the shower room, watched the two men go. The policeman might look like a fool but prowled like a caged animal looking for the way out. Aye, he would have to be kept away from her Yevgrafovna – especially given what had happened with Alexei.

Outside in the rain the two men stared at each other affectionately.

"You've been such an angel Starchenko."

"Why, thank you sir."

"May I kiss you on both cheeks?"

"If you must sir."

The two men followed a long drive flanked by linden trees

toward the nearby *flügel* – essentially a long, elegant extension to the manor house that somehow seemed to have migrated out toward the periphery. As soon as they neared the veranda, Frumkin came flying out to meet them like a puppet on a string.

"What seems to be the problem officer?" he said, hurriedly skipping down from the steps, Nadya in hot pursuit.

"Oh – just doing my rounds," said Tutyshkin, smiling broadly. "Taking in what the Yellow House has to offer."

"Well, you can see why our guestbook is full," said Frumkin, watching the rain pour from the guttering. "Um, I'd invite you in, but with the contamination risk, it, ah…"

"Oh no – no need," said the inspector, holding his palms up. "I think that Starchenko and I have seen what we need."

"It's just that – wait, you don't want to come?"

"This fellow and I need to go inside and get dried out, and then a dash of lunch, I fancy. Perhaps after that everybody might gather in the library – we'd better get this business of the Superintendent sorted out."

"The library? Isn't that a little… premature."

"Oh I just need to establish times and places, that kind of thing."

A face appeared at the window but Frumkin shooed it away behind his back.

"Sure, sure, I just need to finish off here." Frumkin examined the bald pate of the special inspector suspiciously. "We'd also like to hear some news from the outside world. For all we know Kersensky is back in the winter palace."

Tutyshkin gestured dismissively. "Oh, I'm not one for politics…"

"Who is? But I still like to know who's pointing the gun."

The inspector shrugged. "You know what they say about the police: nobody likes us except for prison wardens and they don't like us too."

"I'm sure you're on the workers' side, Comrade Tutyshkin…"

"Is there any other? But now Starchenko and I need to get out of these wet clothes? Eh, my lad?" and the Special Inspector winked.

"I'll escort the inspector back to the main house," said Starchenko, his Imperial wig now no more than a dishcloth.

"I'll look forward to reviewing current affairs later my dear doctor."

"I'm just the *feldsher* – but, yeah, sure. After lunch. Let's hope that Shishkin has caught something kosher in his trap…"

Nadya whispered something in Frumkin's ear and Frumkin whispered something back. Fortunately the two men were already leaving, Tutyshkin trying to avoid the pointed edges of the parasol, Starchenko like a clockwork toy winding down, his parts rusted, the mechanism clumsily jammed.

Uncharacteristically the inspector splashed back to the house in silence. Despite his extensive tour of the grounds, he felt himself no closer to understanding the true nature of the place than he had upon his arrival. Refuge, prison, asylum? Of course, one might say the same of Russia herself…

Zvonkov had been moved in with Shiskin, and Tutyshkin had been billeted in Petr's bed. The room was in the very attic of the east wing, in an alcove high above the carriages. The room was filled with hunting paraphernalia of all kinds: snares, wire, odd bits of rope, some kind of fishing tackle and a jug full of hooks. The only really interesting thing was a large heavy bear trap, the jaws newly greased and cleaned. Propping up the table was a copy of Tate's classification of Russian birds, and a fusty old book on animal husbandry. Other less reputable volumes – mainly spicy reflections on the goings on in the Imperial court – were hidden under Zvonkov's bed.

By Petr's cot was a collection of carved wooden birds, presumably whittled by the lad himself. Tutyshkin idly picked up a woodcock and turned it back and forth in his hands. The boy clearly had talent: it was a shame how everything had turned out. Tutyshkin placed it back on the shelf and footered around beneath the boy's mattress. A moment later he retrieved something wrapped in a doubtful looking rag, the inspector holding it disdainfully between two outstretched fingers. Beneath the wrapping was another carved creature, albeit rather different from the game birds: this one had the torso of a naked man, and the head of some kind of horned bear. Tutyshkin examined the figure carefully. It seemed like something glimpsed at the far side of reason, yet the carver was unquestionably the same as the one who had whittled the perfectly proportioned partridge and snipe. Petr? Tutyshkin suddenly had his doubts.

Outside the rain threw itself against the window, seeming to search for a way in. Above it, the sky resembled a great black dam, the walls just starting to burst.

In the washroom beneath the alcove, Alyona held Tutyshkin's jacket up to the light. As well as various tears and rips, it had a large bullet hole positioned just above his heart. Alyona stared through it, her pretty lips pursed. On the other side, Zvonkov stared back intently.

3

Only Aleshin could provide a detailed account of his movements and appointments in the hours preceding Lepinov's disappearance. Frumkin had been busy in the *flugel* whilst Zinaida had made what she called "her usual rounds". The three graces merely stared sullenly while Nikolai gnawed anxiously on his pipe. "By night I guard the door, by day I shovel your shit. And when should I sleep, eh? In the grave?"

Nor could anybody seem to remember the last time they had seen Lepinov alive. Starchenko believed that Alyona had delivered his final meal, but Alyona claimed it had been Churkin. Nor could Shiskin recall the dish: something involving buckwheat perhaps. Zvonkov mentioned seeing Lepinov collecting herbs and mushrooms in the woods, but wasn't exactly sure when: "before the rain" he suggested, dismissively. Finally, after many furtive glances, Polina told the tale of Lepinov's assignation with Shemiakin the bagman, although she carefully avoided any mention of suitcases or fancy goods.

"A bagman?" asked Tutyshkin. "Dear, oh dear. Shady characters. What did Comrade Trotsky have to say? 'These speculators are drinking the blood of the people...' Eh, Comrade Aleshin, was that it? Class enemies and betrayers of the Revolution?"

Hidden behind his spectacles, Aleshin merely shrugged. The inspector winked and continued. "And this bagman – he traded with Lepinov you say?"

"Inspector Tutyshkin," said Yevgrafovna, in a voice generally reserved for only the most stupid of children, "I am sure you are aware that transportation and communication has all but broken down in this province. Our vegetable plots are not sufficient to ensure the nutrition of either guests or staff. Under such circumstances, I hardly think that…"

Tutyshkin smiled and made a gentle, conciliatory gesture. "Calm yourself, sweet doctor – I meant no offence. So, Nurse Polina – you saw this piquant scene, but overheard not a thing – am I right?"

"They were arguing about money sir."

"What else do bagmen do? And our Master Shemiakin: he said he would return, yes?"

Polina nodded.

"And yet nobody has seen him since? Our sweet yardman: no suspicious knocking at midnight?"

Nikolai jumped as if whipped. "I don't let anyone in I shouldn't, damn you…"

Zvonkov and Alyona exchanged glances but said nothing.

"Well, all this is most perplexing," said Tutyshkin. "So nobody saw our Chief Superintendent make his way to the monastery for a final sup?"

No one said a word.

"And how often do people travel to this well?"

"Well, Nikolai or Starchenko are there twice a day, orders of the Tsar."

"The Tsar?"

"One of the guests thinks he's Nicholas the second. He's still agonising over the abdication."

"A most colourful character, I'm sure. But I don't see…"

"Asks for holy water twice a day – for his son. Special orders from Rasputin."

"And you humour him?"

"Lepinov was very fond of the old Emperor," said Starchenko, gravely. "A true gentleman, not like some of the refuse we've had to sweep up…" The old retainer scowled. "Indeed, the last time I can recall speaking with the Superintendent was on the way to see Tsar Nicholas; the two souls often liked to converse."

"And our Imperial Emperor – who is he really?"

"A shop-keeper from Lipetsk. He lost his reason sometime during the October Revolution. Superintendent Lepinov organised his admittance personally. And a most convincing replica of our departed Tsar, if I may say so."

"I see, I see. And what about on the way to the monastery? Might somebody have done him in on the path, and hidden his body?"

"Well, it's pretty exposed, but, maybe. I mean, the Superintendent was no lightweight and you wouldn't want to carry him far. But there aren't any boot-prints…."

"Besides our gallant yard man, you mean…"

"Not even his."

"I lost my boots, curse you!" yelled Nikolai. "Is it a crime to take a drink once in a while? Does that make me a murderer? Damnation upon you all! I'm off – you can shave somebody else's chin."

And with that the enraged *dvornik* started to take his leave, the smell of samogan rising up with him.

"Sit down you old goat," hissed Zvonkov. "Can't you be quiet just for a moment?"

"What have my boots got to do with anything? The devil take that Jew and his footprints."

"Just sit down if you know what's good for you."

Nikolai glowered but slowly lowered his haunches. "The devil take their boots…"

"He's a lively fellow," sniffed Tutyshkin.

"There's no evidence of anyone heading along the path," said Frumkin, "Lepinov, Nikolai or the Angel of Death. I mean, sure it was raining pretty hard but even so – anyway, a better question is how a dead man ate his meals and chatted with the Tsar without anyone noticing. I'm not kidding: his remains stunk like he'd been dead for a month."

"But he died from a blow to the head?"

"Well, some drummer had been to work on his skull, that's for sure…"

"Inspector," said Yevgrafovna, "I'm sure that our esteemed *feldsher* is trying to help, but the fact remains that the time of death is extremely hard to determine. I've been running some tests and I can confirm that there was a high degree of poison in the superintendent's system – ingested in the form of hallucinogens."

"Tests?" For the first time Aleshin stirred himself from his seat, shaking his long, blonde locks. "On whose authority did you undertake such 'tests'?"

"Dr Aleshin, you may be operating under the fantasy that you are the new Superintendent here, but let me remind you that as the most experienced physician here. I…."

"This is an outrage, Dr Yevgrafovna. You had no right to interfere with Superintendent Lepinov, whose mortal remains are now the property of the working people. This is appalling, unacceptable! I assure you that I shall be underlining key passages in my official report."

"Your report, your report – and who shall read this report? We are a long way from the people's army and the Whites are approaching. My duty as the senior physician is…"

"Your duty, Comrade Yevgrafovna, is to the World Revolution…"

The doctor furiously scratched at a scab in her hair.

"Dr Aleshin, I…"

"No, no, I will not countenance this; I simply cannot tolerate such individualist…"

Tutyshkin clicked his fingers. "Ah, doctors, if I may?"

Yevgrafovna turned to the inspector, blowing hard through her nose. "Although Lepinov's system was overflowing with dangerous toxins, he nevertheless died from blows received to the head and gut. If you would like to view the body then…"

"The corpse? Oh no, there's no need to…"

"But surely an inspection of the deceased is part of standard procedure inspector…"

"Is it? Well, I suppose. Not too messy is he? This gown is borrowed…"

Tutyshkin was now wearing some kind of servant's garb leant to him by Strachenko, the high neck making his bald head resemble the last egg in the nest.

"His body remains in the cold room at the rear of the dairy. We were awaiting your arrival before interring the remains."

"Well, if you think it's really necessary…"

"Besides, perhaps it might be best to keep some of the medical information confidential."

"Indeed. What a clever thing you are."

As the doctors got up to leave, Aleshin pushed his way between them. "You haven't heard the last of this, Comrade Yevgrafovna. Interference with state property constitutes anti-revolutionary and petit-bourgeois activity."

"All my investigations were carried out with the express aim of revealing the objective truth. The fact that you yourself failed to undertake such necessary testing only illustrates that your position here in the Yellow House is fundamentally a subordinate one."

"Subordinate to who?" snapped Aleshin. "You? I hardly feel that your ideological credentials…"

"Come on, let's go look at the stiff" said Frumkin. "Make sure that our inspector doesn't pass out too."

The last few days had done no favours to Lepinov at all. The green hues of his skin had started to turn black, his torso expanding rather than contracting, like the remains of a whale upended on a beach. Angry pustules had erupted around his mouth, his tongue had shrivelled, and his nails dropped off. He emitted a foul, almost unbearable smell, somewhere between rotting herring and the trapped wind of a cow. Only his eyes remained human. I know, I know, they seemed to say: a fine catch of fish is this…

Yevgrafovna prodded the bruising, Frumkin looked in his ear, and Aleshin studied a blood sample. Only Tutyshkin refused to come near. "Terrible, awful," he said, holding one of Starchenko's antique handkerchiefs up to his nose. "Your superintendent has really let himself go."

"Do you want to see the wounding, inspector?"

"No, no, you carry on my darlings," choked Tutyshkin, cowering behind his embroidery. "For my part, I have seen enough of death,"

"So," said Aleshin, setting down Yevgrafovna's papers. "The poison – mushrooms?"

"Given the high degree of hallucinogens and the chief superintendent's proclivities, I would think so."

"So the question is: when did the subject consume the toxins?"

"With the equipment to hand, very hard to say. I would say that Lepinov had been taking these things for months – his luck must finally have run out."

"So what are we saying?" asked Frumkin, staring at Lepinov's boils. "He flies to the monastery, then trips down the well?"

Yevgrafovna scratched at the sore patches on her skin. "Not at all – the head wound is the result of a collision with a blunt object.

His spine might have been broken in the fall, but otherwise…"

"Poisoned, clubbed to death and drowned," said Frumkin. "He's a regular Rasputin. You're telling me that poisoned mushrooms did that?"

T'was true: In death, the superintendent seemed to have assumed even more monstrous proportions. His belly was the size of an unwieldy piece of furniture, filling the room and no longer supported by its long, broken limbs. Lepinov's skin was swollen, his neck bloated. Though clumps of hair had been pulled out, the dark locks of his beard seemed to spread like ivy.

"What about his hat?"

"Hat?"

Aleshin tossed the strange padded helmet to Tutyshkin, the pot a cross between a post box and a gas mask, obscurely obscene, with its hideous tubes and broken mouth-bit.

"A piece of psychiatric ephemera," explained Aleshin, "dating from the middle of last century. The superintendent amassed a great deal of such junk, squirreled away in his study. He was a man of strange, bourgeois tastes…"

"Bourgeois? Rather selective if you ask me," said Tutyshkin, fingering the holes. "And this was rammed on his head?"

"The idea is to exclude disruptive visual or aural stimuli whilst soothing water is applied."

"Well, water was applied, sure enough. And the tubes?"

"A means of restraint, I would imagine."

"How peculiar. And this relic was taken from the super-intendent's study?"

"Well, I imagine so…"

Without his stopper, the superintendent seemed to have expanded, like a genii from a lamp. Indeed, he barely seemed to fit on the slab, a slug the size of a pig. Zinaida hung back at the rear of the room, as far from the box as possible.

"And has anyone examined the superintendent's collection? Or searched for clues in Lepinov's study?"

"Well, you're the investigator," said Frumkin, regarding Tutyshkin with open scepticism.

"Yes, yes, I am. Well, shall we adjourn to somewhere more amenable? I think our work here is done. Besides the superintendent's aroma is sadly inimical to clear thought."

"Yes, what is that smell? Amonia, spores, faecal matter?"

"Oh my dear doctors," said Tutyshkin. "What a mystery the human body is…"

Lepinov's quarters were by far the most luxurious in the Yellow House, consisting of the old master bedroom, a spacious reception room, and a large, book-lined study. There, Phillippe Pinal's *A Medical and Philosophical Outline of Mental Illness* nestled alongside tomes on demonology, the transmigration of souls, and recipies. Many of the books were in foreign languages, their yellowed pages smelling strongly of damp. On Lepinov's desk was a bottle of expensive French cognac, a miscellany of papers, pens, keys and coins, a human thighbone, an amulet of protection, and the carving of a voluptuous female figure possessing the head of a goat.

"Just look at all this trash," tutted Aleshin. "Reactionary, counter-revolutionary and contrary to the will of the people. One should knock the bourgeoisie out of their nests…"

The room fell silent.

"Well," said Frumkin, "I'm sure I saw Lepinov's stash back when we were hiding the Graces."

Tutyshkin pulled a face.

"The nurses had to seek refuge here when the soldiers came," added Aleshin. "Purely a precaution Comrade Inspector, of course."

"But of course," said Tutyshkin, smiling. "Who can tame the

Revolutionary spirit?"

Pushed behind an oriental divan were a whole series of boxes containing masks, manacles, shirts that tied up at the back. Tutyshkin made a cursory pretence at looking at the goods and then wiped his hands.

"What an inspired collection! Do you think anything might be missing?"

"How would we know?"

"Well, just so. Are you all right my dear Dr Yevgrafovna? You look quite unwell."

"I'm fine, Inspector."

"Ah – good, good."

Lepinov's study was itself an historical exhibit of an earlier time, the ancient habitat of lawyers, doctors and academics – all those doomed people of the past. Ah, the bourgeois melancholy of cosiness! Tutyshkin sank down into Lepinov's handsomely upholstered chair and surveyed the superintendent's domain. On the desk was a mass produced handbill of Bolshevik propaganda. "Our people demand that we crush the accursed vermin! The graves of the hated traitors will grow with tall weeds and thistles, covered with the eternal contempt of all honest people..." The words seemed as out of place in this sleepy den as a steam engine in a cathedral.

"Mysteries within mysteries," said Tutyshkin, picking up the goat-woman from Lepinov's desk.

Aleshin's weak eyes peered out from behind their golden cages. "Inspector, I have several questions regarding the paperwork surrounding Sikorsky's transit to the Yellow House."

Tutyshkin held out the figure like Aristotle contemplating Homer's beard. "My dear doctor, I really don't think that this is the time to..."

"Several pages seem to be missing Inspector, torn from the

original dispatch."

"As I explained," drawled Tutyshkin in his most languid tone of voice, "our little group came under attack. Things might have become lost or confused – I don't know. But all the official seals are attached, all signatures correct – not that it matters now, in any case."

"And what of your Sikorsky?" asked Frumkin. "You say he's dangerous – why shouldn't he make his way to the Yellow House and cave in Comrade Lepinov's roof?"

"It all sounds very unlikely," said Tutyshkin with a yawn. "I mean, how could he enter the estate without anyone noticing or leaving any footprints?" For some reason Tutyshkin patted his head like a monkey. "I wouldn't worry about our missing Sikorsky – there's no way the scamp could travel over field and marsh."

"If I may say so," said Yevgrafovna, "you seem surprisingly unconcerned that such an individual should find himself at liberty, still less that…"

"Sikorsky? Oh, he's less trouble than you think. Besides, I saw him wounded in the shoot out – though I saw no body, his bones won't be so very far away."

Yevgrafovna advanced on Tutyshkin's sheared head, peering at where a variety of nicks, cuts and bruises pitted the lunar surface.

"Sikorsky is dead? So why didn't you share this information…"

"My sweet princess, I didn't say dead: I merely saw him hit. But you can sleep well, dear heart, I'm sure that our Sikorsky…"

"*Our*? Hey, it was your job to get him here," snapped Frumkin.

The rash on Comrade Yevgrafovna's neck shone angrily. "Inspector Tutyshkin, why did you not inform us that…"

"It's simply not relevant that…"

"Not relevant? Inspector, in what sense is it not relevant that…"

"In the sense that Sikorsky is not here."

"Comrade Yevgrafovna, let us return to the paperwork," yelled Aleshin, "which is by far the most pertinent matter in this case. Pages two, seven and thirteen are plainly missing – and not as a result of any so-called attack either…"

"Well, I don't see…"

"These pages detail key aspects of the prisoner exchange and…"

"Yes, yes, I'm sure…"

"… and have obviously been tampered with in a manner contrary to…"

Tutyshkin stared across Lepinov's desk like a teacher addressing a classroom of unruly pupils. "My dear doctors, calm yourselves: there's really no need for such dissent. Sikorsky was shot and wounded in the leg: there is no possibility that he might have found his way here to murder your esteemed superintendent. All the paperwork setting out Sikorsky's crimes and transferral is complete and correct – authorised by the revolutionary authorities in Davydovka. Whether certain sections were or were not completed by the relevant clerks seems rather an affectation given the current circumstances."

Aleshin looked ready to speak but again Tutyshkin cut him off.

"Your young man, Petr, informed me that you were in need of assistance in regard to the murder of Chief Superintendent Lepinov. If you wish this matter to be investigated then I must be assured of both your assistance and your patience."

For a moment, Lepinov's study felt as dark and silent as winter. Realising nobody else was going to make a move, Frumkin looked around, clapped Tutyshkin on the back and said, jovially, "Of course Inspector, of course – these times make everybody jumpy. After all, we're all on the same side…"

"Why yes, but of course…"

"Of revolutionary justice I mean…"

"What else?"

Frumkin sidled up to the inspector and blew dust from the desk. "So what are they saying in Davydovka – are Denikin and the Whites getting closer?"

"How is one to tell? All anybody talks about is the Terror: the Bolsheviks did this, the Don Cossacks did that, but in the meantime the rye husks are mixed with goose fat, the loaves all yellow and bitter…" The inspector put down the figure, picked up the Superintendent's cognac, but then seemed to think better of it. "The only constant is the constant rain of declarations and decrees: the Germans are coming back, the Poles are invading, the Jews are stockpiling food. After a while one stops reading. One fellow told me that some faction had got hold of a kind of death ray, a deadly violet light, and if the colours were to seem different one morning then one shouldn't venture out of the house."

Aleshin scowled. "The only authority is Red Authority."

"Well, yes, yes, but people are sheep. The latest whisper was that Jewish merchants were putting something in the soup that made people sick – mukhomar, death's cap mushrooms." Tutyshkin glanced at the *feldsher*. "All nonsense of course…"

"Of course" said Frumkin, without expression.

"I mean, who believes you can still find mushroom soup?"

"And what is the news from Moscow? Some say that Lenin has recovered, others that he died and a double has taken his place."

"Oh – I imagine that one of these two statements is true. No, no, I'm sure that Comrade Lenin's shoulder is still to the wheel of progress."

"And in Voronezh?" asked Frumkin.

"Mm?"

"What's happening there?"

"Oh: the usual. Looters, food hoarders, corrupt bankers" At this he glanced at Aleshin. "Honestly it's hard to know who to arrest."

"And you Inspector?" glowered Aleshin. "To whom do you

answer?"

"Oh my sweet lad, the flame of law isn't quite yet extinguished."

"So who is in control?" asked Frumkin. "Still Korostelyov?"

"Hm."

"And Yanovsky in charge of security? The old man still holding the fort?"

"Yes, yes…"

"Footerov running defence?"

"Who else?"

Frumkin smiled curiously and for the first time seemed to notice the strange figure by Tutyshkin's paw. "Well, I suppose we should be glad there's still somebody here to protect us – we're grateful for your assistance, Inspector."

There was an awkward pause as Frumkin waited for Aleshin and Yevgrafovna to join in, but the two doctors merely scowled. "If there's anything we can do…"

"Thank you my dear Moises. I think I'll take a trip out to the monastery next, perhaps take a peek down the well." He tapped his egg. "Helps complete the mental picture, you know…"

"That's outside the walls of the estate," said Yevgrafovna. "In such circumstances, you'd better take Zvonkov."

"No need, no need, I'm sure I'll be…"

"Oh, we insist Comrade Inspector," said Aleshin.

Tutyshkin nodded. "As you wish." With that he stood up and pushed the chair back in to place. "Till suppertime then. Tell Shishkin there's no need for anything special – whatever the good earth grants us…"

For several minutes after Tutyshkin's departure nobody spoke. Finally, Aleshin coughed, wiped his glasses, and marched over to Frumkin.

"What was the fool saying about Davydovka? Yanovsky was

shot in the spring."

"Mm."

Yevgrafovna nodded. "So who's Footerov?"

"The door man at Polonsky's restaurant."

"I see."

"Well," said Frumkin, clapping his hands. "I guess we've all got things to do...."

4

"What is it Dostoevsky says? There is nothing more unbearable than greenery and wooden huts in the rain, 'neath a horrible sky."

Zvonkov grimaced and refused to reply. Tutyshkin was a policeman, and as far as Zvonkov was concerned, the purpose of the revolution was to do away with those. Besides, the man was responsible for his son running away – the devil knew how, but Petr would not have abandoned his father otherwise.

"Eh Zvonkov? Or do your literary tastes tend elsewhere?"

Zvonkov aggressively picked his nose and Tutyshkin looked away. The track led from the Yellow House past the small copse of beggarly trees, and then rose sharply along a muddy rise. The muck grabbed at their ankles like a lunatic, the rain falling unceasingly. Far away in the distance, the burnt out windmills of Serezha could just be seen. The meadows looked more like dirty puddles, the outline of the forest an ugly black stain.

"Yes, yes, unbearable," Tutyshkin muttered, mostly to himself.

The rocky outcropping slowly wound its way up above the estate, affording a view of both the Yellow House and the meadows surrounding it. The grass was wild and uncut, flattened by rain. You could see a few dirty sheep, heads bowed, as well as the wreck of Lepinov's automobile, more like a becalmed boat than a horseless carriage. The shell of the old *banya* looked like somebody had sat on it. From up here the spikes of the perimeter fence resembled matchsticks, offering no protection at all.

On the other side of the path one could just about make out the start of the post road, as well as more unkempt fields, the old telegraph wire (now cut) and what might have been the distant railway line – though it may simply have been another embankment or ditch, who knows? The river looked like a great brown line, wiped unpleasantly across the ground.

Meanwhile, the muck on the post road was as deep as a horse's belly, the ruts on the monastery path the height of a man's shin. Progress was slow. Though Zvonkov successfully sought out stepping stones and well-placed branches, Tutyshkin struggled as if he had never set foot outside the city before. "I have made a perfect mess of Starchenko's britches," he lamented.

Exactly what the inspector was searching for seemed unclear. There certainly were footprints – but quite possibly dating from when Zvonkov and Petr had transported the Chief Superintendent back to the Yellow House by cart. Just six days later, such conveyance would be impossible: the *rasputitsa* had done its work. Holes filled with rainwater, streams replaced walkways, and the mud pulled at everything like a drowning man. Searching for clues in such a place was like searching an elder's beard for lice. Despite this Tutyshkin made a great show of inspecting the endless holes and furrows – like a fool looking for his echo, thought Zvonkov. After a while even the inspector was forced to make his way to the surrounding hillocks, his garments painted an ugly shade of brown.

From here, the outskirts of the old monastery could just be seen. The stone cross that had once stood by the east gate had been torn down by the Bolsheviks – indeed, it now formed part of the path, creating a kind of bridge across the muck. The guesthouse, originally intended for supplicants, was the only building still whole: everything else had been burnt down and demolished. The avenue was scarred with dead trees, fallen masonry and collapsed bits of wall. The chapel and the monks' cells had been completely flattened. Broken glass, chopped up wood and ancient stonework lay scattered like droppings, and yet it was still possible to walk through the old monastery grounds and make one's way to the grotto containing St Leonilla's well, descending the hefty stone steps gouged into the rock.

Zvonkov wordlessly lit a lamp and showed Tutyshkin the way. Although it was good to get out of the rain, the drips and cold pursued them like the flu. Instead of being magnified by the cavern, the sound seemed muffled, as if covered by a cloth. In the centre of the chamber stood a plain, unadorned well, its rope and bucket a human flaw amongst the eternal.

"Aha!" said Tutyshkin, clapping his hands. "So this is where our dear Chief Superintendent washed up. I wonder if behind these walls lie Starchenko's lost tunnels?"

The Inspector nosed around in the dirt, sniffed the edge of the well, and then knocked on the grotto wall. Pure pantomime, thought Zvonkov.

"Are you done?" the orderly barked, his expression thoroughly bored.

"Done? Ah, I'm afraid that police work is a slow and painstaking business," trilled Tutyshkin lightly. "Now if you'd be so kind as to bring that light over here…"

Grudgingly Zvonkov illuminated the well shaft and the two men stared down into the gloom. At the bottom, the holy water glittered like treasure.

"And like a salmon he made his way to the source," recited Tutyshkin.

Zvonkov grunted.

"Milk from Saint Leonilla's bosom, eh?" Tutyshkin winked, but Zvonkov chose to ignore him.

The walls of the well were smooth and unmarked, but the shrine was obviously very ancient. There was no smell, no sound, no breath of air. One might have been looking into the very eye of eternity.

"Mm," said Tutyshkin. "Could you angle the lamp a little, please? There. No, no, a little further down..."

Zvonkov was forced to lean awkwardly over the lip, holding the lamp by its hook.

"No, no – further. That's it, just there..."

Whilst Zvonkov's behind struggled awkwardly, Tutyshkin moved silently round behind him, arms outstretched.

"Mm, yes, just lean a little more toward the wall if you can..."

By now, the inspector was right behind him: one push and the medical orderly would be in.

"Yesss..."

Zvonkov drew himself back up. "There's nothing there, damn it."

Tutyshkin shrugged. "I thought I could see something. Some kind of letter or mark. Oh well, probably nothing, right enough."

Zvonkov shot Tutyshkin a look of pure hatred and tucked his shirt back into his pants.

"Done?"

"Well, I suppose so. We can say a prayer to Saint Leonilla and then be off. I don't suppose you could secure a vial of *Christy* water for me, dear soul? Purely for investigative purposes you understand."

Grumbling, Zvonkov once more turned his back on the inspector, hauling up the bucket on a rope. Tutyshkin closed in behind him, gently licking his lips.

"A saint's labour is always rewarded," he intoned.

His shoulders straining, Zvonkov wrestled with the rope whilst the inspector practically perched on his shoulder. The orderly's arse was very close. When Zvonkov turned back round, both men gave a little jump. The orderly stared at the inspector suspiciously.

"Your holy water," the orderly growled sarcastically, holding out the bucket as if to a sow.

"Most kind," said Tutyshkin, mildly. "You will see that I have brought my own bottle."

The bucket fell back like a guillotine.

Outside it was still raining, a tub that could never be filled. Tutyshkin wandered here and there among the ruins but soon lost interest. All the monastery's relics had either been stolen or smashed, the few remaining monks taken away at gunpoint – this nearly two years ago by now. It was only the presence of the Yellow House which had enabled the shrine to hang on this long, the monks little more than washroom attendants. For all that though, there was something striking about the place, even in its ruined state. The broken masonry resembled great black letters, spelling out some unknowable mystery. When Tutyshkin glanced back at the entrance to the shrine, it looked like a wound. Neither man stood on the cross on the way back.

5

Instead of returning to the main house, Tutyshkin instructed Zvonkov to escort him for an audience with Tsar Nicholas II, the Emperor sequestered above the aging guests in the old gymnasium. The orderly wasn't keen.

"The doctors said nothing about…"

"The doctors are not in charge of this investigation. Lead on, my darling, lead on…"

The bottom floor of the mustard coloured building was low and flat, like a pie left out in the rain. For the second time that day Tutyshkin crossed the uneven wooden floor, the yard now deserted save for one lost guest endlessly stacking chairs before slowly taking them back down again. In the rafters, a wet sparrow watched him, his head cocked in ironic encouragement. There was no sign of any nurses and all the doors were locked.

"The Tsar's up here," said Zvonkov, begrudgingly. "He gets his own suite for some reason. Well, I suppose with him being the imperial majesty and all."

The stairwell was painted with scenes from *Ruslan and Lyudmila*, all dancing peasants and sleigh rides through the snow. On the landing, a white horse pawed the ground uncertainly, while off to one side a dwarf watched the Inspector with an expression suggesting either tragic loss or bellyache. Rather incongruously, an angel was painted high up on the ceiling, his mouth open as if to ask who the hell had let that dwarf and horse in here.

"Well, it's not every institution that is honoured with the presence of such a distinguished occupant," said Tutyshkin, smirking.

"You'd be surprised," grunted Zvonkov.

Odd remnants from the days of the old count – a bow-legged grandfather clock, a green vase, a broken lamp with dusty glass tschotchkes – adorned the corridor, forming almost a parody of Imperial splendour. Damp spots and grey mildew spattered the walls. The curtains were full of holes. There may once have been frescoes here too, but only a cow's arse remained, floating in space like some mysterious planet.

"He's just through here," said Zvonkov, unlocking yet another metal gate. "We're supposed to ring the bell when we enter,"

"Oh – follow imperial protocol by all means," said Tutyshkin.

The Tsar was sitting at his desk in the reception room, dressed in the same blue and white gown as the other guests, but with a large Caucasian hat propped up on his head. In front of him lay a great screed of paper and a pen; his majesty was at work on his abdication speech, as always.

"Yes?" said the Tsar, surprised to see the orderly standing there and not his loyal *prizhivalschik*, Starchenko.

"Somebody to see you your radiant majesty."

"The Minister for Education?"

Zvonkov pulled a face. "A policeman – an inspector…"

The Tsar pulled the same face as Zvonkov. "Oh well, bid him enter."

Tutyshkin and the Tsar carefully examined each other, each searching for signs of deception. Even Tutyshkin had to admit that the guy really looked the part – right beard, handsome features, slightly vacant eyes. Of course, he was too old and his hair had turned white – otherwise he would have made a perfectly respectable waxwork dummy.

"So Inspector," said the Tsar, his eyes flicking nervously back at his papers. "What can Imperial Russia do for you?"

Tutyshkin bowed. "I am here to speak of Lepinov, your majesty."

"Alexei?"

"Lepinov – the Chief Superintendent. I believe that he would visit you here at your palace."

"Palace?" Nicholas' moustache twitched mirthlessly. "I would hardly call these rooms a palace ... well, what does this Lepinov say? Am I to return to Petersburg?"

"Peter? Ah, no..."

"I cannot return until the speech is done. And then there is the Imperial family to think of..."

"Well, yes of course."

The Tsar gestured down at the endless scroll washing across the desk like a waterfall. "What can I say, what should I tell the people? It is necessary that I should abdicate for the good of Russia, I am ready for it, but the people – the people will not understand."

His face was grave and drawn, enigmatic thoughts passing across his mind like clouds across the sky. He stared not at Tutyshkin but at some invisible spot just behind him, a place only he could see – the very heart of *Rus*, perhaps.

"The people, well yes indeed," said Tutyshkin, looking down at his muddy clothes. "And you discussed all this with Lepinov?"

"But of course: the future of this land lies heavily upon my soul. I have been born for misfortune. God punishes me, you know: punishes me for ruling too meekly, for staying the Imperial hand. I have should have ruled like Ivan the Terrible, but instead I governed like a lamb. Only autocratic power is divine power. I permitted the mice to play too many games... No, no, don't contradict me. I allowed myself to become blinded by love."

"Love?"

"For the people. They are children, the Russian race. Absolute power is required to restrain their childish ways. That's what foreigners do not understand … democracy cannot take root here, the people do not want it…" The old man's voice trembled. "Like Romanov and Susanin, the people and I are bound together for eternity. Do you have any cigarettes?"

"And Superintendent Lepinov agreed?"

"It is not a question of agreement, but rather recognition of the truth. French, English tobacco, I really don't mind."

Tutyshkin watched the Tsar's eyes flit nervously from papers to window to door, like a bluebottle looking for the way out. Only when they settled upon some abstract symbol inside his skull did they finally find rest.

"It is my duty before God to maintain the principle of autocracy as firmly and as unflinchingly as it was preserved by my unforgettable father. People do not influence events – God directs everything. The Tsar, as God's anointed, does not take advice from the masses, but only from the Holy Spirit. And yet God now tells me that I must abdicate, step aside in favour of my son. How can this be? How can I place this burden upon the brow of a helpless child?"

Tutyshkin nodded.

"Last night I dreamed that blood ran from Alexei's side all the way down the streets of Moscow, stopping off to buy cigarettes along the way. What do you think it means, *herr doctor*? Afterwards I dreamt that the Imperial procession was moving past series of dry, yellow fields, all baking in the sun. In one, there was a solitary tree from which a naked man used a scythe to carve the side of a whole rack of beef. When he opened his mouth his tongue was the same colour as the flesh and Alexandra asked to borrow my *lorgnette*."

"Most perturbing, I'm sure. Beef, you say?"

"When a peasant dreams, he dreams of a soft, white bed. But when the Tsar dreams he sees only omens."

"And you discussed your dreams with Lepinov?"

"But of course! Once I dreamed that I was a lowly shop-keeper from Lipetsk – dry goods, straw, grain, material for hats. Can you imagine it? Ladles for ladies and hats for cats. I dreamt that I was sitting at a great desk, filling in ledgers, recording figures … and I had a wife and daughters too. Daughters, my dear fellow! Now what do you think of that?"

"Most mysterious, your majesty…"

"Susanin gave his life for the Tsar: therefore the Tsar must give his life for the people. What little strength I have, I draw from serving Russia. But my son? He is not well. When stricken, he cannot even rise to his feet. And this, this … babe, is to rescue *Rus*? Alexei is a sweet lad but cannot find his trousers… 'where are they? Wither are his britches? And over Russia I see a quiet, far-spreading fire consume all."

"Well, quite," said Tutyhskin, looking the Tsar in the eye. "And when did you discover that you were really the Imperial Emperor of Russia, my angel?"

The Tsar took Tutyshkin's hands and rocked from side to side. "Why, Lepinov told me! He explained to me that I had been moved to this place for my own safety, while the rest of Russia believed me to be dead. What was it he called me? A vessel waiting to be filled."

"And the Tsarina?"

"Yes, yes, close by."

"And Alexei?"

"Alexei?" At this the Tsar's whole face seemed to quake. "Why, he's to be found in the sanctuary, of course. Have they moved him? Is he back in Moscow? It is not safe there – the Germans attack from the West. The boy cannot walk – how then can he command our troops? Yes, the sickness grows worse. At times he cannot rise from his bed. His skin is the colour of milk. His blood pours from the winter palace – bagmen sell it in bottles, twelve kopecks a jar. He must not be moved – the slightest scratch could prove fatal. It is a punishment – a punishment from God. The Heavens tell me that I must abdicate – but how can I transfer such a burden to my son?"

"I also bring holy water, your Imperial munificence..."

"The water? Why, yes, I..."

"*Christy* waters, from Saint Leonilla's well..."

"You are a great comfort to me, my friend. Whenever I am in trouble or plagued by doubts, I need only talk to you and I invariably feel at peace."

"Why thank you, your majesty."

"I fear that without this life-giving elixir, poor Alexei would have passed to the Lord's care long before... I shudder to think of it! And the Tsarina ... if her son were to be plucked from her ... well, best not to say... my thanks, dear fellow ... you are a good, simple-minded Russian... your Father Tsar blesses you..."

With that, the Old Tsar moved his hand across Tutyshkin's bottle in blessing; for once his hand didn't seem to tremble at all.

"Take the water to Alexei in the sanctuary," he said. "And tell my dear Alexandra that I think of her and long to be reunited."

"But of course..."

"Of course. Now hurry – the future of Russia depends upon these holy drops."

At this, the Tsar nodded curtly and returned to his eternal drafting of his speech. His expression was focused and concerned, his pen suspended in space like a hawk. Tutyshkin turned back to look at Zvonkov.

"I fear our audience with the Tsar is at an end."

"If it pleases you, inspector," said the orderly, weighting his words with as much sarcasm as they could bear.

"What a marvellous performance," said Tutyshkin as they retired to the mildewed corridor watched over by the bandy-legged clock. "Do you think all that stuff comes naturally to him or does he have to practice?"

"If a cock opens its mouth then something is bound to come out."

"You're a philosopher my dear Zvonkov, a pearl."

Descending back past the frescoes Tutyshkin peered through one of the barred and locked doorways and spotted the mischievous old man he'd observed earlier that morning – the old goat with the ball, Dr Bezenchuk, the chief superintendent before Lepinov. Now the old man lay slumped in a chair like a discarded dressing gown, his eyes dull and his lips slightly parted; Tutyshkin paused and pointed him out to Zvonkov.

"Your old boss, if I'm not mistaken. A little less lively this afternoon though."

Zvonkov glanced at him without interest.

"Him? Yes, that's Bezenchuk right enough...."

"And were you employed here at the Yellow House during our darling Bezenchuk's reign?"

"Mm."

"And Lepinov? Did Bezenchuk ever meet him?"

"Lepinov? It was Lepinov who had him locked up. For the good of his soul, he said. Nu, I'm not sure about that... it was all to do with that mess with Orlov, if you ask me."

The old man softly blew a raspberry, but seemingly without malice or intent. His eyes were as empty as a coalscuttle.

"You didn't think he was ill?"

"What do I know? As long as madhouses exist then someone has to be locked up in them. But Bezenchuk was no more crazy than Lepinov, not from where I'm standing."

Tutyshkin nodded and walked with Zvonkov back into the rain
– Holy water itself, at least of a kind. Zvonkov sneezed and the
inspector passed him a rag. The building watched them like a
toad. For a moment, you could almost hear it croak.

four

1

"Historically, of course," said the historian Radek, gratefully receiving his husk of bread from Frumkin, "madness has always been seen as something to be dealt with by the religious authorities, monasteries the proper place for internment..."

"Well, they're right next door," said Frumkin, licking his lips.

"In this one must remember that lunacy was rarely seen as an ailment or even an impediment. Rather those that were touched were also seen as blessed."

"Blessed?"

Radek's eyes glowed. "Fools for Christ whose naked souls required the protection of the church. In Europe, the mad were seen as possessed by unclean spirits, just as the Greeks pronounced. Only in Russia was madness seen as holy."

"Really?" said Martynov from under his moustache. "I'm not sure Ivan the hunchback was treated like a saint on the streets where I grew up."

The professor, the *feldsher* and the actor were settled around the stove in one of the *flügel's* elegant reception rooms, slumped on seats that had once supported more aristocratic behinds. The actor, Martynov, tall and handsome with a strikingly noble nose, sat opposite the venerable historian whose crazy hair, long arms and curiously short body made it look like somebody had half-heartedly tried to shave a monkey.

"No, no, of course: but at least the church recognised the need to protect such souls. After all are not the most dirty and downtrodden of men in truth the closest to God?" Radek patted his hair down as if donning an imaginary cap. "Nakedness, public urination, spitting, defecation – the German sees these as diabolical, the Russian as proof of the sinner's proximity to the divine. Even Ivan the Terrible wrote under the pseudonym of Porfeny the Fool."

"Mm, there's a couple of guys in ward five who are particularly reverent," said Frumkin, passing Martynov an onion. "So what are you saying – the monasteries took in the otherworldly 'cause they couldn't make it on the outside?"

"I thought that was the universities," said Martynov winking at the professor.

Radek smiled toothlessly (he had lost his dentures during his flight) and waggled the crust in the actor's face. "Well, there are many similarities. Both can be seen to provide shelter for, shall we say, visionary or unpopular ideas. Even today, only in an asylum can a man cry 'God Save the Tsar' and not get arrested."

"All this sounds very idealistic," said Frumkin, watching Martynov wipe the onion juice from his shirt. "But aren't both institutions just places to dump troublemakers? Call somebody a lunatic and you don't have to listen to them – it's the same with academics."

"You're far too cynical my dear Frumkin…"

Frumkin made the universal gesture for disgust. "Really? Okay, who sets up the Yellow Houses in the first place? Our supreme Queen of the Enlightenment, Catherine the Great – just around the time she was setting up the secret police. If you claim to be acting for reason and good sense then your enemies can conveniently be written off as maniacs. Lunatic, lunatock – the next thing you know the guards are turning the screws."

The professor pulled at his wild hair and regarded Frumkin

ironically. "Oh you doctors have always been such liberals! I suppose like the Reds you believe mental hygiene to be purely social."

"Who's mad? The guy who eats his soup with a fork or the radical whose ideas don't sit well with the state?"

"And under Bolshevism the new man will be strong willed, optimistic, free from uncertainty?"

"Unfortunately not" said Frumkin, glancing ruefully out of the window. "They'll just lock up a different class of people."

For a moment the three friends fell silent, the only sound Martynov's exuberant munching. Seated by the fire, surrounded by whatever relics of the old life had yet to be sold or burned, they looked just like a painting by Kiprensky, albeit a little faded at the edges. Only in the *flügel* were guests permitted to keep their own clothing, Radek in his professorial gown, Martynov dressed like one of Shakhovskoy's nobles. As a consequence of fleeing the city in their best clothes, the occupants of the *flügel* looked as if they were just heading out for a ball, albeit a provincial one everybody else had done their best to weasel out of.

Martynov finished his onion and sat back in his chair like Oblomov. "I played Lear in Kazan once, wearing only a loin cloth. Bloody cold. 'Poor naked wretches, wheresoe'er you are, that bide the pelting of this pitiless storm' – then someone opened a door, a breeze blew in, and everyone got to see my Tom's a cold... Gave the ladies in the front row something to weep about, I can tell you."

"I'm just saying," said Frumkin, "that when I started out in psychiatry, all anybody cared about was examination and testing. Was this a crazy person or not? Was there still evidence of reason? And the only boxes to tick were yes and no."

"Well, yes, crude empiricism, but..."

"So, could this guy hold a pen or the next grip a hoe? But all anybody really wanted to know about was loyalty. Could the citizen fulfil his duty? Was he any benefit to the state? That's all anybody asked me. Crooked or straight? Broken or whole? And that's how you decided whether the poor sucker was useful."

"And what did you tick my dear Frumkin?"

"The same box as everybody else – what do you think I am, an idiot? But you can see where this leads – only a crazy person would bad mouth the Tsar."

"My point exactly!" said Radek, picking absent-mindedly at the stuffing of his chair. "Only the fool is permitted to speak the truth."

"Mm – if he wants his jacket to tie up at the back. But who's listening then?"

"Nobody's listening now," grumbled Martynov, growing bored. "I thought you wanted to hear about our dreams."

"It's all a dream..." said Frumkin, wearily.

"Now you listen to me Frumkin, I've got a good one... last night I dreamt that St Isaac's Cathedral was filled with caviar and Lenin was standing there with a big spoon..."

The *feldsher* looked tired. "I'd say you were hungry..."

"Well, that's the benefit of your university education. Did I say Lenin? I meant my mama, her apron full of rainwater, smelling of warm bread."

"With her moustache, they're easy to mix up."

"The spoon turned out to be a ferry on the Volga, where I once spent a magical night with a young gypsy called Zdenka. Ah, what a dame – like sugar on a plum! The moon like a pie crust, the stars reflected in the water, millions of tiny teeth..."

"The stars or the girl?"

Martynov's own teeth were rather yellow, but large and strong, like those of a horse.

"Then I pulled up her skirt and..."

At that moment there was a knock on the door and Nadya entered, smelling of a mixture of iodine and detergent.

"Sirs? Madame Semenova wishes to speak with you. She says it's about Tutyshkin."

The three men exchanged glances.

"Okay, okay – send her in."

"Um, she, ah…"

"Oh, don't worry, just…"

Madame Semenova entered the room as if dancing a polka at some unearthly ball; only when Nadya slipped away did she come to a rest and address the learned assembly directly.

"Professor, doctor, my dear Martynov. Please forgive this intrusion. You were asking about an Inspector Tutyshkin."

"You've heard of him?"

"Heard? Well, I've had dealings. One of our clerks was attempting to embezzle stock and Tutyshkin helped bring the reprobate to court."

Before her arrival at the Yellow House, Tatiana Semenova had owned a whole chain of *perfumèries* in Voronezh, as well as sponsoring a regular series of artistic *soirees* known for their aesthetic daring and a pungent cherry liqueur that was 92% proof. Madame Semenova was a middle-aged woman with striking black hair, tiny dark eyes and remarkably wrinkle-free skin, as if her outer layer had been stretched out on a drum. Her *soirees* verged on the *avant-garde* and the painter Lazimir had once broken her down into geometric forms before an aghast crowd.

"So what was he like? Tall, big chin, shaved head?"

Madame Semenova wrinkled up her nose. "Shaved head? Oh, how awfully droll. No, no, he had a full head of hair, like, like – how did Ketola put it – a tree full of starlings. Or was that Ivanov's beard?"

"Young, old?"

"Why, neither: middle aged I supposed. But very vital. Almost an animal magnetism."

"This can't be our joker," said Frumkin. "I wouldn't put him in charge of his own shoes."

"Well," said Madame Semenova, colouring slightly. "There was something quite eccentric about him – more like a poet than a representative of the authorities."

"Wasn't there some famous case involving a Tutyshkin?" asked Professor Radek, offering his seat to the dark-haired *perfumière*. "Something in the papers regarding a murder?"

"Don't ask me," sighed Martynov. "I only read the reviews and only then if good."

"Why yes," said Madame Semenova. "About six months after our dealings I spotted his name in print: Tutyshkin had been instrumental in the arrest of Sikorsky, the head of the Voronezh City Zoo."

"Zoo?"

"Hadn't he been feeding his victims to the animals – or did I dream that? Either way it was a sensational case, you must remember it…"

The three men all looked blank. "I was writing my book on the Old Believers of Solovky at the time" said the professor, palms outstretched. .

"Sikorsky was some kind of zoo keeper?"

"Yes, yes, fed his rivals to the lions – was it his family or just passers-by? Anyway, it was the talk of the town."

Frumkin looked at Madame Semenova curiously: her dark eyes shone and her plump, pinkish skin looked younger than ever.

"I had a dream I was a lion once," said Martynov. "The Tsarina was attempting to coax me out of my cage with a bone and …."

"Okay, so this Tutyshkin," said Frumkin. "Even if he'd have his head shaved, you'd recognise him, right? I mean, this wasn't so long ago."

"Of course I would – I haven't completely given in to our madness," replied Madame Semenova with a smile. Only the skin under her chin looked flawed, as if she'd been buttoned up like a cloak.

"Right. Um, our session is later this afternoon. At two, right?"

"I'll be counting the hours my dear doctor."

"Till later."

"Adieu."

After the *perfumière* departed, the three men returned to the meagre remains of their lunch.

"I'm not sure this place is all that good for her," said Frumkin. "Do you think craziness can be catching?"

"Neurasthenia?"

"Nerves? Nerves were last month. Who's got time for nerves? Now it's morbid anxiety."

The elderly professor rolled around a hard egg on his plate. "These are morbid times. Death, dying, disappearances late at night. Is it any wonder that the suicide rate is so high?"

"To a Jew, doom isn't news," said Frumkin. "Only the Reds believe in the future – which is why they're going to win."

"The important thing is to vary one's repertoire," said Martynov, sleepily. "*Tartuffe* for the noble folk, then dress up as Gorky's *Mother*."

"Fire and blood. The Bolsheviks love all that sort of stuff. Do you know what's painted above the entrance to the jail in Davydovka? 'With an Iron Fist We Will Lead Humanity to Happiness'"

"And what were you doing outside the jail?"

"Don't ask. At least I was outside. The important thing is not to be a class enemy. Nobody knows what it means, but it's definitely not a compliment."

"I still don't see why I wasn't permitted to play the role of doctor," said Martynov, grumpily. "In my youth I played the physician in *The Healer of Souls* to very great effect."

"Trust me," said Frumkin. "The role of committed narcissist suits you much better."

"Aye, I'm too famous, 'tis true. What's that quote by Polonius? 'To define true madness – what is't but to be nothing else than mad?'"

"I had a colleague at the University for whom everything was a matter of historical determinism," said Radek, tapping his egg, "a German philosophy to which we fatalistic Russians are particularly prone. Nerves, depression, suicidal tendencies: all bourgeois traits, he believed, vestiges of the old order yet to be expunged from modern life."

"This bread tastes of birch bark," said Martynov, scowling. "Do you have any paté?"

"Aleshin's very down on suicide," said Frumkin. "Takes it personally. A bourgeois betrayal, he calls it. Not like our much-missed Superintendent. He gargled with suicide like a glass of fine wine. Of course genuine depressives rarely take time out to fleece their guests."

Radek threw up his arms as if to say 'nobody blames you for that, dear fellow', knocking over his plate and bowl in the process.

"Yes, my colleague and I had many arguments regarding the so-called suicidal personality. He blamed poets and thespians." Here Radek winked at Martynov. "He felt that only after all these were successfully liquidated, would the New Man be truly able to breathe…"

"Hm, what's that you say?" asked Martynov, his mouth full of onion.

"This colleague of yours must be celebrating now."

"Not really – he was executed for hoarding bread. Or so

people said…"

At that moment the doors to the reception room flew open again and two small round figures in expensive suits burst in, pursued by Nadya.

"I'm sorry Dr Frumkin," she said, "I tried to stop them, but they insisted."

"Frumkin, we have to talk," yelled one of the men, his face flushed and his brow furrowed. The other's little goatee nodded in agreement and Frumkin rose to his feet.

"But of course, gentlemen. Thank you Nadya. Nadya? I'll take it from here."

The two businessmen suddenly seemed to register the nurse's presence and started to crow like cockerels. Fortunately, they stopped the minute she closed the door.

"What's all this about some Inspector, Frumkin?" one demanded. "We're paying you good money to…"

"You're not paying me anything," Frumkin snapped. "You paid Lepinov, but he's gone. Now we all need to keep our heads and…"

"So why is this Inspector snooping around? We can't afford for…"

"Look, I've met this Tutyshkin – he couldn't find his toes in his sock. Petr found him wandering about in the woods and his horse led him back here. Trust me: he's got no idea about our little arrangement or the *flügel*. All he's worried about is who bumped off Lepinov – which, let's be honest, could be anyone…"

The two-headed businessman exchanged glances, as alike as two playing cards in the pack.

"Well, how can you be sure? This Tutyshkin: he's some kind of big shot. Back in Voronezh, his name was all over the papers. He's some genius detective like Inspector Dupin. If he catches wind…"

"Believe me, our prince is no genius: I've had smarter coats. Just keep your heads down and your traps shut. Tutyshkin is sniffing down a different rabbit hole entirely."

Back in Davydovka, Balashov had owned a paper mill and Yurovsky some kind of copper-works. In their best suits and neckties they looked like they'd just been turfed out of their box in the theatre.

"All I'm saying," growled Balashov, eying up Martynov's onion, "is that we're counting on you to fulfil your end of the bargain. Don't tell me that a *zhid* like you isn't making a little something on the deal. And if this Tutyshkin finds out…"

Yurovsky's goatee shook like a bell rope. "Say what you like, Tutyshkin's no dope. He smashed the Sinegub case – and caught Sikorsky too."

"Yeah, yeah, the zoo-keeper, I heard…"

"Zoo keeper? Sikorsky was a jewel thief. But they caught him at the zoo: he was hiding in the lion cage."

"Near the lion's cage you goose," growled Balashov. "But what does it matter? You've got to make sure that this Tutyshkin stays away…"

"You know him?"

"Not personally. But this Tutyshkin doesn't waste his time chasing butterflies. Lepinov told us that Denikin would be here within days. You've got to keep him out of our hair until then."

"The Whites? Lepinov had a direct line to Admiral Kolchak, right? Listen you play your part and I'll play mine. With Lepinov gone, we've got more to worry about with Aleshin than this Tutyshkin."

"Anyone who cracked the Sinegub case…"

"Tutyshkin's performance as a master detective is as convincing as Martynov playing Ophelia. The guy belongs on the *cinematograph*. Now go back to your ward and hope that Denikin's men show up rather than the People's army. Just remember to cluck whenever Nadya's in the room."

As soon as Balashov and Yurovsky closed the door, Frumkin collapsed back in his seat and Radek and Martynov regarded him silently. Then Martynov said, "What did you mean about my Ophelia?"

Frumkin stared at the fire like a chicken looking at the pot.

Eventually Radek said in a quiet voice "Do you think the White army is close? Lepinov said that…"

"You think that Lepinov knew? Okay, he might have heard things from the bagman, but really, how can anyone this side of the Volga really know?"

"But Denikin has taken Odessa, Kiev…"

"Perhaps…"

"Come on Frumkin," said Martynov, standing by the fire like a Turgenev hero. "The tide is undoubtedly turning. In Voronezh the Reds rule by sufferance rather than the people's will. The Bolsheviks are scruffy, drunk and violent. They loot shops and rob citizens in the street. How long can this go on? There's talk of a St Bartholomew's Night for the bourgeoisie – the Bolsheviks are already sharpening the knives."

"And your Denikin will be any better?" said Frumkin, still staring at the fire.

"How can you say that? The University has been closed, the Mensheviks and Socialists rounded up. The posters talk of a bonfire of capitalists, kulaks, bourgeois intellectuals. Private homes are looted on the pretence of searching for hoarded goods."

"Well, I've heard some pretty hair-raising things about Denikin's army too – and I don't just mean for the Jews. If towns won't hand over their food supplies then…"

"Of course during war-time…"

"Sure, sure, hangings, executions, villages burned to the ground. A Russian loves nothing more than destruction. But why should peasants flock to the Whites? They'll just give the land back to the rich. And that's all the peasants care about."

"What do you know of the Russian peasant?" demanded Martynov. "The peasant loves their Father Tsar, their priest, their *bárin*. No creature on earth is more tied to Russia than a true son of the black earth."

"They certainly didn't love Ryabovsky," said Frumkin, gloomily. "And their love of bárin didn't stop them from burning down his bedroom."

"With respect Frumkin," snapped Martynov. "You're an urban Jew ... you don't know the Russian soul. Of all the races on earth it is by far the most spiritual, the most, ah ... what did Radek say: the dirtiest peasant is closest to God."

"The Whites are telling the peasants that the Bolshevik regime is a Jewish conspiracy: that all its leaders are Jews – well, excepting Lenin's bald head. For them Pogroms are simply revenge for Red terror. The Reds shout 'Death to the *Burzhoois*', and the Whites yell 'Death to the Yids'. I don't know about you, but for me it's not a comfortable place to sit."

"Frumkin, Frumkin, Frumkin," said Martynov. "You and I have been friends for many years, and I'm very grateful for all you've done. But we all know the Jews have got rich from speculating on the economic crisis. Little wonder that the Whites believe such wealth should be used for the war effort instead."

"Well, that's the great thing about being a Jew," said Frumkin bitterly. "There's always a stash of gold hidden someplace between your gums."

"Awful things are going on," said Radek, positioning himself between them. "But Frumkin, you're a doctor, a psychiatrist, a member of the *intelligencia* – there's only one side to be on."

"Ah, but I'm just a humble *feldsher*," said Frumkin, refusing to look at either man. "You must be mixing me up with somebody else."

At that moment the door was flung open a third time, Nadya entering alongside Simanovich, the banker. Simanovich was tall, smartly dressed, with a long but neatly trimmed beard. Only his eyes rolled crazily, as if somebody had knocked over his hen house.

"I'm sorry doctor, but he pushed his way past and…"

"It's okay Nadya, we're used to it. My dear Mr Simanovich, what can we do for you?"

"Tutyshkin, Frumkin – a dream!"

Radek and Martynov looked at one another. Frumkin licked his lips

"Thank you Nadya, we can take it from here"

"But sir…"

"Go, go, it's fine."

The nurse closed the door but Simanovich continued to stalk about the room, his expression wild and haunted.

"It's okay Vassily, you can knock it off now, she's gone."

"What? No, it's true, Frumkin. Two nights ago I dreamed of a shaven head riding a dead horse – and then I saw you talking with him, doctor, just outside the door."

"The horse?"

"The baldie – the man from my dream. I've seen him before, Frumkin, in some place terrible … From his head came enormous antlers, tall and wide as an elk. Gentlemen, gentlemen, you can't imagine the sight. And in his saddlebag, the heads of the fallen – severed at the neck." Simanovich's eyes bulged like a rich man's pockets. "From mud it came, the horse pulling itself out of the grave, flesh falling from its flank. And the horses's muzzle, why…" At this, the banker stared at Frumkin's sceptical expression and abruptly stopped. "You don't believe me."

"Look, maybe you saw his sketch in a paper – something about a zoo…"

"A zoo? Don't mock me, Frumkin. This Tutyshkin is a creature from another world… a demon!"

"Hey, look, nobody likes the police, but you need to get a grip Simanovich. You're letting this place get to you. Remember what I said: act a little crazy but don't draw attention."

"He's here to open the gate. I know this. The very gates of Hell!"

"Vassily, I've spoken with this guy; he's as human as you or I. I mean, a little clinked in the noggin, but, listen: definitely no antlers. They're hard to hide even under a hat."

"Don't let him in here Frumkin. He's the Angel of Death. He's come to destroy us."

"He's come to figure out who stiffed our Superintendent. How many times do I have to say it? He's got no interest in the *flügel*. Our arrangement is completely beside the point. Let him sniff around for a couple of days and he'll be off: we've got other things to worry about. At the moment the roads are so bad nobody is going anywhere. When they dry up, we'll have to find out whether it's the Whites or the Reds digging our graves. Until then, belts tied. And don't scare Nadya – the last thing we need is for one of the other nurses to be assigned here – never mind one of the other doctors…"

At this Simanovich seemed to calm down.

"But my dream…"

"We'll talk about it later."

"That man: he was the same…"

"You remembered the face but forgot the name – maybe some fraud case, who knows? If you can think of anything that doesn't involve antlers, let me know. In the meantime, try and get some rest. The Yellow House is no place for craziness."

Nodding, the banker reluctantly took his leave, closing the double doors behind him.

"Well, that was strange," said Radek. "And to think, I always considered Simanovich the most sober of individuals."

"Madness," said Martynov. "It's the Russian disease."

"A dead horse?"

"Dead tired."

Radek's gums smiled as he warmed himself by the stove. "And yet who would have thought our dour banker would be capable of such visions! Just like the Holy Fool! Just like Gogol's Madman. What was it Herzen said? Though lost in concentration, the madman may be more independent, more original, closer to true genius. And are his dream worlds in any way inferior to the real nightmare outside?"

Frumkin shook his head while Martynov assumed a noble pose. "Talking of dreams," he said, "I had a dream where instead of a pen I was trying to write with a perch ... or was it a chub, I forget... Anyway, this fish, it..."

Frumkin wasn't listening. Outside, the rain fell without pause, the clouds clasped like a murderer's hands. Despite Frumkin's flippancy, something about Semanovich's dream bothered him. The severed heads in a bag and proud, erect antlers suggested a sexual meaning, but the dead horse threw him. Yana? Russia? Staring out of the window, he imagined Tutyshkin's face grinning back at him, a perfectly round smile, like a child's drawing of a fool.

2

Although Aleshin pored over the papers till well after midnight, their secrets still eluded him. Either some pages were missing, or the papers had become confused, or somebody had muddled two different reports – whatever it was, nothing seemed to make sense. Was there a second prisoner, whose transferral details had somehow been mislaid? Or was it that the information regarding Sikorsky was itself contradictory, no matter how many official stamps and seals it bore?

One thing was sure: the cold, dead hand of Lepinov touched everything. The prisoner exchange was not only authorised by the late Chief Superintendent, but had been initiated by him as well. According to the papers, the killer Sikorsky was to be brought to the Yellow House 'for psychiatric treatment and observation'. The document acknowledged (albeit in a rather vague manner) the receipt of funds covering the costs of this transfer as well as a not inconsiderable sum relating to the employment of armed guards, apparently for the purpose of safe transportation. Money – and quite possibly a great deal of money – had obviously changed hands: but why would Lepinov want somebody like Sikorksy in the first place? Aleshin could see no logic. Several years before the young doctor had arrived, another patient, a certain Orlov had fled the treatment room, assaulted Yevgrafovna, and tried to murder one of the orderlies. Feh, who needed another Orlov? Not even Orlov's mother. No, nothing made sense. The Yellow House had neither the facilities nor the correct procedures to deal with an individual such as Sikorsky. And why, during a time of revolutionary class conflict, should such a wolf be transported across a wild and unstable region anyway? Aleshin shook his head – the whole thing was a tangle. Like Shiskin's tea, the waters only got murkier the more you stirred.

Cleaning his spectacles, Aleshin once more sought out first principles, solid ground. Sikorsky was identified as belonging to the bourgeois class, his official designation 'an enemy of the proletarian struggle'. Before the revolution, he had worked for an import/export business, primarily in jewellery and precious metal. In cold blood, and with absolute premeditation, he had murdered two other employees of the firm of Tager and Woytinksy: employees, whom, the prosecutor claimed, lay in the path of his professional advancement. Before his apprehension, he had also murdered his father (who'd confronted him with evidence of his homicidal activities) and attempted to dispatch his wife and two young daughters. In regard to the latter butchery, he had been prevented only by the quick thinking of an Inspector Tutyshkin, who had apprehended Sikorsky during a family visit to the district zoo (curiously, although Tutyshkin's name was mentioned in relation to Sikorsky's arrest, there was no explicit reference to his having any official involvement in the transferral: for the moment Aleshin let this pass). Whilst in custody, Sikorsky had also admitted his involvement in a series of other murders: a student friend, a deliveryman, a passenger on the Tula – Penza railway, even his landlord during a stay in Moscow. Sikorsky's only denial involved pushing his daughters into the lion cage: he assured the authorities that he was simply assisting them through the bars for a better look.

So far, so bad: but at this point, the sheath of papers began to mysteriously unravel. There were also charges of embezzlement, fraud and impersonation of a government official: how these related to Sikosrky's other crimes remained unclear. There were references to crimes of an indeterminate nature committed in Saratov, seemingly dating from six months after Sikorksy's committal, but these too were vague and insubstantial. Despite the number of references to Sikorsky's capture amongst the wild animals at the zoo, in at least one report he was apprehended attempting to board a train to Perm. His conviction accorded once in the Spring, and then twice more in the Autumn. His patronymic kept shifting. A missing cache of cut-diamonds appeared in one draft, but then disappeared again, like a mirage.

Aleshin, whose own bookkeeping was so meticulous, was appalled. In one entry, Sikorksy's age was entered as thirty four, in the next forty three. Somehow, he was simultaneously both six foot two and five foot eleven. His beard came and went, like the wind. Was such carelessness a clear indictment of bourgeois capitalist inefficiency, or proof of a counter-revolutionary campaign of sabotage and gross falsification? The more he read, the angrier Aleshin became.

Other aspects of the case worried away at Aleshin's mind too, in particular the act of patricide. Sikorsky had stabbed his father with, of all things, a paper knife, the slim blade piercing his father's heart and killing the bourgeois element on the spot. Despite this mortal wound, the dead father had somehow managed to appear in court six months later to testifying as to the accused's bad character, low morals and general lack of filial respect, orating for more than an hour in what was described as a "rich and authoritative voice". Speaking from the witness bench – and presumably from beyond the grave – Sikorsky senior angrily lambasted his offspring for his idle temperament, his dubious acquaintances and for bringing shame to the family name. The accused had been given everything in life – wealth, education, a loving home – and thrown it all to the dogs. His actions had destroyed his family, his reputation and his sanity. From this day on, his name would be struck from the family bible, never to be spoken of again.

Aleshin leapt up from his desk and marched around the room. How could a dead man declaim these things? What right did the deceased have to speak? Let the young dead bury the old dead: a corpse should remain in its grave. Running his hands through his hair, Aleshin forced himself to take a deep breath and return to his seat. The unreliability of the text was truly shocking: how could such errors be allowed to slip through?

When he glanced down, he saw the report had turned itself into an account of Sikorsky's visit to the zoo: another aspect of the case which seemed peppered with inconsistencies. To start with, the mention of the lion's cage seemed rather spurious: did the zoo at Voronezh even possess such beasts? Thinking back to the times when his own mama and papa had taken him there, Aleshin could only remember the deer park and a cage of green parrots - more of a menagerie than a zoo. It was alleged that the defendant had transported his family to the African exhibit with the express intention of homicide: but of all the places to commit such an act, this surely seemed one of the least likely….

Struggling to recall the zoo, Aleshin allowed his mind to slip ever backward: the dark avenue of trees, the blue sky, the cry of the parrots. All at once, an incredibly clear image – almost a vision – appeared inside the comrade doctor's head: Gregory, age four, dressed in a blindingly white sailor's suit and riding a carousel at the zoo, his beloved mama watching him from afar. His horse was white with a red scarf – Sasha, was that it? Mama had promised him that if he was a brave little soldier she would buy him an ice. Aleshin remembered the horse's crooked teeth and fierce expression. But why was his mother looking so angry? He was still pondering this mystery when the sound of knocking brought him abruptly back to earth.

"Gregory?"

"What?"

"Gregory? Dr Aleshin? Are you awake?"

Marya trembled in her thin hand-made gown, one hand holding a candle while the other played nervously with her hem. Aleshin said nothing as Marya moved closer.

"I'm sorry doctor, but I couldn't sleep. And my bed is ever so cold."

"Yes, yes," said Aleshin, brusquely. His hand shook a little as he held open the door. "Come quick, before someone sees."

Entering the doctor's sparse but scrupulously clean apartment Marya felt as if she were crossing some boundary between the everyday world and someplace finer and more meaningful. Aleshin was as beautiful as an angel.

"Oh Gregory, I've been so scared…"

"Scared?"

"Of the murderer. And that Tutyshkin. His head is like a serpent's egg."

"Mm."

Marya glanced at Aleshin's papers and then made her way toward the bed. Stopping by the bedside table, she glanced down at the phonogram.

"Gregory – can we play something? Some music, I mean. It's so beautiful and…"

Aleshin shook his head.

"But why not? Why have a machine and never play it? Music is so pretty. It makes me think of pretty things."

The doctor pulled a face.

"I can't listen to music any more. It makes me want to say kind, stupid things and pat people's heads. But I can't. During war time you have to beat them on the head – beat them without mercy."

Aleshin's expression was hostile and angry. For a moment he sensed Sasha's dead wooden head looking up at him.

"Don't say such things," said Marya, her own eyes downcast. "It's a sin."

"Sin?"

Aleshin's speech was cut short by the fact that Marya had removed her gown. Except for the two dark circles of her breasts, her skin was very pale. She trembled by the candle like a second flame, the hair between her legs the colour of corn.

Aleshin nodded and started to remove a prophylactic from a drawer. Marya, however, was already upon him. With a kind of swoon, the doctor allowed himself to be swept over to the bed, his breathing fast and his lips awful dry.

"But Marya, I need to, ah…"

"There's no need," said Marya, rolling on top of the doctor like a hay bale. "No need, my love."

In this, she was correct. Marya was already three months pregnant, carrying Aleshin's child. Thinking of the World Struggle, the good doctor closed his eyes and allowed Marya to claim him.

3

So: had Nikolai the yardman murdered the Chief Superintendent or not? After a bottle of plum brandy and a quart of a bucket of grain alcohol, even the *dvornik* wasn't so sure: Zvonkov's words stayed with him like a hornet's sting. Exactly what had the yardman been doing during the night? All that remained were flashes: a rack of wine jugs, a broken bottle, the shadow of a cat. It was like kneading soup with your hands – nothing seemed to stick. Only one clear picture remained: the sight of the Superintendent's oddly adorned head colliding with Nikolai's pole at the bottom of the well. But where had this meeting twixt Mr Pole and Master Head taken place? Had Nikolai tossed Lepinov down the shaft and used the pole to drown him? Or had he innocently discovered him there, stinking like last week's fish? The more Nikolai thought about it, the cloudier things became. Why kill Lepinov? A dog doesn't bite the master if its' paws can't open the door…

Shaking his head, the old yardman lit his pipe and stared gloomily at the gates. The rain fell incessantly, like the complaints of a woman. Nikolai puffed on his pipe and scowled. His nose was blocked, his eyes ran, his knees ached like a bastard. For some reason he felt a terrible compulsion to howl at the sky – better a dog's life than this.

His station was no more than a forlorn clapboard hut with a tin roof which succeeded only in making the rain sound even louder, like a herd of cows being driven across his head. It stank of smoke, piss and booze. In one corner was a filthy mattress, crawling with life. The guests' rooms were cleaned but not Nikolai's: who would dare? A single shelf held half-eaten pots of jam, honey and a peculiar kind of gooseberry relish, still containing the corpse of a summer wasp. Elsewhere a table, a lamp, and a Muscovy chair reclined slovenly: not even Lenin's revolution could hope to move them. No, the yardman's station would remain thus until the end of time. Even in death, it was hard to imagine Old Nikolai changing his ways.

Was this better than his old life in the fields? But of course; here he could idle away his time drinking, sleeping and mooning over Alyona – the House was large enough that he could avoid most duties, performing those he was unable to escape as badly as possible. Unlike back in his village, he would not be whipped for failing to doff his cap at his masters: the doctors here were liberal and weak, their words unable to harm him. The loons he stayed away from; to Nikolai they were no more than human cattle, slow-witted and ungainly. Though his rheumatism made him testy and short tempered, the yardman was not without compassion: he never hit or mocked those in his care and watched them eat their kasha without comment. God had made them after all, just as he had planted thistles and nettles amongst the crop. Nikolai of course hated Frumkin the Jew, and mistrusted Yevgrafovna, who acted as if she had a dick between her legs. But doctors were doctors. Red, White, Green: whatever the regime, Nikolai would be at his post for longer than Saint Peter. Since Solokha's death, drink had been his one true friend, closer to him than a mother. Without drink, each night would last longer than a year, his watch unbearable. No, it was worse than that – without a drink the night would swallow him whole.

Solokha, his last pointer bitch, had died last winter. He had tried carrying her to her bed, but she had pulled away and staggered away to lie in the cool snow 'neath the porch of the *flügel*. When Nikolai found her, she was already on her side, helpless and finished. She died after two or three small shudders, without any yelps or cries, as good in death as life, the best of all companions. Nikolai would have buried her in the woods but the ground was too hard and the yardman too old. Instead, he placed her under a rough canopy of spruce, knowing full well that during the night other animals would come and take her away. What else should he do – toss her in the mire with the bones of the old cow? No, let her return to the forests that she loved. And yet the thought of Solokha all alone in the woods often came back to grieve him. One last thing she had asked of him, and he had been unable to do it. O Solokha! She had a little white mark on her head and grey paws. Her eyes were brown with a dash of black, as deep and kind as the Virgin's.

Since Solokha's death, Nikolai had oft reflected upon the difference between a dog's life and a man's, by no means certain that such a comparison was to man's credit. A dog stayed devoted for life whilst women demanded all sorts of things – money, sugar, fixing the roof. And a man? A man would knife you for a goose of vodka and a chaser of bread and onion. A skull for an eye and the whole mouth for a tooth; such was the true meaning of life. Nikolai's mother had carried him in her belly like a warm loaf of bread but she too had beaten him, sometimes with a plank. When Nikolai had married he had beaten his wife too, and when she died he found himself a fresh widow and began to beat her as well – and her brood of brats. A child needs a firm hand, but to beat a faithful dog – for such a crime a man would pay with his soul. Solokha would wake Nikolai by licking his face, and during their long nights would curl up and warm his feet. Whatever he ate he would share with her; if he were too drunk to find food she would never complain but rather nuzzle his fingers, rubbing up against him as if for warmth. How different to those ungrateful brats of Motka's! Always hungry, always crying, always making a mess. Finally he had tapped little Viktor a little too hard and had to leave the village. Still, the Yellow House had taken him in. Better to sleep by a door than plough the fields outside.

Nikolai smoked his pipe and stared out at the gloom. Without a nip the night stretched out like a rope. All sorts of thoughts come to a man in the dark heart of the night: Nikolai's mother, little Viktor, Solokha lying alone in the woods. Without a little stinker, a man could easily end up like those guests inside, soiling his pants and screaming at the walls. The night was long and a man's arms short: like reaching for Lepinov at the bottom of the well. Had Nikolai killed him? Zvonkov seemed to think so – but why should he care? A goose is not a pig's friend: let them hang somebody else for the Superintendent's bath. It was Churkin that Nikolai felt sorry for – a good lad even if he was a little cracked. Who then had strung him up like a woodcock? Not I, thought Nikolai, not I. Had he thrashed Solokha when he came back and found that she'd eaten the last bit of rabbit? Not at all. A man who takes a whip to a faithful dog is no man at all…

At this the drip drip drip of Nikolai's thoughts was interrupted by the sound of a loud banging at the outer gate. The yardman almost lost his pipe. No one had come to the gate at this hour in all the days since Lepinov's death: why choose tonight of all nights to return?

The knocking continued and Nikolai reached for the rifle, even if, given his current state, he was unable to either cock or load. What did they want? Why had they chosen now to return? Nikolai stared at the door as a rabbit stares at a hunter. Beyond the bars, he could see nothing, just the endless cloth of night. No trees, no outbuildings, no figure: a nothingness so absolute one could drown in it.

"Be gone! Clear off! Lepinov's dead and in no need of visitors."

In response to the yardman's words, the knocking fell silent. All Nikolai could hear was the sound of the rain and his own hot breath. Then the banging started up again, a little louder if anything, the rhythm swift and urgent. Instead of taking the lamp and advancing toward the gate, the yardman blew out the flame and hung back in the darkness.

"Bugger off I say – I will not open…"

The knocking continued, insistent as the rain, and Nikolai felt a wave of heat travel from his bladder to his heart. The Yellow House's rifle was aimed vaguely at the door but Nikolai had yet to load it. Instead, he retreated to the far corner of his hut, almost tripping over his chair in the darkness.

"Can't you hear? Lepinov's dead. I won't open this door anymore."

The hammering paused before coming back even louder, as thunderous as the tolling of a bell. Then it occurred to him: what if it were Lepinov's ghost that was outside the door, angry, lost, seeking revenge? All of a sudden, tears started to run down the yardman's cheeks.

"I didn't do it, curse you. Did any eye see me, any tongue wag? Be gone and leave me alone. That Zvonkov is a lying shit. Leave me alone! I didn't do it even if I can't find my boots."

Alas, Nikolai's words seemed to do little to calm the vengeful spirit located just outside. Instead, the raps fell like falling stones, the whole hut seeming to shake.

"So I found Lepinov's hide: does that make me the tanner? Let me sleep, you dirty corpse."

Was it Lepinov or some other unquiet shade? His first wife Olga or even the widow Motka – may dandelions grow over her bones. Little Viktor? No, no: no child could pound the gates like that.

"For the sake of my soul let me be."

The hammering stopped and Nikolai heard a scrabbling at the door like the paws of a dog. The old man was sobbing openly now, the rifle lying forgotten at his feet.

"Please…"

The silence was deafening, as if deep underground. Only when Nikolai gathered his wits did he understand that whatever had stood at the gates had gone. The yardman had pissed himself and his britches were wet and cold. His hands shook like the guests in ward four.

Scrabbling around his desk, Lepinov retrieved a match and lit it. A tiny prick of light appeared, its feeble circle making the darkness even deeper. With a second match, Lepinov lit his lamp. Nothing. It was perfectly dark, like placing your head inside a cow. He took a few more steps and finally arrived at the fence. The rain poured down and soaked his beard. Here he could see the outlines of the trees and the hump of an outhouse, but nothing else. Whatever had visited the Yellow House that night had gone. Once more Nikolai began to weep. If only Solokha was still by his side! Cold and wet, the yardman returned to his post. He possessed no timepiece and had no idea as to the hour – only that there wasn't even the merest crack of light in the east. Still shaking, he sought out the remaining finger of surgical spirits. His thoughts seemed lazy and sluggish. What had happened the night of Lepinov's death? Had he opened the gate to some unearthly visitor? Was it Lepinov's usual appointment, or another? But the yardman's memories refused to be squeezed into a single thought. All he wanted to do was tear off his clothes and stretch out like Solokha under the branches, his nose pointed toward the woods. All of a sudden a great and profound pity – for Solokha, for his mother, his wives, even for little Viktor – swept over him and Nikolai's very soul seemed to ache with sadness. When he opened his eyes it was still night.

five

1

When the visitors arrived the next morning, Nikolai was nowhere to be seen – sleeping it off in some barn no doubt. Rather than the yardman, it was Polina and Nadya, who spotted them from the top floor: two weary and bedraggled soldiers, their uniforms foreign looking and ragged, the men as blank-eyed and foul smelling as a pair of goats.

They were bread hunters, both desperately thin, with skin the colour of lichen and beards full of twigs. They limped toward the Yellow House as if they had travelled many miles, both barefoot, their mud-spattered knees giving the illusion of long galoshes. Nadya hung back but Polina pushed open the doors, one hand on her hip.

"Miss? Miss? Help us in the Saviour's name."

"There's bugger all for you here," Polina yelled. "We have nothing either."

"Please miss – we're starving, miss. Spare us an egg or a little bread, to save your soul…"

Polina regarded the pair with open contempt, remembering the last soldiers to enter through these gates. One wore a long trench coat with no buttons and cotton poking out of the holes; the other an army jacket with no belt, sleeves bound with white handkerchiefs.

"Be gone, I say. The Yellow House is full."

At this, the two tramps stared at each other, whispering

underneath their breath. Their gestures were those of sheep traders, their accents strange. Both were unarmed with long greasy hair and burrs stuck to their clothes. Eventually, one produced a brown and dirty bag, the pair of them pointing hopefully at it.

"We have goods to sell or swap – things you need. Please let us in, little sister."

Now it was Polina and Nadya's turn to exchange glances.

"Should we tell the doctors?"

"What can these crows have? Lice and scrofulous. Let them be on their way."

"But they might have news."

"They don't bring news but the weather. Soldiers are worse than wolves. They can all starve for I care."

The two graces looked back at the twin supplicants. The men's caps looked like drowned cats, earflaps unbuttoned. Everything about them spoke of ill fortune.

"We should still tell someone…"

"Why waste our breath? These two stink from the head down."

"But Polina, they…"

"Let the wolves take them. It's no concern of ours."

Despite Polina's protestations, Aleshin was sent for, Zvonkov accompanying him with an axe.

"Comrades," said the shorter of the two men, "in the name of Lenin I ask you grant us aid. Our unit was cut off by the Cossacks and…"

"The Cossacks are close?" asked Aleshin.

"No more than three or four days ride from here. Please, comrade doctor, an egg and a slice of black loaf."

Aleshin looked the men in the eye and nodded. "Open the gate" he said.

Zvonkov stared at him sceptically. "Balls. These are deserters or worse. Why should we listen to them? Send them on their way – we're no hostel to the lost."

Aleshin glared angrily at the orderly's moustache.

"Let them in, Comrade Zvonkov."

"Feh, they…"

"I told you to take them in."

Still grumbling, Zvonkov reluctantly let the pair inside. The soldiers looked more like corpses than men. They were deathly pale with patches of green skin under their eyes. If a worm had crawled out of the smaller one's nose, no one would have blinked.

"Bless you comrades, in the name of the Workers' Revolution…"

The orderly wiped his nose on his sleeve and snarled. No good could come of this.

As Zvonkov guessed, their news was sketchy and contradictory. The soldiers' had been ambushed somewhere between Davydovka and Chulm – by Cossacks, they said. The shorter one claimed to have seen their tunics, but his companion was more circumspect: "shooting" was all he said. Along with several other 'comrades' they had taken refuge in the dense woodland nearby. After their rations had run out, they had been forced to eat their horses; later they'd snuffled for roots and berries like pigs. Several of their party had been injured in the skirmish, and were in desperate need of medical attention. They had very little ammunition remaining – certainly not enough to defend themselves from the Whites, who were everywhere, like lice. If the Whites caught them, they would torture and then hang them. The woods were full of bodies hanging like broken branches, their ears and noses cut off. The survivors required food and the ministrations of a doctor: fortified, they might just make it to the Red Army camp at Tayda.

"And this skirmish," said Yevgrafovna. "When did it happen?"

The two soldiers looked at one another.

"A week," said one.

"Two months," said the other.

Embarrassed, they stared at Tutyshkin and the doctors with dull expressions. "'It's hard to remember, Comrade Doctor".

"Why do you have no boots?" asked Aleshin.

"The Red Army has no boots."

"And why do you wear foreign uniforms?"

"The Red Army has no uniforms, either. These were taken from the enemy – the British."

"The British? The British are here too?"

The two tramps shrugged. "The whole world is against us."

"Well, Inspector?" asked Frumkin, watching the two men squirm like pike in a net. "You've been out in the wilds – what do you have to say?"

For his part Tutyshkin – dressed in a blue *kostroma* tunic, dug out by Starchenko from who knows where – looked profoundly bored with the whole thing. "Well, I'm sure that these are honest and decent gentlemen, but I saw no Whites – only deserters and thieves."

"What was your regiment?" barked Aleshin. "And who was your commanding officer?"

Both men replied spontaneously, though their answers meant nothing to the doctors.

Aleshin nodded. "And how many of your corps remain?"

"Twelve sir – as long as no one else has croaked."

"Quite impossible," said Yevgrafovna, inspecting the men's dirty hands and nails. "We barely have any medical supplies for the House, never mind giving it away to passing brigands. Give them food, rest, and send them on their way. The Yellow House cannot help."

The men shifted uneasily, like a horse waiting to discover

whether it was to be saddled or whipped.

"Gentlemen, it's no use – the larder is empty," said Frumkin. "If the Whites are here then why go to Tayda? They have no boots or uniforms either."

"This is defeatist talk, comrade," hissed Aleshin.

"Oh, I'm sure these fellows have little intention of heading to Tayda," said Tutyshkin with a yawn. "The Red Army are the last folk they wish to meet…"

The taller of the men looked about ready to cry. "Please sirs – we work for the Revolution, just like you."

"Work by running away you mean? Doctors, the woods are awash with such cowards."

"We're no deserters…"

Tutyshkin smiled and made an aristocratic gesture intended to indicate that the audience was over. In panic, the two men stared at Aleshin, now their only hope.

"Please sir – we're workers, right enough. We need medicine and bandages if we're to make our way back."

Aleshin shifted uneasily. "Under revolutionary conditions … which is to say, the dictatorship of the proletariat…"

Desperate, the smaller one handed over his dirty, cow-skin bag. "We have things to swap – in exchange for your help."

"Bag men and deserters," said Tutyshkin, dryly. "A very dangerous combination."

The little one opened up his bag and spread its contents out over the table. For a moment Frumkin thought an armful of severed heads was about to tumble out, but no, the contents were much more mundane: some copper wire, a handful of cheap jewellery, a large golden cross obviously looted from some church. And alongside it – Petr's amulet of protection, the chain now rudely broken.

"Where did you get this?" demanded Aleshin.

"Some of our men ran into bandits – they took it from them…"

"Bandits?"

"Yes sir."

"Anarchists, greens?"

"I don't know, sir. It's yours if you want it."

Tutyshkin and the doctors looked at the bag and then looked at the men. Aleshin blinked. "Yes, yes I see. Starchenko, take the men to the barn, and give them food and water – but not a word to Zvonkov. The rest of us will retire to the Superintendent's office to discuss this further…"

When they walked out of the door the rain was waiting for them like a carriage.

An hour later, the argument was still in full swing. Aleshin insisted that as part of the Bolshevik movement, the Yellow House was obliged to lend as much assistance to the Red Army as it could, while Yevgrafovna argued that these two were jackals and dogs and should be pushed back under the mire.

"Doctor Aleshin," she explained, falling back in to her familiar hectoring voice, "do you truly believe that these men are trained, disciplined soldiers? That they honestly seek to make their way to Tayda and the Reds? These are deserters and runaways, thieves in the woods. Given half the chance they would cut our throats – just the way they cut poor Petr's."

"We can't know that for sure," said Frumkin. "The kid could be anywhere."

"There are no deserters," screamed Aleshin. "This is a war to the death against those henchmen of the bourgeoisie who seek to drown the Revolution in blood."

"No deserters? Who shoots at the Yellow House at night? Who prowls the woods?"

"Bandits, anarchists, Menshevik traitors. All the enemies of the working class who shall be destroyed and crushed by the proletariat boot."

"My dear sweet doctor," said Tutyshkin, drifting over to the doctors like a child at a party, "the peasants flee the Red Army by the hour. The Bolsheviks spend more time shooting conscripts than kulaks. The new recruits pick up their greatcoat, pack away their rations, and then leg it as fast as their legs will carry them."

"Dirty White propaganda," Aleshin spat. "Why would a peasant flee the worker's army? What peasant wants to give his land back to the Tsar?"

Tutyshkin's eyebrows arched. "Why fight? If a peasant dies, he doesn't get any land anyway. Why take another hilltop? Make peace at the bottom and everyone can go home to their fields."

"The peasants are the bedrock of the Revolution."

"If the peasants are such ardent revolutionaries why must they be signed up at gunpoint? No, my dear doctor, all they want is to go home and share out the land they got after stringing up the squire. Is this their field, their wood, their pond? If not, why get killed over it? The fields are filled with weeds. Whether it's the Tsar, Kaiser Wilhelm or Lenin sitting on the throne, the land is all that counts."

"Your class origins blind you to the historical circumstances," snapped Aleshin, strands of golden hair sticking to his brow. "The Red Army is engaged in a merciless class war, laying the foundation of a new Socialist…"

Frumkin knocked on the desk. "Okay, okay, we get the point. But what are we saying? We've barely got any gauze, medicine or dried food ourselves. Can we really afford to give it away?"

"Our first priority is to our patients," said Yevgrafovna.

"Our first priority is to the Revolution," barked Aleshin. "Anything else is treason."

For a moment, all fell silent. Rain drummed on the windows as in the time of Noah. The sky was the colour of a depressive's dreams.

"And what of Petr?" said Yevgrafovna finally. "Are we to feed his murderers?"

"Yeah, Petr," said Frumkin. "Poor kid."

"He might still be alive."

"Perhaps."

The doctors again fell silent.

"I say again: we must give assistance to the Red Army," growled Aleshin. "Are we kulaks or capitalists busy hoarding our goods? Everything must be sacrificed for the workers' struggle. I will go with these men and do what I can. To do otherwise would be to betray the blood of freedom fighters and martyrs."

"You're a fool, Aleshin," said Yevgrafovna. "You're digging your grave with your bare hands."

"Tsk, worry not my princess," said Tutyshkin, stirring himself sleepily from his seat. "I will accompany our esteemed doctor and ensure that no harm befalls him..."

"You?" sneered Yevgrafovna.

"Perhaps Lepinov's assassin is linked to these fellows – perhaps not. But your young man was kind enough to grant me assistance and the use of his steed. The least I can do is to help you find him."

Frumkin looked at Yevgrafovna and then at Aleshin. "Well, in that case Zvonkov should go too. Petr was Zvonkov's kid after all – there's no reason to leave him in the dark."

"Oh," said Tutyshkin with studied nonchalance. "I'm sure that the doctor and I can cope just fine."

"No, no, Comrade Frumkin's right," said Yevgrafovna. "If you insist on going then Zvonkov will accompany you. But perhaps best not to mention that these two tramps have Petr's stone; not until we know the truth."

"Comrade Yevgrafovna," said Aleshin. "We travel to assist the

Revolution, not search for some lost youth. Petr disobeyed orders and struck out on his own: our concern is not for the individual but the cause."

"Yes, yes" said Tutyshkin, bored. "The cause…"

"It is war, Inspector, life or death…"

"Mm," said Tutyshkin, "one or the other."

"If you must go, then take as little as possible," said Yevgrafovna. "Winter is coming. We can't spare the supplies and we can't spare the food."

"It is our duty to eat less."

"Is it our duty to starve the guests too?"

"Hey, don't look at me," said Frumkin. "I ate yesterday."

Despite Yevgrafovna's protestations, it was agreed that Yana should be loaded up with food (black bread, dried biscuits, cakes made of linseed oil and straw) and emergency medical supplies, the party to set off in the morning.

Walking back over to the wards, Frumkin took Yevgrafovna's arm and playfully pinched her.

"So what do you think?" he asked. "Aleshin finally going to get his campaign medal?"

"This is madness," she muttered. "What do they think they'll achieve out there, walking into a bandit's camp? They might as well leave their boots behind and tie themselves with bind. weed…."

Frumkin shrugged. "Well – maybe they'll find out something – whether the Whites are out there anyway. And what about our Inspector? Why's he so keen on this stroll?"

"Tutyshkin knows exactly what happened to Petr – and to his Sikorsky too. I say it again: Aleshin is putting his head inside a bear. And not through the front hole either."

Frumkin steered Yegrafovna away from a puddle and nodded.

In the *flügel* he could see the anxious face of Simanovich the banker peering out as if about to weep. Who was he looking for – Satan in his top hat? It wasn't hard to believe. On days like this, the whole estate looked like a preliminary sketch for the eternal realm of the dead.

2

The party departed at first light as planned – Aleshin, Tutyshkin, Zvonkov, Yana and the two nameless tramps. Nikolai was there to see them off, having finally emerged from whatever hole he'd crawled into. The yardman didn't look well. His beard fell from his chin in foul knots and tangles and his skin was the colour of corn oil. Opening the gate, he growled at the assembly half-heartedly, like a very old dog. His breath could fry onions. He still had no boots.

By way of contrast the two bread hunters looked a little more human – washed, fed, their feet clad in wooden shoes. Zvonkov kept his gun pointed at them at all times. This was a fool's errand and no mistake: the doctors were as cracked as the guests. Yana too was uneasy, shifting her head from side to side, trying to rest her lame leg. The supplies were heavy and she bowed her head against the endless river of rain. 'Why all this sorrow?' her eyes seemed to say. 'Why climb up, when the top is as tedious as the bottom?'

After days of constant rain, the post-road had been transformed into a quagmire, the filth as high as your thigh, with water streaming over the stones. Nor were the grassy banks any better, their sides collapsing into deep ruts whenever anyone tried to evade the road. Progress was agonisingly slow, the mud sucking at the travellers' legs, pulling them down into an oozing sea. From time to time one could hear the melancholy song of passing geese.

By midday, the Yellow House was still in sight.

"The World Revolution seems bogged down," said Tutyshkin. "Shall we rest?"

"The World Revolution knows no rest," said Aleshin, though in truth all five men were now sitting on the bank.

"This is a very poor place," said Zvonkov. "No shelter."

"From rain?"

"From bullets."

According to the two bums, the decapitated unit was to be found in the woods somewhere to the north east, some three days walk from the House. The two men constantly scanned the horizon, muttering to each other like an old married couple. After a tense, whispered debate, they proposed heading off across the unmowed and unloved fields, thus avoiding the periphery of Ryabovsky's old estate.

"By all means" said Tutyshkin. "Anything to get away from this road."

"Something you wish to avoid, Comrade Inspector?" asked Aleshin. Tutyshkin pulled a comic face. "A woman's tongue and the Devil's stare" he mouthed, with a wink.

Alas, the fields were as treacherous as the road, and progress was painfully slow. The land, dark as oil, stuck to everything. What had once brought forth crops now sucked and pulled, as if attempting to swallow up the puddle of the sky. Goose grass and scrub poked up from the mire. A line of trees could be seen but didn't seem to get any closer, like a stripe drawn on Aleshin's glasses for a joke.

Unused to such conditions, it was the soft, pampered representatives of the intelligentsia who struggled the most. The doctor's exercises could carry him only so far, while the Inspector seemed out of place as a princess in a sty. Tutyshkin's knees buckled and feet slipped; his story of having walked for a week to reach the Yellow House seemed as likely as a snail reaching Tula.

"I'm sorry chaps," said Tutyshkin, "I can't help but feel that I'm slowing you down."

"Concern duly noted, Comrade Inspector…"

"Me and the little horse – perhaps we should head back to the Yellow House. You stout fellows can manage with the supplies. Foo, Yana and I are an awful nuisance."

Zvonkov looked at Aleshin and Aleshin looked at Zvonkov.

"It's getting dark," said the orderly. "If we can make it to the long meadow there's a hay rick, which should provide some shelter. We can rest there. There's no sense in one of us heading back now."

"Look at the poor horse," said Tutyshkin. "He sinks deeper with every step…"

"To the barn," said Aleshin. "Desertion is not permitted."

In truth, Aleshin was also exhausted; his legs trembled and the ground pulled at him like a mother. Fortunately, his anger at Tutyshkin drove him on. Class struggle required iron determination – not the soft wheedling of bourgeois elements.

"But I fear my stockings…"

"The barn, Inspector. We can take stock there."

The hayrick was no more than a few rotting planks nailed together beneath a balding roof. Much of it had collapsed last winter, the remnants leaving barely room for the five men to shelter, never mind poor Yana and her leg. The search party ate their linseed oil cakes with a little pickled gherkin, the rain dripping spitefully through the cracks.

"Doctor Aleshin," said Tutyshkin, drawing close to the fire. "Aleshin, Aleshin, Aleshin … yes, I remember your father and mother well. A magnificent house – though I don't believe I ever saw you there. Perhaps you were away at university? Ah, but I heard all about you – the apple of your family's eye, your mama's darling boy."

The doctor refused to meet Tutyshkin's gaze. "I have no interest in this topic, Inspector."

"A beautiful room with a grand piano. A piano? Two pianos! Pianos everywhere! And a painting of some lady arriving at a ball – though your own mother was incontestably more beautiful."

"Such comments bear no connection to our current circum-stances," said the acting Chief Superintendent. The fire made Aleshin's golden spectacles look like two small lanterns and he refused to look up.

"Long golden hair, as fair as Penelope. We drank fruit tea and looked out at the acacia blossom near the cathedral. And that voice! Like a drop of honey in one's ears."

"These are entirely irrelevant remarks."

"Oh come now, Comrade Doctor: I see where you get your pretty looks from! Oh, to have had such a mama; when she wiped your arse, it must have felt like being caressed by an angel…"

"Under Socialism," said Aleshin, "all children will be taken from their parents and taught to love the People instead. There will be no need for pianos or flowers or coddling. Over every child's crib shall be written 'Down with the Capitalist Tyranny of Parents!' The party will provide."

Tutyshkin smiled like the Devil. "You won't get much milk sucking at Lenin's tits."

"I warn you Inspector: evidence of sedition will be passed on to the Commission for Struggle against Counter Revolution and Sabotage. And the Cheka delivers revolutionary justice without any papist-Quaker babble about the sanctity of human life…"

"Please don't distress yourself," said Tutyshkin, mildly, "I'm merely chattering to pass the time. We're all on the same side, are we not? Of justice, I mean. Why, I recall saying as much to your father."

"My father is no concern of yours."

"Oh, don't worry yourself, my darling. I have no intention of bringing up his, ah, indiscretions here. He was the most charming of men – a better dancer than financier perhaps, but then wouldn't the world be a more pleasant place if that were true of everyone?"

"I warn you Tutyshkin…"

"Didn't I hear that he had moved to Paris – with Olga Tarnova, the wife of a colleague? O, your poor mother! Or was she shacked up with Count Solokov by then?"

"I will not allow myself to be mocked, Comrade Inspector. I am the senior physician of the Yellow House, and as such…"

The tufts of hair growing back on Tutyshkin's skull made it look like a map of an unknown kingdom. Across his face, the beginnings of a moustache floated as if a little boat were moored atop his lip.

"Yes, yes, your mother was such an angel. How is she, my darling? I imagine she finds the revolution most trying…"

Aleshin leapt to his feet, trying to decide whether to break the policeman's jaw or burst into violent tears. Instead, he swayed spasmodically from side to side, pumping his arms up and down in a kind of manic salute.

"I have nothing else to say," he concluded, through tightly clenched teeth. "I'll go check on Yana. The poor beast has no shelter at all."

"Yes, yes, you go," said Tutyshkin. "Lenin can spare you for a moment." When the doctor had gone, Tutyshkin looked across at Zvonkov and winked. "A rather sensitive young man don't you think?"

"You're a son of a bitch, Tutyshkin."

"Indeed."

With that the Inspector closed his eyes and huddled down in his blanket. The two tramps looked on silently, sharing a crooked smirk. The smell of wet clothes and sour breath was almost unbearable. When Aleshin returned a few minutes later, his clothes were soaked, his eyes as red as his first day at school.

When Zvonkov checked on Yana in the morning, she was lying down and only reluctantly got to her feet. It was obvious to all that the horse would not be able to carry the supplies over such uncertain terrain; even without it, it was hard to see how she could manage another day's walk. Yana's eyes were soft and resigned, her movements affectionate – she had let everyone down.

"Well, that's settled then," said Tutyshkin triumphantly. "I'll return the horse and you stout fellows can…"

"This is lunacy," said Zvonkov. "We can't carry these supplies for two days through the mud. The saddlebags are too awkward and the packages too heavy. Give these men their due and send them on their way – we can do no more."

The two soldiers – if soldiers they were – blinked at Zvonkov unhappily. Once again, they realised that Aleshin was their only court of appeal. One of them prostrated himself before the doctor while the other pulled earnestly on his sleeve.

"Comrade, please. Our men are hungry and hurt. The Red Army requires your strength…"

Aleshin nodded as if an adjunct had just delivered an important report. In his mind's eye he thought: what would Rakhmetev do? Not betray the revolution through shameful capitulation, that much was sure.

"No one will return to the Yellow House. We will leave Yana here with half of the supplies. Then we will deliver the first half to the men and return."

Zvonkov looked incredulous. "You think Yana will be waiting for us when we get back? This area is crawling with thieves.

Besides, even carrying half the food is folly."

"The fellow's right," said Tutyshkin. "Let me escort Yana back and you can hide the rest of the supplies in the rick. Without a horse stationed outside, nobody will find it. I can't help the revolution in these shoes."

"The people's decision is final," said Aleshin curtly. "We will leave Yana here with half the supplies whilst the rest of us go on – including you, Comrade Inspector. Weakness is a petit-bourgeois affectation."

"My dear Aleshin…"

"Where do you truly wish to head, Inspector? Not back toward the old estate, I think. Is there something you've left undone out here? Or something you do not wish us to see? Yes, Inspector, yes – you are not the only one with questions to ask!" By now, the doctor was warming to his theme, his boots tramping up and down on the dirt. "The liquidation of the enemies of the people is the only justice now. Do not think that your position will save you…"

Tutyhskin's smile was thin and tight. "Sweetheart, angel – let's not fight. We're all sailing in the same boat. I've been asked to discover the nature of the misfortune visited upon Comrade Lepinov, and that is what I shall endeavour to do."

"It's agreed then," said Aleshin. "We shall take what we can carry, and move on. According to our comrades we still have far to go."

Zvonkov shouldered one of the saddlebags and cursed. What was he doing here, plodding around in the muck instead of making eyes at Alyona by a nice warm stove? Even the rain mocked him. The world was a cold, malignant place, populated by lunatics. If the doctors and the guests were to change places, what would alter? Neither the rain, nor the mud, nor fate.

For the rest of the day, the men trudged on without words, Zvonkov in a foul temper, Tutyshkin uncharacteristically mute. Only Aleshin, picturing himself as a Red commander leading his troops to victory, marched with any real sense of purpose. By the afternoon, however, even this brave representative of the People's Struggle was flagging. The men were muddied as if crude clay figures, their feet great pats of muck.

Mid-afternoon, the two soldiers began to squabble over the correct route, the taller arguing that they needed to locate a beck by a fallen tree, the shorter that the swiftest route would be to skirt the forest edge and then seek an old forester's trail. Zvonkov was of the opinion that the two men had been bumming around the wilds for months, and all this talk of a Red camp was so much stale air. Who were they anyway? Peasant conscripts who had trousered their first month's wages and then fled: they no more wanted to get to Tayda than he did. Besides, Zvonkov had other things to think about. Had Petr really set off to join the Bolsheviks as Tutyshkin said, despite his Papa's warnings? Of course, the young were easily taken in by fine words: just look at the Comrade Doctor, barely needing to shave, yet already liberating the workers. Whites, Reds, Greens: mix them altogether and all you were left with was a shitty mess. What was he even doing here? Alyona's bosom – that was Zvonkov's cause…

A finch flew out from a thicket and Zvonkov recalled the times he had hunted near here, alone and free, his own man for once in his life. He remembered searching for bustard and woodcock, chewing on cured hare as he walked. If only he were out hunting now, rather than on this damned fool's errand. The gun nestled easily against his shoulder, trying to trick him into thinking this was just another jaunt, a pleasant little shoot in the countryside.

Behind him, his fellow travellers stumbled around in the mud as if they'd never stepped off the Nevsky Prospect.

"I'll go on ahead," Zvonkov said. "Shelter 'neath that larch till I'm back."

"In the People's Democracy, I give the orders, Comrade Zvonkov."

"Do you want to rest or don't you? I'll scout ahead. You dry your doctor's smock."

As if set free, no sooner had Zvonkov left the others behind, then he began to breathe more easily. Whistling a peasant tune, the orderly passed a copse of elderflower and spear-grass, then skirted a black, partially hidden, bog. Yes, this was the old forester's trail: he recognised the rotting timbers of what had once been some kind of shack. To his right were a line of wrecked beehives, all faded blue, while from a ditch protruded the shaft of some long abandoned cart. Aside from the rain, the woods were strangely quiet here, just the occasional thrush or finch hopping here and there amongst the mud. A squirrel scraped up a tree and Zvonkov had to restrain himself from shooting it. Instead he opened his hunter's pouch and filled it with berries and pine nuts; something to come back with, at least

Near a small clearing, there were signs of recently dug holes, now topped by mounds of wet, black dirt. Zvonkov felt no desire to investigate. The dead outnumbered the living in this world: who could name them all? Besides, how old were the graves – a month, a week, a day? No crosses, no stones, no branches, just a series of small black hills, a humble mountain range of the dead. From a nearby tree dangled an old coil of rope. Zvonkov picked at the knot and shook his head in disgust. What, couldn't they even hang a man properly? The end of the rope had been hacked at with a blunt knife: other than that there were no signs of activity. Perhaps all that had taken place here had occurred a long time ago – or perhaps it had taken place yesterday and the rain had hidden everything. There was no way of knowing, or reason to linger. Dig a hole in Russia and you're bound to find some bones.

From the patch of open ground, Zvonkov headed deeper into the woods. He'd been gone for almost an hour now, but what did it matter? If the others followed he'd hear them blundering about like boars. True, he could no longer make out any way-stones, but that was of little consequence – he could retrace his steps any time he liked. Above the tree line, the rain came down like an unstopped tap. By the base of an old, bent elm, Zvonkov spotted a circle of pale, bone coloured mushrooms, the like of which he'd never seen before. He kicked one over with his boot, revealing a dull, tarnished red. He picked it up and sniffed: awful.

It was getting boggier now, the way clogged with leaves, some green, some red, like the Duma. No whites though – at least not before the first snow. Dark, wilted nettles poked out between wet leaves, the smell of mulch heavy and intoxicating. The forest hit him like a sharp shot of vodka. O, to be free! In that instance, Zvonkov entertained a wild fantasy about never going back, tramping to the ends of the world with just his gun and a good pair of boots. Why not? What was the point of this fool's errand anyway? The light played hide-and-go-seek amongst the branches, the gloom stealthily darkening. Carved into the hollow of a trunk was the figure of a man with the head of a bear and the horns of a stag. Had Petr been this way? Zvonkov remembered seeing such a figure on his son's shelf, though he had no idea as to how it had got there. Maybe his son hadn't gone off to join the Reds – perhaps he had run away to meet someone in the woods… but was that better or worse? Now was not the time for skipping through meadows. For all its faults, the Yellow House provided at least a measure of sanctuary from all the ills outside. There were walls to keep out the wind and a roof above one's head. The Reds hung anyone with soft white hands, the Whites those with dirty nails. This was no time for foolishness: one cannot reason with fire. The priest at Chernavsky had had his nose and ears cut off and his eyes gouged out during mass. Not even God knew the future. In the meantime: wait.

The general gloom was deepening into twilight now: time to turn back. Now they were on the forester's trail, it wouldn't be long before they found the camp, if indeed any camp was to be found. Zvonkov strained his ears but could hear nothing: no soldiers, no deserters, no Cossacks. For a moment he imagined himself the last man left alive in Russia, if not the world. There were still birds and animals and bugs, but every other human-being had been swept away by an enormous broom. There were no more houses, no estates, no classes. Perhaps it was the only way for the war to end – who knew?

As before, the scouting party spent most of the night grumbling and quarrelling, Tutyshkin joking about Aleshin's 'maidenly hands', while the two tramps jibber-jabbered in the corner like Old Believers in a prayer huddle. Zvonkov would rather have spent the night with Yana: less foolishness and a sweeter smell. An Old Russian joke: during a storm a peasant brings his prize goat into his hut. 'But what about the stink?' demands his wife. 'She'll get used to it' says the peasant.

The orderly was tired after his expedition and soon fell into a deep sleep. Let somebody else keep watch. A policeman, a revolutionary, two soldiers – surely somebody could keep one eye open? That night he dreamed of his dead wife, her sick bed abandoned in the forest. The sky came all the way down to the ground, while a row of heads, like winter cabbages, watched from their graves.

Aleshin woke him with a sharp kick to his leg.

"They're gone," he hissed.

"Gone?"

"The tramps."

It was true. During the night, the two bread hunters had absconded, taking with them as many of the supplies as they could carry. Nobody had heard anything. The pair had vanished like kindling on a fire.

"How was this allowed to happen?" demanded Aleshin. "Who was on watch?"

"The gentlemen in question" said Tutyshkin, dryly. "Perhaps a poor choice in retrospect…"

"This is simply unacceptable," said Aleshin. "We travelled all this way in order to assist the Red Army. Why would they…"

"You don't still believe their fairy-story about the camp do you?" asked Zvonkov. "These were bums, pure and simple. If they were part of some Red brigade then they fled it long ago…"

"Not at all, that is simply not the case. No, no, no. Perhaps they feared repercussions for becoming separated from their unit. Or perhaps they were mobilised against a White attack."

"Balls. Let's find Yana and return to the Yellow House. If our friends haven't cut her throat already."

"But look, Zvonkov – tracks. We can follow them. In this mud, it should be child's play. Those fellows can't have gone far. Yes, here – here is where the pair of them headed off along the trail…"

"We can follow," said Zvonkov, crouching in the mud. "But to what end? There's no point beating the cow after the milk is spilt."

Aleshin glared at the orderly as if at a class traitor. "We follow along the track. There is to be no going back, no surrender. The Revolution cannot retrace its steps."

Zvonkov sighed and Tutyskin held up his hands. But what else could they do? At least when it all went belly-up they wouldn't be the ones to blame. Besides, as every Russian knows, a stupid order was better than no order at all. The branches quivered, the leaves fell, the trees swayed. Nature itself seemed to shrug. Outside the shack it was raining. Maybe it always would.

3

Despite the slow progress of the police inspector and the acting Superintendent, Zvonkov followed the trail easily and without impediment, drawing closer to the bread-hunters all the time. A crow came to watch them, settling down on its branch as if with a fat novel. Dead leaves fell, the rain spoke in tongues. For their part, the frogs stayed in the background, grumbling like critics. A squirrel watched the men from afar. Of mud there was no end.

By the time Zvonkov reached the meadow, the tracks were fresh. On the far side of the clearing, around fifty feet away, was a second, even denser section of forest. Smoke curled up from a camp and there was a spot over to the right where several trees had been felled, not so long ago. 'I'll be damned,' thought Zvonkov. 'So there is a camp after all…'

From the look of it the pasture had been cut back years ago, though it was hard to imagine why. Now the barren ground was home to a scab of wild flowers, ringed by thickets of fierce looking brambles. Nevertheless, living souls had once been here, and fairly recently too. There were broken bottles, spent cartridges, and several trees had been dragged off in the night. The ground was tramped down and there was a low, muddy ditch where somebody in the forest had hauled the trunks away.

"Doctor?" said Zvonkov. "If they're bandits or deserters, they won't take kindly to us visiting unannounced. Let's skirt this place and…."

Aleshin's smooth chin nodded seriously. "I will attempt to make contact. It was my decision to come here and my responsibility to see this operation to its end"

The young doctor's expression was determined and sober, his glasses spattered with rain. He hiccupped, silently. "One has to know how to talk to soldiers. It is all a question of psychology…"

"Listen, I…"

"I repeat: I will make contact." And with that Aleshin strode out into the clearing, waving his arms as if seeking to stop a runaway train.

"Comrades!" he yelled as loudly as he could. "Comrades, workers, memembers of the proletariat! I greet you in the name of the Revolution and International Socialism!"

"Our good doctor's going to get his head blown off," hissed Tutyshkin. Zvonkov said nothing, but stayed as close to the ground as possible.

"Comrades, come forth! We have travelled from the Yellow House at Bezumiye in order to assist with your struggle – the struggle of all working people. We come in peace, bearing crucial medical supplies" – in his excitement Aleshin had forgotten that the two bread hunters had already taken their supplies from them – "in order to tend to your ill and wounded. Comrades, there is nothing to fear from our party: step forth!"

Aleshin paused and trained his eyes on the trees on the far side of the clearing. He was now a good ten feet away from Zvonkov and Tutyshkin, with no possibility of finding cover.

"Soldiers of the Red Army, where are you? There is no reason to conceal yourselves. I am unarmed and in possession of drugs and food. I come in the name of fraternal peace!"

"He's done for," muttered Tutyshkin. Blades of goose-grass tickled Zvonkov's nose.

Aleshin stopped and listened. Nothing. The clouds were low

and oppressive. Rain poured as if from a broken keg.

"Comrades…"

The doctor was about to return to his companions when a figure in green slipped out of the tall grass on the other side of the meadow. He was bearded, weather worn and filthy. Like the bread hunters who had arrived at the Yellow House's gate, he resembled nothing so much as a corpse, disinterred by a fox.

"Who the hell are you?" he yelled.

To the amazement of Zvonkov and Tutyshkin, Aleshin actually saluted. "Comrade Doctor Gregory Aleshin. I bring you greetings from the Yellow House. Your companions travelled to our institution requesting assistance, though we lost them someplace in the woods…"

The stranger, rifle in hand, stared at the doctor as if at a rhinoceros, or some other fabulous beast. Everything about his bearing suggested that although he had heard of the existence of learned doctors, he had never truly believed in them. He wore a foul *armyak* and a green hat made from the felt of some looted billiard table.

"Companions?"

"Yes, yes…" Aleshin suddenly realised that he had no idea as to the two bread hunters' names. "Your fellow soldiers. They came to us to ask for aid. We have come to tend your fallen…"

"We? Tell the others to come out."

Aleshin turned round and made a quick gesture. For a moment, he couldn't spot them, but then set eyes on Tutyshkin and Zvonkov, lying in the mire.

"Ah, yes, indeed … they're coming…"

Zvonkov shot the doctor a look of pure hatred, but nevertheless followed Aleshin into the meadow alongside an obviously petrified Tutyshkin. Although Aleshin held out his bare palms in supplication, the orderly kept a firm grip on his rifle, its safety catch released. There were several other figures concealed amongst the trees on the other side, all of them fully armed and hostile. If this went badly then the doctor would be dead in seconds.

"Where do you say you come from?" yelled the figure in green.

"Bezumiye. The Yellow House."

"Never heard of it."

"Your two soldiers…"

"Never heard of them either."

Zvonkov figured that he could shoot the green one first, but that wouldn't save him from the others scattered among the trees. The only cover was a rotting log situated near a low ditch. Perhaps he could throw himself over it and roll toward the tall grass. Apart from this, his mind was blank.

"Citizens, what will happen to Mother Russia if no one acts to defend it, if people think only of themselves? The World Revolution promises land and freedom for all. My friend, our common enemy is the capitalist and the exploiter, the bourgeoisie…"

Aleshin seemed almost touchingly unaware of the difference between his own soft features, tailored clothes and educated accent, and the bedraggled representative of the People standing there before him. Zvonkov wanted to shoot him himself.

"Both our patriotic duty and our class duty is to the cause…"

"And what do you say you want?"

"To help with any medical needs you might have. I am a senior doctor. We are here to help…"

The Green Man turned around, obviously to seek orders from another. This was Zvonkov's last chance: should he shoot him now or no?

"Why should we need your help?" yelled the Green Man.

Aleshin genuinely looked confused. "Why to further the

dictatorship of the proletariat…"

The first shot hit Zvonkov in the neck, his head twisting to one side as he fell. The second missed Aleshin by a whisker, the bullet whizzing somewhere just past his scalp. The Green Man leapt back toward the trees, cursing loudly. Immediately a more general crackle of gunfire started up from the other side. Aleshin fell to his knees and rolled childlike through the tall grass. He heard a cry from nearby – Tutyshkin, most likely – and found himself by Zvonkov's corpse, the gun lying at the orderly's feet. Without thinking, Aleshin picked it up and fired: astonishingly a yell from the opposite side suggested that his aim was true. Emboldened, he fired again. Then the ground erupted close by him, and Aleshin stumbled backwards over the log, rolling down the ditch in an awkward and unheroic fashion.

More firing commenced. Aleshin had no idea as to what had happened to Tutyshkin, but assumed that the Inspector too was dead. Without looking back, the doctor flung himself into the undergrowth and fled as best he could. He could make out a loud and indiscriminate swearing, but heard no more shots. The adrenaline made him feel sick and dizzy. He'd already lost Zvonkov's rifle.

Running blindly, he snagged his ankle on a root. As he fell, a perfect, almost luminous, vision of his mother appeared before him, her clothes radiant, hair bright burning as the sun.

"Mama?" he said.

Before she had a chance to reply, the vision waivered, breaking into a million shards. Something cold and hard hit him 'cross the cheek like a slap.

4

When the doctor came to, the forest was silent, the frogs, birds and animals, all mute. The doctor picked himself up and realised his hair was streaked with filth and his ears were full of mud. But where was he? The world seemed composed of brown, green and black patches. Fuzzy clouds came down from the sky to mix with the fog. Sky and canopy had merged. It took a few moments before Aleshin understood what had happened: his gold-rimmed glasses were gone.

Without them, the doctor could make out only shadowy lines and blurs, a world without purchase. In the place of shacks or way-stones appeared blobs and black holes. These holes hid yet other holes. Straight lines collapsed. Objects hid. No longer capable of forming solid shapes, the things of the world seemed to bleed into one another, an odd tangle of blotches without pattern or meaning or sovereignty.

Aleshin blinked. Had the fellows from the clearing followed him? If so, they would be able to pick him off like a bird. The doctor strained his ears but could hear nothing but a steady drip drip drip, as if through a leaky roof. There was no sun, little light. Gloomy shapes separated and then came together again, like an opening and closing of gates. Shape, size, colour – all these things were fading from the world, replaced by a single sticky cobweb stretching from the clouds above to the mud below. Perhaps he had sustained some kind of head injury, compromising his mental faculties. Or perhaps he had died in the clearing, and this was some outer region of the underworld, a foretaste of the annihilating nothingness to come. For once, Rakhmetev had no answer.

Lacking any plan, Aleshin began to walk. It was hard to say how far he marched, or for how long: time seemed to have fallen in on itself like an old dead tree. He pulled at some dark berries, but found them bitter and inedible. Two years spent amongst the peasants at the kolkhoz in a village near Panino, and yet he knew nothing! In his lodgings, an old woman called Pelagea had brought him soup, stews and fresh meat, but the good doctor never once thought to enquire as to how such a miracle was accomplished, day after day.

Instead what he remembered was the way the headman doffed his cap and called him 'honoured sir', Old Semyonova offering up her daughters like fruit, peasant women shaking like saplings whenever he walked past. What was the name of that girl who was in love with him? Aksinya, the dairy maid. Once he found her waiting outside his shack holding his scarf she'd stolen.

"Doctor? Doctor Aleshin?" she'd said. "I've got a painful boil on my bum."

"Well, ah," said the doctor, protecting himself with his bag.

"Please sir," said Aksinya, blushing. "It won't take a moment and it's ever so red."

The girl was besotted, but she really did have a bright red spot on her bottom: probably a spider bite of some kind. Aleshin dabbed some ethanol on it and administered a clean rag. By the time he'd finished, both parties were flushed and giddy.

"That spider might have carried me off," said Aksinya, panting.

"Yes, yes, very good," said the doctor, edging toward the barn door.

And yet in many ways it had been the village which had concluded his education. Peasants kept their animals in their homes and slept on the stove, the wooden huts clustered around the *mir* like chicks around a hen. The fields were stony and badly tended. Most men were *otkhodriki* – seasonal workers, who worked for most of the year in the factories at Voronezh, returning home only at harvest time. The peasants were still paying off the landowner for their freedom and would be until the Seventh Seal was opened. Debtors were regularly flogged and whipped. Once a month the bailiff, accompanied by two drunken police officers, would come and extort whatever they could from whichever peasants they chose to ambush. Those who resisted were thrashed and had their passport to work outside the village taken away. Such was the way of things in the village: unless one removed one's cap for the bailiffs, they set about you with sticks.

"Good morn Gentleman Sir!" yelled the headman. "'Tis an honour to have a young gentleman like you…"

How far was Panino from here? It was impossible to say. The forest, the sunken meadows, the swamps: to Aleshin, it all looked the same, ugly as the devil's arse. As the day went on, a dull grey gloom, heavy as a restraining blanket, descended inexorably upon him. The doctor's throat was dry and his head throbbed incessantly. There was no sign of the shack they had stayed in on the way here, or any sort of landmark at all; the forest was stuffed into the gloom like a pillow. At some point, the Comrade Doctor became convinced that a figure – and perhaps more than one – was tracking him through the undergrowth, stopping when he did, and crouching behind bushes like a thief. Was it one of the anarchist band? A bandit? For some reason, the doctor thought of Tutyshkin's escaped prisoner and the Inspector's words: "a man like Sikorsky isn't used to the wilds…"

Finally, Aleshin found a small, brackish-looking brook and drank greedily. Then he lay down and rested. When he closed his eyes, shapeless blobs floated across his vision and when he opened them, the blobs remained the same. How strange the world was! Blocks of light and shade collapsed into one another, lacking any sense of independent existence. Lines became vague and confused. Something touched his fingers and when he looked down a small brown rat looked back at him with a certain degree of suspicion.

"Hello," said the doctor. "Hello Comrade Rat."

The doctor knew that he ought to catch, kill and devour said rat, but could not for the life of him imagine how any of these processes might actually take place. Instead, he stared uncertainly at the creature while the creature looked back at him. Aleshin had once had a cat called Miska, but she had made him sneeze. Then he had a horse called Sasha ... but no, Sasha was a machine, from the day he had got lost and brought shame upon his mama... Besides, there was no place for sentimentality in the people's dictatorship. Only courage, resilience, positive values.

The rat faded back into the murk, and the murk faded also. Like the direction of modern art, everything was moving inexorably toward abstraction. The doctor felt a little non- representational himself. Still, there was little option but to press on. After a while, the scribbled trees seemed a fraction further apart. Was this a sign that he was near the outer limit of the wood? Or had he simply circled back on himself, stumbling blindly back toward the bandit camp?

And then he saw it: a heavy black shape, perhaps some kind of forester's shack. Way-stones lay on the floor like giant's teeth, the mud pitted and disturbed. Had Aleshin and his party passed this way once before? Yes, yes: this must have been where they had spent the night. Aleshin crawled in eagerly; if this was the same shack, then he must be going in the same direction. Within minutes, the doctor was asleep.

When he awoke, it was already night. Outside things were buzzing, croaking and crying. The darkness was absolute, every last shape annihilated. What was out there? There wasn't even a 'there'. Only the rain, more constant than time.

Aleshin climbed painfully to his feet. Inside his body, white blood cells were fighting counter revolutionary forces and recidivists, bands of kulaks hiding behind his eyes. It took him a few moments to realise that the banging was coming from outside rather than from inside his skull.

The doctor jumped like a mouse. Another bang – or was it a knock? But who would come knocking in the middle of such nothingness? No light penetrated the cracks, nor could any lamp or torch be seen. But something was out there in the emptiness, pushing up against the door. Who was it then? Tutyshkin, Zvonkov, somebody from the enemy camp?

"Hello?" whispered Aleshin. "Hello, is somebody there?"

The visitor – human, animal or spirit – paused before throwing itself against the frame even more insistently.

"Tutyshkin? Inspector? Stop fooling around, curse you…"

The knocking continued, as insistent as the rain, and the doctor felt his revolutionary courage begin to desert him.

"What's that? Speak up man! I will not open this door."

Something heavy seemed to slump alongside the walls, causing the whole shack to tremble. For some reason Aleshin thought of his slender, delicate mother. Was it her shade out there, his Mama's spirit somehow haunting these woods?

"Who is it? Answer me! For pity's sake, let me be."

That very second, the banging stopped. The silence was deafening, as if the shack and its occupant had moved to some place deep underground. For a moment, Aleshin allowed himself to believe that the stranger was gone. Then he felt the whole lodge shake, as if whatever was out there were pressing themselves ever closer.

"Who are you? What I did, I did for the revolution, curse you. I need not answer to you..."

When Aleshin flung open the door, he saw an enormous black head with two bulbous brown eyes. For a moment, he failed to place it. Then he understood: Yana.

Whether someone had released Yana or she had somehow pulled herself free, the doctor had no way of knowing. How far could such a horse have come – surely not so very far? Aleshin pulled Yana and permitted the horse a comradely caress. Did Yana know the way back to the Yellow House? Ho, she had carried that damned Inspector on her back; why not a member of the revolutionary vanguard just as well? Yes, yes, a man in possession of a horse possesses the whole world. Yana was uninjured and unmarked, though her saddlebags – and the remains of the food and medicine – were gone, presumably left back in the hay rick. Little matter: the horse would lead the way...

The doctor took Yana by the reins and informed her to return to the Yellow House without delay. The horse looked left, looked right, and then released an enormous stream of piss. Shaking his head, Aleshin reminded the horse of her responsibility to the workers' struggle, whereupon she began to move, albeit limping a little, and listing slightly toward the left. A strong smell came from her rear end and her back seemed to steam. But at least they were moving now, following the old forester's trail as best they could, Yana's tail flicking from side to side like a commissar's whip.

Good Yana, kind Yana, true Yana! The doctor longed to climb atop her back but he knew as little of animals as he knew of berries. Besides, the horse looked as exhausted as he was. He considered whispering some affectionate name in her ear but felt that such a course of action was, at best, un-revolutionary. Instead, he murmured, "Yes, yes, one must proceed in an efficient and determined manner if one is to secure the rights of the people…"

Morning arrived like a grim faced-nurse. Though the world remained as indistinct as ever, Aleshin sensed that they were heading back toward the house, the fields opening up before them like a corpse on a dissecting table. The black line of the *opushka* gave way to the white and green of meadow grass, though the density of things no longer seemed commensurate to size or scale; weeds grabbed and tripped, whilst rocks and banks disappeared into nothing. Only Yana was heavy, solid and dependable. If she vanished then the whole would disappear too.

From here, it should have been no more than a day's travel back to the Yellow House but their progress was still agonisingly slow. One of Yana's feet – hooves! – became stuck in the interminable bog and the doctor spent the best part of a black hour struggling to pull her free. First Yana fell in a hole and then Aleshin. How much mud could there be in the world? Enough to drown Man and all his dreams… Aleshin had misjudged the bread hunters, led his companions to their deaths. What would he tell Yevgrafovna, Marya? He pictured himself limping back half blind through the mire, at best a comical figure, at worse, a scoundrel. And all the time this endless plod, like a heavy book which one must somehow get through. How many steps must a man take? Always another and another and another. And at the end of it: mud, rain, the nothingness of night.

Night? Yes, without the doctor even noticing it, the earth had turned on its axis once more. Sensing the gloom, Yana started moving toward a distant smear of trees, her ears twitching. But was this another forest or the same? To Aleshin the thought of bandits seemed less terrifying than the notion of having to make this awful journey all over again. Another ditch, another bank, another shit hole... no, it was unacceptable, inconceivable: not even Lenin fleeing to the depths of Finland had had to put up with such a thing...

Plod, plod, plod went Old Lady Horse, until both man and beast seemed swallowed up entirely. What the trees gave in shelter, they took away in light. But in time the darkness shifted and Aleshin sensed they had entered some kind of clearing, maybe even a lawn. When his hands touched some kind of a wall, doctor and horse came to an abrupt stop. What was this, some kind of a ruin? Whatever the construction might be, it had to be better than the nothingness all around. The pair halted and lay down as best they could amongst the infinite emptiness. One hand touched the remains of a windowsill while two fore-legs rested against a dismembered table. O, a place to rest, a place to halt! But were they safe here? It was impossible to know: it was impossible to know anything.

Despite the cold, sleep came swiftly, like a flood.

Aleshin awoke to a terrifying vision of the destruction of all things. Collapsed walls, broken windows, gutted buildings: it was as if the little horse had led the doctor to the ruin of all Man's dreams. For a good minute or so, the doctor was speechless. Every scrap of furniture had been dismembered, every last beam hacked in two. What misfortune could have visited this place, what timeless calamity? And then the doctor understood: Ryabovsky's estate, ravaged by the mob. Yes, torn curtains, soiled bed linen, caved in pots. What did Pushkin call such violence? *Puganchevschina* – the savagery of the Russian soul.

Still half-asleep, Aleshin picked his way amongst the broken glass and splintered timbers like Ryabovsky's ghost. Had this once been the landowner's study, his art gallery? Everything had been ripped out, smashed, visited by shit. Of course, Ryabovsky was in every way the embodiment of the class enemy, every last possession evidence of his aristocratic crime, and yet, and yet… hadn't Aleshin himself grown up in such surroundings: his father's estate near Yamskai, the orchards he had played in as a boy, his beloved children's *dacha* hidden at the edge of the meadow? Again: guilt, shame, disgust. On this lawn, Ryabovsky's children might once have romped and played; but just a few miles away peasant children had died of diphtheria and tuberculosis – where then did the true tragedy lie? One's sympathy can only be with the whipped and hungry – anything else was a spit in the face of the Party.

Deep in thought, Aleshin drifted further and further from the ruins. Where was he? His weak eyes could make out only smudges and marks, the bare trace of things. The body, he virtually fell over. It had been stripped of its clothing and lay awkwardly amongst the weeds, awful in its nakedness. On its belly, ants scurried to and fro, one entering the chest through a bullet hole, another exiting carrying something red and sticky. The man's expression was annoyed, but not surprised. For some reason his lips had turned black like a dog.

The second body was down by the main road, wearing a policeman's uniform and a surprised expression. Death lay on his shoulders like a saddle, his cheek crushed against the ground, eyes pale and oily. Again, the cause of death was a gunshot wound to the chest. A little further along, stuck in deep mire and completely blocking the post road, was a large black carriage with bars on the windows and a broken back door – a police wagon, Aleshin surmised. So this was where Tutyshkin had been attacked. Tutyshkin? Aleshin compared the inspector's height to that of the cloth-less corpse and shook his head. No, Tutyshkin was no police officer. Tutyshkin was not even Tutyshkin. It was all becoming clear to him now. Sikorsky had not been shot. Sikorsky had disguised himself as another. The murderer had come to the Yellow House wearing a dead man's name.

And inside the cart? Either the interior of the carriage had been looted by the transport's assailants, or else somebody had been through it with an eye to disguising their tracks. There were neither supplies nor bodies, though several bullet holes could be found in one side. The harnesses for the horses had been smashed open, the animals gone. Climbing inside the stranded carriage made Aleshin think of climbing into Baba Yaga's cauldron; he half-expected bird legs to grow out from the sides. His eyes were too weak to undertake a thorough, forensic examination, but what did it matter? The carriage had obviously been attacked – perhaps by the bandits he had himself encountered, perhaps by some other hooligan band – and in the confusion, the prisoner had engineered his escape. Aleshin imagined Tutyshkin hiding amongst the ruins, surreptitiously returning to strip the uniform from the corpse when he was certain his assailants had gone. Tutyhskin or Sikorsky? It was obvious now: they had been deceived. The man they called Tutyshkin was a rank impostor. Little wonder he expressed such counter-revolutionary views! He was a murderer, a parasite, a class enemy: how could they have allowed him to escape?

Stepping away from the carriage's becalmed hulk, Aleshin had a sudden sensation of being watched. He stared from left to right but could sense nothing. And yet for some reason the feeling persisted, an instinctive warning of the presence of a predator or foe, class-related or otherwise. His thoughts raced back to the anarchists' camp: had he truly seen Tutyshkin fall? He remembered a body stumbling, a cry – but had he really witnessed his death? If the doctor could have escaped from the bandits, why not a hardened criminal? And if Tutyshkin – Sikorsky – had followed him back through the woods, what if he were observing him now? Aleshin squinted but could see nothing: beyond his elbow, everything turned to fog. Nevertheless, he hunched his shoulders, ducked his head, and made his way back toward the old estate. There were enough corpses here already: why plant another? Let the rain water the weeds. A dead man does not grow.

Aleshin rounded a corner and came upon the remains of a damp bonfire. Where was he? Toppled statues, hacked up benches, weed-strewn flowerbeds: and again that unbearable feeling of being followed.

"Yana!" yelled the doctor. "Yana, come!" Nu, where was that oaf of a horse?

He had forgotten to tether her to any post and most likely she had wandered off, distracted by the sight of tasty bracken or acting upon some equine whim. What did Aleshin know of horses? Less than he knew of murderers, or the working class.

"Yana! Yana, where are you?"

Only one building remained unscathed by the rampage, the Ryabovsky family chapel, its door still locked. Aye, peasant superstition had prevented its sacking, the stained glass dull and lifeless, just one pane broken by somebody's stray brick. Aleshin circled the chapel, fearful that some malignant force was following him along the other side. Uncertain, he attempted a peculiar half run, half retreat, moving away from the main garden like a lame man attempting to walk.

"Yana! Yana, I need you now!"

The rain continued to fall, albeit a little half-heartedly now, turning into mist and drizzle. Shapes grew and shrunk. To one side was darkened hole, smelling of sweat, piss, and something worse. Should he hide? The whitewashed walls were covered in stains, tubs of foul smelling straw overturned on the floor. It was some kind of bathhouse. On his hands and knees, the doctor made his way between the tubs and a sort of wooden platform, coming across Petr's body in the process.

Petr?

Aleshin stared hard at the boy, allowing his physician's training to take control. The boy had been dead quite some time – strangled by the look of him. There were signs of a struggle, but obviously to no avail. The lad's cheek was bruised, his lip split. Like father, like son, thought Aleshin: death had claimed them both.

The truth of the situation was now clear. The lad had encountered Tutyshkin, presumably already dressed in the outfit of the fallen police officer. In accordance with Yevgrafovna's foolish advice – not his! – the lad had asked the inspector to travel to the Yellow House to assist them. Tutyshkin – no, Sikorsky – had agreed, but then, when Petr wasn't looking, the swine had assaulted and asphyxiated him. The lad had struggled but his assailant had the element of surprise. Afterwards the killer had coolly taken his mount and headed toward the Yellow House. But why would he do such a thing? The answer was simple. Sikorsky had been handed the perfect disguise. Why not use the Yellow House as a sanctuary, somewhere to lie low for a while? And then, once rested, slip away into the disorder of war...

Yes, there were signs of a temporary camp here, some kind of refuge from the rain: perhaps the assassin had sought to murder the boy whilst he slept. In one corner, Aleshin discovered some kind of fabric torn from the carriage back on the road and used as a makeshift blanket. Was this where Sikorsky had lain low and plotted his foul deception? All of a sudden, Aleshin heard movement beyond the *banya's* blackened door. The comrade doctor froze. Somebody was waiting outside - the same thing that had been shadowing him through the murk. Oh, if only he had a gun! Or at least his spare pair of glasses... Then a hoof moved outside the bathhouse, followed by another and the flick of a tail.

Yana? Yes, it was Yana. The horse was waiting outside the *banya*, her expression melancholy and wise.

"Comrade Yana" said the doctor, sadly. "It is my duty to inform you that we have found the boy…"

Doctor and horse spent the rest of the day and night in the ruins of the Ryabovsky estate, having located an interior room whose ceiling was still, more or less, in evidence. Neither slept very well. Aleshin stared into the boundless gloom, straining to detect any trace of his pursuer, while Yana stared at a blank wall thinking of who knew what: Petr, the rain, her stall?

In the morning, the pair of them set off along the post road, circling back toward the Yellow House and open ground. Aleshin had felt too exhausted to bury the lad, and his cadaver was too stiff to load upon poor Yana. Instead, he covered Petr in straw and left him in the *banya*.

The going was difficult, the road knee deep in mud. If Aleshin's shadow was carrying a gun then they were easy prey, but the doctor felt too tired to care. With every step, they sunk deeper into the gruel. A thin drizzle covered everything with spit. Time had slowed down to a dribble.

As they walked, a thin sickly mist, stirred up by the wind, came upon them, rising up to the top of the trees before falling back to earth. Yana found her way with some difficulty, snorting and slipping, her nostrils almost touching the mud. A dense bush of greyish burrs stuck to her flanks, her coat steaming. The leaves on the trees trembled, something fell from above, the mist turned blue then green then white. Was the world heavy or light? Such distinctions seemed to be breaking down, each thing turning into its opposite, as life turns to death.

And yet for all that, somehow they walked the rest of the day and night without stopping. At some point, the doctor climbed up upon Yana's back and allowed the little horse to carry him. His thoughts mingled with the mud and the cold. Once he saw his mother fording a ditch in a beautiful white gown; another time he glimpsed Tutyshkin's bald head in the gloom, glowing in the darkness like a star. The inside of the doctor's head seemed to have leaked out into the world – or maybe it was the other way around.

"*Mamoshka*" whispered the doctor, "*Mamoshka*, where are you?"

The night stretched and yawned and eventually the outside world returned from the murk like something left behind by the tide. The *opushka* – the edge of the forest – was now far behind them, the meadow grass wet and flat, turning from green to brown to black, torn by scrub and spear-grass. The road led between wildflower meadows directly to the edge of the estate and the Yellow House itself. There was the avenue, there the outer fence, the out-stretched palms of the alders. And yet, as Yana turned in between the trees, Aleshin felt as if something undefinable had changed. Yes, yes – something about the place was different, something he struggled to put into words. Ho, what was it? The buildings, the colour, the light? The doctor wiped his eyes and looked up at the sky. The rain had stopped and a pale, white light shone down from the heavens, strange and unearthly. So that's what it was – the first day of dry weather. No rain, no sleet – why, it seemed impossible to believe! Was this why the illumination seemed so eerie, or was it something else? Hadn't Tutyshkin said something about a death ray? Yes, some mysterious new invention, the absolute transformation of the earth's atmosphere. Was this what had happened? And if not, then what did this uncanny light portend?

Aleshin rocked from side to side, Yana snorting. The light lay on the house like a cloak.

SIX

1

What they say is true: alcohol spoils everything except the glasses. And so it was that Shemiakin the bagman was finally pinched outside Makeyevsky's tavern, calling out for his pissed-up horse: "Myushka, Myushka, where tread your dainty feet?" So bad were the roads between villages, that the bagman had resorted to adding a mixture of beer and *eau de cologne* to his horse's feed, just to keep her going. A little tapped, Myushka had sleepily drifted away from the tavern to join the crowds in the Prishchepa market where she bumped into Fasolnikov the bone-man, trampling on the frock coats of deceased gentlemen and upending a cart of pears. Thus, the old proverb was proved right: a horse has four legs and still it stumbles.

Nor did it end there: in the back of Shemiakin's cart were four sacks of grain, a barrel of black market oil, and a consignment of German rifles. All bread can be smoothed over with a little honey, but Shemiakin had the misfortune to arrive just as the Red Guard were arresting Fasolnikov, who accused the bag man of parasitism and the horse of worse. Even more unfortunately, the desk clerk at the clink had been stiffed by Shemiakin just the week before, his grain alcohol cut with petrol. "What kind of a shit gives his best booze to his horse?" asked the clerk, and not without reason. Inevitably Shemiakin was locked up for the night, but what of it? It rains, it snows. True communism was still around the corner, and a box of cigars and a goose of vodka normally sufficed to secure a prisoner's release. Instead, to his great surprise, Shemiakin was taken from his cell to the Institute of Beaux Arts, now occupied by the Cheka.

"So," said Chief Investigator Karnivsky, rolling a cigarette. "What's all this about Sikorsky?"

For both domestic and professional reasons, Shemiakin kept two homes; one with Lyala, a seamstress, the other with Isolda, a professional blocker of hats, The Cheka had visited both, arresting Shemiakin's two wives, and scooping up his children in a cart. The reason, it seemed, had little to do with German rifles or Myushka's little spree. Rather, the seeds of disaster had been sown with the arrest of Chief Officer Kuptsov, some two weeks earlier.

That Chief Officer Kuptsov was on the make wasn't news: what Chief Officer wasn't? An honest man was like a yellow cow: rare and well worth milking. No, it was less his dishonesty than his lack of discretion that had led the Chief Officer to the ditch behind the lumberyard at Gurin's place, flat and skinned like a rug. But such is the fate of all recidivists and class traitors in the zone of Revolutionary Justice...

What had happened was this: so many draftees had run away from their commission that the People's Army had been forced to piss in other pots, swooping on stockades and prison camps all the way from Glum to Voronezh. But when the Reds turned up to enlist the hardened criminals rotting in the Mukholovka or 'fly-trap' clink, they'd discovered the cells virtually empty: whether the prisoners had paid for their freedom or whether they'd been sold to the Whites, remained unclear. Either way, the Cheka were called in, graves dug. When the Chekists examined the paperwork, they discovered the prison's most famous inmate, the killer Sikorsky, had been purchased by a Dr Lepinov of Bezumiye, for three hundred roubles in fancy goods. But what would the chief superintendent of a remote sanatorium be doing with a gift like Sikorsky? When Karvinksy applied the screws to Kuptsov's chief clerk, the bagman's name was mentioned, alongside other counter-revolutionary individuals. The call went out, and though Shemiakin's rabbit was not so easily caught, then Myushka had gone and over-done it with the booze.

"Sikorsky?" said Shemiakin. "Sikorsky the lion guy? Comrade, is it my fault if his cage is empty? Try sending someone out with a big hunk of meat."

Shemiakin spoke like a Tartar, dressed like a Turk, and bartered like a gypsy. He had large bulbous eyes with dark, heavy lids, like some sort of animal roused from hibernation.

"Comrade, I am a poor man, a worker. Look at the calluses on my hands! These are not the hands of a princess on her way to the ball…"

In this, Shemiakin was right. He was not a princess; the neat, smooth shaven Karvinsky could fit inside Shemiakin's cheek like a small plug of tobacco.

"This Sikorsky does not sound like somebody I would care to make the acquaintance of. Why would I buy such a man? I sell only quality items: cold pancakes, sweet buns, pies stuffed with butcher's waste. Who buys and sells maniacs? Only if a maniac themself."

Shemiakin did not like the comrade investigator's silence. The Reds he'd dealt with before had been bought off with a slab of millet: Karnivsky was a fish of a different colour.

"I am no bagman, no bourgeois – search my coat, my children's rags. Do I hoard? Do I steal?" Shemiakin paused. "Okay, some goods maybe I keep for a rainy day, things best kept beneath floorboards or behind a barrel in the *banya*: there are thieves and bandits everywhere. But comrade, I am no kulak growing fat on somebody else's grain. There are no crumbs in my beard nor rings on my toes…"

Certainly, the fellow in front of Karnivsky was no recruiting agent for the bagman's life: his teeth were brown, his shoulders stooped, he had large yellow patches under his eyes. Shemiakin was a sack into which many things could be placed: but who would want to buy them?

"Comrade Inspector, am I a killer, an assassin of the night? Would I stick a man? I mean, if he owed, then fine – we are Russians, after all. But my hands are clean. Okay, okay, Gurtsov, I know – but a snout like that, he had it coming."

"Your wife is here to see you," said the Inspector, without the faintest trace of emotion.

"Wife?" said Shemiakin, suspiciously. "One or Two?"

Lyala entered in tears and a blue headscarf, the scarf curled tightly against her jaw as if suffering from toothache.

"My dove, my sweet!" boomed Shemiakin. "Fear not, for Shemiakin still lives!"

Lyala removed her scarf, spat, and slapped the bagman across the chops. "If I had a knife I would stick you right here," she hissed.

"My angel, my treasure: the other one, she's not my wife. How can a man saddle two mules? Sure, she puts some business my way once in a while, and I have to sugar the buns ... but wife? Pff. You are my reward from Heaven..."

At this Lyala laid her head on the table and sobbed.

"Lyalushka, I need you to be strong for the little ones, tell them that Papa is helping the revolution, that the hour of the proletariat is near... also, to ask Fialkin for a little horse meat, that crook owes me dear..."

Karnivsky pushed a piece of paper across the table to Lyala, his nail-less pinkie tapping the top word dispassionately.

"Inventory?" sobbed the seamstress. "I don't know, I don't know. You mean the stuff he hides in our bedroom? Pff – such

173

junk. But 'an Inventory'? If you say so. The Devil alone knows what he's got in there."

Shemiakin's eyes skipped up and down the list of impounded goods, looking for whatever might get him shot: ladies' jewellery, fur coats, theatrical costumes, cocoa, pain killers, first edition manuscripts, rare stamps, sweet vinegar, ecclesiastical vestments, a balalaika, ladies' underwear, French novels.

Karnivsky licked his lips and handed Lyala a pen. "I don't know, I don't know," she sobbed. "If you say so. Who can count all the nuts he has squirreled away?"

"Sign, sign," said the bagman. "I'm just looking after these things for a friend…"

The seamstress made her mark and Karnivsky nodded.

"Shemisky, my husband," moaned Lyala from beneath her headscarf. "When they take you out and shoot you, don't let that bitch take all your teeth – think of your children, Shemisky, and leave us the poor horse too."

Lyala was escorted out and Shemiakin once again faced Karnivsky across the table.

"What do you expect me to say?" demanded the bagman. "To beg, to weep? Comrade, the people are in need. Supplies are low, spirits too. These things" – he pointed to the list – "are bourgeois trifles. I take them from the rich and hand them to the workers…" Shemiakin's eyes shone like candles. "Comrade, these things I have liberated from our class enemies – actors, lawyers, intellectuals. I wouldn't compare myself to Comrade Lenin, and yet…"

"Bring in the other one," said Karnivsky.

Isolda looked so much like Lyala that you might have thought the seamstress had simply changed scarves. Why the bagman felt the need to have two wives upon his cart was a mystery – but that was not the concern of Revolutionary Justice right now. Isolda entered, nodded to Karnivsky, and immediately began striking the bagman about the head with a long wooden stick.

"My kitten, my dear, my love..." begged the bagman.

"A seamstress?" she demanded. "Some pretty slip of a thing I imagine – silk knickers to blow her nose..."

"Everything you've heard is a lie," said the bagman, protecting his beard as best he could. "My enemies spread filth as a slug leaves a trail. A seamstress? Married to a man of good standing like me? Slander! Besides – think of the children. Is it right that they should see Mama beat Papa about the face?"

If anything, Isolda swung the stick even harder. "The children? The Reds went and pocketed them too. You bastard, you swine! They've taken everything – even the dresses from the Samosov Theatre, the ones you promised for me..."

"Comrade Inspector," said Shemiakin from beneath the heavy rain of blows. "I promise you I have never set foot in a theatre in my life."

Karnivsky nodded, tapped Shemiakin's wife on her shoulder, and handed her a second piece of paper. Breathing heavily she lay down the stick, and picked up an even more dangerous implement – a pen.

"With this I sign your death warrant!" she snapped.

"My dove, my prize..." Once again, the bagman eyed up the list like a rabbit looking for snares: ball gowns, cloaks, an inlaid jewellery box, a gramophone player – oh, and another case of German rifles, this one with ammunition too.

"What would a man like me be doing with a case of German rifles?" he asked Karnivsky, ingenuously. "With these eyes I can barely see my toes."

"He's a liar and a dog," screamed Isolda. "He told me that that other woman was his sister ... the painted tart with her brood of pups..."

With some effort, Isolda was removed from the interrogation room and taken back to the cells. Karnivsky sat stiffly on his chair whilst Shemiakin leaned back like a pasha. "Perhaps now the women are gone, we can talk about serious things," said the bagman, shoving the piece of paper to one side.

"This is all very ... disagreeable," said Karnivsky, lightly clicking his tongue. "Tell me, Comrade Shemiakin – is there any reason why I shouldn't order you to be shot right here and now?"

At this, the bagman pinched his nose. "Shot? Why shot? There's no reason for the People's Army to waste a bullet on a bird like me. Here, let me tell you about Sikorsky..."

The story Shemiakin tapped out on his pot was this: the deal was between Lepinov and Kuptsov: he was the middleman, the *facilitateur* (for some reason he pronounced this in French), not the horse, just the cart. Three suitcases of bourgeois gold – or if not gold, then silks, coats, gramophones. And where did these cases come from? Fleeced from the guests, of course – except that this was good stuff, schmancy, stripped from the back of a better class of lunatic. In return, Kuptsov agreed to Sikorsky's carriage, and even threw in a couple of guards to sweeten the tea. What the Chief Super-intendent wanted with a nut like Sikorsky was none of Shemiakin's affair: for all he knew Lepinov's beams were sagging too. All the bagman had done was to lug the suitcases through the mud from the Yellow House back to Davydovka: this was Kuptsov's deal, not his. Shemiakin hadn't even laid eyes on this Sikorsky: "In all of this I am only the porter."

"A porter who took his own cut?"

"Purely for expenses," said Shemiakin. "The rest: straight to the poor."

"So why do you have the goods, not Kuptsov?"

"What good is a gramophone to Kuptsov? All he needs is a

winding sheet and somewhere to lay his head."

Karnivsky nodded. There was little else of merit to be learned here. True, he could have had the bagman tortured, but what would have been the use? Instead, Shemiakin was taken back to his cell, whilst Karnivsky and his adjunct reviewed his case.

"Up against the wall or the ditch at Gurin's yard?" asked Matveyich, indifferently. Karnivsky flapped his wrist.

"Fetch me what you have on Lepinov – anything in the old secret police file. These trinkets are not the droppings of lunatics. Perhaps the Yellow House is shielding counter-revolutionary or bourgeois elements. Or perhaps our Chief Superintendent is cooking up another dish. Where is this Bezumiye?"

"Where? Everywhere."

"I mean the Yellow House."

"Some thirty versts – but the roads are impassable in this weather."

"It won't rain forever. In the meantime, let the bagman stew in his juices. We might even take him with us: see what Lepinov says with the pair reunited."

Matveyich nodded and retreated, leaving Karnivsky at his desk. Straightening the items on his desk, the Chekist reviewed his revolutionary motives. Was there any reason to allow Shemiakin to live? Bagmen were swindlers, parasites and vestigial capitalists: their correct home was in the grave. Nor did he require the bagman's evidence. The Cheka was not some court, or tribunal, but a fighting organ: it did not judge, but destroyed. Lepinov could be shot with or without the bagman's words – and yet there was something else going on here, something not quite on the page. Was the bagman a goose or a fox? He knew much more than he was letting on, the Devil take him. And then, what of Lepinov, the so-called Superintendent: why spend a fortune securing the freedom of a fiend? There were too many bones in this soup: one needed more than a spoon to eat.

But should he travel to the Yellow House? Who knew how close Denikin's volunteers were, or worse still, the Cossacks. And yet it was not the time for doubt. The Red Army would defend the supreme power of the workers through merciless class war. True, all the evils of the world were rooted in the free market: but for all that, Shemiakin might yet be useful in the eradication of some larger conspiracy. The dictatorship of the proletariat must not delay. When the rains stopped, they would go. Let the mud bury Shemiakin and Lepinov – and the remains of the old world too.

seven

1

At first all that Aleshin could remember were shards: a spinning carousel, a white sailor suit, Sasha the horse and his bright red scarf. But what was the meaning of these things? They seemed poised somewhere between a memory, a dream, and something else entirely. Aleshin remembered his mama passing him to his nanny, promising that if he were a brave little soldier, she would buy him an ice from the stall. The carousel was bright and a box near the front played pretty music but Sasha had scary teeth and hollow eyes and Gregory was scared to go closer.

"It's a nice horsey," said the nurse. "Don't make such a fuss..."

Sasha the horse was hungry. The wood was chipped between his teeth and his tongue was long and black.

"I want to stay with Mama..."

"Your *Mamoshka*'s just there ... don't be ungrateful to Mama ... look, I've paid the man already..."

Unlike Aleshin and his Mama, the man in charge of the ride was bent and dirty: a gypsy, maybe.

"I don't like this horse..."

"Shh – all the other boys are starting to stare..."

The next thing he knew he was holding Sasha's reins beneath a round painted sky, the clouds dotted with tiny balloons and stars. Then the stars started to turn and the contraption started. The mechanical parts were rusty, and the horses whined and squealed.

"Mummy, where are you?"

Gregory didn't want to look at Sasha, so he turned his eyes to the sun instead. The sun was pretty. All the ladies' dresses were glowing. Gregory's sailor suit was glowing too.

"*Mamoshka!*"

Gregory searched anxiously for his Mama, but everything was a blur now, the shapes streaked as if they'd grown a long tail. Straight lines collapsed. Objects hid. Where were Aleshin's glasses? The World Revolution had no time for glasses. Frightened, Gregory searched for *Mamoschka* and Nanny amongst the blobs and flashes. His Mama was wearing a white dress, bright as the sun on snow. If you stared at it long enough, the white turned to something else.

"Mama," said Gregory. "Mama, I don't like this horse…"

If anything Sasha seemed to be running faster and faster, the machinery screeching like a parrot in a cage. Where was the man selling ices? Where were the zoo and the lions? Where was Mama? Gregory's cheeks were wet and flushed.

"Mama, this horse has sharp teeth…"

The next thing he knew the ride had stopped and grown-ups had appeared from nowhere, plucking the children from the machine like fruit from a tree. The dirty man helped Gregory down from his horse. There was no sign of Mama or Nanny anywhere.

"Please sir," said Aleshin. "I can't see a thing…"

The dirty man led Aleshin over to an old woman in a smock. "Sit down, my dove," said she, "your Mama will be here in a minute. My, what a pretty one, you are!"

The woman stroked Aleshin's beautiful hair and gave him some kind of sweetie. He felt rather sick, but took the sweetie anyway. For some reason, the world was full of flashes and holes and blocks of light. If he closed his eyes, it was as if everything was still moving. Perhaps the world was a carousel too.

"Pretty as a princess! But, of course, a young gentleman too."

Was this to be his new Mama? Perhaps he could stay with her on Mondays, Wednesdays and Thursdays, going back to his old house in between. She was awfully dirty but very nice. Maybe she would let him play with her chickens and spoon him porridge from a big, brown bowl. After a while, the man who ran the carousel came over and the pair of them talked very quickly in an accent Aleshin couldn't catch – something common, no doubt.

Something worried him though: if the man was here, then who was looking after the horses? Gregory imagined Sasha breaking free from the machinery, searching for children to bite. Naughty horsey! The man would have to chase it with a whip.

"Can I stay with you?" asked Aleshin. "Do you have a painted finch? Nurse says that all gypsies have a painted finch. Perhaps I could put one of his feathers in my hair…"

The woman smiled and stroked his locks with her long, bony fingers.

"Shhh – your Mama will be here right enough."

And then, just as if in a dream, Mama was there, red in the face and holding on to Nanny as if suddenly taken ill. She looked at the couple holding her son and said something Aleshin couldn't catch: thank you, most likely. Then she handed over some coins in a bag and snatched her hand away. Had she sold him? No – Nanny took his hand and they smartly walked away. *Mamoshka*'s dress was still very bright. What did white turn into when it was too white? Violet, maybe.

When they returned to their bench, Gregory's mother knelt down, looked her son in the eyes, and said in a voice hot with anger: "I have never been so ashamed! Never, do you hear me? To give those foul thieves money – it's disgusting, horrible! I have never been so embarrassed in all my life. It's just so hateful, so horrid – I can't bear it. When your father gets home, I'll tell him all about what you've done to your poor Mama. Oh, it's too beastly! Those nasty looking peasants, their hands out-stretched... I never want to think about them again..."

Gregory did think about them though, and about Sasha, and his mother's shame – not just that night but for many days and nights to come. Indeed, like a single tune played by an idiot, as the years went by it became the most important motif of his life.

Aleshin's fever lasted for seven days, and he slept another four. Initially Yevgrafovna had attended him, but when it was clear that he was no longer in any real danger, she permitted Marya to take over his care. Marya wrapped him in wet towels and rubbed vinegar on to his chest. At night, she kissed him all over but still could not rouse him; instead, his blind eyes stared up at the ceiling, his lips white and dry. In his delirium, he murmured something about Tutyshkin, that Marya couldn't catch: murdered, perhaps.

"My name..."

"Gregory..."

"Code name..."

"Gregory, what..."

"Zhelezin..."

"Doctor Aleshin?"

"Inform the Minister for War immediately..."

Aleshin's mouth opened and closed as if he were breathing feathers.

When the doctor awoke, the rain had gone and a weak sun looked down upon a cold, half frozen landscape. The doctor felt terribly tired and thirsty. Marya burst into tears and held his hand. "Thank you Lord for saving him..." she murmured.

When Yevgrafovna and Frumkin arrived, he told them

everything: how the party had been ambushed by anarchists in the forests, how Zvonkov had died, Tutyshkin shot, the two bread hunters fled. Then he told them of his investigations at the Ryabovsky estate, his discovery of Petr's body, the truth about the inspector.

"Sikorsky played us like a violin," hissed Aleshin, reaching for his spare pair of glasses.

"That clown was Sikorsky the murderer?" said Frumkin. "I don't believe it – he had two feet in one boot. Besides, why travel to the very same clink you're being taken to?"

"I saw the uniforms" said Aleshin, "Petr's body. There is no other explanation. The Menshevik traitor Sikorsky has deceived us."

"And Petr was strangled?" asked Yevgrafovna.

"By that bald fiend…"

"But perhaps it was the same assassin who murdered Lepinov and Churkin?"

"Tutyshkin, I tell you – by which I mean, Sikorsky."

Aleshin's voice was that of a choirboy pretending to be a general: and yet there was no doubting his sincerity.

"We must make contact with the Revolutionary authorities. A conspiracy is afoot…"

Frumkin nodded. "Well, isn't there always?"

After the other doctors had left, the acting Chief Superintendent laid back on the bed and thought about his mother. Marya changed his pillow and brought him fresh water. How kind she was! Marya smelt of ethanol and antiseptic, milk and rye. Inside her apron was a peasant's hut, and inside the hut, a soft bed and a stall filled with hay…

Was this place a haven or a trap? When he had run into problems with the authorities over a bundle of Leftist pamphlets, his mother had arranged his transferral to the sanatorium at Bezumiye, a highly respected institution engaged in both scientific research and the care of the nervous: her own Aunt had once been a patient there. The Yellow House would both take him away from his political difficulties and keep him safe from the war. He would move in the right circle of physicians and guests, and meet a number of significant and influential people. He should thank his Mama for her kindness and forbearance: no dissent was permitted.

O, how tired he felt! All of a sudden he had a vision of the moment he had seen the Yellow House for the very first time: the mud, the bowed trees, the rain unceasing, like regret. The clouds were heavy and oppressive, the colours – green, mustard, ochre – bleeding from the stuccoed walls into the earth and the sky. As the young doctor approached the main house, he remembered seeing a pale blonde man in golden spectacles looking out from a window; only when he got closer did he realise that it was only his reflection. Aleshin started to wave and then stopped: what was he, a child? Then Nikolai picked up the doctor's case, and the gates closed shut like a book.

2

Madame Pimenova dreamt that a great field of pale mushrooms had appeared on the lawn, cockades planted jauntily on their little roundy caps, while the jeweller, Chalikov, announced that the Imperial Eagle had flown three times over Petersburg, carrying a bright red snake in its beak and shitting roses on the crowd. Not to be outdone, Countess Rybnikova reported that she had seen the trees in the courtyard move like the parts of a timepiece, their branches marking out the fatal hour. For once the omens were in agreement: the white army was now no more than one week's march away. Denikin was here.

Frumkin threw up his hands. "Dreams aren't like telegrams," he despaired. "You might as well leaf through the entrails of a goat."

"But my vision..." intoned Countess Rybnikova.

"Keep your vision fixed on the gates," said Frumkin. "If you see a Cossack hat, yell."

Most vexing of all, the *flügel* was gripped by rumours of a mysterious letter outlining how Davydovka had already fallen to Marmatov and his Cossacks, with Denikin and the White Army advancing from the South.

"A letter? Delivered how?" asked Frumkin. "We've had no supplies and the roads have been impassable for weeks. What, some postman decided to take a stroll?"

Nobody wanted to listen. According to the letter, the Jew Trotsky, had been found murdered in the Ministry of War, the

Tsar's brother was on his way back to the Winter Palace, and a stockpile of tobacco and tea had been discovered near the bridge at Pysostrovo.

"Lysevitch told me all about it," said Madame Pimenova. "The envelope even bore the Imperial seal…"

Such were the laws of psychiatry: the longer the guests stayed in the Yellow House, the crazier they became. Yes, lunatics build castles in the air, and then the psychiatrists charge rent. Frumkin cancelled all his appointments and went to see Radek and Martynov instead. The professor and the actor were usually to be found in one of the old reception rooms or another, playing *Podkidnay Durek* or discussing literature. When Frumkin told them of the elusive missive, the old professor shrugged his shoulders like a lawyer.

"What was it Gorky says? A scratch lights up an empty face. The human imagination needs something to gnaw upon, and in the absence of the real, one is forced to invent what one can."

"Yeah, well, it's all getting out of hand. Dolzhikov has stitched his St. Anne ribbon to his jacket and Pimenovsky is dressed up as if the Tsarina is going to call any minute."

Radek placed a long academic finger up his nose. "If a garden doesn't grow radishes, then it grows weeds. What can one do? The longer the House stays cut off…"

"The longer the house stays cut off, the safer we stay. Let the whites slaughter the reds and the Bolsheviks liquidate the Mensheviks: we'll stay here and dust our *tschotchkes*." Frumkin scratched his woolly fleece, his demeanour that of a sheep sniffing at a burnt offering. "In the meantime nobody gets any crazy ideas. No visions, no signs, no imaginary letters."

"What's that, the letter?" asked Martynov, idly fishing through a basket of old clothes. "Yes, yes, I've read it. The Cossacks are just outside of Chulm…"

"There is no letter!" yelled Frumkin, "Who delivered it, Elijah and the Angels? You're as crazy as the next man. Which in this place...."

"Calm yourself doctor: Lysevitch told me all about it. The Red camp at Chermavka has been over-run, the Bolsheviks scattered. As soon as they saw Marmatov's beaver, the Reds all shat their pants and pledged allegiance to the crown."

"Yeah, yeah – and they say they milk chickens. Radek: tell him..."

"This letter: do you still have it, dear fellow?"

Martynov pulled out a long peasant cloak made of thick cloth and a broadcloth jacket lined with batting. "I had to give it back to Lysevitch. He wanted to show it to his sister..."

"You ask me, the goats have eaten all your greenery," muttered Frumkin. "I get more sense from the chronics in ward five."

To think it had come to this. Just a few years ago and Frumkin had had a thriving practice treating the frayed nerves of the intelligentsia of Davydovka; now he was hiding in a nut house, pretending to be a *feldsher*, and discussing the fine print of non-existent letters. And these were just the flowers – the berries would come soon enough.

"Look at this!" bellowed Martynov. "A magnificent crimson shawl – just right for playing Ivan the Terrible, or perhaps Genghis Khan."

It was a universal psychiatric truth: the longer one stayed within an institution, the more neurotic symptoms one displayed. Craziness was catching. Without strict quarantine, pathological symptoms spread like bacilli.

Take the guests in the *flügel*: Frumkin asked the tenants to show a little lunacy whenever Nadya came near and now they gibbered like monkeys even when the nurse was on her break. Why should he listen to any of them? Madame Semenova had spied on the Inspector as he set off on his ill-starred jaunt and whispered "No, not Tutyshkin: too tall, too bald." Did that mean he was Sikorsky? Frumkin had his doubts. One wouldn't put a chicken in his hands but – a murderer? Feh.

"The people dream of order as an answer to chaos," said the old professor, trying on an astrakhan hat. "Which is madder: the one yelling or the one who started the fire? Yes, things have come to a parlous state. What was it Kornilov said? We must save Russia even if we have to destroy it. The language of victory has been replaced by the rhetoric of annihilation. Such brutality touches everyone."

"That hat makes you look like a toothless old woman," said Martynov. "It suits you."

Martynov was right: without his housekeeper, students and books, the professor was wasting away. Instead of intellectual debate, he muttered about the extermination of the gentry and the revenge of the serfs. Green bags hung under his eyes and his clothes gave off a sour stench.

"Like a forest fire, the Red Terror will consume itself. Do you know, I heard of a scholar at the University – a professor of architecture – who named his daughter Terrora. Can you imagine? And all the time soldiers are free to attack and rob peaceful citizens, breaking into homes and murdering and looting."

"Well, obviously the Cossacks will put an end to that," said Frumkin, sardonically.

"A friend of mine, Dr Brod – some civilian turned up at his door wearing a pitiful face, and begging for medical help. But when the doctor opened the door, four hooligans set about him, pushing a pistol against his temple and beating him so badly that he could only lie on his stomach."

Martynov made a face as if he didn't believe a word.

"And that's the least of it. A list of Davydovka's wealthiest businessmen was drawn up, the individuals ordered to present themselves at the Grand Hotel with five million roubles in two weeks otherwise they would be taken as hostages of the state. The Cheka roll prisoners around in a barrel full of nails – if they aren't shot straight away."

"I'm sure this can't be true."

"A proclamation was posted that the bourgeois should be used instead of horses to pull heavy loads. Those who fell would be whipped."

"Calm yourself dear professor," said Martynov. "The dogs may run wild in the cities, but at least here we're safe."

Frumkin winced. The good people of Davydovka had paid handsomely to be transported to the Yellow House but the deal was with Lepinov, not Aleshin: when the Red Doctor recovered from his jaunt, he'd start sticking his pretty little nose into everything. Frumkin didn't trust him: inside every revolutionary was a policeman. Besides, all the guests' goodies – suitcases full of jewellery, furs, deeds and antiques – had been handed over to Shemiakin. What was left was junk and trinkets: religious relics, broken frames, paintings of ugly relatives. One wouldn't pick such things out of a ditch.

"Just look at this coat," sneered Martynov, "it's been through so many hands it's turned from a bear to a dog."

Eventually the Yellow House devoured everyone, like straw in a fire. When Frumkin, then a lawyer, had visited the house some six years earlier, Lepinov had impressed him as an efficient manager and sharp businessman. By the time Frumkin had come to disguise himself as a *feldsher*, Lepinov had transformed into some kind of unholy fool, talking of spells and amulets and the delicate wine-like taste of the soul. What had happened? The superintendent stank of brimstone and juniper. His nails curled like old roots. Whenever he ventured outside blackbirds swooped around him, dropping twigs on his head. "The body is best understood as a vessel for unquiet spirits," he told Frumkin conspiratorially; "when the spirit burns the body suffers also."

For Frumkin, everything came down to the head. Madness was a disease of the mind, a malady of consciousness. If one could only straighten one's thoughts then one's spine would follow. Bleedings, sweatings, the draining of bile: all this was torture rather than medicine. Reason was the only cure.

"Fancy a game of fool?" asked Martynov from beneath his Imperial wig.

"If you have the roubles then I have the pockets," said Frumkin.

In truth, the *feldsher*'s position was becoming increasingly parlous. The two businessmen, Balashov and Yurovsky, demanded some kind of insurance on their investment. They'd given nearly three thousand roubles to this bagman – could Frumkin guarantee the Reds would stay away until Denikin and his forces arrived? But the money had gone to Lepinov, the roubles flown like sparrows. What the hell had Lepinov spent it on anyway? Where could one spend such a sum in the middle of a waste dump? Unless he'd hidden it away somewhere – or Shemiakin had stiffed him on the deal.

"No, no, let's play *Vint*" said the old professor. "A much more civilised game."

Radek had come to the Yellow House after radicals set fire to the University. The institution had been closed for more than a year but it took the burning of his books to bring home the severity of the situation.

"First they lynch the bankers, then the shop keepers, finally anyone who wears glasses or tries to read a book. Everything is reduced to the lowest possible level. Of course, Russians have always believed that manual labour is the only thing of any real worth. But this belief in the moral superiority of poverty has now taken on a new form: the war on wealth. If the Bolsheviks cannot make the poor any less miserable then at least they can make the rich more miserable still."

Spittle appeared on the old man's lips, stretching between them like glue.

"This levelling has its own logic of which looting the looters is only part. Who are the *burzhooi*? Employers, officers, priests, students, anyone well dressed, carrying a satchel, capable of following a thought to its end."

Martynov abandoned his box and slumped down on a chair. "Ask a hungry worker who the bourgeois are, and he'll say those crafty, grain-hoarding peasants. Ask a villager and he'll say those thieves in the factories with their fancy factory goods. The term is meaningless. Who are these *burzhooi*, who?"

"You, you big ape," said Frumkin. "Now, are we going to play or not?"

Radek shuffled and the men examined their hands.

In truth, the *feldsher* feared the Cossacks much more than the Reds. When the Whites seized a town, one of their first acts was to paint a red star on the synagogue and string up the rabbi. Afterward it was standard practice for White officers to permit their soldiers two or three days discretion to rob and kill Jews at will – a Jewish holiday, they said.

"When you can buy hand-grenades at the market but not meat, it's a sign that civilization has fallen apart," said Radek. "As for the alcohol: the Reds drunk it all as soon as they nationalised the liquor stores. Russia is an Asiatic country, primitive and backward. Though the Germans failed, Western troops will soon march in – and a good thing too. The Enlightenment never caught on here – what a Russian likes is destroying things. Our greatest military achievement was to burn down Moscow. Give a Russian an axe and he'll plant it in his neighbour's head."

"Am I the only one playing? Two hearts."

"Calm yourself Professor," said Martynov, examining his cards. "The Whites will sort things out, and they'll be back queuing in the stalls. Why, according to Lysevitch's letter, the fortifications at Tayda have fallen and the Reds are fleeing like ants…"

"Oh yeah, yeah, this mythical letter," said Frumkin with a sneer. "That's right: Denikin is just about to ring the bell. Listen, the snail is coming, who knows when it arrives. In the meantime, three hearts…"

Frumkin was still in a foul mood when he sat down to eat with Yevgrafovna. The talk with Radek and Martynov had depressed him; what did those two clowns know about anything? Put the pair of them in a bag and they'd be talking until the Day of Judgement. Besides, all educated Russians loved to go on about Russia's primitive, Asian soul, especially if it meant they could put on a uniform and wield a big stick.

Yevgrafovna's eyes glowed with a strange intensity and she reached out and squeezed Frumkin's arm. "So: you think that whoever clamped that helmet on Lepinov, also killed him?"

"Well, it's a novel way to block a hat…"

Zinaida moved from Frumkin's arm to his cheek. "Aleshin felt that the bodies of the police officers were well over a week old. Could Sikorsky have shot them, made his way to the Yellow House, murdered Lepinov and Churkin, and then retraced his steps to the Estate to strangle Young Petr?"

"I don't know – it sounds a busy day. Besides, who commits a murder and then comes back to investigate?"

"The perfect alibi…"

"And he's got his own key? I know that Nikolai is hammered as a nail, but even he isn't in the habit of admitting homicidal maniacs. Nor did Tutyshkin act as if he'd been here before, or knew anything about the Chief Superintendent. Unless he's the world's greatest actor then I just don't buy it..."

"We accepted that he was a police officer."

"We all said there was something screwy from day one. A liar's hat always burns. I don't think he'd ever set eyes on our beloved Lepinov in his life."

"He didn't want to look at the corpse."

"Who does? Lepinov looks like something from Shiskin's spleen stew. But that doesn't make him a murderer. Quite the opposite in fact."

Yevgrafovna pulled on one of Frumkin's ears then absent mindedly scratched herself with her fork. "Say what you like doctor: there was something about the shape of the man's skull which spoke of criminality."

"What, we believe in feeling heads now? If we're talking of psychiatric principles then it's the inside of the skull which counts."

Yevgrafovna's lips curled back in a sneer. "Oh yes, I forgot: you can cure a patient just by talking them around."

"So, consciousness is where exactly – a quarter of an inch up from the sphincter? I can't believe that in the twentieth century you're still trying to instil reason by monkeying around with somebody's juices."

Yevgrafovna's voice was that of a teacher explaining something extremely simple to a very stupid child. "That the causes of mental distress are physiological is a scientific fact."

"Yeah, yeah, it's all in the digestion: or is it the lungs these days? Maybe we should just try tapping the scalp with an axe..."

"Madness is a degeneration of the brain. The belief that the dreams or ravings of the demented have any meaning is pure sophistry. "

"And speaking of dreams..." The *feldsher* looked down at his milk pudding and dug at it with his spoon, "have you heard anything about a letter?"

"A letter?"

"Yeah, a letter – sent to one of the guests."

"Sent to whom? Delivered by whom? How would a letter make its way to the Yellow House?

"I know, I know, I just…"

"The roads are impassable and crawling with bandits. Enemy combatants are everywhere…"

"Okay, okay, I hear you…"

"A letter?" Yevgrafovna pulled a face. "You've been in this place too long…"

"Well, that's the truth…"

Frumkin waved Yevgrafovna away and went back to his pudding. He had a headache and his chest felt very tight. Perhaps he was coming down with something after all. I mean, who was he trying to kid? He would never leave this place. Rather than some kind of hiding-place or sanctuary, it was just another trap There's no way out, Frumkin reflected, no matter how many times you knock.

3

True, Frumkin was a quack and a charlatan, but for some reason Zinaida couldn't imagine the Yellow House without him. Quite why she felt this way was a mystery. Frumkin's belief in some kind of whimsical 'unconscious' was divorced from any clinical understanding of the brain, and his arbitrary distinction between reason and instinct as 'categories of the mind' lacked any grounding in scientific practice. And as for his unhealthy interest in dreams, fornication and fantasy – pff, better not to talk of it.

Yes, Frumkin was a sly one. Officially, he was the *feldsher*, the medical assistant, but everyone knew that he had owned his own analytic practice in Davydovka, tending to the rich and gullible. Why then the pretence? Frumkin had come to the House before the outbreak of war, so he wasn't hiding from military service. Nor, as far as Yevgrafovna knew, was he in trouble with the Reds or wanted by the police. He joked, he winked, he played cards, and despite his junior role, Lepinov indulged him like a prince, allocating him the least damaged of patients and allowing him to treat them via 'analysis', his so-called talking cure. Needless to say, none of his practices had any basis in physiological fact: after a while the guests either grew bored with the chatter or became dependant upon him and moved in on his couch. Something else was going on too. It was abundantly clear that the other doctors (and nurses too, except for Nadya) were quietly but conscientiously being kept away from the *flügel*, the old estate annexe. Wealthy guests (many, old acquaintances of Frumkin's from the city) arrived displaying few if any immediately apparent symptoms. Rather, these new guests arrived bearing expensive *objects d'art*, jewellery and clothing, all of which went straight into Lepinov's pocket. On the night when the Superintendent had argued with Shemiakin the bagman, Polina reported seeing Churkin lug at least two great chests of booty from the *flügel* to the tunnels beneath Lepinov's study. Was this why Lepinov agreed to shield him from public view as a mere assistant? But why did Frumkin need hiding in the first place?

Yes, when it came to Frumkin, Yevgrafovna felt torn. As a physician, her philosophical disagreements with Frumkin were profound – but she also liked to touch his curly hair, and take his arm after dinner. In the end, their arguments always came down to the same old question: did those in the Yellow House suffer from maladies of the mind or disorders of the brain? The most common delusion was that the patient was at the centre of some kind of conspiracy or sham, that they'd been tricked into entering the Yellow House by actors masquerading as family or friends. For many, everyone in the institution, whether doctor, nurse or inmate, was, in reality, some kind of detective, spying on them and poisoning their food. They saw the institution as an enormous masquerade, each member of the cast disguised as someone else.

Yevgrafovna couldn't care less: if a guest believed that he was a speck of corn about to eaten by a large hen, it was of no concern to her. The degeneration of the nerve fibres, malformation of the skull, the flow of blood to the brain: only these were of legitimate concerns to medical science. Everything else was rank foolishness. (At times, she wondered whether Frumkin was even qualified as a doctor. She'd heard that he'd been a lawyer before entering psychiatry, and his clinical practice was atrocious).

In their heart of hearts, both Lepinov and Frumkin saw

themselves as doctors of the soul – a typically Russian misapprehension. The idea that psychiatry was the science of human essence, an invisible soul, hidden from the human eye – ho, such stupidity made Yevgrafovna want to bite and kick. After all, it was such primitive thinking which had resulted in Yevgrafovna's expulsion from the Moscow Clinic of Psychiatry in the first place. True, though an injection of rat bite fever had proved detrimental to patients in the short term, it also revealed something of vital importance: namely, that temperatures, fever and infection altered the physical make up of the brain, leading it to function in a profoundly altered manner. After all, fever produces hal-lucinations, fantasies and intense emotional mood swings – all the traditional symptoms of the mad. Sickness makes the brain work differently. One question was how to turn the brain's functioning back to normal. Another was how such sickness was spread in the first place.

If madness displayed strikingly similar symptoms to cholera and syphilis, then might it too be a contagious condition, spread by as yet unseen agents? As all doctors knew, hysteria was infectious: fainting fits, tears, delirium – all of these could migrate from hysteric to hysteric like wildfire. Likewise, the frenzy of the mob could touch even the most rational or reserved of individuals. Could then a form of monomania sweep the country, a general mental epidemic? Yevgrafovna had seen this first hand in the soldiers she'd treated for nervous exhaustion. Those who had suffered actual bombardment seemed to inculcate symptoms in those further back along the line: fainting, headaches, dizziness, a loss of speech or movement. A soldier who had never seen shelling would react just like a captain who had lost his limbs. Depression, anxiety and hallucinations were almost universal. Of course, conditions on the front were hellish – but why should cooks and clerks moan and grind their teeth as well? For Aleshin such derangement was a reaction to social turbulence, a transitional period as the Old World was replaced by the New. But what if some other kind of plague stalked Russia, physical rather than emotional, a mental Black Death? Madness was the Russian disease: but what if it was an actual disease after all?

Before disturbed soldiers had begun to arrive at the Yellow House Yevgrafovna had been obliged to work on elderly guests suffering from dementia and confusion. Only with a regular supply of stupefied combatants could Yevgrafovna finally put her theories into practice. As Wagner von Jauregg had shown in Austria, the intro-duction of typhoid fever – counter-balanced by the administration of quinine – could both replicate and treat fevers of the brain. All Yevgrafovna had done was take this theory to its logical end – and, foo, who could blame her for that?

When the revolution came and the Russian army collapsed, the patients were re-assigned, and unceremoniously shipped out. Fortunately, the process was chaotic and unaccountable and nobody looked at the numbers too closely. Even after the end of the war and the beginning of Bolshevik rule, Yevgrafovna was able to continue with her experiments – albeit 'with one hand under the covers'. Did Lepinov care? No, no, he did not. By this stage Lepinov was consorting with demons.

After bidding farewell to Frumkin, Yevgrafovna went to meet Polina in the vestibule to the rear of Ward Four. Most of the vestibule roof was missing and the rain came in like time.

"How are they?" Yevgrafovna asked curtly, stroking Polina's hair.

"The same, the same"

"Have you checked the blood?"

"But of course…"

"And?"

"No good."

Yevgrafovna pulled a face and took the lantern from the nurse. Behind a locked door, a whitewashed stairwell led down to an underground passage cut off from the main house. From there, dark intestinal passages twisted left and right. A strange whimpering could be heard from behind a closed door, accompanied from time to time by a frenzied bark.

Polina flinched. "Dr Yevgrafovna … Zinaida … we have to talk about Alexei."

"There is nothing to be said."

"But we both know he was wearing…"

Yevgrafovna shook her head and carressed Polina's cheek. With her pointed nose and pinched features, the lantern made her look like some kind of gargoyle.

"No, Nurse Popova, we don't know anything."

"But Alexei is still missing…"

"Missing? He cannot be far."

"Zinaida, these passages…"

"Silence, I say!" Yevgrafovna's arm fell to her side and she glared at the nurse with flashing eyes.

How far did the passages go? Half way to Minsk and twice around the world, a labyrinth without end.

Science moved slowly, like a stone.

eight
1

When it came to how the Devil arrived in Chulm, nobody seemed to be able to get their story straight. Some said that he walked into the village of his own accord, appearing in the middle of the night, naked, save for a crown made from animal bone. Others claimed that Dusya had conjured him from the ditch in Oboski's field, summoning him from Hell to play the role of teacher and consort. Granny Ona swore that she had dug him up in her vegetable patch, buried up to his chin amongst her radishes. Either way he was the first man to enter Chulm in months.

The Reds had accused the men of the village of hoarding grain and taken them away by cart. The head of the village council had been held for ransom for six weeks and then shot; the rest of the men were given stolen uniforms and unusable muskets and conscripted into the fighting vanguard of the proletariat. That was the last anyone had heard of them. Three weeks after their transportation, another brigade of Red soldiers arrived, this time accusing the men of Chulm of evading compulsory registration as well as providing material assistance to the Counter-Revolutionary cause. When they discovered that the villagers had already been taken, they set fire to Voloshyn's barn and took away the peasants' pots and pans. Late that night several drunken soldiers retuned intending to rape any unprotected women. No one would say what happened, but the soldiers' bodies were hidden in the clover behind the midden heap, their heads caved in with hoes. No Red ever returned to find out what had happened: either nobody gave a rat's ass about their comrades, or the unit had already moved on. Whatever the case, after the Reds left, the women took over the labour of the absent men. They tended the fields, looked after the livestock, and repaired the huts. For a time they continued to trade with the nearby Yellow House but as the roads deteriorated and the woods became ever more dangerous, even this connection began to fray. It was as if their village had been visited by a great flood. Only Dusya continued to follow the old paths through the woods – but then as everybody knew, Dusya was protected by eldritch powers.

Of course it was Dusya who came upon the stranger among the trees, his bald head in one pile of leaves, his torso and legs in another. She'd used black magic to put him back together again: this was why he walked like a Frenchman, one leg limping behind the other. He was a police inspector, he said, set upon by brigands in the course of his duties.

When Dusya asked his name, he whispered "Inspector Aleshin. District of Voronezh."

"Aleshin?"

"No, no, what am I saying? Tutyshkin."

To Tutyshkin, the girl seemed very young – no more than sixteen at the most – yet she looked him up and down with the expression of a bitter old woman. Dusya was small and flat chested, skinny as a hair. She had a single witch's brow and her long, black hair reached almost to her navel, dark as a crow's dreams. Was she human or no? Her eyes were a mixture of green and violet unlike any colour he'd seen before. On her *sarafan* she had drawn occult circles, flowers with mouths, fish with human legs. How they had travelled from the forest to the village he couldn't say – on a sparrow's wing, perhaps.

At least the hut was clean and dry, covered in odd off cuts of rugs and carpets purloined from who knows where – Count Ryabovsky's estate, most likely. The stove was small and well tended. Herbs and strong smelling plants lined a series of roughly made shelves, strange wooden figures peeping out from behind the foliage. There was no smell of food or tobacco, but rather something bitter and earthy the Inspector couldn't quite identify. Odd metal rings were suspended from the roof, chiming whenever a breeze happened to stir. There was no mother, no Auntie, no Granny, no animals, either. On the ceiling was a crude picture of a tree growing from between a woman's legs. Lying in Dusya's bed, the sheets pulled at him like quicksand.

"I'm in Heaven," croaked Tutyshkin, though in truth he suspected the opposite.

Still, he needed to rest. After the ambush – and the murder of Zvonkov and Aleshin - Tutyshkin had wandered around the forest in a kind of dream. One bullet had narrowly missed his skull, while a second grazed his thigh. Lost and confused, the Inspector had drifted through the woods in odd concentric circles, taking flight at the slightest sound. The forest was like the prison at Kursk: the crows looked on like warders, the branches thick black bars. Once he thought he glimpsed the spirit of Aleshin, searching for the door to the next realm.

Had he died too? When Dusya him back to her hut, she removed his clothes, washed him in some kind of oily broth, and rubbed a handful of foul smelling moss on his wound. Afterwards she gave him a large bowl of mushroom soup that made him sick.

"Please…" he said, but the girl shook her head and pointed to the bowl. When she sat down opposite him, she stroked her hair like a cat. Her nails were very long – especially those on her feet, which she scraped against the bed frame in stripes.

"You're a sweetheart," he croaked, "an answer to prayers…"

The girl examined him like a jeweller sizing up a stolen piece.

"Eat," she said.

Ho, what snare had he landed in? The hut was full of jars containing odd foodstuffs: bright green fruit, yellowy broth, pickles shaped like members. Some contained dried insects and poisonous looking roots. One bottle was full of tiny mottled eggs; next to it, a bright red cockroach peeped from the top of an earthen jug.

"I don't think I…"

"Eat."

Afterwards he slept fitfully. When he woke there were two wrinkled heads looking in through the doorframe.

"Hello," he said. "Hello, my dears, don't be shy."

The two women glanced at each other and made the sign of the cross.

"Why you look like two angels just hopped down from Heaven."

In truth, both women looked more like sacks of potatoes stuffed into felt boots. Dusya's hut was built half underground and the women had to bend uncomfortably, their backs protesting like an old barn roof.

"Yes it's definitely a devil…" said one, turning to the other..

"Horrible…"

"A demonic spirit."

"Oo, yes…"

One of the old women advanced a little closer, wanting to see the fiend close up. Yes, yes, just as they'd heard: dark eyes, soft mouth, head like a skull. Was he naked under those covers? They imagined his scaly back and long tail, the hidden patches of coarse, black hair.

Tutyshkin tried smiling one of his ingratiating smiles.

"O dear Granny, I…"

"The Lord curse you…"

"Dear lady, I promise…"

"Angels take your hat."

Yes, he was a devil right enough. Everything about him suggested satanic powers. His eyes were dark and hollow and his skin looked like a bruised pear. Even the tufts of hair growing from his craggy skull seemed somehow unclean.

"Do you think I might have some water? I'm terribly parched…"

"Devil! Beelzebub!"

"Dearest Granny, I'm no devil, but an inspector of the law…"

The women stared at him in fright. "The law?"

"A police officer" said Tutyshkin, smiling.

"Swine!" cried one of the grannies, smacking him one with her stick.

"My dear…"

"Pig! Dog! Shit!"

"My dear, please…"

The Granny tapped him again and the two old ladies fled like bedbugs. Tutyshkin held his head and groaned. Nothing good could climb out of this hole.

Exhausted, the Inspector closed his eyes. There was no icon in here, no holy lamp. One jar contained salted nuts, another, the corpses of tiny baby birds, embalmed in brine. The wind chimes played a melancholy tune, and all the time the woman with the tree between her legs looked down indifferently, her eyes as blank as snow.

After that a steady stream of onlookers came to stare at the devil or (as some whispered) *policeman*. The women were thin and dirty, the children with bloated bellies on rickety legs. They looked at him with frightened eyes in pale, anaemic faces, necks distended from scrofula. Tutyshkin waved like a duchess and winked at the tots.

"Come in, come in," he said. "Come see the monkey."

The children pointed and giggled, some blowing raspberries, others waggling their bottoms.

"Yes, yes, that's it," said Tutyshkin. "Come in, I won't bite…"

At this Dusya returned, chasing away the children like chickens. The grannies crowded round asking questions, but Dusya remained silent, pulling a tattered curtain across the doorway as if ending the first act. She made an odd gesture before the door and kissed her fingers twice. Then she turned to the inspector and handed him a husk of bread, smeared with goose fat, and tea tasting of sage and dust.

"A real feast," said Tutyshkin. "I'm feeling better already…"

The girl lit a fire and settled on her stool, running her nails through her long black mane.

"Why did you say Aleshin?" she asked softly "I've heard of a doctor by that name…"

"How extraordinary" said Tutyshkin, eyebrows arched.

"At the Yellow House. Have you been there? It is only a day or so from here."

"You mean there's somewhere else apart from here?"

The girl shrugged. "There was once."

"And this Yellow House – what happened to it?"

"The devil took it and put it in his sack," she said, "taking all the doctors with him…"

"Ha ha, yes indeed. The doctors, quite… perhaps you know of the Chief Superintendent?"

"Lepinov?" The girl's hair covered her face like a veil, or a cloak. "Why ask about Lepinov, Inspector?"

"Why because I'm here to investigate his murder…"

"Murder?"

"The poor fellow was found at the bottom of Saint Leonilla's well. Done in, as we say in the police force."

"I see." Dusya's voice sounded very far away, as if hidden behind her dark curtain of hair.

"Murder, yes, yes, yes…"

Dusya was silent.

"Did you know him, my dear? Have any dealings with him? I understand that the Superintendent often took long walks near here. Perhaps you met him? Or perhaps you had some other kind of business at the House?"

The hut felt very warm, the air very sour.

"But what would a girl like you be doing at the Yellow House? Eh, my lass? What would anyone want there?"

The girl didn't answer. Her hair was dark as night.

"Have you been there, my dear? At midnight, perhaps. Did Nikolai let you in? Lepinov waiting in his chambers…"

"I played near there as a child," she said. "With my little brother."

The hut was so gloomy, Tutyshkin wasn't even certain she was still there. The fire flickered and the shadows fell. For a moment, he suspected that the girl had somehow disappeared behind that great black waterfall of hair.

"One day a naked man came out of a hole and strangled him."

"Um…"

"He was called Orlov. My mother and Lepinov were chasing him and Lepinov shot him like a dog."

"Orlov?"

"They dumped his corpse in a ditch nearby. My brother was buried in a hole in our garden – he was only small and the hole wasn't very deep. After that, *Mamochka* fell ill. A few days later she was taken up into the Yellow House, and I never saw her again. 'She's not well,' people told me, 'not well in her nut.' I didn't understand. My brother and I had been playing 'Heaven and Hell' with a nut and a stick…"

Tutyshkin scratched his nose. "Orlov, you say? Well that's very interesting, my angel. How old were you my sweet? Was this…"

"Your name isn't Tutyshkin," said a strange, old voice from behind the black veil. .

"What?"

"And you're no police officer either."

A pair of violet eyes appeared from behind the curtain and Tutyshkin felt a strange pressure, right between his ears.

"My dear, I…"

"Who are you?" said the voice. "Who are you, really?"

Tutyshkin blinked and his mouth felt as if filled with dust.

"No, no, my dove – 'tis true! A lad from the Yellow House – Petr, I believe - asked for my assistance…"

"Petr?"

"That's the fellow! He came to Davydovka, seeking aid. Chief Lepinov murdered – his body blackened and bloated, horns growing from his head."

"And Petr? What became of…"

"Oh these young scamps: who knows? Gone in search of adventure or Socialism or heaven knows what. Do you know the lad, my dear? I had no idea…"

Dusya's voice now sounded normal again: the voice of a young girl.

"Yes, I know Petr," she said, her voice as soft as mouse fur. "Now sleep."

"Well, it's been a long day…"

Dusya turned and moved toward the door.

"Dusya?"

"Shhh, sleep, sleep."

When he awoke, night had settled in like a large, heavy sow. The hut was black and empty, Dusya gone. The Inspector pushed away his blankets and struggled to his feet. Terribly weak, he fell into a potted plant and knocked over some kind of carved figure: a woman of some sort? He felt sure the figure was sister to the ones found in Lepinov's study and under Petr's bed, but it was too dark to see. He gripped it in both hands and trembled: he too was naked. Exhausted, he climbed back into Dusya's bed and let the night wash over him. Darkness seemed to lap against his legs like floodwater. The bed floated on a sea of nothing. Wind chimes whispered.

"Sikorsky," he whispered. "Old friend, if you could but see me now."

2

In the morning, Tutyshkin was visited not by Dusya, but by Ludmilla, the village headman – or woman, in this case. She was a handsome Auntie in her mid forties, with strong teeth and a formidable chest. She wore a peasant's blouse over a pair of man's trousers, unstitched at the hem.

"Well – they smeared your beard with mustard," she said.

Ludmilla sized him up like a slab of meat at the market.

"So how come you aren't dead?" she said, pulling on his ear.

"It's not as easy as you think."

"Mm."

She grabbed the bottom of the blanket and took a look under. "Police?"

"An inspector."

"We know all about police here," said the woman. "They come, collect taxes, steal food, flog anyone who hasn't washed their hands."

"Sweetheart, I…"

"Police is them, not us. I don't know what Dusya was thinking…"

"I'm enormously indebted to your kindness."

"I bet."

Ludmilla fished in her pocket and retrieved a Bolshevik decree printed in large red letters. She then poured a rough kind of homemade tobacco into it and lit up.

"She said you'd come…"

"I'd come?"

"That it was fated." Her eyes were lively and cynical.

"Well…"

"You a Red?"

Tutyshkin pulled a face. "Foo…"

"The Reds took our men away. Not that it was any great shame. Thieves and piss artists, the lot of them."

"Ah, I'm sure…"

"Only good for drinking, fighting and thieving."

"Well, yes…"

"A woman needs a husband like she needs a tail. It's just something that gets in the way…"

Ludmilla's husband had been a cantankerous old goat some twenty years older than his wife. He had run her ragged with all his chores, giving her a smack to the head if she so much as forgot to wipe the crumbs from his plate. When first married he'd been fiercely jealous, and whipped her naked in the street, in full view of everyone. He would get drunk and set fire to their furniture. Afterwards he pissed on the ashes, no matter which way the wind was blowing. In short, no pearl.

"When the Reds took him, I thought, 'Oh, some peace and quiet – let him be yelled at for a while'. Why men? We can sew, reap, clean, mend. Men are good for one thing and they're usually too pissed to do it."

Tutyhskin made a funny, fluttery gesture with his wrist. "You have nothing to fear on that score, my dear…"

Ludmilla snorted and pulled his other ear. Her grey eyes were the colour of smoke.

"Some folk say that you're a devil…"

"An inspector…"

"There a difference?"

"In dress uniform, yes."

"You looking for deserters?"

"Pff."

"Kulaks?"

"Not at all."

"Bagmen?"

Tutyshkin raised himself up on one elbow. "My dear, I am here to investigate the murder of Chief Superintendent Lepinov of the Yellow House."

"On your own in the woods?"

"Evil lurks in many pots."

The ashen end of the decree fell onto Tutyshkin's bedclothes, but both chose to ignore it.

"You've got your nose up the wrong arse, Inspector. The roads aren't safe to travel on and there's bandits everywhere. Besides - the mud's high as a horse's belly. Even the Reds have gone back to the Devil. The nearest village is twenty miles away and there hasn't been a market since the Germans."

"Germans?"

"The war, I mean. 'Aint nothing to do with us. You think life would be worse with a German Tsar than a Russian one? Same mud, same soil. And the same goes for the Reds. Is Lenin coming to sweep the streets here?"

"They swept away the old estate…"

"That's right. And do you know what our sainted men-folk did? Set fire to the roof and took an axe to everything inside. 'Did the Lady have a sewing machine?' says I. 'Damn right,' says my man, 'broke it into tiny bits…' It was all I could do not to strangle him there and then."

"So no one goes to the Yellow House?"

"Not any more."

"But once?"

"Yes, once."

Ludmilla stared at the man's potato-like skull. He wasn't one of them; why should she tell him anything? But then Dusya had prophesised that such a man would come…

"Dusya seemed to know a lot about it."

"Well, Dusya would. Until my pig of a husband stopped her, she would go to the House on errands, bartering food from the village for kerosene and tools."

"So why did your husband…"

"He accused her of sleeping with Lepinov, kissing the Devil's arse, all kinds of depravities. But really it was jealousy, pure and simple. I knew what he did to her in Lorinov's barn at night: couldn't stand the idea of somebody else doing just the same. So he started sending Slow Pavel in her place, although we all knew she still went there, under the cover of night."

Tutyshkin looked at where the ash had formed a little pyre on his bed and rubbed his head.

"Last night she mentioned somebody by the name of Orlov…"

"Orlov? Never heard of him."

"No? He was supposedly taken away from the Yellow House after some kind of incident. To be honest though, my dear, I'm not sure whether he wasn't in fact, secretly transported back and…"

"Never heard of him. Who knows what goes on in that place?"

Dusya's mother, Nadezhda, had worked at the Yellow House back when it was still a rest home for gentlefolk; cleaning, washing, serving food. But one day she returned to the village with a full belly and Dusya came along a few months later. The other villagers scorned her and she was flogged, but it did no good: a year later another child was born, a boy. Nobody knew who either father was. Certainly, no man in Chulm would own up to anything; maybe she'd gone back to the Yellow House, maybe not. Either way Dusya's mother moved here, where she collected herbs and made potions. If anyone got sick or got a rash, they'd go to Nadezhda. Womens' problems or childbirth too: she could also tell fortunes and conjure up the spirits of the dead.

"She called up the shade of my own mother," said Ludmilla, indifferently. "She told us where she'd left the jar of cooking oil and how to fill honeycombs with plumb jam."

As the years went by, Nadezhda was accepted back into the bosom of Chulm; what would the dead do without her? But once again God had other plans. Whilst Dusya and Mikhail – her brother – were playing in the woods, Mikhail was killed and Dusya's mother went mad and was taken up to the Yellow House. Dusya herself never said a word about what happened to her brother – some whispered that the girl was a witch and she'd killed him herself and eaten his heart. But in time Dusya took over her mother's role, mixing potions and fashioning charms and protective stones. Once an itinerant priest came and told her she was doing the work of Satan but the villagers chased him out and stole the wheels from his cart.

"Dusya once told me that her mother's shade would come to her in her hut, whispering about her death. She told Dusya that Lepinov had had her locked away and then murdered her. And when the old Superintendent found out, Lepinov had him locked up too."

Tutyshkin shook his head. "So why would Dusya go to the Yellow House?"

"She goes wherever she pleases. She has an amulet of protection – the woods cannot harm her."

"She didn't come back last night."

"Dusya does not sleep. No one knows where she goes: the other world, perhaps…"

Ludmilla carefully re-arranged a fold in the blanket, and looked Tutyshkin in the eyes.

"And what about you, my dear? Can you sleep? I mean, without a husband there beside you…"

"I'd sooner sleep with a pig," she said, running her hands over Tutyshkin's chest. "What are these? Tattoos?"

"Youthful folly…"

"I heard of a man who came back from the flytrap with marks like this…"

"Yes, yes," said Tutyshkin, "they're all the rage."

Ludmilla held onto both ears and stared at the inspector's odd shaped head.

"You're a strange policeman, Inspector," she said.

"I'm not a policeman," said the inspector softly, "I'm the Devil."

nine

1

It took the small matter of Zvonkov's death to transform the orderly from lascivious pest to sainted gentleman, the very noblest of souls. Alyona prayed for him nightly. She longed for his voice, his touch, *The Night Orgies of Rasputin*.

"Such a kind, good man," she sobbed. "A true Russian prince…"

Nikolai and Shiskin were more circumspect in their praise.

"What fell off the cart is gone," said the yardman with a scowl. "Besides, that Zvonkov, he was no catch. Feh, you could have chopped sticks on his head."

"Sit, sit," said the cook, "there's no need for sorrow. Once there was Zvonkov, now there isn't. What can anyone do? Here – try this cucumber, it's marinated with juniper…"

"You dogs, you have no souls!" yelled Alyona, her eyes bright red. "Why couldn't you have died instead?"

"God watches over those who are careful, and the crows watch over those who aren't," said Nikolai, warming his feet by the fire. "The clod was a fool to go. Now come and sit by the warm with me…"

"I'd rather sit in the fires of Hell."

The yardman was certainly no prize. His beard was matted with mud and leaves and his yellow alcoholic eyes oozed an odd kind of pus. It was hard to know what had happened to him. Coarse black hair covered his hands, an eruption of boils on his neck like an amulet.

"Why waste your tears over Zvonkov?" sneered Old Nikolai. "If you go in the forest, expect wolves. And the same goes for that Red doctor! Let them chop off their own heads, for all I care. Somebody else can open the door at midnight – I'm tired of being treated like a serf."

Shiskin offered Alyona a pot. "My girl, tears don't flavour the milk. Here, try some soup – it's flavoured with lung…, there, there, don't sip at it like a German…"

Alyona knocked the pot from his hands and fled. Why was she surrounded by fools and dogs? What they said was true: grey hair into beard, devil into rib. If only she could find a place to go and cry. Why did the Good Lord call back his lambs and leave the goats in the fields? Ivan, Petr, Sergei: all those closest to her had been taken. Still sobbing, she threw open a door and squeezed herself into Churkin's mouse hole of a room. Yes, there was his little bed, his tiny lamp, the Red Corner with its ancient, battered icon. What a good soul Ivan was, what a saint! Her face pressed up against the icon, Alyona wiped away her tears: the Virgin's face was fading back into the wood just like the monastery was falling away into the hillside. She crossed herself, pulled her shawl over her head and dropped to her knees. Immediately a sharp pain shot through her leg. A floorboard had been pulled out just in front of the icon, one of its nails upended. Angrily rubbing her knee, Alyona looked at the nail a little more closely. Someone had pulled out one of the floorboards, and then replaced it in a hurry. But why? She levered back the board and rooted around in the dark, unwelcoming space. In the hole lay a long candlestick, strewn with webs. Alyona pulled it out and examined it. The stick was brass, heavy, and very old – the property of the monastery no doubt. Churkin had loved his 'Holy Castle' as he called it, spending hours there, praying, dancing, and singing songs to the lamb. But why bring the stick back here? What would he want with it? It was tarnished and cumbersome, one end badly damaged and covered in rust. No, not rust: blood.

Alyona dropped the weapon on the bed and staggered to the door. This was where they'd found poor Churkin - had the murderer left something else here too? The thing was badly hidden, as if it had been stowed away in a hurry. But if hidden, then by whom? Alyona didn't suspect poor Ivan for a moment. He was the sweetest, kindest, most considerate of souls; there wasn't the smallest trace of malice within him. So what did the candlestick mean? Had whoever hung poor Ivan bashed in the head of the Superintendent too?

Overcoming her distaste, she picked up the stave and carried it at arm's length back down the stairs toward the main house. There she met Marya carrying a large basket of soiled dressing.

"Marya!" cried Alyona, breathlessly. "Come look at this!"

The nurse inspected the ingot without understanding. "What…"

"I found it in poor Ivan's room, hidden under the Red Corner. Look, look here, where the brass is damaged. Blood, Marya, blood!"

Marya handed the candlestick back and covered her mouth in fright. "But…"

"Whoever killed poor Ivan must also have caved in Lepinov's roof. Don't you see? And after hanging up dear Churkin they must have hidden it."

"Hidden it? But why would…"

Alyona waved the stick under Marya's nose. "How should I know? Quick, take it to the doctors. They'll want to know…"

"Take it?"

"Yes, yes, take it - the doctors need to see it, right away."

Marya took the baton from Alyona's hot little hand and carried it away to the house and up another series of steps.

"Oh dear," she said, "the Lord save us, yes, such a thing…"

Holding it aloft like a burning torch, Marya raced up the stairwell and banged on the door to Aleshin's chambers.

"Doctor, Doctor!" she cried.

Aleshin opened his door looking rather dishevelled, golden spectacles all askew.

"The murder, doctor! We've found the thing that did it!"

"What the devil are..."

The doctor saw the candlestick in her hand and trembled.

"Alyona found it, sir. The very thing."

Aleshin blinked. The blood drained away from his face and his skin was pale as milk.

"What's that? This thing, what..."

"Take it sir, here..."

"But..."

"Take it."

The doctor gripped the candlestick uncertainly.

"The very thing..." he whispered.

2

Although the road from Davydovka was again more or less passable, few travellers chose to break their journey at Dymov's: where would such a traveller be going anyway? For the most part, only bagmen and bread hunters plodded their way between the petrified waves of mud, exchanging goods from the city for grain or potatoes or beets. Such trade was illegal, but speculators were very unlucky to be shot; everyone knew that the further you got from the city, the more frayed the Red banner became. Instead of soldiers, the lanes were clogged with vagrants and beggars, cold and filthy refugees from Voronezh seeking food and sanctuary. These were in short supply; most of the barns or hayricks had either been set fire to or chopped into pieces, the livestock also. Amongst the fields one could occasionally make out makeshift camps, the huts blown from place to place like autumn leaves. It was cold and filthy, the ditches full of rubbish, waste and disease. Yet even so, few chose to spend the night at Old Dymov's.

The Inn was situated on the old post road, at a point where once upon a time horses had been rested and modest refreshment served. Now the stables were empty, the horses eaten. A bed for the night was cheap, but the menu somewhat limited: millet cakes, millet bread, thick millet broth. An egg or a lump of cheese was an extravagance. The vodka was radiator fluid, but not so bad. Meat was limited to whatever had wandered into a trap.

"Beggars can't be choosers," said Dymov. "A wolf feeds on his feet."

Dymov ran the Inn with his wife and their three sons; they had taken literally the old saying that one son is not a son, two sons are half a son, only three sons a whole lad. The three boys seemed more like old men than teenagers, stooped and grey, with thin, ravaged faces. Only Dymov and his wife retained any sense of vitality, constantly bustling around, moving tables and changing beds, still busy despite the lack of guests. In addition to the owners, the Inn was home to two black dogs, Danya and Vanya, who spent their days barking at the old stables and baring their teeth; they were supposed to deter thieves, but in truth kept most customers away as well. A long fence, topped with nails, surrounded the house, the wood bent and warped. One out-house had collapsed, the roof of another sagged like a kulak's bed. This was not the Astoria. The gate had been hit by a dairy man's cart and hung askew across the entrance like a hastily crossed out word.

Karnivsky and his Chekists, along with Shemiakin the bagman and their drivers, had been forced to stop there, defeated by the roads, the mud, and a cart of rotten sheep left abandoned on the road near Lvonsk. The cart had become lodged in a deep hole, preventing Karnivsky's carriage from passing. When the soldiers tried to move it, the whole load tipped over, sending a wave of liquefied mutton across their boots. After that, even Dymov's Inn didn't seem too bad.

"I know the old dog," said Shemiakin. "He'll do us a good deal."

"We don't need to do a deal," said Karnivsky. "We are the representatives of the People's justice. We will take whatever we need."

"Yes, but Old Dymov, he..."

"Free trade is the root of all corruption. Parasites, speculators and free marketeers will be exterminated." Karnivsky looked across at Shemiakin and nodded humourlessly. "No offence to your good self, of course..."

When Danya and Vanya came racing out under the horses' hooves, they were answered with whips, the hounds turning tail and retreating under the veranda. Hearing the howling, Dymov's wife, Margarita, bustled out to greet her guests, her smile dropping the instant she recognised the uniform of the Counter-Revolutionary Guard.

"Gentlemen! Comrades! Come in! Miska, take the horses – come on, you clod, be quick about it. I'm sorry sirs, my son's as slow as he is stupid – and he's the brightest of the three. Miska, the horses! Oh, you pup..."

The tavern was surprisingly large, clean and well heated, dry thyme scattered on the floor. From behind a counter old Dymov shuffled forward, his lame leg dragged behind him like a mop.

"Esteemed guests! Visitors! Representatives of the glorious Red Army!" Then Dymov spotted the bagman lingering at the rear like a shadow. "And Shemiakin, my old friend! I didn't know that you'd joined the Bolshevik cause too."

"What other cause is there?" muttered Shemiakin, obviously embarrassed.

"Well, come, sit. There's no truth in feet..."

In the shadows, Dymov's other sons stared at the soldiers open mouthed. They had heard all about the Bolsheviks from their mother and father; it was as if their parents had opened their doors to a bear.

"Here, here, pull these tables to the stove... let me fetch you something for your thirst..."

Dymov returned not with radiator fluid but rather samogan vodka, cut with hair tonic. Aside from Shemiakin there were twelve Chekists and barely enough alcohol to go around.

"And something to eat, my friends? Bread, eggs, a little fat?"

"You have all these things?" said Karnivsky.

"For you? Of course, of course! Let me just talk to my wife…"

It was a dilemma: if they produced too much, they could be accused of food hoarding and then shot. But if they had nothing to give the Reds, they could be shot too. The Dymovs decided to slice open the egg and let the Reds decide.

"Jacob! Tolya! Don't just squat there like toads – plates, plates!"

All they could hope was that they weren't going to spend the night: especially with Yegurov coming round on his nag. Had Shemiakin really gone over to the Reds? The bagman looked sheepish and had a great red welt on his bonce.

"Captain, O Captain," said Old Dymov theatrically. "I feel safer just having you and your men here."

"Safer?"

"Safe from the Whites, I mean. I've heard that Cossack outriders have been spotted further down the road."

Karnivsky stared at the innkeeper without blinking. "I see. And who provided you with this information?"

"Information? Well, I wouldn't call it information … I mean, I just hear that … ah, Shemiakin, what do you say?"

"I hear nothing," said Shemiakin. "Sparrows have made a home in my ears."

Dymov was saved by his wife's millet broth, flavoured with bacon rind and a generous lump of liver.

"So you and your fine lads," said Dymov, handing out the spoons. "What are you doing out here on the post road?"

"Looking for Counter Revolutionary activity," said Karnivsky dismissively.

"I see, well…"

"Conspirators of the old world."

"Ah, but of course. And for you sir?" Dymov offered the jug to a strange rat-faced little man, but the fellow stuck out his tongue and hissed like a snake.

"Um…"

"He's fine," said Karnivsky.

"Nu, nu, but of course…"

Over on one of the side tables, one of the soldiers tasted the broth and began to bawl.

"Just like home!" he yelled. "It tastes just the same – and you, Auntie" – here he grabbed Margarita by the elbow – "you look just like my own sainted mother. Beautiful, beautiful!"

Margarita blushed and slapped his hand as it slipped down to her knee.

"Foo, it's only millet broth," she said. "The least I can do for brave soldiers like you…"

"It tastes like Angel's milk," the soldier moaned as Margarita removed his paw. "And you, the very mirror of my beautiful *Mamoshka*!"

"Oh, hush…"

"The most beautiful woman in the world…"

He made another grab for Margarita, but she slipped out of his grasp just in time.

"So I hear you two are old friends," said Karnivsky to Shemiakin and Dymov, the two men throwing up their arms as if each were the mirror image of the other.

"No, no – more acquaintances…"

"Business partners?"

"My inn is open to all," said Dymov, nervously following Karnivsky's spoon. "Prince or peasant."

"Prince?"

"Well, in a manner of speaking."

It had been a long time since the Inn had been so busy. The Chekists drummed their spoons on the tables and kicked over the stools. Jacob, the squattest of the three sons, passed a bowl to a soldier with a large, red beard.

"Feh – are there no serving girls here?" the Chekist snorted contemptuously.

Jacob stared back at him dully.

"And such an ugly lad too."

"Only our three lads," said Margarita, pouring drinks. "Girls steal and gossip and chase anything in britches…"

"A shame, right enough," muttered Red Beard. "Couldn't you at least put a dress on one of your lads … paint his ugly mug…"

Margarita laughed a little uncertainly. The soldier stroked his beard and removed his boots. Jacob continued to stare.

"Eh lad, what do you say? You'd make a better looking lassie than you do a goose!"

"Oh you boys," said Margarita, "always thinking of pretty things! Now Jacob – you go outside and help your brother with the horses…"

And with that she whisked Jacob away.

"See if there's any sign of Yegurov," she whispered. "If you see the old ram then tell him to go round the back."

"Yegurov?"

"Shhh. Go and check on your brother. Tell Yegurov to hide everything under his hat…"

Jacob wiped his nose on his sleeve and drifted outside. It was getting dark now, crows gathering in the trees. His brother was nowhere to be seen and the dogs were still whimpering beneath the porch. A Red Guard spotted him and called him over.

"Hey lad, what's in that shed?" he said, pointing to the last out-house still standing.

"Nothing" said Jacob shiftily.

"Nothing? Open it up then."

"'Aint got no key."

"Go and fetch it then."

"Don't know where it is."

The guard lifted up the butt of his rifle. "I said, go get it, you pup..." In truth, the Chekist was no older than the serving lad, but only one of them had a rifle. Jacob pulled at his hair and walked away slowly. Where had his brother gone anyway? An evening gloom descended, thick as broth. His brother seemed to have vanished into thin air.

Back inside, Karnivsky questioned the innkeeper about passing trade.

"Oh the roads have been awful, ah, Comrade Captain. Mud high as Peter. No, no carriages have been through. Just beggars and little kids asking for alms..."

"I see. And before the rain: any carriage bearing prisoners?"

"Ah, yes, yes ... a *brishka* with police and some prisoner, his head shaved from the prison."

Karnivsky placed his spoon in his bowl as if filing away an important piece of paperwork.

"And did they stay the night?"

"No sir. A pot of barley coffee and then off. Didn't want to get stuck in the mire."

"And who was at the head of this party?"

"A very sociable fellow called Dovlatov was in charge – a policeman, though I don't hold that against him. Taking the prisoner to Bezumiye – the nut house. Not that the prisoner seemed too cracked – I mean he ate with a spoon and fork and sat at the table right nicely."

"And there was only one prisoner you saw..."

"Only one came inside the Inn, sir. Whether someone else was kept in the *brishka*, I can't say. When my boy Jacob tried to take a look, the police shooed him away. They asked for a bowl of soup to be taken outside, but that might have been for the guard – who can say?"

"And do any of the staff of the Yellow House frequent your establishment? The doctors? The Chief Superintendent?"

"No sir. It's a long way to Bezumiye. At the start of the war, you'd see carts of wounded soldiers going along the road, but since the Revolution, the shutters have come down. To be honest I'd heard that peasants had burned the place to the ground, but this Dovlatov, he said no."

Karnivsky nodded calmly; the captain seemed more like a librarian than a Chekhist, his face as impassive as an unwritten form.

"And this was when?"

"Oh – I'd say, maybe three weeks ago, sir."

"And have you seen anyone travelling in the opposite direction – perhaps with a cart load of goods?"

Dymov glanced at Shemiakin, but the bagman's face was as beatific as Saint Ignatius.

"No sir, can't say that I have."

"I see."

One of the Reds came in from outside, his heavy coat smelling of pine needles and the night. The fellow whispered something in Karnivsky's ear and the Comrade Inspector rose with a nod.

"Please remain here," he said, marching outside.

Red faced, Margarita rushed over with a tray of pancakes and jam. "Is everything alright, my darlings?"

"You may continue to attend the People's army," said Karnivsky, dismissing her with a wave.

Outside, the Reds had nabbed both Yegurov and his horse. The latter had been apprehended hauling a cart filled with grain, the former gesticulating wildly and blinking back the tears. Yegurov was pulled from the saddle and punched in the face. Karnivsky glanced at the sacks and then at the sagging barn.

"Where are you going with this grain?"

Terrified, Yegurov rubbed at his mouth. "Sir…"

"All food stuffs are the property of the people. What are you doing transporting prescribed goods?"

Yegurov shook and made a vague gesture with his hands.

"Oh for heaven's sake," said Karnivsky, bored with the whole thing. He made Yegurov kneel down, took out his revolver, and shot him between the eyes. "Open up that barn," he said to his adjunct. "And go and fetch the inn keeper."

Margarita heard the flat pop of the gun and jumped. Empty glasses littered the table, upended on greasy plates. One of the soldiers had produced a guitar and the mood was becoming steadily jollier. Margarita rubbed the tables with a dirty rag, trying to avoid any stray hands. Where were Jacob and Tolya? If Yegurov came now then all their geese were cooked.

"How your cheeks shine, Auntie," said a soldier. "Just like my own dear Mama with a drop of the warm inside her…"

"I'm sure she's very proud," said Margarita, swatting away his mitt.

"Where's that lad of yours?" roared the Chekist with the red beard. "I want to see him in a bonnet!"

Without Karnivsky watching over, the men started to grow restless and wild. A table crashed to the floor, sending glasses tumbling.

"Dearest husband," said Margarita in a strangled voice. "Could you help me with something in the pantry?"

"Of course my love," said Old Dymov, too deaf to have heard the shot.

As the pair shuffled toward the kitchen, two Chekists grabbed them and roughly marched them outside.

"Sirs, what…"

Jacob stood by the open barn, dangling a great ring of keys. He looked older than ever, like some ancient Uncle struggling to keep himself up.

"Comrade Captain," said the innkeeper. "This food is being stored here, until the cart comes to take it to Davydovka. The peasants always keep their produce here. We've just been waiting for the roads to dry a little, for the cart to be able to get through…"

The Red Guards took Dymov and his wife into the barn and shot them. Their bodies were dumped next to those of Yegurov and Miska, their eldest. Jacob watched without moving. He was still holding the heavy ring of keys and seemed to be slowly sinking into the ground. A Chekist handed him a shovel and kicked him. The lad looked at the shovel and blinked, his body closed up like an arthritic hand. When the Chekist yelled again, the lad still didn't move: everything felt too heavy and too hard. Finally, the soldier stabbed the boy's boot with the spade and pushed him to the ground When Jacob got to his feet, whimpering and crying, the soldier offered him the shovel once more.

"Do you want the wolves to take your Mama and Papa?" he said. "Dig."

It was cold and dark outside the inn, and the coat-less Karnivsky hurried back to the warmth. Pots and tables were turned over like moneylenders' in the temple. The soldiers had emptied all the bottles and the Chekist with the guitar was singing a revolutionary song. Karnivsky ignored the chaos and sat down by the bagman. Shemiakin looked up with the sad eyes of a donkey.

"I trust tonight has been instructive to you," said the commissar, pouring a cup of coffee from the pot.

"In this war, every day is a lesson."

"Revolutionary justice is swift and merciless. We have no need for courts or tribunals. We act in the interests of the proletariat."

"Dymov was no count – is this any palace?"

"All property has been wrested from the hands of the working people. Private trade, bourgeois possessions: all this will pass away. Besides, Dymov was a profiteer, a grain hoarder. Whilst honest working people starve in the cities, scum like Dymov grow fat on their secret reserves. They are like rats, vermin, devouring the precious resources of the revolution."

Shemiakin held up his hands but Karnivsky went on. "You protest, but I have seen it, Shemiakin. Mothers mixing bark with their flour, while their children starve in the streets. Labourers in the cities faint from hunger whilst these dogs fill their bowls. Do you think these stupid peasants understand the processes of historical change? Left to their own devices they'd turn the whole harvest into booze."

Shemiakin looked round at the Chekists looting the inn and nodded. "It's a mercy you're here to protect us."

"I come not to protect, but to destroy your kind, root and branch." Karnivsky sipped his vodka and watched the bagman carefully. "Dymov was a sponge, a capitalist and a speculator. All those who profit from the misery of others will pay – including you Shemiakin."

The bagman's smile was like honey. "I am here to help with your enquires, my dear fellow."

"So tell me – were there two prisoners or one?"

"Two? Why do you say that? Two by two, as in the days of Noah?"

"Are you sure your deal was just for Sikorsky?"

"I've told you before – the deal was between Lepinov and Chief Officer Kuptsov. I was merely the mule…"

"Carrying a murderer?"

"Murderer, thief, lunatic: when it rains, whose hat is dry?"

By this stage, the Cheka had liberated all the food and drink they could find, and were starting to look a little weary – the day had been long and the drink highly potent. The third son, Tolya, was marched in at gunpoint and told to heat the rooms. He had been hiding in the attic but heard the shots clear enough. Tolya's eyes were red and his hands shook like a grandfather. Of Jacob and his spade, there was no sign.

In the morning the People's Representatives of Red Terror departed the inn and continued along the old post road. Two guards were given the task of guarding the grain, whilst the rest of the department went on, their carriages rising and falling with every rut. Tolya's body – dressed in his dead mother's clothes – was left by the back door: none of the soldiers could be bothered to move him and Karnivsky seemed to have forgotten. Shemiakin glanced back at the broken gate and spat. It was cold and overcast, the mud half frozen. The black dogs, Danya and Vanya, watched the soldiers from beneath the veranda. Only when they were absolutely certain that the soldiers had gone did they dare to come trotting out, sniffing uncertainly at the back step. One howled, the other barked. There was no answer, no movement. Vanya span round and round by the door, pissed on the step, and bit Danya smartly on the ear.

ten

1

Instead of Dusya, Tutyshkin was visited twice daily by Masha, her scarf embroidered with little red birds, her hands as brown as ditch water. Little Mother Masha brought food, drink, and emptied his pot. She also changed the dressing on his leg and washed the wound with vinegar. Like a nightingale, Masha appeared twice a day, once at dawn and then again dusk. One time when the wind chimes rang, Ludmilla appeared instead.

"Still on your back?" the head-woman asked, poking him with a stick.

"Just clinging to this world," said Tutyshkin, with a wink.

In truth, the inspector was growing stronger day by day. When no women were around he liked to climb out of his bed and explore Dusya's hut, which was full of strange and curious things: dried tubers, a petrified star fish, coloured dust, the shrivelled remains of a salamander. And the figures, of course, hidden behind plant pots or crouched awkwardly behind jars, their torsos adorned by horned heads of all possible kinds. On the base of each, one could be found some kind of letter or rune: occult gobbledygook, no doubt. Many of the male figures were in a state of arousal, the females' legs wide open. They certainly didn't look like the handiwork of a young girl, but then Tutyshkin knew very little about the lives of peasants, their existence as alien to him as that of creatures on the moon.

On the fourth day, Tutyshkin felt well enough to take a tour around the village – his legs no longer buckled, and a weak sun had decided to smile. The Inspector appeared among the huts and shacks of Chulm like an ill omen. Women made the sign of the evil eye and licked the tips of their fingers.

"Good morning ladies," said Tutyshkin, playfully doffing his hat. "The sky is open and the sun is singing a little song."

He was dressed in the rags of the village blacksmith – the only garb which would fit him here – complete with soot coloured smock and apron. Passing a dark door, in blackened clothes, it seemed as if his bald head were floating there of its own accord. Bald? No, his hair was growing back as a dark pelt, odd tufts sticking up like thistles. The back of his head was striped and a black beard sprouted on his chin like rye.

Tutyshkin halted before a plain plank of a woman and bowed like a poet. "Hello my dear, how beautiful you look in that head scarf – like a wonderful head of cabbage."

The women of Chulm scowled and hurried away. Just who was this 'inspector' and what had he come to inspect? Yes, the man was a fiend, right enough – or was he one of the mythical *burzhooi* they'd heard so much about?

Tutyshkin waved goodbye with a filthy rag. "Don't run, my dove, don't flee … the earth turns like a mill…"

The village had but a single, unpaved street, with a rough wooden walkway laid out on just one side. There was mud everywhere, but the women kept the walkway and the front of the huts scrupulously clean, sweeping away rubbish into the weeds in the middle of the road. Pots of geraniums and pansies in old earthen-wear jugs sat prettily out on sagging sills. There were few chickens, no cows. A beady-eyed goat strolled along like the mayor.

Tutyshkin clapped his hands like an infant: what a marvellous place this was! All that was missing was a flock of cranes and the sound of church bells. After all, what was Russia without her bells? But, alas, the Reds weren't so keen on such things these days...

Behind the huts were little strips of gardens, turning to fields of rye and clover as the land became common ground. Empty hovels and pigsties lay marooned amongst the mud. A well, a pond, the headman's house. Outside the *mir*, Ludmilla sat mending a pair of leather boots, a trumpet of rolled up tobacco clamped between her lips.

"What a wonderful place, my darling," said Tutyshkin gesturing with his hat. "Why, it doesn't seem as if you need men at all..."

"It's easier for the mare when the man is off the cart," the head-woman said, watching as the inspector negotiated his way around a puddle. "You'd better come inside. If someone sees you they'll fetch stones."

"It's all so marvellously restful," said Tutyshkin, bowing his head in Ludmilla's doorway. "Only in the countryside can one find true peace."

The head-woman snorted. "There's some mowing needs doing if you're feeling better."

Ludmilla's house consisted of two parts. One contained the parlour and her bedroom, whilst the other was made up of the kitchen and laundry room, which also housed a grey cat, an old dog, and a hen turkey under a bench. There were no children: Ludmilla's daughter had grown up, married, and departed many years before. Her daughter's husband was a footman and they lived with their four sons in Voronezh. Who could say how the war had treated them? No worse than if they'd chosen to remain here, that was for sure.

The unpainted furniture had been roughly fashioned by

Ludmilla's absent husband, and his hunting gun, whips and game bags still hung rather crookedly on the wall. His rifle was one of a very few the villagers had managed to hide before the Reds had come to strip the village bare; now Ludmilla used it to shoot game. The red corner contained a dilapidated board more like an upended tabletop than an icon. The ceiling was the colour of soot and bits of straw poked out of the window frame. Yet for all that, the place was dry, clean and well scrubbed. Ludmilla sat Tutyshkin in the parlour and brought him tea, bread, and a slab of cold millet.

"How lucky your husband was to find a jewel like you my dear."

"Aye, and he'd thank me with his belt."

"Oh, I'm sure you two had a merry old time."

"Merry? Like two corpses dangling on one rope." Ludmilla blew her nose on a rag. "Well, the Reds own him now – maybe they'll teach him better manners."

"Aye, they're great ones for lessons, right enough." Tutyshkin squeezed himself into an over-stuffed, under-sized chair. No, maybe this place wasn't so bad. With the sun shining in, Ludmilla's parlour felt bright and cozy. The cat came over and nestled against Tutyshkin's knee, the dog begging for crumbs, Ludmilla chasing the turkey hen with a broom. What more could one ask for? A smell of bonfires and pine blew in on the wind.

"Can I ask you a question, my dove?"

"You're the policeman…"

"You said that Dusya knew where to find me. That she foretold I would come."

Ludmilla wiped the crumbs and ash from her apron. "She said a stranger would come – a monster, his skull like the angel of death…" Ludmilla bit into the cake with her strong yellow teeth. "I don't know Inspector, does that sound like you?"

Tutyshkin gave a coquettish wave. "Oh you'll turn my head…"

"And this stranger's arrival, it would be a sign … a sign of great change … not just for Chulm but all of Russia."

"Foo, I fear that horse bolted a long time ago," said Tutyshkin, languidly pulling the cat's tail. "A Revolution cannot be undone. And there's no putting the Tsar back on his chair, no matter what the Whites might think."

"Well, of course you work for the Reds…"

"Feh – Lenin and I play fool every night. What, you don't believe in the Revolution? Oh, the Bolsheviks came and robbed your village, I forgot. If the Black Hundreds rode into town you'd kiss the hem of their cloaks."

"If the Whites come then Ryabovsky will be back in his house and we'll be back ploughing his land." Ludmilla's teeth snapped like a trap. "You ask me, we're better off without any men, Red or White, commissar or noble. Ours was the land, ours is the land: no police, no army, no bailiff. You ask me, we don't even need elders – just a cow to milk and a strip of land to tend."

"Count Tolstoy could not ask for more."

Ludmilla stared at the inspector with an unreadable expression on her face. Was Dusya right about this one? Nothing about him seemed to add up: his prison tattoos, his flirtatious gestures, the way he stroked the cat. When she handed him a rough earthen-wear mug, he held it like some Polish princess.

"The Whites, the Reds, the Greens," she said contemptuously. "The only thing that matters is the black earth. Everything is either ours or theirs. What else is there? Any thief can put on a uniform. Wouldn't you say so, Inspector?"

"My dove?"

Shaking her head, the woman collected up the tea things and took them over to the sink. Behind her back, Tutyshkin transferred his knife to the palm of his hand, quietly following her.

"Oh come my darling, surely you don't doubt..."

"If you're a policeman then I'm the Tsar. That disguise fits you as well as that blacksmith's smock."

Tutyshkin paused and toyed with the knife.

"No policeman bats his eye-lids like you," said Ludmilla from the sink. "Or flounces into a room like a courtier."

"Oh, my sweet."

The knife dug into his palm as he moved it into position.

"And no policeman has hands like you, neither."

"Hands?"

He was right behind her now, one hand behind his back.

Abruptly she turned, looking him straight in the eye. "Eh, Doctor Aleshin?"

Startled, Tutyshkin took two steps back. "Ah, well..."

The head-woman bared her strong, yellow teeth. "Oh, Dusya told me all about Doctor Aleshin at the Yellow House – Aleshin the Red Doctor. So what were you doing wandering about the woods, Comrade Doctor? Not picking flowers, I bet. So why Inspector, Aleshin? One wage not enough?"

"Doctor Aleshin, ha ha, yes indeed."

Tutyshkin paused and a newfound look of sincerity appeared in his eyes. "But Chief Superintendent Lepinov really is dead, my angel. Murdered."

"Oh – and *Inspector* Aleshin plans to catch his killer?"

Tutyshkin nodded, slipping Ludmilla's knife into his pocket. "My darling, my sweet ... an unsolved murder, escaped prisoners ... none of us are safe."

"There's a war going on, Comrade Doctor – or haven't you gentlefolk at the Yellow House heard?"

"There's been some talk..."

"You're out looking for a murderer when Russians are hanging from trees like pine cones? Now tell me who is the crazy one,

Comrade Doctor Aleshin?"

"Ho, isn't that the real question," said Tutyshkin, tying up his smock and putting on his hat. "Many thanks for the tea, my sweet … delightful, simply delightful. Perhaps you could ask Masha to drop off a little jam. Oh, and some black bread to spread it on…" Tutyshkin stooped and kissed Ludmilla's hand as if she were the Empress.

"All this must remain our little secret," said Tutyshkin softly. "To the good ladies of Chulm I am Inspector Aleshin of the detective. Doctor Aleshin must remain in the Yellow House."

Ludmilla put one hand on his chest as if seeking to trace the tattoos. But what would a doctor be doing with tattoos? Perhaps the Bolsheviks were different. Or perhaps they really were the marks of the devil after all.

"Good afternoon, my love. I can't tell you when I last had such a wonderful time."

And with that Tutyshkin bowed and took his leave, whistling the Red anthem, 'You Fell Victim to a Fateful Struggle' as he struggled with the gate.

Ludmilla retrieved the butter knife from where it had fallen. Why had Dusya visited this fiend upon them? My dove, my pet, my sweet: perhaps it would have been better to poison him with mushrooms after all.

Instead of walking back along the muddy road, Tutyshkin wandered through Ludmilla's vegetable patch and then along the track to the clover field. Nu, why had he called himself Aleshin when Dusya had found him in the woods? Well, you can't put the milk back in the cow. To the ladies, Inspector, to Ludmilla, Doctor: Life was a jolly game when all was said and done.

Tutyshkin picked his way through the mud and the weeds like a minor nobleman taking a tour of his estate. A whole village of women – what a fascinating thing! True, the steps were swept and the fences mended, but how could these hens survive the winter? It wasn't so much the lack of men, as the lack of food: if the Reds had taken everything, where would a second harvest be found? Things were looking bad. It wasn't just the chickens who were looking skinny; many of the children had swollen middles and blotchy skin. Nor was it a simple matter to forage. The fields weren't safe, never mind the woods. Ludmilla had fierce eyes but even she could only shoot so many cocks. Still, what did he know? Everything he knew of the countryside came from Turgenyev and *A Sportsman's Sketches…*

Could he weather the rest of the storm hidden away in the cozy nook of Ludmilla's parlour? No, the walls were made of straw – only the Yellow House offered any real chance of protection. Better locked inside with murderers and lunatics than locked outside with worse. Besides, who *had* murdered Lepinov? It was like reading a tremendously exciting novel.

Tutyshkin paused at the line of trees and watched where a small cloud of brown birds rose up like smoke. It was cold but dry, the invalid sun venturing out for the first time in weeks.. Aye, Chulm was delightful, but no place to wait for Deniken and the Whites. What had Dusya said to him? "Who are you? Who are you really?" That wasn't the tongue of a young girl– it was the voice of the grave itself.

Tutyshkin drew the blacksmith's smock around his shoulders and shivered. The woods lay before him, leaves falling like notes in a romantic ballad. Was this where Dusya had lost her brother? So, this maniac Orlov had not been sent away after all, and Lepinov was in someway involved. Had he then interred first Dusya's mother and then the current Superintendent, all to cover his tracks? A delicious quiver ran through Tutyshkin's body, and he felt a sudden desire to find paper and pen. O, the trees, the webs, the sickly sun: who could fail to be inspired by such things? But then he suddenly remembered that Masha was coming to deliver his broth and he hurried back toward the village, rubbing his hands together in delight.

2

While one Dr Aleshin strode purposefully in the direction of Chulm, a second stared at the candlestick on his shelf and scowled. How the devil had Alyona come across it? The girl had a nose as long as a fox. What was she doing there in the first place, poking around in Churkin's things? Bloody servants! He should have buried it or thrown it in the pond, not hidden it under a floorboard. No wonder it had come back to mock him.

The doctor recognised the thing as soon as he pulled it out of Churkin's jacket, long and heavy and speckled with blood. Whilst Starchenko was off looking for Zvonkov, Aleshin prised up one of the floorboards and shoved the stick inside. Churkin's bag and satchel, he threw in the room next door – he struggled to find a reason why. They contained Churkin's religious paraphernalia, a cross, a holy bone, pages torn from some old Bible. Could Churkin read? Aleshin doubted it. No doubt the idiot had collected such brick-a-bac from the monastery, or the tunnels near St Leonilla's; he was always scrabbling about down there, up to his nose in dust. The caves were full of junk, squirreled away by the monks. Icons, amulets, consecrated cups: nu, such superstition would be swept away by the clean broom of the Revolution! Yes, under the revolutionary rule of the proletariat, recidivist religiosity would not be permitted. The irrational would be outlawed. And yet, and yet – in the cold light of day, the doctor's own actions seemed quite without reason. Why had he hidden the candlestick? What had he been thinking? Aleshin squinted balefully at the stick. How had it tricked him into such lunacy?

Ho, it was all the fault of Churkin himself - nothing about the oaf was right. Churkin talked like an old peasant but looked like a youth: red cheeks, healthy skin, a shock of blond hair. Just how old was he? He seemed to have been at the Yellow House since Catherine's time, but he could have passed for twenty. He never spoke of his village or parents. His past was a mystery - nobody seemed to know whether he'd started out as a servant or a patient or simply wandered in like a cat. Wherever he'd been, he had the run of the place: only Starchenko knew more about its nooks and crannies than he. Churkin collected firewood, mopped floors, wiped arses. The nurses and Alyona adored him. He was humble, cheerful, gentle. True, you couldn't stop his damnable singing, but then the same could be said for the birds. "He's an angel" said Marya, "the very soul of goodness." Even Yevgrafovna treated him like a pet.

The doctor had Nikolai bury him in a shallow grave at the back of the dispensary.

Asphyxiation: but what was the cause? Suicide seemed impossible – nothing in Churkin's character supported it. But equally, why would anyone want to murder him? Ah, it was all a fog! Despite all the uncertainties, Aleshin ordered that his body be disposed of before anybody else should take a look. It was better that way: safer. But just why did he feel so guilty? Why this feeling of shame, of disgrace? Oh, it was all lunacy from top to bottom...

The doctor sat on his bed and watched the weak sun illuminate the brass. The candlestick looked very old, almost ancient. Aleshin adjusted his glasses and examined the point where the stick had collided with Lepinov's head. It had been a moment of madness, a crazy mistake. He had panicked, that was all. Hiding the candlestick had only heaped suspicion on his head when he would have been better off shovelling it elsewhere. Such stupidity, such misjudgement! Fortunately, nobody suspected him of anything – if they had, why would they have brought the stick to his door? He would present it to Yevgrafovna and explain how Alyona had found it in Churkin's room. Nothing in the case in any way pointed to him. He hadn't strung up poor Ivan. Any culpability he felt was both irrational and bourgeois. His secrets were all his own.

Churkin had taken Aleshin by surprise, the doctor lying on his bed, a picture of his mother by his side. The devil knows what the idiot wanted – one of the guests was in need, no doubt. Aleshin tried to hide the portrait under his pillow, but was too late.

"There, there," said Churkin. "It's your Mama, is it? She's in Heaven now, sitting with the Good Lord. Shh, don't cry sir. Nothing can happen to her there, she's protected by the wing of the Dove."

Churkin's face was round and red, like he'd just been licked clean by a cow. Aleshin didn't like his tone. Didn't he realise he was addressing a senior comrade and qualified medical practitioner?

"S'alright doctor," said the orderly. 'Ain't no harm in lamentations. Didn't our own good Lord weep? Shh, come with me, sir, we can pray a while in my room. There's no burden the Lord can't shoulder. That's it sir, bring your mama. No, there's no shame in tears. Christ weeps with those who are grieving and rejoices with those that sing."

For some reason Churkin's funny little sing-song voice reminded Aleshin of the woman who'd rescued him from the carousel – the woman in his dream. Hadn't she spoken in just the same kindly way?

"Tears are the balm which washes away our woes. A man can cry as much as a child: more, maybe. This world weighs heavy on us all. But this 'ain't the only world, sir. No, there's a place in Heaven where there's no more crying or wailing or gnashing of teeth. And your dear Mama's there now, partaking of the feast and singing songs to the Holy One. There's no need to feel bad about her, sir. She's gazing on the countenance of the Lamb, sitting in His palaces of silver and gold."

Churkin smelt of animals and stables and sweat. His hair was stuck to his head as if he'd been anointed with oil.

"Let's go pray in my room, sir. Prayers are like honey poured in the Lord's ear. There's nothing he likes so much as the prayers of his believers. I have a special candle, sir – let me light it and we'll pray to Heaven for your Mama, let her know that her little boy is thinking of her and sending his supplications up unto the Lord."

The next thing Aleshin knew he was sitting in Churkin's tiny, coffin-like room, Churkin lighting a candle in a tall brass candlestick.

"That's it sir, you bring your woes to Heaven. There's nothing He hasn't heard up there, 'ain't nothing surprises Him. It's alright sir, don't worry – you don't need no priest or have to be sitting in any church. God hears everything – sees everything too."

Aleshin remembered sobbing and sobbing, the words refusing to come out.

"Sir? Sir? Go ahead and take it to the Lord, sir, His door is always open."

"Mama."

Churkin nodded.

"My Mama."

"Go on, go on…"

"My Mama hid me in the Yellow House," whispered the doctor. He shook and rocked. "To keep me safe. But then the Red Army came. And when they left they were going to take all the doctors with them. Do you understand Churkin? They were taking the doctors away. What could I say, Churkin? There was nothing else I could do."

"Sir?"

By this stage his father had left for Paris with his strumpet, while his mother sought refuge with that reactionary bastard, Count Solokov. She sent her son money and jewellery, Aleshin repaying her with revolutionary pamphlets and angry invective. But she was right: the Yellow House had protected him from the Revolution, from War. Until, that is, the call came for all doctors to be mobilised, posted forthwith to the front.

"Mama," he cried. "*Mamoschka.*"

Oh, if only there was a Father in Heaven who could hear him. Or better still a gentle mother on whose lap he could lay his head.

"S'alright sir, 'ain't no sin that can't be forgiven…"

Was that true? No. What he had done to his mother was unpardonable. But they were going to take him away…

"Your Mama, sir, yes…"

"I told them, Ivan. I told them everything."

Churkin stared at the doctor as if he didn't understand a word. "Sing with me, Doctor Aleshin," he yelled. "*I long for my eternal home, no longer in the world to roam…*"

Aleshin sobbed and shook, great rivers of snot flowing from his nose.

Ah, might I pass through Heaven's door…"

Churkin's singing was toneless and loud. Aleshin imagined the entire House listening on.

"I told them," the doctor repeated, "told them where they were…"

"*To Gaze on God for evermore…*"

Aleshin shook his head as Churkin looked at the doctor with his kind, good eyes. "God bless you doctor, sir. Don't you worry about your Mammy. No evil can befall her now. She's sitting up there in the lap of the Lord, right by the Lamb she is, shining like a light."

Aleshin grabbed the picture of his mother and looked wildly up and down the stairs.

"No," he whispered. "No." His code name was Zhelezin. He was a member of the party and an agent for the Bolshevik cause. Bolsheviks did not sob or say prayers. Bolsheviks transformed the old world into the new.

"No," he said again. "No, I think not."

"What's that?" asked Churkin.

"No, I tell you…"

"Sir, I…"

Aleshin looked at the idiot with hatred in his eyes. "I warn you Comrade Churkin – if you persist with such counter-revolutionary devotions, the Department of Religious Affairs will have to be informed. You know what happened to those black crows at the monastery. Such primitive practices have no place in the dictatorship of the proletariat."

Churkin looked back, a guileless smile on his face. Fearing he was about to launch back into song, the doctor took his photograph and fled. Oh, why had he even gone to that idiot's room? What Lenin said was true: some heads would only learn the truth when it was beaten into them…

And now the candlestick was here, in his very chamber, sitting alongside his revolutionary books and his medical dictionaries, as out of place as a cassock. No candle, of course: that had been snuffed out long ago. But why had he taken fright on seeing the cursed thing again? And why had he hidden it and then hastened to hide Churkin's body in the ground too? Dead men sang no songs – the fool would never speak to anyone of what had happened to his mother. O, what a fool he was! The old sour tune of guilt and shame followed him like a rag tied to a boot. Only the blood of the Revolution – not the blood of the Lamb – was enough to wash his sins away.

3

Varva sniffed the air, wrinkled her nose, and tried to work out just where the smell was coming from. The scent was overpowering, maddening, a combination of musk, spoiled meat and something else – fish, vegetable matter, glue? Whatever it was, it drove the little cat wild.

Padding her way across the kitchen, Varva sniffed in Shiskin's pots and pans seeking out the aroma's source. Alas the smells emanating from Shiskin's cooking failed to come close – not even the remains of lung stew.

O, what was it? A rotting mouse, the head of a perch, something squitted sideways by a fox? For the first time in many months, the odour tempted the little cat out of the warm kitchen and out into the cold, damp corridors of the house. The smell pulled at Varva like a string, and she walked flush to the wall, her flattened shadow no more than a paper toy. Every once in a while she would stop outside a door and sniff, thinking 'no, not there'. This room smelt of disinfectant and bicarbonate of soda. And not there either: dirt, mould, the sour stench of alcohol. But if not there, then where? Just what was this odour? Whither this arresting perfume? Varva licked her whiskers and followed her nose along the long, dusty corridor, her tail held aloft to reveal a round red eye.

Only one door was open, that of Polina, the nurse – Yevgrafovna was sitting with her, the two of them arguing furiously. 'Alexei', whispered one, 'Alexei' snapped the other. The smell of medicine was strong, but it wasn't the bouquet Varva sought. The two women argued and the doctor kept standing up and sitting down: then the two started to embrace. But was this of any concern to a small grey cat? No, no, it was not. Neither woman had ever given her titbits or thought to share the contents of their plate. Varva sniffed at their pale, meagre spirits and went on, ears pricked, her eyes as wide as tea cups.

The next room was Marya's; a wet patch on the floor indicated where the nurse had thrown up and washed the stonework clean. The scent still lingered, but still didn't have the right tincture – too human. Varva licked at the stain and guessed Marya's secret straight away. But did the little cat care? No, no, she did not. Marya had once given her the remains of a bowl of *kasha* but she wasn't there now – off with her mate, perhaps. Bored, the little grey cat prowled out of the room. No, not here. Then where?

Like a duchess, Varva picked up her dainty paws and made her way across the cold and filthy courtyard. By far the strongest aroma came from the stable, a mixture of fodder, horses, and dung. Yana the horse looked at the cat with her big, wise eyes, and farted softly. The most powerful smell in the place emanated from Nikolai, who lay sprawled in the straw as if he'd just fallen from the moon. Mewing softly, Varva walked over and snuffled between his toes. Yes, yes – this was more like it! A tangy green mould grew betwixt the stubs, the flesh from ankle to toe topped with a bitter, scabby crust. Sweat, filth, sores: but beneath these, other notes too. Whatever Varva had smelt was in Nikolai too – not quite the same, but close, related. The yardman rolled over, breathing out noxious fumes, and the cat jumped back, alarmed. Then, seeing that Nikolai was still unconscious, she padded a little closer, paws barely touching the ground. Settling herself down by Nikolai's large crooked toe nails, she began to nibble intently, not really biting, but allowing flakes to come away on her tongue.

Nikolai stirred and Varva bit a little harder, her sharp little teeth tasting flesh. Abruptly one fat foot lashed out, but Varva was too quick; instead she moved from toe to instep, pulling at the meat like something she might have found in the garden.

This time the yardman woke up.

"The devil take you!" he cursed. "Go find another corpse to prick."

But why should the little cat listen? The yardman had driven a cart over her tail and kicked her in the air one Easter time. Besides, his stench made her think of the stink and tang she'd sensed earlier. Not identical but close: its sister, maybe.

The cat took another nip but this time Nikolai brought his leg around and booted the cat out into the yard.

"Leave me alone! Let a working man have a little peace, God curse you…"

The cat yowled and gazed at the yardman with open hatred. Should she go back and claw him? No: his fists were too big and his feet too bony. Besides, she could still scent the trail, leading not to the stables, but the dispensary, its infuriating fragrance drawing her in like a net.

Nadya was in there, scrubbing the tables with carbolic soap, and Varva slipped between her legs, more like a puff of smoke than a cat. Nadya let her drink milk from the pail, but she was busy with her chores now, her face pale and tired. Besides, did the little cat care? No – she did not. The source of the emanation was close now, a smell unlike anything the cat had smelt before.

The stench – ancient, fishy, like something enormous had died in the sea – was coming from behind the door where the doctors kept the cold meat. The cat pressed her face to the bottom of the door and sniffed. The meat in there usually smelt of chemicals and soap, but this was different; this smelt of decay, sweetness, the tang of some creature. The cat quivered as if stroked. The scent was almost unbearably pungent, sweeping over her like a flood. Varva pawed at the door and cried. Why wouldn't they open it? Why couldn't they hear her? She yowled louder and paced this way and that, driven mad by the piquant flavours just inside.

Nadya arrived and yanked her away. Varva hissed and clawed. Who was this little bitch to refuse her? She squirmed in Nadya's arms and set her teeth into one hand, just by the knuckle.

"You demon!" Nadya yelled.

Varva dropped to the floor and ran back to the closed door. Why couldn't somebody just open it? Whatever was vexing her senses, lay just within. It called to her and reached out its arms. Why wouldn't Nadya open it?

"Out, you little shit," howled Nadya, and with that she grabbed the little grey cat and flung her out of doors. Varva spat and wailed and Nadya shook her fist.

"What's got into you, you horror?"

Realising that her cause was hopeless, the little grey cat slunk away. The smell still vexed her though, a constant itching in her skull. Whatever was behind that door was something beyond her wildest feline imagining – better even than the sweet memory of chicken…

As she crossed the courtyard, she spied Ilya the cock, parading about and pecking at bits of straw in the mud. Without thinking, Varva leapt on him and drove her teeth into his neck. Ilya struggled and flapped his wings but was taken by surprise: he couldn't use his claws or beak to save him. The cat bit into his soft throat and then let go. Ilya flopped drunkenly to one side and collapsed. In an instant Varva pounced on him and frantically began to claw. The cock was dead within seconds, but still fluffed his feathers convulsively. Varva pushed her head into his neck and breathed in. The meat was warm, rich, sticky. But even there the smell followed her, tickling her, stroking her, licking her all over like a mother. Ilya the cock looked at her as if to say 'Varva, my darling, my angel, what's got into you?' but Varva was too busy to notice.

eleven

1

Should Shemiakin throw himself from the cart or no? The ground was boggy and soft, but it would be difficult to get away, especially with Karnivsky watching like a hawk. Well, either it'll rain or it'll snow, thought the bagman: Fate doesn't listen to words. There were two carriages, ten Chekists, two drivers, all armed. According to Comrade Lenin, bagmen were thieves, criminals, and drinkers of plebeian blood. If Shemiakin was still breathing then Karnivsky obviously wanted him alive. Why jump in a hole? Better to stay on the cart than water the ground like the Dymovs.

"It's nice to have a chance to see the country," said Shemiakin, pointing at the mud. "Normally people are shooting at my head."

The trees were drab and increasingly bare. Leaves fell from the sky like public notices. Somewhere off to the right a woodpecker banged his head against a trunk over and over again.

"These woods are very bad. Full of cut throats, bandits, dangerous fellows."

"Hm," said Karnivsky, not looking up.

"Why, a band once tore the coat from my back. They'd have taken my skin too if they could…"

"The perils of your bourgeois trade," said Karnivsky, indifferently.

Shemiakin blew out his cheeks. "Bourgeois? I don't know such people from lions or bears. I am a simple, working man, Comrade

Inspector. If someone needs a pot to piss in, then I get him such a pot. If someone wants a little salt for his porridge, I fetch the salt too. What is it your Lenin says? To each according to his needs. You think I'm a wealthy man? Some Strogonov, sitting in his palace? I must brave bandits, wolves, the mud … you should pin a medal on my chest, my friend… I too am on the side of the working man…"

"Like your friends, the Dymovs, I suppose," said Karnivsky, mildly, "who steal grain and sell it for profit whilst workers in the city go hungry."

"Friends? Feh, like a razor to a throat. You malign me, Comrade Karnivsky! I am here to help. The soldiers at Chermovka lack boots – I can get boots. Quality leather too, like slipping your foot inside a cow…"

"I think not…."

"Uniforms too – German ones, true, but if you reverse the lining…"

"The People's Guard does not barter."

"Barter? Who said anything about barter? For my enemies a snake, for my friends, miracles…"

It's true, thought Karnivsky: only the grave will cure the hunchback. Explaining the Revolution to one such as Shemiakin was like explaining collectivism to a cat. Besides, why lecture a bagman, a speculator? Karnivsky had no interest in lectures, instruction, or political enlightenment. The ideological differences between the two men were such that the pair belonged to virtually different species. Shemiakin did everything for himself, Karnivsky everything for the party. Shemiakin strung along two different women, siring children like signing his name. But Karnivsky – Karnivsky kept himself clean for the fight.

He knew the bagman looked at him as if it were Shemiakin who was the worker and Karnivsky the bailiff, but none of this was true. The Chekist's class origins were impeccable. His father had been a foundry worker, his mother had mopped floors with a rag. Karnivsky had seen the treatment of the workers first hand, and in response he had educated himself, become politically enlightened, cultivated an iron discipline. It was a bourgeois luxury to treat life as if it were a game. He was no hypocrite, no Red clerk; for crimes against the Tsar his finger nails had been pulled out by the secret police. Karnivksy knew that it was the urban workforce which was the backbone of the Revolution: the peasants were too primitive, too selfish, still lost in the Russian darkness. Kulaks, like the Dymovs and Shemiakin, disgusted him. In thinking only of themselves they caused untold misery. Stealing tools from factories, grain from depots, boots from soldiers: who could count the damage done to the country at large? Thieves would ruin Russia. Only a sharp whip could steer the horse.

"Why shiver with winter coming? A good lining, that will keep you right…"

Such patter! Shemiakin's words buzzed and distracted. Only the Bolsheviks and the Monarchists understood the Russian character. The Mensheviks, the Socialists, the Liberals: they organised committees while their seats caught fire beneath them. Democracy had no place in Russia. Faced with hardship, a Russian's first inclination was always to do nothing – a passive, almost philosophical refusal to do any work. What was it Trotsky said? Discipline cannot be maintained without revolvers. And Shemiakin was the same as any other peasant: he averted his eyes, lowered his head, and waited for the storm to pass. Like fruit trees, they bent in the wind, first to the right, and then to the left. And if one could gather up some apples in the meantime – so much the better.

"This lining is soft as goose feathers yet strong as iron at the same time. Now I'm not saying that it will stop bullets – but, maybe? Now take this fabric" said Shemiakin, picking at Karnivsky's sleeve. "Poor quality, no good. You need something nice and warm for the winter – like a mother's hug. Inspector? Comrade?"

Confused by the Inspector's silence, the bagman fell back into silence. All horses can be bought, Shemiakin thought, sourly. It's just a matter of fixing the price.

Minutes later they rounded a corner and came upon the wreck of a carriage. The wagon – one wheel stuck in the mud, the other splayed out to one side, like a drunk – blocked the road entirely. Nearby it a corpse looked up at the sky as if disavowing the mess once and for all.

So much for the wagon transporting Sikorsky. The Chekist looked down at where the bullet had entered the policeman's chest and nodded, ticking something off inside his head.

"Well Shemiakin, what do you know of this?"

"Know? Who can know of what goes on in these woods? I tell you, Chief Inspector, this is a haunted place – I am only glad I have the Cheka here to keep me safe."

The guards fanned out and discovered a second body, this one stripped of his uniform, on the way to Ryabovsky's estate. Hoof prints could be found around the old bath house and leading off into the woods. There were signs of some kind of camp and the remains of a bonfire. A few spent cartridges, of indeterminate age, littered the garden; more than one party had obviously spent the night here, sheltering amongst the ruins. Whether this included whoever attacked the carriage, or any number of escaping prisoners, was impossible to say.

"Is this your doing?" Karnivsky asked evenly. "First you arrange the transport and then you arrange their escape?"

"For what reason?" asked the bagman, indignantly. "A deal is a deal, my friend. Lepinov bought himself a lunatic and I licked the stamps. This is a matter of ethics, Comrade Inspector. Besides, why would I want a sick dog like Sikorsky wandering from pillar to post? This Sikorsky is not a character I care to meet…"

"And the other?"

"Other, Comrade Inspector? I told you before, I…"

"All the paperwork suggests we are dealing with two prisoners, rather than one. True, the name is missing, but there are clear references to some kind of petty criminal, a fraudster, who had already spent some time at the jail at Mukholovka…"

"This is a very interesting development, but…"

"What are you trying to hide from me, Shemiakin? Did Lepinov purchase one maniac and receive another one for free? "

The bagman looked down at the policeman's corpse and realised just how precarious his grip on this world truly was.

"I swear, Comrade Inspector, I'm as puzzled as you are. Am I accountable for the paperwork? Do I have forms to sign? Lepinov purchased your Sikorsky and I carried the purse. This is the beginning and this is the end." The dead man at Shemiakin's feet looked up at him sceptically. "My dear Karnivsky, I did not kill these poor unfortunates. None of this carnage is my doing. Why shoot the delivery boy? My deal was with the Superintendent. I know nothing of what followed…"

Karnivsky believed him, but was tempted to shoot him anyway. Shemiakin was beginning to bore him, and he was by no means convinced of his usefulness. Still, he could dangle until they arrested Lepinov. Let the two men condemn each other and then share a grave.

"Perhaps you had better get back into the carriage," said Karnivsky. "For your own protection, of course."

One of the Chekists handcuffed the bagman and led him away. The others examined the bullet holes, the bodies, the various indentations in the mud. Finally the Chekists hauled the carriage out of their path, struggling with the broken spokes and the half-shattered shaft. The bodies of the two dead policemen were laid onto the rear carriage and wrapped in crude blankets. Karnivsky was no monster: the guards knew nothing of Lepinov's misdeeds. Let their mothers have something to mourn over. He would arrange for a Bolshevik funeral in Davydovka. Of course, he would not treat Shemiakin's corpse so kindly.

For his part the bagman watched the Chekist activity with only one thought – how could he escape? Alas, flight seemed next to impossible. They had hand-cuffed him to the carriage, next to the guards and the rotting carcasses. Soon he too would be with the Lord or the Devil, unless he could give the Reds the slip. What would happen when they reached the Yellow House? Lepinov was a slippery character, with a belly full of lies, but not even Lepinov could talk himself out of this – and when the fat man fell, he would drag the bagman down with him.

Nu, thought Shemiakin, it had all been madness from the start. When he had first traded with the Yellow House, exchanging drugs and medicines for money or kerosene, all was well and good. Lepinov paid well, and the bagman had been happy to fill his sack. But the plot to buy a murderer – why would anyone do such a thing? And why had Shemiakin allowed himself to go along with it?

"This is folly," he had warned the Superintendent, you bring misfortune upon your head. This Sikorsky – why store him under your roof? You think he will bring you presents, a pie? This Sikorsky can only bring ill luck."

"There is no luck," said Lepinov. "Everything is written by an invisible pen."

"You want to buy a prisoner? Let me go to the ladies' prison at

Shulem. There are beauties there that…"

"I need a wolf not a bird."

"A wolf? Be careful, my dear Lepinov. Who keeps company with wolves will soon start to howl…"

Truth be told, Lepinov had started to change long before this. His nails were curled, his skin tinged green, his jowls hung from his skull like empty purses. Had he already shaken hands with the Devil? There was an odd smell about him, like a mouse dug up by a cat.

"Okay, okay," said the bagman. "But I warn you – this will not end well".

What could he do? Another man's soul was darkness. So Shemiakin had done the deal, and shaken hands with Kuptsov. Let the cook decide what to put in his stew – the taste was no concern of his.

And then this. Shemiakin gazed at the wrecked carriage and regretfully shook his head. So Lepinov had been telling the truth: Sikorsky had never been delivered. When Shemiakin had arrived at the Yellow House expecting payment, Lepinov had thrown up his hands and denied that any such exchange had taken place. No police wagon had arrived at Bezumiye; no new guest admitted to the house. Shemiakin had flown into a rage and threatened to sever Lepinov's ears from his head – only a case of stolen wine glasses had placated him. Finally it was agreed that half the goods from Davydovka should be handed over now, half upon receipt. Both men were sure that the other was trying to trick them, but then relented; if neither chicken nor man is happy then something is wrong with the soup.

Unfortunately by the time Shemiakin had made his way back to the Mukholovka, Kuptsov was already sleeping in a ditch. With the Reds poking their noses in, it was best to lie low – until that fool of a horse had sauced herself up and gone to market without a bag. O Myushka, Myushka, what have you done? But it was now too late to blame the horse. A deal is a deal. What's written with a pen can't be undone with an axe.

And yet, all this talk of a second prisoner confused him. Had the Superintendent been out to stiff him after all? The deal with Kuptsov was for Sikorsky, not some conman or nameless forger. Why would Karnivsky think that there were two feet in one boot? No, none of it made sense. One murderer, stamped and delivered. There was no second man. Perhaps Karnivsky had lost his reading glasses in the war. Or perhaps Lepinov had some other bird up his sleeve. Shemiakin gussed that they would find out when they arrived at the Yellow House – just before Karnivsky shot them both.

2

After Polina left, Yevgrafovna sat brooding in her room. What the nurse had said about Alexei was ridiculous, absurd – nothing about her interpretation of events rang true. So what if 'The Tranquilizer' had made its way onto Lepinov's skull? This fact, in itself, meant nothing. Such a thing was easy to remove, unscrew – besides, Zinaida reminded herself, she must not think about Alexei right now. The important thing was that the remaining guests were still locked up, none of the others any the wiser. Polina's fantasies were of no concern to her. The guests' condition was serious but essentially unchanged. The experiment could continue.

It was now nearly a year since the rest of the soldiers had been moved out of the Yellow House, for Yevgrafovna a year of intense clinical investigation. True, the remaining soldiers persisted in a state of some derangement, and – from an objective point of view – their delirium might even be said to have worsened, but this in no way diminished the importance of Yevgrafovna's experiment, or the value of the intellectual benefits which would inevitably follow. Did their ravings mean anything? No, not one jot. One believed that if he were to urinate he would drown the whole world; another heard mice whispering to him in his hair. Signs and portents? Foo – one might as well listen to the chattering of rooks.

The doctor forced herself to get out of her chair and walk over to the little mirror. Yes, her wound was healing now, virtually invisible beneath her hairline. She administered a dab of iodiform and winced. Of course the incident with Alexei couldn't help but bring back memories of when Orlov had set about her with a stick: afterwards Orlov had been taken away from the Yellow House for good. Was it then that the previous Superintendent, Bezenchuk, had begun to lose his mind? Though Orlov had been Lepinov's patient, Bezenchuk was in legal charge of his custody, and the subsequent investigation had served to unhinge him for good. Months later he reported that Orlov had returned to the Yellow House, attempting to break down his door. A week later, he told Nadya that Orlov had appeared in the bathhouse, crawling out from a hole in his tub.

Should Orlov have been taken away? Despite her injuries, Yevgrafovna could not bring herself to agree. Such a specimen permitted the doctors to study mania in its most naked form: where else should an investigation be conducted if not here? Moreover, the decision to forcibly remove Orlov and terminate the proceedings echoed the doctor's own painful expulsion from Moscow only a few years earlier. Once again, the timidity of those in power had failed to recognise the value of a clinical examination of the physiological origins of lunacy. A pox upon philistines and imbeciles! After all, what was her work in the Yellow House if not the culmination of all that she had started at the Advanced Psychiatric Institute many years ago?

The problem with fever therapy lay in maintaining the correct temperature: hot towels, sweat baths and steamed mud could only do so much. Treated with such methods, the illness was at best suspended rather than cured. Malaria injections were more effective in cases of psychosis, but posed their own problems. Sulphur mixed with peach oil initially produced a strong calming effect, but also led to muscle necrosis, immobility and severe pain.

As many as one in five died – often in terrible agony. And yet even these failures taught Yevgrafovna an important lesson. If fever could cure hallucinations and degenerate behaviour, then it proved that such illnesses were caused not by inappropriate impulses or disturbed thoughts, but rather by a physical source – a spiral-shaped micro-organism akin to a syphilitic worm. This bug, Yevgrafovna believed, burrowed its way into the patient's brain, its presence manifested via psychological symptoms of schizophrenia, mania and distorted vision. Madness was not an ailment of the soul: madness was an infection.

When Yevgrafovna's twelfth patient died, the official investigation begun. When those infected with rat fever began to degenerate and turn violently psychotic, a tribunal agreed to expel Yevgrafovna from Moscow, her connection with advanced medical procedures broken forever. It was decided that the ambitious doctor should be transferred to the Yellow House at Bezumiye, her radical therapy program immediately terminated. Zinaida Yevgrafovna hissed and bit, but it was no use: her time at the clinic was over. There then followed disgrace, exile, boredom. Only when the traumatised soldiers started to appear did she suddenly start to realise that the Yellow House might actually enable her to put her plans into action.

Many of the soldiers returning from the front were afflicted with malaria, and Yevgrafovna carefully bled them, storing the infection in bottles hidden deep in the wine cellar, and marked for special use. When eyes were averted, she administered the blood intravenously to shell-shocked soldiers, sometimes via direct injection through the skull. The results though were disappointing – either fatal or inconsequential, with very few cases in-between. Rat bite fever was more effective, but Nikolai drew the line at collecting rats. What then to do? A great cloud of uncertainty seemed to hang over her. Yevgrafovna lost weight, neglected her patients, bit her nails. But then, just when she considered abandoning the study entirely, she met Alexei, a captain from the Seventh division, discharged from the frontline for 'air trauma' – which is to say, for nerves. And it was Alexei who would show her the way.

Initially Alexei's symptoms seemed no different to those of any other military patient: dizziness, disorientations, bouts of acute anxiety. When this disquiet was at its worst, he became paralysed and unable to speak; when words returned, he spoke of a sharp stone lodged some place between his eyebrows, a sliver of dark granite pressing down upon his brain. The certainty of his report, coupled with the specificity of the infection, made her think of the faded print hanging in Lepinov's study – Ivan the Fool, with the pebble growing out of his head. In medieval art, idiots were frequently portrayed with a large stone protruding from the middle of their forehead, a physical manifestation of their derangement. It was, of course, possible that the captain might have come across such a picture some place and unconsciously internalised the image– but possible too, that this visual representation of idiocy hinted at the existence of a tangible, physical cause.

In his lucid state, Alexei was kind, courteous and sincere. He asked Yevgrafovna about her time at the Yellow House, and was modest and dismissive of his experiences at the front. He had seen little conflict, he said, certainly not the heavy shelling which other battalions had been victim to. His illness was a mystery to him. He was not a conscript but a voluntary combatant. He believed in the war, in the necessity of defence. He had no desire to be invalided back home; rather he sought a cure so he could re-join his regiment. He was no coward nor shirker: his paralysis was a source of profound shame and personal mortification.

"Doctor Yevgrafovna, you have to believe me. All my actions have been in defence of Mother Russia."

Zinaida believed him. His voice was low and dignified, his hair a sweep of black paint.

They discussed the war, the political situation, the somatic nature of mental illness. Later, when the relationship had become more intimate, they discussed childhood vacations by the Black Sea, the cafes and restaurants of Moscow. Side by side they took a tour of the formal garden, the allotment, the meadow by the well. Alexei Voskresensky was tall, reserved, serious; whenever he spoke his words were carefully considered, as if he had weighed them first in his hand.

"My dear Zinaida, I am filled with boundless admiration and respect for the work which you and your fellow doctors undertake here. The degree of care, of concern, the dignified way in which you conduct your relations with the patients... the Yellow House is a remarkable place, my dear doctor."

"Yes, yes," said Yevgrafovna sadly. "If only Nikolai could catch more rats..."

Should she have lain with him? Well, yes, why not? Zinaida had never understood this moral squeamishness regarding the existence of one's body. Bodies were bodies: anything else was emotional claptrap. "Do you think consciousness is dependent upon intense ontological awareness?" she inquired during lovemaking, but the captain was unable to reply.

The first time they made love was in the tall meadow grass at the back of the dispensary, the second in Yevgrafovna's private room. After the act Voskresensky began to judder and shake, and the doctor examined his body dispassionately, as if checking a cart for a broken wheel. The limbs which had once been so full of purpose and ardour, now twitched spasmodically, as if an army of ants were marching somewhere beneath the skin. When the current stopped, his body cramped into a distorted shape which he held as if playing some demonic game. His eyes twitched and his fingers curled. "Alexei Voskresensky," Yevgrafovna said. "Could you describe to me the passage of electrical energy along your nerves?" Alas, he could not.

Sometimes they made love in the meadow, sometimes in the sick bay, once on the backseat of Lepinov's stranded car. Fits and seizures did not always follow copulation; more often than not the captain was gentle, respectful, kind. He was deeply embarrassed by such immobilizing episodes and rarely talked about them: perhaps a mention of "that damn stone between his eyes" – but no more. Once he recounted a dream where mushrooms had sprouted on his chest and neck: clear psychological indicators of some kind of invisible growth. Another time he mentioned an itching inside his skull as if some creature were moving in there, laying invisible eggs. All soldiers knew about lice, he said, but this thing felt different – as if some bug were gnawing away inside his mind. Most times he refused to discuss his illness at all. Besides, there were other things to talk about: the abdication of the Tsar, the collapse of the provisional government, the rise of the Bolsheviks. News of the revolution and Lenin's peace policy had confused him, but he still felt a profound desire to fight. This, Yevgrafovna felt, had as much to do with personal anxiety as the political context. He feared his paralysis might prove permanent, leaving him dependent, like a baby. "Shoot me between the eyes if that happens" he gasped, and Yevgrafovna nodded, looping his hair back behind his ears.

As their relationship deepened, the doctor was extremely tempted to infect her lover with malaria. Might the contamination burn out the illness, freeing him from all his ills? Unfortunately, malaria was dangerous, unpredictable – rat bite fever even more so. And yet the captain was changing. There was something frantic about him now, his ardour increasingly incautious. What if she fell pregnant? What if the other doctors – or the military authorities – found out? They made love in the barn, in the allotments, on the floor of the old bath house. "Am I a mad fool?" he cried during one passionate embrace, and Yevgrafovna took a deep breath before answering. "No, no, not at all," she said. "Your symptoms are neurological in nature and linked to a definite somatic cause"

As well as the act of copulation, they discussed their favourite spots in Moscow, the view from the Sparrow hills, Spring in the Izmailovsky gardens. Miraculously, Alexei's apartment had been only three streets away from the Institute for Advanced Psychiatric Research.

"To think," said Yevgrafovna, "I once collected a dead cat from that very street."

"Perhaps I saw you," he smiled. "Perhaps I even tipped my hat."

"I don't know," said Yevgrafovna. "It was pretty dark".

They embraced under the low wall of the *flügel* annexe and cross-examined Gromov's *The Forensics of Mental Illness*. The Captain was increasingly interested in the fundamental principles of psychology and desperate to believe that the cause of his distress was corporeal rather than mental in nature. "A worm, or some kind of bug? Yes, yes, I can see how that might have happened". Nevertheless, his faith in his own sanity had started to falter. After one particularly severe fit he was unable to move for two days, his muscles taut, his teeth ground down to their stumps. No, he no longer resembled the dashing infantryman who had first been admitted to the Yellow House. He became impotent and depressed. Holding his penis in her hand Yevgrafovna inquired as to whether there were underlying causes of his physical deterioration. Yes, he said, the order had been given – patients from his regiment were to be moved out from the House and back to Moscow. He would be gone within the week.

What could they do? One war was over and another, even more terrible conflagration, was about to begin. Yevgrafovna knew that things were coming to an end. When Alexei Voskresensky returned to revolutionary Moscow, she would never see him again, the captain swept away among the rags of history. If she was going to act, she would have to act now.

Fortunately the captain had a debilitating attack that very same day. With Polina and Churkin's help, she had him transferred to the maximum-security wing where Lepinov had once housed Orlov. There Yevgrafovna took a scalpel and buried it deep into Alexei's neck. She drained the blood – carefully preserving it in an old cognac bottle – and administered a transfusion using infected blood she had kept hidden in her suitcase from Moscow. Afterwards, Voskresensky fell into a deep sleep for seven days. When he awoke he thrashed from side to side and attempted to chew his arm. His eyes were yellow and wild, and his gums bled from the ferocity of his grinding and chomping. Still, all was not lost. When the other soldiers in his regiment were moved on, Alexei was permitted to remain, too ill to be moved, and conveniently absent from the military register. As the weeks went past he was joined by others, who were also administered Yevgrafovna's remaining stocks of poison. Blood was taken out, and blood was introduced. The results were not entirely conclusive, but in a sense, this did not matter. Yevgrafovna placed the blood taken from Alexei's veins under a microscope and studied its viscosity, searching for some element of the so-far invisible worm.

A worm? Well, perhaps that was not quite the right term. A microbe or bug then, akin to syphilis, but transmitted amongst the serving soldiers, manifesting itself via symptoms mistakenly labelled as 'shell shock'. An infection – possibly airborne, certainly capable of moving from host to host via bodily fluids– which was responsible for the plague of anxiety, horror and mania overwhelming Russia and the *Rus*. Yevgrafovna squinted at the dark, liquid universe, searching for the presence of some entity, a falling star or dust trail, an ancient comet presaging disaster. Was it to be found in that swirl, secreted within that spiral? The strange thing was that despite their uninhibited love-making, she never questioned whether she too might have been infected. Her own thoughts were clear, logical. The blood held all the answers – the body's inescapable truth.

3

The *flügel*, late at night. Martynov had come to the study brandishing a bottle of schnapps and loudly proclaiming that today was his birthday – not that anybody believed him, of course. Martynov wore a sailor's hat, Radek was in an academic gown, Frumkin was dressed as a doctor.

"This unconscious of yours, yes, yes, I see…," slurred Radek. "But where exactly is it to be found? In the skull, at the top of the throat, behind the brain?"

Frumkin took a finger of schnapps and loudly smacked his lips. "In Martynov's case I'd try further down."

"But if a thing is not materially present then how can one cure it? Unless there is a physical cause then…"

"The body is a clue, but the answer is the mind."

"The mind? Ah well, I…"

"Dreams."

Martynov nodded. "Last night I dreamt that my private parts grew to an enormous size and floated above the *flügel* like an enormous balloon. A magnificent sight! What do you think this means, dear doctor? Fear of impotence?"

"Well, it explains why Galina Yevgueniyeva has a crick in her neck…"

Martynov wrinkled his nose. "Ola, yes, yes – I've spied her making eyes at me, the hussy! Of course it's hard to resist an actor's magnetic effect – she's seen my *Seagull* of course…"

"I bet."

"What woman can resist the sight of a man in make-up. All they want to do is take out their handkerchief and give you a quick dab. Yes, yes, everything they say is true. Women are to actors as honey is to bees."

Both Radek and Frumkin tried to work out if this was the right way round.

"Nu, what woman wouldn't want a man who can play a thousand different lovers? Onegin on Monday night and Cyrano on a Tuesday…"

"And who are you by Friday – Lear?"

"You're just jealous Frumkin. How do you doctors get women anyway? With a bottle of formaldehyde and a sack?"

"Our minds are on higher things."

Martynov dipped his nose in his drink and leered. "That's not what I heard in Davydovka…"

"Well you know what they say – Gossip needs no carriage. Though if he's a Jew he'd better have a cart waiting, just in case."

"We've heard that tune before," said Martynov, swaying unsteadily and grabbing hold of the book case. "And in the meantime there's a queue of young ladies outside your door, just waiting to unburden their sins."

The *feldsher* made a modest gesture. "You're getting me mixed up with the Archbishop next door. He's the one with the beard."

"Oh come on, Frumkin," said Martynov, winking. "All those respectable ladies discussing their fantasies, their secret thoughts – you must have been fighting them off."

"You think? Well, times change. Once it was young ladies and their desires and now I'm sowing you into your straight jacket. Besides, Davydovka is long gone now – all those unhappy young ladies are Bolsheviks now, learning about socialised labour."

"Yes, yes," said Radek, suddenly waking up. "No unhappiness

under Socialism! We're all optimists now…" His behind released a tiny fart. "Compulsory happiness: the great Bolshevik dream! The new man is healthy of body and healthy of mind. Melancholics need not apply."

The professor seemed to have sunk into himself like a badly risen cake. His ears seemed too high up while his brows and nose had fallen into a ditch. "Culture, history, values – all gone. The Reds have buried the lot."

"Uncle needs more medicine," said Martynov, propping the professor's chin on a pillow.

"Why would anyone need a professor of Russian history now?" lamented Radek. "Russian history is on the pyre. The new dead are burying the old. Soon all of *Rus* will be in the pit."

Radek's eyes were sunk in his skull like last year's potatoes, his skin a ghastly green. What had happened to the vigorous academic of yore? He'd lost so much weight, there was nothing left but his name.

"When the Reds shut the University they called out *nikchemyi* – useless person…."

"That was your students."

"You'll be joking in the grave Frumkin. But the Reds will come for the doctors too, take my word for it. Anyone with a mind is a danger."

In Frumkin's estimation, Radek's depression, like that of other petit-bourgeois intellectuals, derived from an inability to adjust: without his seminars and symposiums and departmental meetings, he was lost. Red and White, White and Red: both doors led to tyranny – only the hat size was different. Or was that too simple? Despite the ugly rhetoric, something in the Bolshevik cause spoke clearly to the *feldsher* – a breaking down of centuries of misrule. If this was history, why mourn?

"My dear professor," said Martynov, consolingly, "You think it's tragedy, but its only melodrama … besides, our friend here has promised to keep us safe, has he not? Everyone thinks that war is the end of days. But if we can just sit out the Revolution a little longer then the White front will reach us. Do you think the Western Powers will allow Russia to be ruled by the mob? The British, the French … no one believes in a country ruled by factory workers and peasants. The Great Patriotic Army is on its way. All we have to do is keep our brains inside our hats."

All three knew that their time in the Yellow House was coming to end. Martynov believed that the Whites were coming to liberate them, Frumkin that Aleshin would discover his deal with Lepinov and have the inmates of the *flügel* shot. The contract had been an expensive one: all one's worldly goods in exchange for sanctuary. But with Lepinov dead and Shemiakin gone things were unravelling like a tramp's coat. Whether anyone really believed that all the lawyers, businessmen, bankers and theatrical types were clinically nuts was no longer the issue; you didn't have to follow the cart to be able to smell the shit.

"Well it's late," said Frumkin, uncomfortable with talk about the future.

Martynov pulled a face. "Late? Phah. The night is long – longer than a horse's tooth. Sit down and you can tell me all about that fancy piece of yours in Davydovka – the one who got you into so much trouble."

Frumkin made a dismissive gesture. "The professor doesn't want to hear about that."

Radek lay gathered in a heap like last winter's snow.

"He's sleeping like a baby – an old, ugly baby. So tell me my dear doctor, what's the story with you and Bella Zinovieva: a grand affair or …"

"What am I, crazy? You're mixing me up with the guests. She was one of my patients – a troubled woman."

"A married woman."

"That too. Also, a *shiksa* – my rabbi wouldn't approve."

Martynov dipped his long yellow teeth in his drink. "Come now Frumkin – that Old Testament beard doesn't become you. We're all men of the world here. The heart wants what it wants – isn't that what you Jews say?"

"I try to employ a higher organ. Besides, Bella Zinovieva was a mess – a sweet, beautiful mess. Her big problem was knowing where her fantasies ended and the real world begun..."

"I heard her big problem was taking her clothes off."

"Well, there you go: why would I get mixed up with such a person? I was running a nice respectable practice. Dreams interpreted and neuroses rinsed for fifty roubles a pop. Do I think I wanted Zinoviev hammering on my door? Jewish doctors have enough problems without such affairs. If we're not interfering with gentile women then we're cutting up Christian babies for Hanukah."

"Frumkin, why do you sweat like you're kneeling before the judge? I've seen Bella Zinovieva and I tell you – if she were sitting on my couch, the hypocritical oath be damned..."

"You're a paragon of virtue, Martynov."

From out of nowhere Varva the cat appeared, rubbing herself up against the actor's legs and settling on his shoes.

"So there's no truth, Frumkin, really?"

"There's no truth. Bella got a little mixed up and her husband made a scene. With her imagination she could pluck Lev Tolstoy's beard. Who knows what poison she poured in her husband's ear?"

"The story was he chased after you with a loaded revolver..."

"I don't know if it was loaded."

"Ah."

"Anyway, who cares? All this was another age. Once I was an analyst and now I'm the *feldsher*. Things change. Look at Radek –

one day he's an esteemed academic, the next he dribbles in a cup. Do you think that when the Whites come everything will go back to how it was? History can't be stopped. You can't put the ink back in the pen."

Martynov fussed Vanya and stared at Frumkin dreamily. "So one day you listened to ladies' dreams, the next you wipe maniacs' bottoms. How do you do it Frumkin? Dealing with the mad all day?"

"Hey, you work in the theatre". Frumkin fingered his cuffs. "Besides, I'm a doctor, it's my…"

"The last time I looked you were a lawyer."

"I retrained. First day of class: psychiatric evaluation. Who are the normal and who are the clinked? Once you've ticked that box you're home and dry."

"You make it sound like easy work."

"What is it Chekhov said? 'The hospital is an immoral institution, harmful in the highest degree to the health of the people'. Just don't get your uniform confused."

"You don't miss all the sad young ladies?"

"I don't complain. Lepinov flipped me out of the pan and I'm grateful for that."

"I thought you hated him."

"Let's say it was a marriage of convenience."

"Ho – you didn't bash his head in then?"

"Me?" Frumkin held up his hands. "When it comes to caving in our Superintendent, I'm at the back of the queue. Listen, I had to leave town for a while and Lepinov leant me a nest. If I have to play the *feldsher*, so what? It's you gentiles who are obsessed with tables of ranks."

"And when the soldiers came?"

"Luckily, somebody had sewn their bodies back together before they got here – all I had to do was stitch up their minds. What, you think they shiver and shake 'cause they got a piece of shell squirreled away? Some of them hadn't even seen battle. It's the mind not the body, Martynov. But you actors don't have to worry about such things – just whether the glue sticks down your wig."

The two men stared at the hearth where a log smoked and glowed. The outside was black and charred, while inside was a hidden kingdom of fire.

"So what became of Bella Zinovieva, do you suppose? Still forgetting her clothes?"

"Her husband took her away – a one way ticket. She's probably a sergeant in the Womens' Patriotic Battalion by now – or maybe a Red Guard."

The log popped and sparked and a great crack appeared in the centre. How long was the night? Longer than a hangman's noose. Martynov straightened his hat and pinched the end of his nose. "I saw Bella Zinovieva at a party once – a magnificent creature. Only she was with some cavalry lieutenant and I couldn't get close."

"Mm."

"If only I could have showed her my *Seagull*."

"Well, she was spared that."

When the two men turned back Varva was sitting on Professor's Radek's head like a kind of ill-shaped beret.

"Do you think he's still alive?" asked Martynov.

"Who knows?" said Frumkin. "It's how we'd all like to go."

With a soft pop the log fell apart, tiny sparks escaping from this world, each one dreaming of heaven.

"Chin up, Frumkin. We all have our lost loves."

"Love?" said the doctor. "That's just another form of delirium."

"Ha! So you were in love with her!"

"Let's talk about something else," said Frumkin softly, "like about your dreams."

"My dreams? Why yes, now you're talking!" Martynov straightened up as if marching on stage. "Now where were we? Oh yes, I was performing at The Yapping Dog when suddenly the whole set started moving – scenery came up and down, furniture slid from side to side, the musicians played madly, and the next thing I knew a great pit had opened up just like the last act of *Don Giovanni*."

"This doesn't sound like you," said Frumkin. "Nothing about the contents of your trousers?"

"One minute the back cloth was a country estate, the next a great grey city, and then an endless forest. And all the time bit-players came and went, mumbling in some language I couldn't understand. Most disconcerting, let me tell you! No script, no direction, no end. And all the time props being wheeled from place to place like the insides of a clock."

When Martynov looked over, Frumkin was no longer listening but staring at the old professor.

"You don't think he really is dead, do you?"

Varva was squatting on Radek's head, licking at one green ear. The wind whistled in the flue and the flames cowered and hid.

"Radek? No, he's just sleeping…"

"Sleeping? Ah, well…"

"You know what they say about Russian intellectuals. They never die – just turn into old books."

Varva purred, the flames waved, and somewhere out of earshot another load of coal rolled into the night.

twelve
1

Tutyshkin was somewhat perplexed to find himself waking up in Ludmilla's bed, her soft round lump by his side. Well, like a wolf's egg, the world was full of surprises; Tutyshkin pulled his naked body from the bed and went to retrieve his clothes. Of the night's entertainment he could remember nothing.

The day was the colour of old putty. Flakes of plaster fell silently from the sky.

'A walk,' thought Tutyshkin. 'A short perambulation to clear my head...'

The Inspector felt better as soon as he put on his boots. Yes, a tour of the town and then back: who knew what delights Ludmilla might cook up in her pot?

Chulm was already abuzz with feminine activity. Grannies in colourful scarves busied themselves collecting vegetables from the allotments, while dun-coloured women fixed tools or herded geese up and down the streets. A pig wallowed in a dip in the middle of the street, unresponsive to the cries of women. Small brown birds typed their thoughts in the dirt. Yes, thought Tutyshkin, a picturesque sight! O, the countryside was a marvel! On one side a cart had lost its wheels. On the other, the walkway sagged like a peasant's back.

"Good morning ladies," said Tutyshkin, bowing deeply. "How fares the hen and the cock's red plume?"

The women crossed themselves and fled. A water-carrier in a

mustard-coloured head scarf staggered past with two buckets on a pole, swearing loudly. Tutyshkin smiled and crossed over to an old Auntie selling bread from a bag.

"Beautiful, just beautiful," said Tutyshkin, tapping the loaf against the wall with practiced skill. "Tell me, my angel; are you real or a vision sent down from above?"

The Inspector gnawed on the bread like a dog with a bone. Black and sour: the bread of old age. Was it going to rain? He hoped so. It should always rain in the countryside – either that or snow. One woman was busy watering her pots while another fixed a pail. This world without men was perfect, a paradise! Tutyshkin could have stayed here forever.

The Inspector passed an old, gloomy cowshed and a large pile of rubbish, the waste heaped up like a bonfire. Half buried amongst the peelings and manure was a headboard with an old family crest: booty liberated from the old manor, no doubt. Tutyshkin poked the heap with his foot and a baby fell out – no, not a baby, a doll. This must once have been the pet of the rich, pampered children living in the Big House: now he would give it to a passing peasant child, some dirty girl with a limp. The doll had lost one eye and its head was caved in, but no matter – what peasant wouldn't be delighted by a treasure like this? He picked the blue doll out of the mud and carefully placed it in an empty trough. How charming it was! Like the Ikon of St Nicetas come fully formed to the world.

When Tutyshkin turned around, a cloud of children had gathered like sparrows: three boys and a girl. They looked first at him, then the doll, then the rubbish heap. The girl picked her nose.

"Come closer, little rabbits," said Tutyshkin theatrically. "Come and see what Grandfather Frost has hidden in his pack."

The girl stared back at him defiantly. "Mama says you're the Devil."

Tutyshkin shrugged.

"And that you and your kind took away Daddy and Uncle Tonka in a box."

"Foo – she's getting me mixed up with Lenin – it's the shape of my skull." Tutyshkin pulled a face, and one of the boys at the back pulled back. "Mummies and Aunties say all sorts of funny things, don't they? Like someone has blown the words – poof! – straight into their heads."

The girl came a little closer and pointed to the blue doll.

"What's that?"

Tutyshkin glanced in the trough and winked. "Shhh – she's asleep."

"What's she called?"

"Petr."

"That's a boy's name."

"Tanya."

"Let me see."

The girl pushed forward and Tutyshkin swept the doll up into his arms. "Wait – she wants to say something." He held the doll's lips to one ear. "Hm. Mm, I see." He nodded. "She wants to know if you're a good girl."

The girl looked at her feet, bare and brown, like two potatoes.

"Eh, my angel? A good girl?"

The boys started to snigger but the girl didn't move. Tutyshkin lifted the doll back up to his ear. "Wait – she wants to talk to you."

Almost reluctantly the girl held out a hand.

"Don't drop her, my sweet – she's very small."

The girl took the doll and held it up to her own pink shell.

Tutyshkin grinned. "Well?"

The girl cocked her head as if listening intently. One of the boys tried to snatch it, but she swiped him away with a well-aimed blow.

"She says that you're not a policeman."

Tutyshkin arched one eye brow. "Really?"

"She says that you're not a doctor, either."

"Mm."

"She says that you have no face at all."

Tutyshkin stamped his foot impatiently. "Give her back then."

The girl demurred.

"I just want to talk to her."

"She says you have horns growing out of your head."

"Ha Ha, well…"

"She says…"

Growling, Tutyshkin pounced on the doll, trying to make her let go. "Give her here!"

From behind the children a sour-faced peasant woman appeared as if from nowhere.

"Ah!" said Tutyshkin. "The Mother of All Russia!"

The woman marched forward and Tutyshkin passed the woman the doll as if bequeathing her a bouquet of flowers. "For you, my dove."

The woman looked at the broken figure and scowled.

"A gift," said Tutyshkin, simpering. "A little something for your cherub to play with – a treasure for her name day. Ho, the child is nearly as beautiful as her mother! Someone should make a doll of you, my sweet, a little toy or …"

"Lizochka, come!" The woman's voice was surprisingly deep, as if wrapped up in straw.

"Oh, my dear: what trinkets can you have in a hole like this? Tch, let the girl have one jewel…"

"Lizochka, come now."

The girl ran to the auntie's side, hiding behind her apron. Tutyshkin shrugged and watched them go. The boys were still there, pointing and whispering.

"Dolly?" said Tutyshkin, showing them the babe.

One boy picked up a clod of earth and threw it at Tutyshkin's head, the others joining in with stones and rubbish. For a moment, Tutyshkin faltered, stumbling over a stack of firewood and row of yellow pots; then Dusya appeared as if from Heaven, scattering the children before her.

"Dusya!" exclaimed the Inspector. "What a marvellous surprise!"

The girl looked at him indifferently, her hair like a shiny black mirror. Was she a doll too? Her hands seemed very small though her head was very big.

"What a jolly place!" said Tutyshkin. "Amusing children, beautiful women, unusual smells … why, 'tis a paradise on earth!"

"Follow me," said Dusya, her voice emanating from someplace behind her hair.

"Now? Ah, I fear that Ludmilla is…"

But the girl had already turned her back to him, disappearing into the forest like smoke. Ah, well! A hen wandered past and Tutyshkin saluted it like a general.

"I'm sorry my darling, but duty calls…"

From behind a merry jumble of pea-frames and wild garlic, the path drifted away to the rye fields and the dark woods beyond. The Inspector walked along, tossing the blue doll in the air as if it were a little ball. Ho, what would Ludmilla be making him for breakfast? Black tea, *kolbasa, syrniki* fried in oil? He tried to remember the previous night's sport, but alas the pail had holes. The good doctor was lucky with the ladies, which was for sure: what a shame he couldn't seem to remember! He would have liked to picture that big, round behind once more.

Tutyshkin picked a flower and placed it in the doll's empty socket – charming, quite charming. The woods were gloomy and dark, scaffolding for a building which would never be built. Peasants had laid wooden planks over the muddiest sections and as long as you kept to the path, the trail wasn't so hard to follow. But where was Dusya? Aye, the girl was some kind of imp, that was sure. Tutyshkin followed the old hunter's trail to where it forked into two, almost identical, paths. But which one had the skinny witch taken? Not for the first time, he wished that he were two men so that he could inspect each avenue to his heart's content. Perhaps one led to a currant bush, and the other to a crop of mushrooms. Or maybe one led to a rabbit and the other to a bear. Having only one life was like having a single hat; a disadvantage and a shame. O, to have two names instead of one! Thus, while one Tutyshkin chose the path leading over stony ground to the right, another Tutyshkin took the boggy way under the broken branches to the left. When faced with a second clearing, different Tutyshkins scattered off in all directions, like a gaggle of children escaping their nurse. Here was one Tutyshkin kicking over a way-stone, and there was another, pushing his way through a thick patch of bracken. Like a mother hen, it was awfully difficult keeping track of them; unless you kept your wits about you, there were Tutyshkins *everywhere*.

The Inspector paused: something was moving in the gloom ahead of him. Sikorsky? No: Sikorsky was either rotting in the Mukholovka or dead in a ditch. The guards had pulled him from the cell, not Sikorsky. He had been given a stale crust of bread and chained to a radiator in the sick room whilst the administrators finished off the paper work. "Sikorsky?" asked the guard and Tutyshkin beamed like a school girl. "Who else, my angel?" Ah, being a murderer was thrilling, invigorating – and such a famous murderer at that!

"Inspector."

As if plucked from a hat, Dusya appeared right in front of him, her *sarafan* the colour of night.

"Inspector, this way."

Tutyshkin followed the girl somewhat reluctantly. Foo, where was the fox leading him? He could swear that he'd been this way before. The broken trees, muddy bog, a hunter's path: ah, wasn't this the way to the ruined estate, what was it called, Ryabovskys? And then he thought to himself: Petr. Was this where Dusya had vanished to? But how could the little minx know?

Her shadow passed through a clearing like a crow. For a moment he thought he could hear her claws clicking on the ground.

"This way, Inspector. There's something I think you should see..."

Tutyshkin held back, fingering Dusya's knife in his pocket. Yes, he knew where he was now. An old ruined wall with the ruins of the manor house beyond it. And to the right, the *banya*.

"Inspector?"

Tutyshkin turned and started to run: ho, no good could come of this. Without looking back, the Inspector plunged into the gloom, his feet slipping in the thick, black muck. Curse the witch! He sensed her someplace close by, cat eyes gleaming behind that waterfall of hair. Ho, what manner of demon was she? His limbs felt heavy, bewitched. All of a sudden the Inspector fell over his own two feet, landing heavily by the side of a bog, the frogs watching over him like a jury.

"Why?" said a voice. "Why did you kill him?"

"Kill him? Not I. No, my angel, you're getting everything mixed up. True, I met the lad just by here. My carriage was set upon by bandits and I took refuge in the *banya*."

He looked up and there was Dusya above him, her toe nails long and black.

"It was there I met your Petr. Ah, what was I supposed to do, my dove? He took one look at the policeman's uniform and , well … a quite remarkable coincidence really … was it my fault he believed me to be some Inspector? Foo, if you put a saddle on a pig somebody will ride it…"

"And he told you of Lepinov?"

"Yes…"

"And asked for your aid?"

"It was really more of a game than anything…"

"And then you killed him and took his horse."

Tutyshkin rose carefully to his feet, manoeuvring himself away from Dusya, fumbling for the knife in his pocket.

"My angel, please … we retired for the night and in the morning he was gone … bound for the railway line at Kastornoc, or so I surmised…"

Dusya's face was unreadable, a mask.

"After that I followed the little horse to the Yellow House. Foo, what else could I do? The forest was infested with criminals. Staying in the woods would be like placing a clod of earth on my head… oh, my darling: I was born under a black star. These are no times for sensitive souls like mine…"

Tutyshkin brushed the mud from his smock and stared at Dusya's black curtain of hair. "Besides my dear, you have had your own dealings with the Yellow House, am I right? And our dear departed Superintendent Lepinov too, I should think… Eh, my chick, what do you say? Somebody was calling on him at midnight every night, crying out for Nikolai to open the black gate … now my sweet, who do you think that might have been? Mm? My dove?"

Dusya looked at him without dignifying his question with an answer. She was as thin as a shadow's shadow, barely there at all.

"What were the two of you cooking up in there? Something to summon a demon, or something to poison Lepinov?"

The girl watched him as a cat does a bird.

"Or am I getting you mixed up with your mother?"

Dusya's voice was like a knife. "My mother? She said you would come. The Devil…"

Suddenly she was on top of him, spitting and clawing, slashing at his eyes. Tutyshkin grabbed for his knife, the two of them rolling into a ditch while the roots scratched like fingers. One moment Dusya was on top of him, her nails tearing through his smock; the next she was beneath him, terribly thin and emaciated, barely more than a sheet. Blood, darkness, mud: and then it was all over.

"Yes," said Tutyshkin. "Well…"

How long did the Inspector spend in the woods? It was hard to say. His beard felt longer and the fuzz itched atop his head – nevermind all his scratches and bites. At times it felt as if he had been in the woods for days, or even years; at other times it felt as if all this were just a dream, something that had happened to somebody else: Sikorsky, perhaps. But there, just beyond the boggy ground, lay Chulm nesting like a grouse.

Alas, the sky was so grey 'twas impossible to tell whether it was morning, dinner or dusk; only the Inspector's belly acted as a timepiece. As Tutyshkin opened the gate to Ludmilla's plot, his voice boomed out like a shot.

"Ludmilla, Ludmilla, your swain has arrived!"

When he saw her lump still snuggled beneath the covers, Tutyshkin paused; what was she doing still in bed, slumbering like a sow?

"Ludmilla? Awake my sweet, for your prince has, ah…"

The Inspector stopped. The head woman's throat had been cut by a large serrated knife. Blood soaked into the sheet like jam, a large blue-bottle squatting merrily among the mess.

"My dove?"

Tutyshkin backed away, patting down his pockets as if looking for a key. When he was sure no one was about, he quietly closed the door and walked back toward Dusya's hut. This time he did not call out to any of the women, or whistle any song. When a small boy flung a stone at him he said not a word.

At Dusya's, Masha was waiting with a large steaming pot. The wind chimes tinkled.

"Where have you been," she scolded, "out singing with the birds?"

Instead of entering, Tutyshkin hung back by the door, an innocent expression on his face. "Oh, enquiries, surveys, observations and the like. You know what police work is like…"

"Come in then, what are you doing? Life goes out through an open door."

Like Masha, the pot was round, brown, and smelt of herbs. Fingers of steam escaped from under the lid as if something were attempting to climb out, or the pot was trying to open itself.

"Ah, if only I could – alas, the case calls me away, my angel. Certain evidence has, ah, come to light, which, that is to say…" For some reason Tutyshkin couldn't seem to drag his eyes from the pot. A thick brown dribble escaped down one side, and the lid seemed to rattle and jump. "Some really quite extraordinary clues, though I shan't bore you with the details."

The pot squatted on the table like an enormous toad. It smelt of earth and moss and the forest. The woman scratched her chin.

"Sit, sit. The food won't jump into your mouth."

"Thank you my dear, but …"

There was some kind of hubbub going on outside: women's voices, urgent and angry. Tutyshkin's hunger had evaporated, replaced by something like dread.

"Delicious as no doubt your stew must be, I must go."

"Whoever sets off on a journey without a thing to eat?" asked the old woman, scowling. "There – I've put out a bowl and everything. 'Tis a sin to waste food – 'specially with the war and the Reds and all. Sit, sit! You look like the stew's about to gobble you, not the other way round."

The Inspector shuffled his feet and peered through the curtains; yes, peasant women were gathering in the street, some carrying sticks and clubs. Had someone followed him from Ludmilla's? He felt the noose begin to tighten.

"O Masha, dear Masha ... but I fear that I have left something behind my dove, crucial evidence..."

So saying, Tutyshkin flew to the back of the house and pushed his way out through a window. Behind him Masha was still talking about soup.

For a moment he thought he saw Sikorsky's face – bald, animalistic, insane – but the vision soon vanished. This was no time for dreaming! Tutyshkin heard angry voices behind him Ho, why had he come to this cursed dump in the first place? Only the Yellow House could protect him now. As the Inspector ran, dark, serried trees squeezed together like bodies in a grave. Rotting stumps, broken arms, and all the time the light spilling out like milk through a cloth. This was no Heaven, reflected the Inspector; rather he felt himself tremble on the very cusp of Hell. Hell? Hell was inside his head. And with that thought, Tutyshkin plunged into the gloom like a rabbit, leaving the women of Chulm far behind.

2

"Lads, lads," said Shemiakin. "I look at you and see my own boys grown into men. Why do you look at me like that? Are we not all Russians? Surely this means something in God's eyes? As the Bible says, if He clothes and tends you, who would give their poppa a snake?"

In truth the Chekists were barely looking at Shemiakin at all. Like the trees, his wheedling voice seemed to go on forever, as grating and monotonous as a wheel in need of oil.

"What's that? You don't have a Poppa? And a thin jacket too. Okay, you wear a Russian jacket, all well and good, sewn together by Grannies, no doubt. But I can get you a good German jacket from Berlin tailors – quality workmanship, beautiful stitching. This jacket – feh, I would not wrap a dead dog in it. Look, the Red Star is already coming unstuck..."

The bag-man's words buzzed around the carriage like mosquitoes. Did he ever rest his jaw? The Chekists had been warned that he had killed several of his rivals in cold blood: by talking, maybe.

"Gentlemen, comrades, listen to me. This war is not like a Bolshevik speech: one day it must end and when it does, a wise man will need a little something put away. Now a medal is all very well, but tin and ribbons don't make for good soup. What, you think your Lenin will give you a nice little pat on the head? A soldier's life is like a dog's tail: it starts near the arse and ends in the shit. No, you need a little sugar put by. Listen, I have set aside some precious items I am personally willing to share with you. Why not? You're all good lads. After the war, we'll all go picking mushrooms together, the Lord knows what we might find…"

At first the Chekist thought it a mirage: two Cossack horsemen, dressed in caftans and red Caucasian caps, floating at the very edge of the road. Then the carriage jolted and – poof! – the horsemen were gone. The Chekist turned to his comrade, but the lad was eating a plum, juice dribbling down his chin. When the Chekist turned back, he saw nothing, the trees going on forever, like a dull and monotonous wallpaper. No, his eyes were playing tricks with him. Mile after mile of drab countryside did that to a man. Cossacks? The sooner they strung up the bagman, and burned down the nut house, the better.

"Gentlemen, I give you my word of honour that what is mine is yours, all spoons in the pot…"

The Red soldier looked down to study a leaf stuck to his boot. In the corner of his eye he half registered a coal black horse moving through the gloom; then he felt a sharp pain in his chest. He looked out of the window and then down at his bloodied shirt: the two things were somehow connected, but for a moment he couldn't work out how. The next he heard was a sound like a loud whine or the shriek of a saw: not rifles, but a machine gun. Holes appeared everywhere. Light streamed in and something gave way with a bang. Then, without warning the carriage toppled over and the world seemed to sway and crash. Shemiakin saw the Chekist fall against the door and heard his neck break with a snap.

"Sonofabitch, sonofabitch, sonofabitch," somebody moaned over and over again.

Fortunately for the party, the other wagon had fared somewhat better. The horses hauled the carriage to the side of the road and the Chekists returned fire. Unexpectedly, the machine gun fell silent. Had it jammed? But if so, where were the bullets coming from? One of the Chekists made a run for the trees but then toppled over, his corpse rolling along the road like an escaped sheet. Gunfire whistled hysterically.

"Dirty bastards," yelled the rat-faced Chekist. "What a dirty trick…"

As if from nowhere, a mounted brigade rounded the corner, the riders screaming and whistling. Mud flew up in large clumps and the air was filled with smoke. Karnivsky, pinned behind the carriage, leant out with his pistol and fired. The lead rider fell, first to one side, then under the hooves of his horse. Karnivsky's hand did not hesitate or quake. The Revolution asked for everything, like a mother.

In truth, the Chekists were lucky. For some reason, the riders had drawn sabres rather than cocked rifles – an act of reckless stupidity. As the horses turned upon reaching the carriage, several more of the Cossacks tumbled, almost comically, to the ground. A Chekist laughed as a tall, sturdy fellow leapt to his feet and ran him through with his blade: the Red's insides slipped out like the filling of a pie. Then the White himself collapsed in a burst of pink mist.

"Hold steady," hissed Karnivsky. "Hold your nerve."

The Cossack horses whirled around and retreated – the carriages had blocked the road and the riders could only attack from one direction. One Red stuck his head out to see what was going on and was shot dead by another. Bullets whistled and whined. Eventually, the riders disappeared back around the corner and the road fell quiet. Horses thrashed about like fish left behind by the tide.

"Filthy sows!" yelled someone. "Look what they've done to Gedali…"

Shemiakin was trapped on one side of the turned-over carriage. Next to him a Chekist spat bloody bubbles and swayed.

Shemiakin pulled at his leg but could feel nothing. It was all a Russian joke: the perfect escape and he was held tight like a louse. Shemiakin closed his eyes and lay still. Perhaps the Reds would forget him. Perhaps his wives and children would forget him too.

Karnivsky stood on the road and surveyed the scene. Half his men were injured or dead, and a second attack was imminent. Worse, the machine gun encampment was someplace overhead. If the Cossacks managed to un-jam the mechanism then they were done for.

"Zabuty – we've got to get off the road and into the woods."

"And the injured?"

"The Worker's State will remember them. This is the enemy, corporal. The White Army cannot be far behind."

The White Army: did he really mean it? It seemed inconceivable that Denikin and his treacherous mob of counter-revolutionaries should have penetrated so far. The last he heard, the Seventh division were sure to finish them off at Novovoronezh. Well, no matter: the shameful forces of reactionary Imperialism would be extinguished like a match.

A series of random shots issued from the woods and the Chekists again took shelter. But these shots too passed.

"We must leave this place," said Karnivsky. "The dog Shemiakin – where is he?"

The bagman was still pinned beneath the first wagon. He had managed to lever half his body out through the broken window but the lower half of his leg remained squeezed betwixt door and seat. His clothes were torn and his hairy belly peeped out like a cat. Although he was obviously in pain, the bagman said not a word: this was no time to be caught singing a song.

Still looking out for snipers, Karnivsky strolled over.

"Cornered, Shemiakin?"

"Only my fool of a leg prevents me from fighting for the cause…"

"I see. Zabuty, Tsydzik – can you free him?"

The Chekists took hold of Shemiakin's shoulders and the bagman began to scream.

"Forgive me, Comrade Captain, my ankle is crushed beneath the carriage. You'll have to go on without me. Don't worry about me, Comrade Karnivsky – the Revolution is bigger than all of us."

Karnivsky looked at the Chekists and the two men shook their heads. "I see," said Karnivsky. He nodded to Tsydzik, and the lad shot Shemiakin in the head.

"Zabuty – marshal the men and get them under cover. The others cannot be far."

As the surviving Chekists crossed the tree line, a second division of Cossacks approached from the same point. A series of un-identifiable cracks echoed eerily, like the snap of a distant whip.

The Reds dodged between the trees and boggy ground, followed by the Cossacks and their scouts. A Chekist span to the left and then fell; another became trapped in a thicket. It was chaos. One Red held up another like two drunken pals heading home. None of the Chekists spoke.

In his flight, Karnivsky soon realised he had left the others far behind. He slumped against an alder trunk, breathing heavily. In one hand he held his pistol, in the other his commissar's cap. There was a splash of blood on his uniform, but he was sure it wasn't his.

When he peered out from behind the trunk he saw a White stalking him like a bailiff. Karnivsky turned and stumbled straight into the rifle of the rat-faced Slinkin.

"Comrade Captain sir…"

"Shut up you fool!"

Karnivsky and Slinkin hid themselves in a ditch, lying as flat as they could. After a while the White youth passed. If you concentrated you could even hear birdsong. It seemed as if the

Whites had passed over, like a cloud.

So, the Monarchists were here already. Karnivsky's first duty was to return to Davydovka and alert the authorities – assuming the place hadn't already fallen, of course. But this was defeatist talk: the fighting forces of the revolutionary vanguard did not countenance failure. Besides, what if the Cossacks weren't part of a major movement, but a separate unit operating out of someplace else – perhaps even the Yellow House at Bezumiye? Was it the Cossacks who had attacked Dovlatov's transport? Perhaps they were anarchists or bandits rather than soldiers – yet, for all their recklessness, they seemed too organized to be merely part of a mob

"What now Comrade Captain?"

"Now? We go on."

A few minutes later they heard two more Chekists stumbling through the undergrowth like horses: how they'd evaded the Whites was anyone's guess. A third cradled his injured comrade by a broken tree.

"How is he?"

"Not good, but not bad either. Like women."

The Chekists had no food and little ammunition. Nevertheless, the Yellow House was not so far from here. Perhaps that was where the Cossacks had come from – or perhaps it might provide aid and medical assistance. Besides, even though Shemiakin was dead, it didn't mean that Lepinov was off the hook.

"Sir?"

"We rest."

"And then?"

"We proceed."

A Chekist extracted the bullet from another's shoulder while the soldier moaned and ground his teeth. Well, no matter: if the Whites were close, all was lost.

"Duplischev? Golovin?"

"Duplischev was shot. Golovin? You might as well look for the wind in the fields."

Karnivsky nodded. Davydovka was four days away by foot, Bezumiye, no more than a couple of hours. The crows had already decided.

After a while, light rain started, threatening to turn to sleet. The Chekists passed the same fallen tree twice. Were these the woods where once Dmitri Donsky had defeated the Mongol hoards? In these woods, anything was possible. Something about the forest unsettled Karnivsky. Though the land did not change, the Chekist felt as if he had crossed some invisible border or line, his brain registering a profound transition in being. Or was he just falling prey to doubt? Karnivsky was a positivist, a rational man. Any fretfulness he felt was no more than a primitive response to the forest and the darkness, an archaic residue of prehistoric fear. Besides, he was no peasant, but a worker. The logical part of his mind knew that the House was close, the trees must end, that the gloom held no secrets. And yet, and yet ... all around him, the trees seemed to silently regroup, always the same and always different, their branches a form of camouflage, hiding something else. The very air seemed squeezed, the dark serried trees as close together as bodies in a mass grave. Rotting stumps, broken arms; and all the time the light spilling out like milk through a cloth...

Karnivsky was ready to retrace his steps when one of the Reds spotted the post road crouched behind the trees, its black line flanked by a boggy track. Gratefully, the Chekists made their way toward it. The road was deserted, the landscape as still as a corpse. The boggy track led across an unkempt meadow, wild grass sprouting out of the black earth. Of course, crossing the road would leave them terribly exposed, but in truth they had no choice. The track was manmade, official. Dark blocks could be glimpsed at the edge of the world. Yes, there was an avenue, buildings. Everything suggested the sanatorium was close.

In the gloom, the Yellow House – not yellow, of course – seemed little more than a thick smear of paint, its deep blue shadows darkened rather than illuminated by the presence of the occasional lamp. A cold rain was turning to ice. Like porridge, the mud was solid on the top, but treacherous down below. But at least here they might learn some answers. What need did they have of the bagman? A gun asks better questions than a man.

Karnivsky reached the outer fence and banged on the large iron door.

"Open up!" he yelled. "Open up in the name of the People's Revolution."

Through the bars he could glimpse movement, hear voices, the sound of something heavy scraping along the ground.

"Open the gate you fools, or I'll have you shot like a dog" cried Karnivsky. "I am an agent of the All Russian Extraordinary Commission for Struggle against Counter Revolution and Sabotage and as such…"

The gate finally opened, and a dirty old yardman stared at the soldiers through rheumy eyes.

Karnivsky pointed his gun at the old fool's beard.

"Did you not hear me? I command you to allow the people's representatives to enter."

The yardman's lips curled and he began to hoot like an owl. The Chekists looked at each other uncertainly while the sky flapped like a back-cloth come loose in the rain. What kind of place was this? The Romans branded maniacs with the words 'Cave furem' – beware the mad thief. Thief of what? Of the whole world it seemed. Karnivsky wiped the rain from his eyes and raised his gun toward the door.

thirteen

1

No, Chief Superintendent Lepinov did not look well. His corpse filled the room like a flood, foul skin stretched tight over distended organs and twisted limbs. The flesh bulged and the meat spoiled. Pustules dotted the lump like a field of mushrooms. It was hard to open the dispensary door, so great was the swelling.

"Just what is going on here?" demanded Karnivsky, holding a rag to his nose. Marya and Polina looked at one another nervously. The Cheka were not pleased with the length of Lepinov's beard. *This* was the Chief Superintendent Lepinov? He was more of a lake than a man.

"This is completely unacceptable," Karnivsky snapped. "Such a position questions the whole nature of this institution…"

Lepinov resembled an unmade bed, a cocoon from which something unspeakable might erupt at any moment. And the smell! Sour, spoiled, foul as a mouldering bucket of fish. Everything about the Chief Superintendent was an affront to Marxist dialectics. How had things come to this?

Karnivsky's first act upon taking command of the House was to arrest the three doctors as 'White Guard Restorationists'. As Acting Chief Superintendent, Doctor Aleshin bore direct responsibility for the ideological purity of the institution: he would answer for any counter-revolutionary activity. The doctors were imprisoned in a barn, Karnivsky taken directly to Lepinov's remains. The Chekist smelt the Superintendent before he saw him.

"This… bloating…" said Karnivsky, gesturing in the direction of Lepinov's gut.

"The doctors suggested that Chief Superintendent Lepinov may have ingested some kind of poison," said Marya.

Lepinov's torso was the length of a table, his beard like spilled wine.

"Poison? What kind of poison?"

"I don't know sir. You locked up the doctors."

Karnivsky had seen many cadavers in his time, but never anything like this. Lepinov's fingers were enormous tubers, his feet big black udders. Ho, what a terrifying landscape he afforded – twelve poods of shit in a ten pound bag.

"And how long has the Chief Superintendent been dead?"

"Two weeks now, sir."

"And the cause of death was…?"

"Strangulation, blows to the head, drowning and poison."

"And you say there has been another murder?"

"Yes sir. Poor Ivan, a servant."

Karnivsky shook his head in disbelief; he imagined Lepinov's corpse spreading and sprouting 'til it burst free from the room and covered the house, the estate, all of Russia. Yes, it was all too easy to picture. Lepinov would continue to grow until he stretched all the way from Finland to Japan. His beard would spread like the Don, his arse grown broader than the Urals. Lepinov would expand until he covered the entire globe. And even that would not be the end.

"I see," said Karnivsky. "Well, let me speak with those who are in command."

The three doctors were ushered out of the barn and into the yard, Aleshin protesting he was a Bolshevik, Yevgrafovna she was a qualified physician, Frumkin merely the *feldsher*. Nobody was listening. Behind Karnivksy three Chekists waited like a firing squad. Like a firing squad? They were a firing squad – death, a brother and a friend.

"You will now explain the exact nature of the events which have transpired here," intoned Karnivsky, calmly. "Comrade Aleshin - do you assume full responsibility for political activity within this institution?"

Aleshin was close to tears. "Comrade Investigator, I assure you … the struggle, ah … I am a loyal party member, dedicated to the cause of…"

"A cause you choose to serve here, far from the front? Tell me Comrade Aleshin: when the Red Army is so short of trained doctors, why do you cower here in your nest? Bolshevik martyrs give their lives for the cause, while scum like you burrow deeper into your blanket like lice … shameful, Dr Aleshin, shameful."

Despite the violence of his language, Karnivsky spoke calmly, almost disinterestedly. It was Aleshin who squirmed like a schoolboy.

"Comrade Investigator, I am a loyal Bolshevik and…"

"Feh, your class origins betray you…"

Aleshin felt confused: how was it his words were coming from another man's mouth? And yet another part knew the truth. He had been found out. His mother's plan to hide him had failed.

"Now explain to me comrade doctor, why did you have the prisoner Sikorsky transferred here in the first place?"

"Sikorsky? Sikorsky was nothing to do with me." Aleshin turned anxiously to his fellow doctors. "Zinaida, Moises, tell him – Sikorsky was Lepinov's treat…"

"And this Sikorsky – where is he now?"

"Dead. Killed in the woods. He accompanied Comrade Zvonkov and I on a mission to make contact with the Bolshevik authorities."

"You took a murderer with you to appeal to the Revolutionary government?"

"Sikorsky informed us he was a policeman and…"

"A bourgeois policeman? Why on earth would you believe that? Are you an imbecile, Comrade Doctor, or is there some other explanation you wish to offer?"

Karnivsky's eyes flicked back to the Chekists and Frumkin quickly butted in. "The fellow who came – he told us his name was Tutyshkin. We still don't know if he was fowl or fruit, but…"

The Chief Investigator regarded the *feldsher* with a certain degree of scepticism. "You did not know the identity of your own prisoner?"

"Listen – I didn't order this dish. Tutyshkin turned up on Petr's horse in uniform. We had no idea…"

"And where is this Petr?"

Yevgrafovna pushed her way forward. "Murdered," she announced, "by the very same Tutyshkin."

"Tutyshkin?"

"She means Sikorsky" said Aleshin.

"Well, maybe…"

Karnivsky rubbed the bridge of his nose. The whole thing was a barrel of tar. It would be easier just to have everybody shot and burn the place down.

"So this Sikorsky – you believe that he murdered your Chief Superintendent?"

The doctors exchanged uncertain glances. "That has yet to be proved."

Karnivsky clicked his tongue. "Yes, yes – a fine establishment you are running here. So tell me, Doctor Aleshin: why did the Yellow House purchase a bird like Sikorsky? And for a not inconsiderable sum, too."

"Lepinov authorised the transfer. As soon as I uncovered the transaction I took steps to investigate."

"Lepinov purchased his own murderer?"

"That has proved difficult to ascertain. He had dealings with a bag man, Shemiakin…"

"Mm?"

"Perhaps the deal went sour. Such criminals are leeches feasting upon…"

"Yes, yes. But why would Lepinov spread this honey in the first place – on a whim? Most peculiar, most peculiar. It is hard to decide who is madder in this place – the inmates or the gaolers. So this Sikorsky…"

"Tutyshkin" said Frumkin.

"Whoever. With whom did he arrive?"

"Ah, Yana…"

"An accomplice?"

"A horse."

"Are you playing games with me Comrade?"

"Um…"

"Tutyshkin arrived alone," said Yevgrafovna, rubbing Frumkin's back. "The Inspector informed us that the other members of his party had been killed and that Sikorsky had been wounded and fled."

"Not dead?"

"Tutyshkin was Sikorsky!" yelled Aleshin. "No one was deceived by his ridiculous charade for a minute…"

"And yet you took him with you?"

"I, ah…"

"I must say all this is extremely irregular, Comrade Doctor. And did this Sikorsky arrive before or after your Lepinov's demise?"

"After," said Yevgrafovna. "He told us that he was here to investigate it and…"

"Here to investigate his own crime!" Karnivsky gave the

slightest of smiles. "Well – a cat knows whose food he has eaten."

"Tutyshkin was no killer," said Frumkin. "Trust me, I've saddled smarter mules. Besides, he didn't meet Petr until later."

Yevgrafovna plucked Frumkin's cheek. "If Sikorsky was the murderer, then it doesn't matter when he met Petr. He may have killed him without exchanging a word…"

"If he did kill him…"

Aleshin flapped his arms. "Who else? Tutyshkin himself admitted that the ambush took place near Ryabovsky's estate. It must have something to do with why Lepinov had him brought here…"

"That's assuming it was Lepinov…"

"His signature was all over the papers. Who else would deliberately plot to store a dangerous individual in a medical facility?"

Yevgrafovna shrugged. "Maybe he believed he could cure him."

Aleshin was red in the face. "Lepinov was a counter-revolutionary figure. He owned a magic amulet. He convinced a shop keeper from Lipetsk he was the Tsar. I hardly think…"

"Okay, he acted the shaman, but underneath…"

"What, Frumkin, he too wanted to cure the mind?"

"Well, at least he didn't just keep pumping out the blood…"

The Special Investigator watched the doctors squabble dispassionately, all the time idly cleaning his boots. Why indulge these *burzhooi*? If you seat a pig, he'll put his legs on the table.

"Comrade Aleshin," he said quietly. "I repeat: do you accept full responsibility for the events which have taken place at the Yellow House?"

What would Rakhmetev do?

"I am the Chief Superintendent and as such…"

"Shoot him," said Karnivsky, and the Chekists raised their rifles. Aleshin fell to his knees.

"Comrade Investigator, I am a dedicated party member and…"

"Get the others out of the way and shoot him."

Aleshin looked wildly at his fellow doctors and then back at the Reds. Shot as a traitor, a bourgeois? Impossible.

Frumkin and Yevgrafovna lingered in front of him, uncertain as to what to do.

"Get out of the way or I will shoot you too."

Aleshin stared desperately at Karnivsky, the impassive face of the People's Justice. Yes, the fellow meant it.

"Comrade, please, please … I was given special leave by the Voronezh Central Committee to remain at the Yellow House. My code name is Zhelezin. I delivered Count Solokov into Red hands. Comrade, I beg you…"

"Count Solokov?"

"Yes, yes. My name is in the files. Without me, he would have fled to the Whites…"

Karnivsky waved at his soldiers and regarded the bourgeois doctor with distaste. "Take them back to the barn," he ordered, mildly. "We will continue our interrogation in the morning."

The Chekists advanced and transported the doctors back to the barn, Aleshin as white as milk.

Frumkin leant over and whispered in Yevgrafovna's ear. "I think Agent Zhelezin has pissed his pants," he said, pointing.

2

After the interviews, Karnivsky installed himself in Lepinov's with the intention of carefully examining the Yellow House's paperwork. It was late but Karnivsky felt no trace of tiredness; rather his nerves seemed on edge, his mind racing with suspicion and conjecture.

The Superintendent struck the Chekist commander as a particularly pitiful member of the bourgeoisie. Was Aleshin an active participant in the Bolshevik cause or a radish – red on the outside, but white in the middle? It was hard to say. Count Solokov had been hiding at an old mill near Davydovka when he had been arrested after the receipt of confidential information: alongside a Madame Aleshkya, if he recalled the affair correctly. Was this the young doctor's mother? So: he had been prepared to put party before family – or was it that he had used this betrayal to buy his way out of military service? Well, he could always be shot later on: there's always a bullet for the dog.

In the meantime Karnivksy had more pressing concerns. Just like the paperwork in Davydovka, the documentation regarding Sikorsky's transfer was a shambles. Whether this was a policy of deliberate falsification or clerical malpractice was difficult to say: nevertheless great chunks of information simply refused to make sense. Some pages referred to an anonymous swindler, arrested for disguising himself as a public official, while others clearly related to Sikorsky and the grisly nature of his crimes. In both cases, the prisoners' psychiatric reports suggested some kind of mental disturbance – though whether it was Sikorsky or the fraudster they were talking about, who could say? Stamps were scattered like chicken feed, but nothing was in order. It might as well have been filed by a bear.

Nevertheless, there was much here to think about. Maybe his earlier suspicion had been wrong. Perhaps there had been only one prisoner at Dymov's Inn, though whether or not this was Sikorsky was still unclear. What then could one know? The wagon had been attacked, its parcel escaped. Then, according to the doctors, the escapee had travelled to the Yellow House under the guise of Inspector Tutyshkin, the renowned bourgeois detective. This plainly pointed to the fake-Inspector, irrespective of Aleshin's assertions to the contrary. But then this Tutyshkin had been dispatched too: convenient for the Yellow House but more than a little suspicious in terms of his crimes.

Was it possible that someone had purchased an assassin precisely in order to liquidate the Chief Superintendent? But no – Lepinov's signature was all over the transferral like a rash. A forgery? If so, a very good one: the scrawl was identical to that found in Lepinov's files and notebooks. From this a number of secondary considerations came to mind. From whence had Lepinov secured the necessary funds to make his purchase? The deal was obviously with Shemiakin, but the capital came from elsewhere. Besides, why purchase a wild beast like Sikorsky in the first place? To cure him or use him? And what use was a murderer in a place like this?

Karnivsky ran his hands through his hair and gazed idly about the snug. Trinkets, baubles, junk. Oh, and books, books, books. Very few appeared to be legitimate scientific research: most were yellowing relics of the old world, concerned with religion, myth, all the superstitions of the Old World. From whence did Lepinov procure such trash? Karnivsky chose a tome at random and leafed dismissively through the pages. Magic circles, ancient rituals, irrational nonsense. Rather than serving the cause of the proletarian struggle, Lepinov consorted with spirits and goblins: this in itself was clear proof of his counter-revolutionary crimes. In Russia, peasants still wore magic amulets, buried dead birds under a neighbour's land as a curse. This was still a primitive country, mired in fear and false belief. Karnivsky turned to a well thumbed page and began to read.

Possession, demons, the transmigration of souls … yes, peasant gobbledygook on every line. One page spoke of the transferral of an evil spirit from one vessel to another, a second of the swapping of souls as if a spare pair of clothes. Did this Lepinov really believe that the mad could be saved through the casting out of demons? Was this why he had purchased the maniac, Sikorsky? To expel some goblin? It seemed awfully hard to believe. Karnivsky picked up a carved wooden figure and regarded it with contempt.

"Sir?" said the figure. "If I may be of assistance…"

Fortunately the voice came not from the figure but from Starchenko, lurking in the corner like an executioner.

"Yes, yes – come in Comrade Starchenko."

This Starchenko was obviously a dyed-in-the-wool reactionary – just look at his clothes! – but Karnivsky knew that servants often knew more than their masters, if only one could induce them to talk.

"So Comrade Starchenko: three murders have been committed here. Chief Superintendent Lepinov, Petr, the orderly's son, and Churkin, an … assistant?"

"Yes sir."

"And in each case there were clear signs of strangulation, blows, and bodily wounds."

"It's awful, sir"

"Although Lepinov was also poisoned and clubbed with a heavy object, while Churkin's body was hung by the neck."

"I shiver to think about it."

"And it was Aleshin who ordered that Churkin's body should be immediately buried? The same Dr Aleshin who discovered Petr's remains at the old estate?"

"It's a curious affair," whispered the *prizhivalschik*, confidentially.

Karnivsky nodded. "And this Churkin – what were his main responsibilities in the House?"

"Oh, our Ivan was a dear soul. He would do whatever was required of him. Mop the floors, fetch water from the well, and help the ladies in the *flügel* with their bags…"

"Bags? And what were in those bags, Comrade Starchenko?"

"Oh, nice things – fur coats, jewellery, paintings and the like. Almost like the old days, sir. Back when the Yellow House was here to serve the gentry, not like the rabble we have today…"

"And Comrade Churkin - he would assist the, ah, ladies and gentlemen?"

"He'd help anyone sir – not like that swine, Nikolai. No, Nikolai moaned and groaned, the bags were too heavy, his arms too short, but Churkin lugged them all the way to the monastery."

"A long way?"

"Oh, Ivan knew the tunnels, sir. Nikolai wouldn't set foot, but Ivan knew the way like a hound."

"And there are many of these … tunnels?"

"Yes sir – though of course most of them have fallen in by now."

"Tunnels – by this you mean secret passages and the like?"

"Indeed, sir. They're everywhere – worse than woodworm. But can one do? All buildings grow roots with time."

"Yes, yes indeed." Karnivsky paused and re-examined the wooden figure. "Now one of the doctors said something strange – that Lepinov had somehow convinced one of your patients that he was the Tsar."

"He does bear a great resemblance, sir. To the Tsar, I mean."

"Tsar Nicholas the second?"

"There's no other, sir."

"Yes, yes, of course, how intriguing." Karnivsky stared off into the middle distance. "Do you think you could be so kind as to bring this Tsar to me?"

"He doesn't like to leave his quarters, sir."

"No? Well, there it is. Nevertheless, I would like to speak to him. Please assure his Imperial Majesty that I bring important news and wish an audience with his munificence immediately."

"I will try and rouse him, sir."

"Good fellow."

As the *prizhivalschik* withdrew, Karnivsky swept Lepinov's books from the table. Devils, spirits, spells – the whole thing stank like a butcher's pail. That Lepinov had groomed some shop keeper to act as the Tsar's double – well, from such mad schemes, wingéd rumours flew. Was it this fake Tsar that the Cossacks they'd encountered in the forest were looking for? If so then the Cheka must be certain that this shop keeper should not fall into Denikin's hands. True, most Russians had danced with delight at the news of the Romanovs' fall, but Karnivsky knew his countrymen: give them a wink and they'd be back rubbing the Imperial arse for luck. Yes, this was the truth; a weak ruler the people devoured like dogs, while for a strong leader they kissed the stick. Karnivsky knew the Revolution could yet falter. If Mamontov's Cossacks were only two hundred miles from Moscow then the situation was even more perilous than the Central Committee imagined.

Karnivsky retrieved the fallen figure from the floor. Was this false Tsar at the root of everything? Did Lepinov somehow intend to transfer Sikorsky's spirit – or perhaps exchange their souls? Or maybe it should be phrased another way: he intended to take the demon from Sikorsky and place it in the Tsar. But for what possible purpose? To replace an idiot with a monster? To craft a second Ivan the Terrible? Ho, this was a tale even Gogol would think twice about....

As Karnivsky toyed with the figure, one of the Chekists arrived and saluted.

"Comrade Inspector? As requested, I searched the acting superintendent's apartment and found this."

Zabuty handed over the candlestick as if transferring a baton.

"I see," said Karnivsky examining the object's damaged tip. "And this was hidden?"

"No sir. On clear display in the window."

"Anything else?"

"Bolshevik literature, weights, *What is to be Done?*"

"Very good. Yes indeed." Karnivsky weighed up the candlestick as if lost in thought. "Go and take a look at the other apartments too – including that *feldsher's* and the *flügel*. Then report back to me. Nobody is to step down. The Whites are close behind us and the House is not yet secure."

Zabuty saluted and departed, leaving Karnivsky and the figurine alone.

So: our man of Iron possessed the murder weapon, but had chosen not to reveal it. Did this mean that he was the assailant? Like cats, men cover up their business. But then why leave the offending item out on display? Still, whether culprit or observer, Aleshin's actions were clearly inimical to the rational functioning of the People's State. The doctor would have to answer for his actions, no matter what connections he claimed.

Karnivsky stared at Lepinov's cognac but then rejected it: the Revolution required strong backs and clear heads. Who could say what was going on here? The walls were honeycombed with crawl-ways. Trap doors opened up like graves. Karnivsky thought of the Superintendent's remains and shivered. It was outrageous, impossible: no mortal remains could grow and swell like that. It was a crime against reason, an infringement of nature...

From nowhere Karnivsky imagined himself lost in the vast cathedral of Lepinov's festering remains, condemned to wander his entrails forever, stuck somewhere between his liver and his spleen. He pictured rotting tubes and festering meat, disease-ridden entrails and putrefying viscera. And somewhere, at the very end of some nameless, unlit passage, the vast decrepitude of Lepinov's mouldering, thoughtless brain.

"Lepinov, you dog," he whispered.

fourteen

1

What did the Reds promise? Twelve months of winter and then summer. They barked questions, yelled orders, stamped their feet, but in the end they too would leave, and Nikolai would be back to shovelling shit with no spade. Reds, Whites, Greens: these were just clouds moving across an endless sky. Down below life went on like before: fires to light, floors to mop, arses to wipe. And so on 'til the pears turned black and fell.

For now though, the Chekists were in charge. They manned the gate and eyed the gloom, leaving the *dvornik* to drink ethanol filched from the dispensary, cut with *Christy* water or something from the wine cellar. The wine cellar – nu, was that where he last saw his boots? Nikolai pictured broken bottles, Varva's teeth, something red and thick, drained from an ancient cask. Perhaps his boots were still there, standing guard over the vault and its treasures. Or perhaps they'd marched away, striding bodiless across the forests and the steppe, leaving big muddy footprints across the whole of Russia. A man can measure his worth by his boots and these were a good pair too, wooden sole and leather uppers. The devil knew where they were now – half way to Arkhangelsk, curse his luck.

Nikolai's skin was turning green, the last few teeth rotting in his skull. Even the cat could smell his stink, as if something had died inside his beard. The yardman slumped to one side, knocking over a bottle of piss. What was going on? The world sagged and swayed as if someone had sat on his hut. Eyes tight shut, Nikolai rolled back on his cot, listening to Solokha's tail banging against his chair. But no, that wasn't right. Solokha had been dead for many years – no, somebody was knocking on the front gate, the noise travelling from outside the house to the middle of Nikolai's ear. 'Well, let the Reds answer,' he thought. 'They're carrying the big stick now.' But even as he poured another finger of booze, the knocking grew louder, like a fence post come loose in his head. 'Why don't they answer?' he thought, 'afraid to open up, are they? Now they know how I feel. The fiend at the gate and his piss in my pot.' Nikolai threw his mug across the room and covered his head with a rag. Let Trotsky get off his Jewish arse: Nikolai the yardman had clocked off for the night. And all the time, bang bang bang, like handfuls of earth on a cheap coffin lid.

Picking up his lantern, the *dvornik* left the squalor of his hut and took a few steps toward the gate. Of Chekists there were none: no Lenin or Trotsky either. Where were they? Nikolai dug his nails into the fierce red pustules on his neck. A thin, cold rain fell all around, supped up by the black, thirsty earth.

"Knock, knock, knock, I hear you," he said, spitting. Then he stopped as if a black cat had passed across his path. Who was out there? That cow Motka, Little Viktor, Solokha wanting in?

"Who is it? Who's there I say?"

"It's me, Nikolai" said a soft voice. "Now open the gate."

"You?"

"Open the gate Nikolai. Open the gate and bid me come."

Was it her? But something wasn't right. The light from the old man's lantern danced across the yard. Where were the Reds, damn their boots? Why had he been left here, all alone?

"Be gone! Clear off! Lepinov's dead and in no need of callers."

No answer.

"Can't you hear? Lepinov's dead and I won't open this door

anymore…"

For a moment all Nikolai could hear was the rain. Then a voice said "Open the door, Uncle. It's cold and I need to come in."

"Dusya?" No: a man pretending to talk like a girl.

Nikolai squinted through a gap but could see nothing.

"Dusya, yes, Dusya," said the husky voice. "Now open the gate."

Nikolai pulled back the bars and held his lantern aloft: what was it? Before he could react, the thing was on him like a wolf. The *dvornik* tried to grab it but to no avail: the thing pulled the yardman's head back and slashed Nikolai's throat with a knife.

The yardman's eyes opened wide. How strange that he wouldn't have to watch the gate any more! He watched his boots climbing the stairs from the wine cellar, tramping across the yard, stepping gingerly over his corpse. Then, without even a pause, the boots left the long muddy drive and plunged dauntless into the darkness of the woods. Somewhere in there was Solokha's remains: she couldn't be far. When the boots found her, Solokha would curl up at the yardman's feet and the pair would finally get some rest. Solokha was a good dog. There was no need to yell at her, or threaten her with a stick. Such a thing was a mortal sin. Yes, thought Nikolai, blood pumping from his throat, a man who beats his dog, he's no man at all.

2

Despite his misgivings, Starchenko hobbled stiffly to the Tsar's chambers in order to inform him of the Red Commander's request. When the servant emerged from behind the mural he gave a great leap: there, sitting by the Tsar's huge desk, in his majesty's dressing gown and Turkish slippers was Tutyshkin.

"Starchenko, my dear fellow," said the Inspector. "How I wish I had been born a day earlier, so I could spend more time with you."

"Inspector?" The *prizhivalschik* looked about the apartment but could see no sign of the Tsar in the gloom.

"A bogus emperor," said Tutyshkin, leaning forward on the desk. "What a peculiar idea! You do know that the Tsar is dead, don't you? So what interest would Lepinov possibly have in growing another one?"

"I have no idea, sir," said Starchenko, his eyes darting this way and that. "Is his Imperial Majesty here, by any chance?"

"The fake one? Foo – no need to worry about him. Off passing secrets to the Germans, no doubt! Now, listen here, dear heart…" Tutyshkin pushed himself back from the desk and strode over to the *prizhivalschik* most familiarly. "I see that we have new guests at the house – Chekists, by their insignia. Now, as you know, I am always on the side of the people, but … do you happen to know what they are doing here, my dear fellow? Hush, hush, don't shake."

"'Tis hard to say, sir." Starchenko took one step backwards.

"They arrested the doctors and locked them in the large barn. One was about to shoot Doctor Aleshin but then thought better of it."

"Really? That's a shame. And the Graces? Alyona, Shiskin?"

"In their quarters, sir."

"I see. Well my friend, it seems as if Marx was right: Socialism is just around the corner."

"Ah, sir? The commander of the, ah, Cheka has requested the presence of the Tsar. Do you happen to know where I might…?"

Tutyshkin looked back at the desk and grinned. "Well, not in these drawers at least. But why are the Reds interested in our own immortal Emperor? I mean, one shouldn't be surprised, but still … well, I feel we should make ourselves scarce, dear heart. These Chekists are no respectors of standing or rank: quite the opposite, in fact…"

"But sir, I…"

"Not another word, my dear Starchenko! We must take our leave of this place: the time of Tsars is over."

Despite the footman's objections, Tutyshkin steered him back out of the Tsar's chambers, the pair tip-toeing across the yard like dance partners.

"Sir … ah, this Red captain was quite insistant. I fear that I must locate our Tsar and deliver him…"

"Shhh," hissed Tutyshkin. "The war's too close for the Reds to holiday here for long. We need to find a hole and…"

He paused. A face was looking at him, floating beneath a little lantern: Marya.

"Inspector Tutyshkin?" she breathed.

"Hush," said Tutyshkin, putting a finger to his lips. "I'm here to save the day…"

Marya looked first at the Inspector and then at the *prizhivalschik*. Then she shook her head and took the footman by his lapels. "Starchenko," she said. "Do you have keys to the barn?"

"The barn? Ah…"

"We have to get the doctors out," said Marya urgently. "If we don't then the Reds will kill them all."

"Nurse Marya I…"

Marya raised the lantern above her head. "The keys, Starchenko. Now."

Tutyshkin shrugged and Starchenko, somewhat reluctantly, obliged.

"O my sweet chick," said Tutyshkin, "let's not be hasty here."

But Marya was already gone, vanishing between the well and the thick mud of the vegetable plots. There were no guards: the Reds must have been busy searching elsewhere. Marya unlocked the barn door and shone a lamp inside. The doctors blinked back like frightened animals.

"Aleshin – Gregory," she said. "We must go."

Zinaida and Frumkin looked at her uncertainly. "Marya, is that you?"

"Yes, yes, it's me. Where is Gregory?"

Frumkin pulled a face. "You mean Agent Zhelezin? He's over there in the corner. But…"

Other shapes appeared behind her: Tutyshkin and Starchenko.

"Inspector?" Yevgrafovna and Frumkin stared at him as if at a phantom. "What on earth…?"

"Oh my darlings, the forces of law and order can never rest," said Tutyshkin with mock modesty. "How are you, my dear doctors? The Revolution treating you well?"

Behind him Polina and Nadya arrived bearing torches. "What's this dog doing here?" Polina snapped

"The devil only knows" said Yevgrafovna. "But…"

"Zinaida, Nikolai is dead and the gate is open."

"Nikolai?"

"His throat has been cut – whether by the Reds or…"

Everyone turned to look at Tutyshkin who held up his hands. "Please, please," he said. "I can only investigate one murder at a time."

"Whatever happened to Nikolai, the gate is unguarded. We must get away, hide until the soldiers have gone."

"Flee?" said Yevgrafovna. "Flee where? I don't see…"

"Into the forest maybe, or to Chulm. At least until the locusts have passed."

"Okay," said Frumkin. "I'll fetch my hat…"

"Out of the question," snapped Yevgrafovna, her hands fluttering around her like birds. "I am the senior physician here, and as such…"

"Please Doctor Yevgrafovna, they'll kill us all," said Polina.

"No, no, no," said Yevgrafovna, shaking her head. "One doesn't wade into a river without first locating the ford. I cannot abandon my patients, my tests…"

"This is our only chance, Zinaida. If not now, then the trap will snap."

The doctor shook her head. "Preposterous. What you propose is unworkable. The Cheka would find us, and in the meantime … the guests need us, Polina, as you of all people should know."

"Zinaida, Alexei is…"

"No, no, I won't go."

"Zinaida…"

"I said no."

At the rear of the barn, Marya found Aleshin curled up in a makeshift nest. When she touched his arm, he turned his face to the wall.

"Dr Aleshin? Gregory? We must hurry…"

Aleshin shrugged his shoulders like a sulky child.

"Gregory? Please Gregory, we must run."

The doctor was immobile. His golden hair seemed almost too

fine to be true, like a painting, or a doll.

"We can't tarry. The Reds will be back. They'll shoot us, Gregory."

"No," whimpered Aleshin. "No, no, no."

"I saw you. I saw what they were going to do."

"The Revolution...," said Aleshin, but then stopped.

"Gregory," said Marya, her lips almost brushing his ear. "Gregory, you must come with me. I am carrying your child. Gregory, we must flee."

Aleshin rolled toward her, his face as blank as a spade. "A child?"

"Your child."

"But..."

"Now my darling."

Marya helped the acting Chief Superintendent to his feet. "This way Gregory, we have to hurry..."

"Nadya," said Frumkin. "If the cats are busy, we have to get everybody out of the *flügel* too. Trust me – the Cheka won't just take names. Martynov, Radek, all the rest – they need to be gone."

Nadya stared at the *feldsher*'s curly head and nodded.

Frumkin smiled and opened his arms. "Nadya, you're a doll. Inspector?"

Tutyshkin winked and pulled the end of his nose. "Don't let me delay you, dear heart. I believe our dear Master Starchenko was about to show me some passage ... wasn't that right, my sweet? Some kind of secret door or some such clue..."

Starchenko looked at him uncertainly. "Sir?"

Frumkin nodded. "Okay. Zinaida, Gregory: let's meet at Ryabovskys' for dancing and champagne. Inspector: hail and farewell. Feel free to catch the murderer on your way out."

As Frumkin and Nadya snuck across the courtyard, Yevgrafovna stared out into the gloom, searching the dark for soldiers. "Polina," she snapped. "We too must see to our guests..."

Polina looked at Yevgrafovna as if the doctor too was an inmate of this place: perhaps she was.

"The guests, Dr Yevgrafovna? The guests cannot survive in the woods. It's no use. We must get out of here now."

"There's no one there. We must find Alexei."

"There's no time, we must..."

"The choice is yours, Nurse Polina: you can choose to assist me or not..."

"This is madness."

"Listen to me: I have no choice."

Polina spat and followed. What else could she do? Marya pulled Aleshin out of the door while Tutyshkin and Starchenko disappeared into the darkness and Frumkin and Nadya ran past the *banya* and toward the *flügel*. Well, to every worm its cranny. The world was full of holes, like a corpse.

3

Marya pulled Aleshin along, the doctor limp and lifeless, like a coat put on in a hurry. The rain was cold and unpleasant, slowly turning to sleet. When they reached the gate, they almost fell over the *dvornik*, his body swallowed up by the dark.

Nikolai? Yes, the yardman lay on the ground in a pool of blood, like a bottle spilled on the ground. Something black and furry supped at the wound: Varva.

Aleshin looked at the *dvornik* without truly seeing. Corpses, murders, wounds? These were more common than potatoes this year. Well, no matter: they could always plant the yardman in the earth, grow another.

"Gregory, Gregory, please…"

Aleshin shook his head as Marya pulled him out through the open gate and toward the lane of trees.

Suddenly a single shot was fired, shaking a nearby trunk. Was it directed at them? The shot came not from the house, but someplace hidden away in the gloom. Marya held Aleshin's hand as the two of them plunged headfirst into the darkness.

"Run, Gregory, run."

More shooting followed.

O, it was too much to take in: the yardman, the gun, Aleshin's interrogation. The doctor blinked his eyes. Was Marya really pregnant with his child? What would he tell Mama? And then he remembered that his Mama was dead, turned in to the Reds. Poor

Mama, poor Marya, poor Russia. What kind of father would he be? He pictured the child with strange eyes and a long black tongue: "Sasha," he mouthed.

After a while, there were no further shots, no cries, no sound of pursuit. Instead vague figures could be seen heading towards the Yellow House, soldiers by the look of them. Aleshin's head rested on Marya's shoulder. The baby lay in her belly like a soft, warm loaf of bread.

"Gregory? Gregory, please help. Pick your feet up, there, that's it. We have to get as far from the House as possible. Do you hear me, Gregory? The House isn't safe. We have to go away and hide."

Hide? Hide where? Lenin had set the torch and all of Russia was ablaze. More shots could be heard now, screaming. Yes, all of *Rus* was falling apart, the Old World swallowed up by the New. But to which did Aleshin belong? He thought about his mother's jewellery, Churkin's candlestick, his dog-eared copy of *What is to be Done?* How could they survive out here, exposed to the horrors of the forest? With a shudder, Aleshin contemplated Marya giving birth and the doctor himself conducting the delivery, yet another thing at which to fail. "Please my darling, we must go…"

The doctor took one last look at the Yellow House and nodded. Ho, even the Yellow House could fall. Time was a mystery. The leaves kept falling and the carousel continued to turn. Was somebody hiding somewhere, winding it all up with a key? But there was nothing anybody could do. There was no way to jam the mechanism, no way to jump from the seat. Nu, escape from the machine was impossible. Once set in motion, the ride would continue 'til the last gypsy sang.

Polina followed Yevgrafovna around the side of the House and toward the secret door. The special guests – did the doctor really believe she could save them? 'Twas madness: better to drown the kittens in their basket. If the Reds got wind of her experiments, Yevgrafovna would be hanging from the same branch as Aleshin.

"Doctor, doctor, please stop."

The vestibule was filled with blackness. Only when Yevgrafovna and Polina were inside did they see the heavy red door lying open.

"Polina, what on earth…?"

Protruding from the lock was a great ring of keys – Nikolai's by the look of it.

"Nikolai – the drunken fool…"

"But what would he be doing…?"

"The wine cellar: a dog always sniffs out the meat. Well, there's nothing to be done. As long as he hasn't disturbed the guests, we can still…"

From the bottom of the stairwell came a long, low moan. The two women swapped faces.

"Doctor Yefgrafovna, we cannot go down there."

"Nonsense. They're my patients and as such I have a duty to…"

"Zinaida, please listen to me. The Chekists will not be distracted for long. We must follow Marya and try to get to Chulm. If the Reds find your guests, they'll shoot us without a thought."

Yevgrafovna shook her head. "No, no, no. If Alexei is down there…"

"We don't know where Alexei is. The captain is lost, Zinaida. There's nothing more we can do. If we try to take the guests with us, we'll die."

Yevgrafovna clapped her hands in front of Polina's nose. "I cannot abandon my charges…"

"We have no choice."

"Then stay here if you must. I'll go down alone."

Polina cursed and stamped her foot. The world was a ship of fools. No good could come of this. The House would devour them all.

Nevertheless, the two women grabbed a lamp and descended. The gate to the special guests was unbarred, the way hanging open. Unfinished shapes shuffled this way and that, like shoppers at a market.

"Zinaida?"

The doctor stood still, trying to take in the scene. Had that fool of a yardman left the whole place unlocked?

"Zinaida, come back…"

The figures rocked and shook, one of them falling into another. To be honest, it was hard to work out where one ended and another of the figures began.

"Please, Doctor Yevgrafovna, please, the creatures are loose."

Creatures? Yes, the injection of rat bite fever, accompanied by transfusions of infected blood, had had a profound effect upon the patients in her care. Whatever tiny microbe had taken root during their time at the front had now grown to control their entire nervous system, like a weed running wild in rank grass. Their skin was white and smeary, their teeth falling out to leave wet holes. The figures were hairless and covered in weeping sores. Their minds? Well, who was to say? Their brains were locked up inside them like little boxes of meat.

"Alexei?" whispered Yevgrafovna. "Alexei, are you there?"

The figures rocked and swayed like old believers. At first they didn't seem to notice the doctor at all, as if fixated on another world, or at least cut off from this. Then one of the patients started to advance, shuffling forward as if reluctantly volunteering for the front.

"Zinaida, please…"

The guest made a grab for the doctor's arm and Yevgrafovna flinched. No, Alexei was not here. Alexei was not one of these things.

"Yes, yes, let's go…"

When Polina turned, she saw that other guests were behind her. They wavered and lurched. Bald heads bobbed like foul tubers, black lips peeled back. A second guest reached out to the doctor and Yevgrafovna took two steps back.

"Nurse Polina, I think we should…"

There was no way back up the stairs, the way now blocked by the things. The guests milled and shook, forming a little half circle. What was it they wanted? What more could the doctors do? Trapped, the women had no choice but to enter the darkness, one backward step after another.

"Zinaida, we…"

"There is a tunnel…"

"A tunnel?"

"A passage, here, through this square…"

Behind them the guests lined up as if at a village store. Was there food for sale, horse meat, a little sausage? One raised his hand, as if answering a question. Another began to cry.

4

Nadya and Frumkin trotted toward the *flügel*, one eye on the Reds, the other on the gate. For the moment, the way remained unguarded, but what then? Time was digging a grave, the Chekists knitting the shroud.

The businessmen, Balashov and Yurovsky were there waiting for them with coats on their backs, like Bobchinsky and Dobchinsky in Gogol's famous play.

"Is it true Frumkin? Have the Cheka arrived?"

"The Cheka, or the Angel of Death."

"No jokes, Frumkin. You swore you'd keep us safe."

As the days had gone by the two businessmen had grown more and more alike: you could have swapped their beards and nobody would have noticed. Frumkin looked from one to the other, as if at a monkey holding a mirror.

"Hey, I did what I could. The deal was with Lepinov..."

"Lepinov? Lepinov, nothing. We bought ourselves someplace to hide."

"What, I invited the Reds? We're all in the same pot you know..."

The two businessmen rounded on Frumkin, fists poking out of their jackets. "You filthy Jews, you're all the same. First you take our money, then you stick in the knife..."

"Listen..."

"Lousy *zhid*..."

Yurovsky lunged for Frumkin but Nadya clonked him on his

chin with a broom. "Get back you stinking dog…"

The *feldsher* pulled Nadya back and threw up his hands. "Okay, okay, let's all calm down. This Karnivsky is no goose. You can't just flap your arms and hope he goes away. Trust me, the Cheka don't fool easy. One look around this place and he'll see you're no crazier than the next."

At that Simonavich pushed his way forward, smacking his lips in Frumkin's face and rocking violently from side to side. "I've seen him," boomed the banker, "his head shaven as the dead."

"Seen him, seen who?"

"The Devil! Beelzebub! Satan has entered the Yellow House."

Frumkin rolled his eyes. "Knock it off, will you? The Reds won't buy this act for a minute."

Simonavich swayed uncertainly, his breath smelling of *slivovitz* and figs. "The Devil is here, Frumkin. I saw him – outside this very window! When he walked past the *flügel*, finches fell from the sky and mushrooms grew in his wake."

"Okay, okay – you sit down while I go get my medicinal mallet. What is it with this place? Anybody who goes into an asylum ought to have his head examined." Frumkin stared wildly around the *flügel*, trying to work out what to do. "Nadya – tell everybody to get their stuff and meet in the foyer. Where's Radek and Martynov?"

"Martynov, I don't know" said Nadya. "But Professor Radek, he…"

"The moment the Reds arrived the professor collapsed," interrupted Madame Pimenova, stuffing furs into a light summer bag. "He heard the news and had some kind of attack."

"Collapsed?"

"He's just upstairs, but you won't get any sense out of him. The professor's not long for this world…"

"He's collapsed?"

Frumkin shook his head.

"Forget about the Prof," snapped Balashov. "We paid you for protection, you shark. Don't think we're about to let you slither out of the deal."

"I hear you, I hear you..."

"We're telling you Frumkin, you better keep this Karnivsky away or you'll be sorry."

"I'm sorry, you're sorry, the Tsar is sorry. Okay, I'll go and see Radek. In the meantime, everyone sing the Red anthem and keep your roubles under your hats."

Balashov and Yurovsky glowered, but the two apes were the least of Frumkin's concerns. Lepinov's scheme to hide the rich and cultured of Davydovka had collapsed with the first blow. What was he supposed to do if the Cheka stared in the window? When Karnivsky checked the guest list, the *burzhoois* would be rounded up like sheep.

Madame Pimenova led Frumkin up the stairs, turning to pat him on the shoulder. "The poor professor; one of the most brilliant minds in Voronezh. I once heard him speak on St Prokopiy of Ustyag for over three hours."

"They lock the doors?"

"Such learning, such erudition. But what do the Reds care? They'll burn every last book in Russia."

Radek was in bed, his beard turning from grey to yellow to green. If anything he seemed even tinier, a wizened *homunculus* left out in the sun. Half his face had caved in, the other half puffed up like a cushion.

Frumkin entered with a flourish. "What's wrong with you, Radek? The History Department taken away your chair?"

Radek's dark eyes glittered. "Tell me Moises," he said with great difficulty, the words climbing awkwardly out of his mouth, "have I told you the story of Basil the Blessed, the greatest of all of

Russia's holy fools?"

"That I missed at *yeshiva*."

Radek's tongue licked at his stumps. "Basil wandered the lanes and fields of Russia stark naked save for heavy chains and manacles. When he came to towns he stole from shops and markets and gave goods to the poor..."

Frumkin pulled down Radek's lids, felt his glands, his pulse. "A regular Lenin..."

"It's said that when he arrived in Moscow during Lent he took a side of lamb and offered it to the Tsar." Radek's lips twitched. "When the Tsar refused, Basil told him it didn't matter whether he ate meat or not, he'd already committed so many crimes, his soul was eternally damned."

"Right. And in reply, Ivan said what?"

"The Tsar declared him a Holy Fool, and after Basil died, Ivan himself acted as one of his pall-bearers."

"Died? Died how?"

Frumkin listened to Radek's heart, and felt his side.

"As Ivan carried his coffin to the cemetery, the poor of Moscow lined the streets, holding up their ragged shoes as a mark of respect."

"Is there a point to this Radek, 'cause I'm..."

"Only the fool can speak truth to evil."

Pulling down the professor's night shirt, Frumkin nodded. "Well, evil's not listening right now". Snuggled up in the covers, the historian looked like a little old baby, spittle dribbling from his soft mouth. "Radek, can you walk? We have to get out of here. Trotsky's at the door, taking names."

Radek shook his head and grinned, his gums black and awful. "For the wisdom of this world is foolishness in God's sight. As it is written: 'He catches the wise in their craftiness.'

"Okay, but you have to help me here."

Radek reached out and patted the *feldsher's* hand. "Who can tell the foolish from the wise?"

"The wise are the ones who brought guns. That's it Professor, let's go get your shoes…"

Madame Pimenova shook her head. "You can't move him doctor. The professor is too ill. This is the last station of the cross."

"Listen, we can't leave Radek to Karnivsky."

"Our dear historian is just too weak. You look at him…"

"Foo, he's fine."

Madame Pimenova plucked Frumkin's cheek. "Doctor, with respect, you're talking like a crazy person."

Frumkin looked at Madame Pimenova then at Radek, then at the window. For a moment he didn't say a word. Then he snapped back into shape. "Wait here Radek. Don't take any wooden roubles…"

Frumkin led Madame Pimenova to one side, wrapping his arm round her shoulders. "Zise, my dove, gather your things and wait by the doors. I need to go and find Martynov. Have you seen him? He's got to disappear too."

Martynov was in one of the downstairs reception rooms, sitting with his box of make up in front of an old mirror. The actor had drawn lines on his face, whitened his hair, blackened his teeth. His moustache was dipped in flour, his eyes two black rings, as if he'd been peering through some key hole.

"Martynov," said Frumkin, "what do you think you're…"

"Frumkin?" said Martynov. "How the devil did you know it was me?"

"You or Kerensky. What do you think you're doing? This is no time for theatrics. The Cheka are at the door."

"Shhh," said Martynov, craftily. "I'm in disguise."

"Yes, as an idiot. Now listen…"

"That's right," said Martynov, smiling. "Don't you see? That's exactly my plan! When the Cheka come to check I'll blend in with the other guests. Nobody will suspect a thing…"

Martynov fished a crazy face out of the air and Frumkin sighed. "Very nice. But the Reds aren't here for psychiatric tests. First they'll shoot the doctors, then anybody not wearing a worker's cap."

"Foo – I shall disappear among the mad. Nobody will suspect a thing."

Frumkin pulled the old man's wig from Martynov's head. "Believe me, this is no time for fun and games. If the Reds find Davydovka's *intelligentsia* hiding out here then there'll be a massacre – although in your case I use the term *intelligentsia* advisedly."

"Please sir," said Martynov, using his old man's voice. "Please sir, Tom's a cold."

"Five minutes," said Frumkin. "Bring only what you need. No props or bound copies of Chekhov. Any longer and we're in our winding gowns."

In truth Frumkin didn't really have a plan. The gate was open, but could he really march his bankers and opera singers out two by two? Noah, he was not. Perhaps the rear wall might be better – across the meadow, then between the barns and the well. True, the spiked fence was a problem – but the railings were rusting to nothingness, their bars twisted and bent. Could Frumkin's motley gang of countesses, artists and lawyers scale it? Not Radek in his bed, that much was sure.

Nadya was waiting for him in the lobby, surrounded by suit cases, steamer trunks and paintings wrapped up in pigskin and brown paper.

"Where is everybody?" snapped Frumkin.

"Getting the rest of their things…"

"Things? I thought we'd sold everything to Shemiakin. How

much stuff have they got squirreled away anyway?" Exasperated, Frumkin looked at the goods: frock coats, ball gowns, a silver champagne bucket, an ornamental basin for the baptism of children. "This is no good. We aren't hiring movers. We have to get out through the bars and into the woods. This much crockery will slow us down."

"They won't listen to me," said Nadya. "They're crazy doctor, they really are."

Frumkin nodded and took Nadya's hands. "Nadya, you're a pearl, but this is it. You've got to go – save yourself. Nadyashka, don't argue, it's true. Go now before the Cheka…"

"Before the Cheka what, Comrade Doctor?"

In the doorway, Karnivsky serenely took in the scene: the bags, the scurrying guests, Frumkin escaped from the barn.

"So," said the representative of the People's Justice calmly. "What do we have here?"

This wasn't good. The Cheka could be neither paid off nor reasoned with. Frumkin had known it from the start: Karnivsky was a believer, without doubt.

"Um, here?" Frumkin said, guiltily.

The commissar's uniform was neatly pressed, his blue ribbon straight as a die. Looking at him there, surrounded by a sea of junk and refuse, one would never have guessed that it was he who was the worker, the other wretches the bourgeoisie. Yes, the world had been turned upside down. Those who were last were now first, and those who were first were about to be shot.

Frumkin looked at Karnivsky's revolver and blinked. "Are you here to help with the removals? Here, take this pillow…"

"This way doctor. You too Comrade Nurse," said Karnivsky, gesturing with his gun. "My men will sweep up the rest."

For a moment Frumkin thought about rushing him, but ach, what was the point? An eternity of darkness was coming: why start early?

"We're coming, we're coming, God forbid."

How did Engels define political terror? Needless cruelty perpetuated by terrified men. But Karnivsky did not look terrified: more like a clerk filing paperwork. Everyone had heard of both Red and White punishments, lynching, castration, eyes gouged out. Frumkin had heard of victims whose hands were placed in boiling water 'till the skin peeled off, producing perfect human gloves. Such was Russia. The night terrors of lunatics and neurotics were as nothing compared to the madness of the truth.

"Doctor…" whispered Nadya.

"Shhh," said Frumkin. "Do as the man says. Let's take a little walk."

Would Karnivsky shoot them there and then or wait for his men? It mattered little. The next world was so close Frumkin could see it bulging behind the screen.

At gunpoint Frumkin and Nadya walked out from the *flügel* and across the yard.

"Okay," said Frumkin. "I guess I ought to explain…"

"Explain what? That the sanatorium is no more than a fig leaf, a hiding place for the scum of the gentry. So, your Lepinov was hiding counter-revolutionary elements – while selling their goods to Shemiakin. Well, one hand washes the other. And what is your role in all of this, Comrade Frumkin? The instigator of the deal?"

"Me?" said Frumkin. "I'm the *feldsher*."

At that very moment machine gun fire peppered the wall behind them. Karnivsky felt a sharp sting and fell to his knees. Had he been hit? No – plaster from the wall had momentarily blinded him. Seeing their chance, Frumkin and Nadya fled, more shots echoing across the yard. Karnivsky blinked furiously, seeking cover while trying to fix his assailants. Yes – the Cossacks had followed them through the forest. The dark forces of reaction were at hand.

Amongst the gloom Karnivsky could glimpse Cossack troops entering the grounds, their red bands burning beneath the lamps. Keeping low, the Chekist moved toward the deeper blackness of the garden. To his left he could hear more machine gunfire and screams. Were the Cossacks gunning down the inmates? Ho, let the dogs slaughter their own. Karnivsky drew his revolver close and followed the path down.

fifteen

1

"Germans!" yelled Shiskin, "Germans everywhere!" When the Cossacks burst in, the cook tried to defend himself with a metal skillet, but the soldiers swiftly threw him to the ground and caved in his skull with their boots. On the stove to one side was a large pot of lung soup. A soldier tasted it and made a face.

"Any good?"

The soldier shrugged. He had a nose which had been flattened by a stick, and unhealthy, oily eyes. "Good enough."

Despite the shouts and shooting elsewhere in the House, the Cossacks put down their rifles and pulled up chairs. There was nothing to drink, but they liberated some black bread, salt, and a pot of yellow lard. The soldiers were hungry and tired. Let the others take care of the Reds; they hadn't had anything decent to eat for weeks.

"What is this place?" asked a hairy-looking fellow in a ragged sheep-coat and a black calf-skin hat. "Some kind of prison?"

"'Tis a place for the sick."

"The sick?" The soldier eyed up his soup suspiciously. At this a second soldier, an old-timer with a grey triangular beard and no teeth, grinned. "No, no – he means sick in the head."

"Oh." The first soldier placed his filthy galoshes on Shiskin's kitchen table and scratched his leg. The galoshes were in a shocking condition, held together with twine. "Is it catching?"

"No more than stupidity."

The soldier smiled like a baby. "Well – that's alright then."

Up above they could hear Shiskin's best crockery being smashed, doors pulled from their hinges.

2

When the shooting started, Nadya took to her heels and fled. Instead of retreating back toward the *flügel*, she pressed on toward the main house, ignoring the bullets and the screams. Only when she reached the dining room did she realise that Frumkin had gone the other way. But what could she do? A soldier was a soldier: each had a gun between their legs. She took the stairs two at a time, her feet quick and certain. Nadya had evaded Karnivsky's grasp: she wasn't about to leap into another pot just yet.

The door to Lepinov's quarters was open but the room was empty. No Reds, no Whites, no wolves. Nadya ran to the false wall and pressed hard. Nothing moved. She pressed again. Still, nothing. Was something holding it shut from the other side?

"Open," she hissed. "Open in the name of God."

Something was definitely blocking it.

"Please," she begged.

"Go away," whispered a voice.

"Alyona? Alyona, open the door…"

"Go away or they'll find us all…"

"Alyona, I beg you, open this door right now."

"Did you open it for me the last time the soldiers came? Find your own well to climb in…"

Nadya could hear footsteps by the stairs, a clatter of pots and pans.

"Alyona, please, they're everywhere … Alyona? Please, on your soul…"

The door opened a crack and Nadya squeezed her way in. "Quick," spat Alyona, "and don't say a word." By the light of her candle the servant girl looked strange, her freckles arranged like some kind of map.

"God bless you, Alyona."

"Shhh."

"Alyona, have you…?"

"Be quiet I say! The swine are right outside."

The women could hear movement, low voices, the sounds of a perfunctory search. Something fell over close to the wall: the book case, perhaps.

"The last time we were here," whispered Nadya. "Polina knew of another passage…"

"But it's so dark…"

"Where Lepinov used to keep his junk… Polina stayed in the corner the whole time, looking for some kind of knob… "

"Nadya, I only have one candle. Let's stay here and be quiet. If they hear us then…"

A thump right by the door. Conversation, tapping. Had they been found out?

"Alyona, it's here…"

"Nadya? Nadya, they're outside…."

"Alyona, now…"

The two women pushed their way through the opening and into a second passage. Making sure there was no one following, they swiftly closed the portal behind them.

"We must keep moving. If they found one door they can find another…"

"But my candle…"

"We have no choice."

Nadya was right. Like a mischievous imp, the candle flame started to flicker and dance. One could almost see it wink.

3

The minute the shooting started, Frumkin fled back toward the *flügel*. Was Karnivsky hit? From man's lips to God's ear. No longer by his side, Nadya had vanished like a rabbit.

"My dear doctor," cried Madame Pimenova. "What's going on? This shooting – what does it mean?"

"The Whites!" yelled one of the guests, staring out of the window, "They've come for us! We're saved!"

Frumkin closed and barred the door. "Are you crazy? Don't start skinning the hare just yet…"

One of the Chekists lay dead in the courtyard, his leg poking out at an odd angle. All around was gunfire, screams, things breaking.

"So the letter was right after all, eh Frumkin?" said Martynov from beneath his false beard.

"Martynov, listen, we've got to get out of here…"

"Out – whatever do you mean? Frumkin, the hour of liberation is at hand."

"Yeah? Well, my watch has stopped. Can't you hear? They're shooting anyone with a nose."

"Nonsense," snapped Madame Pimenova in her seal-skin coat. "It's just the Reds – prick them and they squeal like pigs…"

Other guests tried to push their way past her, but it was impossible to tell what was going on. Everything was too dark, too confusing. Cries and shouts came from all directions, while unknown figures went by, armed with axes and sticks.

"Maybe a *zhid* like you fears the Cossacks," said Yurovsky, maliciously.

"You get the welcome party ready, I'll find my hat."

"Are those flames?" asked one of the guests, pointing at the main house.

"Flames?" said the costumier, Lopukhin. "What, no – a lantern maybe..."

"No, there – smoke. And something dancing in front of it..."

"'Tis Satan!" said Simonavich, clapping his hands. "The Evil One has arrived and the time of lamentation is at hand."

"Yeah, well, I've got tickets for the Marinksy." Picking up his coat, Frumkin strode for the back door. There was nothing he could do for the Professor now. First the Cossacks strung you up, then they asked who owned the rope.

Only Madame Pimenova made any attempt to stop him. "Moises, what are you doing? Can't you hear the gunfire? We're all safer in here. The Whites come to save, not to burn."

"Tell that to the Cossacks". Frumkin shook his head. "Madame Pimenova – Zise – the game's up. If we stay here, we're finished. There might be some way out to the rear."

"Moises, you need to calm down."

"You think that's the Reds screaming for their mummies? If the House is on fire, the *flügel* will burn too."

"Frumkin, Frumkin," said Martynov, smoothing down his beard. "I'll explain everything to them: Lepinov, the deal, sanctuary..."

"You think they're going to listen to you, dressed like Gogol's madman? Trust me, Cossacks are worse than critics."

There was another hail of bullets from the women's *dacha*, and Frumkin bolted for the door, Martynov in hot pursuit.

"Frumkin, what are you doing? Frumkin, come back..."

It was tremendously dark out there, blind as a needle without an eye. The only light came from the flames licking at the outside of the Yellow House – otherwise the world was a deep, dark hole. A small black figure was hacking at a set of green shutters with an axe.

"Frumkin, stop…"

Frumkin took off between the barns and the out buildings, Martynov close behind.

"Frumkin!"

The two men skirted the edge of the allotment, stumbling over the cabbages and the beets.

"Frumkin, stop I tell you!"

The *feldsher* paused and threw up his arms. "Will you quit yelling? This is an escape, not a matinee."

The trim of a Cossack gown could be seen by the barns, along with the red of a hat. Everything seemed to come and go in flashes. The meadow was very wide and very boggy. It seemed inconceivable that the two men would ever cross it.

"Moises, come back. This cannot end well."

"Nothing ends well – that's why it's the end." Panting like a sick dog, the one-time mind doctor squinted at the gloom. "What do you think? This way, past the *banya*?"

"This is madness old friend: let's head back to the *flügel*. Those Cossacks aren't such bad fellows. I played one once – Severyanin in *The Axe and the Pine*. I wore a very tight tunic, and this lady friend of mine, she…"

"Martynov, I'm going now…"

Frumkin could see shapes moving through the ink, letters in a language he could not read. What is it, he thought: Hebrew?

"Frumkin, Frumkin," yelled Martynov. "Wait for me, I'm in character…"

The shot whizzed somewhere just about Martynov's fake pate.

The two men threw themselves to the ground and lay head first in the dirt.

"Was that a bullet?"

"Not a garland."

Slowly, carefully, they crawled their way forward. Something black and solid was just ahead.

"What is that thing? Lepinov's car? Quick get in…"

Frumkin climbed in the passenger's side, Martynov driving.

"What do you think?" asked Marytnov. "Can we get this thing started?"

"Sure, sure," said Frumkin. "You hold the Cossacks off and I'll start cranking…"

In the mirror he could see the shadows of soldiers against the flames of the Yellow House. Ah, if only the car would go! A mouse had made a nest in one seat and moss covered the gear stick.

"Maybe we should have taken Yana," said Martynov with a sigh.

"I'm not sure she could jump the wall."

Behind them, soldiers advanced, cocking their rifles.

"Well, what now?" asked Martynov, plucking a snail from the wheel.

"Now? Petrograd and step on it. I've booked a table for seven and you know Saburov – he'll never hold it."

Bullets whistled through Lepinov's car as if through cheese. One penetrated the upholstery, a second Frumkin's skull.

"Saburov's?" said Martynov, pulling a comic face. "I'd sooner eat from a pail…"

The second burst of rifle fire killed the actor instantaneously. Fortunately, the maestro completely failed to notice. In his final moments, even the gunfire sounded like applause.

4

The candle created its own tiny halo, Alyona's head glowing like a miracle. The corridors smelt of mould and stale air. Once in a while, rats could be heard, packing.

"Why ever did we come this way? This passage will never end…"

"Would you rather wait for the soldiers? Polina was right – all men are beasts."

Five steps down, then three steps up: nothing about this place made sense. Some walls were hewn from rough stone, while others were smooth and dusty. Several openings were in fact painted shadows, others locked doors of awkward height. There seemed no plan, no purpose. Where were they now? Half way to Finland or just outside the *banya*…

"What's that, gunfire?"

"The Tsar coughing. Alyona, come on…"

The candle was low, the flame uncertain. Their foot steps seemed duplicated, as if their shadows had four legs, not two. The darkness was like a great black wall, a new block lowered into place with every step.

"We're going the wrong way, this isn't right…"

"Shhh … when it's all over we can say hello to the sun…"

"Sun? There is no sun. The Reds abolished it."

In truth the passageway did seem a little narrower, Alyona's skirt filling it like a napkin in a ring.

"It's cold. My feet are sore. Who'd live in a place like this? Only the dead."

As they turned a corner, the candle abruptly sputtered and went out. Before the women could react, darkness pounced.

"Light it, light it, what are you doing?"

"Light it with what – a wish?"

Oh, the two women had escaped a snare and fallen into a pit. The darkness seemed to possess weight, mass, physical dimensions. What a terrible place! Nothingness lay on them like snow.

"Nadya, Nadya, are you there?"

"I'm here Alyona. Give me your hand."

"Nadya, what is that thing?"

"My hand. Take it, Alyona, please…"

Nadya heard movement and stopped.

"Nadya, where are you?"

"I'm here, holding your hand."

"But if you're here, who's that?"

Alyona was right: the two women weren't alone. Other feet wandered the maze, their footsteps distant then suddenly close, as if somebody had folded the vault up into a ball.

Nadya spat. This dungeon was worse than a trap, the footsteps closer now, like the space between twilight and the night.

"Alyona?"

A glow, shadows. Nadya wanted to scream but couldn't find her tongue. Suddenly the spirits of Polina and Yevgrafovna materialised before them, the two figures dipped gold as if in tallow. Ghosts? No, 'twas the real nurse and the doctor, though in the light of Polina's lamp, both seemed aged, as if they'd been wandering these halls for years.

"Polina! Comrade Doctor!"

"Nadya, Alyona, is it you?"

Or perhaps it was not so strange after all – simply that the four women had sought sanctuary in the gloom. Nadya told them about the shooting and the soldiers, Polina about the escape of the guests. Yevgrafovna was uncharacteristically quiet, glancing over her shoulder as if listening to some kind of rustling in her head.

"Doctor? Zinaida?"

"I thought I … I … I don't know."

But Yevgrafovna did know: Alexei was down here too, and not so far behind.

"What of the others, what happened?"

Polina shook her head. "We heard shooting, running. It's impossible to say…"

"But the soldiers – who are they? Whites? Bandits? More Reds?"

"Why would Reds shoot the Reds?"

"Didn't the Bolsheviks shoot the Socialists?"

"Give a man a stick and he'll start looking for an eye. We're better off down here. Death's busy enough as it is."

"Did you see Marya? Running off with Aleshin…"

"Aleshin? She might as well tie herself to a log. Take my word for it, the doctor's a fool…"

Throughout all of this Yevgrafovna remained strangely silent; instead of criticising or issuing orders, she hung back in the gloom, anxiously looking behind her and cocking her head like a dog. Not that there was anything to see, of course; as soon as Polina's lantern moved along the passage, the darkness rushed in to fill it.

"Doctor Yevgrafovna, you must keep up…"

"There's something … something I can't…"

"Please Doctor, you must stay with us…"

Were those her lover's foot steps? She imagined Alexei wading through the ink, his black tail following close behind.

"Doctor, please, what's wrong?"

Yevgrafovna's eyes skittered from side to side.

"Alexei, he … "

"We can't stay, we must go."

"Alexei, he's there…"

"Now, Comrade Doctor, now – Zinaida, are you crying?"

"It's Alexei…"

"Stop it, Zinaida, stop it. What's the use of crying? Wait and see what happens. Then we can cry."

The evening of Lepinov's murder, Alexei – Captain Voskresensky – had seemed almost well. His skin looked healthier, the lesions healing. True, without teeth his face seemed to have caved in (a condition not helped by the box squeezing his skull) but his eyes demonstrated sentience, and his expression was calm. Yevgrafovna stroked Alexei's cheek and ran her hands over his chest.

"Alexei?"

His features were kind, his mouth twisted into a vague half-smile.

"Alexei, how do you feel? Any pressure, encephalitis? Can you focus on my face?"

The dashing captain twitched.

"Do you feel dizzy, nauseous? Are you in cognitive control of your bowels?"

Six hours earlier Yevgrafovna had administered her final vial of rat fever poison, the elixir carefully preserved from Moscow, and mixed with the remains of an injured soldier's blood. Where the rest of her supply had disappeared to, she had no idea. Nikolai had been known to prowl about the wine cellar – perhaps he'd pinched them on a spree? Whatever the case, Zinaida's thesis was clear. Madness was a bacterial infection, caused by an almost imperceptible worm: only fever could kill the organism responsible, thereby purging the body of its unwelcome guest. The greater the degree of infection, the closer to the surface the alien entity: to save Alexei it was necessary to take him to the very edge.

"Alexei, are you in possession of your faculties?"

His fingers touched hers, latching onto her knuckles like a baby. Everything about him seemed to express an earnest longing – to be released from The Tranquilizer, if nothing else.

The doctor untied the restraints and started unscrewing the box from his head. Alexei's hand moved from Zinaida's hand to her breast. His breathing increased – hers also. Awkwardly, the captain rose to his feet, searching the box for his nose.

"What is it? Are you experiencing discomfort?"

His body jerked painfully, folding in on itself like paper.

"Alexei?"

No answer.

Zinaida pulled back, her hands patting air. Alexei buckled and slumped, a foul stench coming from his mouth: fish, bile, something peaty. Zinaida backed away. Perhaps it would have been better to have waited for Polina after all.

Rocking violently, Alexei threw up his arms as if attempting to clap: for a terrible moment Yevgrafovna felt certain she could spy his nose growing longer, glimpse whiskers sprouting from the side of his face. His claws were sharp and dirty, his face a lunatic's drawing of a mouse. What was it the Reds called the bourgeoisie? A rat with two legs.

"Alexei?"

The captain crouched as if ready to jump.

"Alexei, what on earth…"

The thing made a grab for her and then all around went black.

When Zinaida awoke, she was lying on the cell floor, the other guests looking down at her impassively. There was no sign of Alexei. Yevgrafovna touched her head and felt a gash – painful, but by no means life threatening. The important thing was to retrieve Alexei before Lepinov found out. The Chief Superintendent's neglect could only be pushed so far.

The red door was still closed, the gates to the special guests securely barred. But where was Alexei? Unless he was still here, of course, watching her from the shadows...

Lamp in hand, she ventured a little further toward the back of the room. There she found baskets of bandages, a slop bucket, a pan containing old pieces of rag. The chamber smelt of idioform and damp. And then, by a soiled rug and a coil of old rope, she saw it – a perfectly black square, not some kind of shadow or a stain, but an absolutely symmetrical shape, a black square in a black frame, like a futurist provocation. Was it a door, a portal? She held her lamp up toward the blackness but could see nothing beyond: no passage, no opening, no reflection. The square seemed cut out of space, as a fissure might be cut out of stone. The doctor took a series of small steps toward it, stretching out her hand. The square neither grew nor shimmered. Then, just as she was about to take one more step, she heard Polina calling out her name some place above her. Cursing, Yevgrafovna turned her back on the square and returned to the stairs.

"Yes, yes, I hear you," she snapped. "No, no, nothing has changed. Everything is perfectly alright. There's no need to carry out any more tests tonight. Polina, are you listening? I told you, you can go..."

Alone in her room, the doctor tended to her wound and tried to re-arrange events into a more reasonable pattern. Alexei was not a mouse. The black square was some kind of secret tunnel, not a diabolical icon. Everything else was an illusion and a fantasy. The important thing was to retrieve the captain and quietly close down her project. Surely such a thing could be achieved without too much fuss or attention; Lepinov was busy with his own schemes and scams, the other doctors too dense to notice. Besides, the hidden soldiers could easily be substituted for some of the guests killed by typhus – at least if the nurses agreed to co-operate. Polina was loyal: she would have to convince the others. The only person who would raise a stink was Aleshin – the truth regarding her experiments would have to be carefully hidden from the young pup at least. Otherwise, she had few concerns. The situation in the country was chaos. The families of the soldiers no doubt believed they had perished long ago.

Just then she heard an incoherent yelling right outside her window. Nikolai, no doubt: the yardman's veins ran with booze. Had he really drunk away her stash of infected fluids? Well, let it pickle him, then. But then a second thought crossed her mind: what if it were not Nikolai but Alexei roaring at the night?

Yet to undress, Yevgrafovna retrieved her lantern and made her way carefully down into the yard. No, no one. She peeked in the yardman's hut, but the scoundrel looked asleep, an empty bottle of *eau-de-cologne* by his side. But who on earth had been out carousing? Or had those been Alexei's cries after all?

Yevgrafovna returned to her room but could not sleep. She hid the wound beneath her hair and burned the photograph Alexei had given her of him as a young man, the one showing the dashing young captain with the sweep of dark hair, Alexei and his uniform, taking the air in Yalta. Then she waited for it to grow light. What would she say to Polina? Nu, the nurse would understand. Polina had assisted in all her experiments. She would help to find Alexei too.

She told Polina of Alexei's escape two days later: it was simply impossible to keep it from her any longer. The nurse paled, but immediately agreed that the situation should be kept from Aleshin. The doctor was a fanatic: he would have them all turned over to the Red authorities and then locked up. No, better to keep the cat under one's hat. The truth about what had happened was impossible to say. The answer, as so often in these parts, was to bury the bones as deep as possible.

"Doctor Yevgrafovna, please, we have to hurry…"

"Hurry?" said Alyona. "Hurry where? The stopper's in the bottle and we'll never see daylight again…"

"These passages lead all the way to the old monastery," lectured Polina. "If we can make our way out and then into the woods we should be safe."

"Safe from whom? The Reds or the Whites?"

"Safe from men."

Was Alexei the killer? When she'd heard of Lepinov's murder that very same evening – and when the cage of The Tranquilizer had been found atop Lepinov's nut – she had thought of him. But why should one and one make two? Perhaps Alexei had removed the box and somebody else had found it. Who? O, what difference did it make? Polina was right. All men were killers. You just had to hand them a knife.

sixteen

1

Two Whites guarded the gate: Karnivsky shot one in the neck and the other in the throat. Elsewhere, gunfire echoed around the estate – the Cossacks liquidating the guests, most likely. Behind the Chekist, glass broke and straw caught fire. It was true: the era of the Yellow House had come to an end.

From the gate, Karnivsky took the pilgrim's road toward the old monastry, his boots sinking deep in the muck. With every step the captain stumbled and slipped, scrabbling from rut to puddle to mire. A cold foulness coated the Chekist's feet, the mud pulling at him like a curse. Were any Whites following? No, it was too dark, impassable by horse. Besides, the Whites were busy with the House: if he could make it to the ruined cloisters then he would be safe.

Time itself had become stuck in the ooze. The Chekist struggled forward, but the monastery seemed sunk beneath the earth. The darkness was total now, a thing. Was all the world a grave? Karnivsky fell to his knees, careful to keep his revolver above the sludge.

When his boots finally found solid rock, Karnivsky pulled himself ashore like a sailor striking land. It was too inky to make out any of the church buildings, but he could trace walls, rubble, ruins, the bare bones of the world. Plucking his boot from the mud Karnivsky heard a satisfying plop followed by a single gunshot, close but muffled – under his feet, perhaps. The captain crouched

350

by a slab and waited. Silence. But then he saw it: light from a lantern, shadows swaying at the bottom of a long flight of stone stairs. Was this the way to the famous well? Perhaps. But who might be collecting *Christy* water at this time of night?

Revolver in hand, Karnivsky made his way down beneath the ground. The steps led down to a round, sandy grotto, St. Leonilla's spring in the centre, a nattily dressed corpse lounging to one side: Starchenko?

Eyes focused on the gloom, Karnivsky made his way toward the stiff. A pinkish star stained the *prizhivalschik*'s shirt, the old man killed by a single shot to the chest. Beyond the circle of light cast by the oil lamp, Karnivsky could see nothing. So the ancient retainer had been killed at the very same place as the Superintendent: how strange. The commander looked down into the well as if expecting to see Lepinov's remains gazing back at him. But no, nothing: though of course the lamplight did not extend so very far. Then Karnivsky sensed movement behind him. Turning around he saw a bald-headed figure dressed in black, arms outstretched as if about to push the Chekist in.

"Stop right there," said Karnivsky, pointing his barrel at the shaven man. "Stop, I say."

The figure halted.

"Identify yourself immediately."

"Me?" said the figure with mock innocence. "Why, my name is Tutyshkin – Inspector Tutyshkin of the detective. Do you have any bandages, my dear fellow? I'm afraid my friend here has been hurt."

The figure moved toward Starchenko but Karnivsky pushed him away.

"Hands in the air. Now back away from the body."

Tutyshkin shrugged. "The poor dove was shot as we made our escape." For the first time the Inspector seemed to take in the

Chekist's cap and uniform. "Ah, from the Whites, I mean."

Karnivsky glanced at the prone functionary: dead as a stone.

"And you dragged him all the way here?"

"Shhh," said Tutyshkin, "don't tell anyone, but there's a passage which leads all the way to the Yellow House." The Inspector glanced in the direction of a large black square. "I know, I know – it's like something from a delicious mystery!"

Karnivsky turned from the dead servant to the bald stranger.

"Your gun, Inspector."

"Ah…"

"Now."

With a gentle smile Tutyshkin delicately removed the revolver from his smock. "Liberated from the Whites, my angel. Purely for self protection, you understand…"

Tutyshkin watched the bald goose intensely: *this* clown was Tutyshkin? Or rather the lunatic who called himself by that name. Shadows from the lantern played across the bald man's head, as if one could see his thoughts moving inside. Karnivsky pointed his gun at his temple.

"So which are you?" asked the Chekist, calmly. "The famous Inspector Tutyshkin or the famous murderer Sikorsky?"

"Darling?"

"Or is there even a difference? First you kill the lad in the ruins then this … servant."

Tutyshkin's lips twitched. "Dear heart, you've got me all wrong. My name is Inspector Tutyshkin, dispatched here to solve the murder of Chief Superintendent Lepinov. Indeed, the good doctor was killed in this very place…"

"Ah, really."

"Yes, yes, it's so exciting! A peasant girl poisoned him, mixing mushrooms and herbs with his potions – but then something came out of the dark and pushed him down the well … a demon or somesuch thing…"

Karnivsky winced: this had been nonsense from start to finish. Was there any reason to allow this lunatic to live?

"A demon, you say. This sounds awfully fantastical, Comrade Tutyshkin."

"Well, demons, spells, magic charms … the peasants are such colourful characters aren't they?"

Karnivsky stared at the Inspector as if at a fish on a hook. Was any of this true? The part about the peasant girl, perhaps. So all the time Lepinov was busy cooking up his magic potions, some bitch was secretly poisoning him – poetic justice, indeed. But what happened when Sikorsky failed to appear? Did the girl somehow lure Lepinov to the old monastery? Did she tell him she'd found the killer someplace wandering in the woods? Ah, it was impossible to know. But this was the place where Lepinov was killed. By the girl? By Churkin? Or by somebody else entirely?

"And why would some peasant girl plan such a thing?"

"One of Lepinov's lunatics murdered her brother. Afterwards he locked up her mother and she died: the Devil knows exactly how." Tutyshkin shrugged. "In my experience, girls take such things to heart. And so the Superintendent came to his bitter end…"

"I see," said the Chekist, his gun never waivering from Tutyshkin's skull, "And after Lepinov's demise?"

"The girl fled back to Chulm. As for sweet Ivan – ah, who knows? Perhaps he belived that the demon had entered him and he took his life in order to save the others – or perhaps this was just what the girl told him, a way of removing him from the picture, as it were. She was an awful cunning girl, you know."

"Was?"

The two men stared at each other as if trying to work out which one was real and which the reflection. Karnivsky tightened his finger on the trigger. Tutyshkin winced. From the tunnels beyond the black square came a vague sound of movement, a faint scraping, something dragging its leg along the ground. Sikorsky? Orlov? Or were these words for something else?

"And what of this candlestick, Inspector – the one used on Superintendent Lepinov's roof?"

"Candlestick?" Tutyshkin shrugged. "You've lost me there, my angel."

"The candlestick retrieved by Aleshin. The one which connected with Lepinov's skull."

"I'm afraid I know of no candlestick, Comrade Captain. Perhaps it was Churkin's, and it accidentally collided with Lepinov's noggin in the struggle – or perhaps the demon grabbed it from Sweet Ivan and did the deed itself?"

"Demon," snarled Karnivsky. "There is no demon. No Sikorsky. No monster loose in the tunnels…"

Tutyshkin arched his eyebrows. "Well … ah, Comrade Captain, can you hear something?"

"So why don't you tell me, what really happened down here…"

"Comrade, there's something…"

"No demon, but a man…"

"I can definetly hear…"

"Be quiet, damn you!"

A foul, pestilent smell emanated from the square, as if something terrible had expired in a deep, wet ditch.

"But Captain, it's here…"

Karnivsky turned his revolver in the direction of the tunnel just as Tutyshkin knocked over the lamp. The cave was plunged into darkness, as if the last light in the universe had been blown out.

"What?"

For a moment, time itself seemed to halt. There was silence and nothingness, neither life nor death; 'twas as if existence itself were suspended, Karnivsky floating in an endless, inky pool. Was the Inspector still here? Starchenko, the well, the monastery? If such a thing were not both empirically and ideologically impossible, the Chekist would have sworn that the universe had come to a sudden and irreversible full stop. But no, this was no more than a primitive fear of the dark. 'Twas just the lantern that had gone out, its flame extinguished: everything else was madness.

Karnivsky felt the knife enter his throat even as his finger tensed on the trigger. Was he dead? Yes, yes, he was. Somehow the sensation of extinction had preceeded the actual act – some kind of mistake, perhaps. But now it was over. A long black pen had removed the Chekist from the ledger, the same black pen that obliterated all names, crossing them out from the Holy book of Life. Scrape, scrape, scrape went the pen. Or was the sound coming from somewhere else?

2

The four women – Polina, Nadya, Zinaida and Alyona – made their way cautiously along the tunnels, the light from the lantern fickle and uncertain. The roof here seemed lower, the air slightly colder – but was this a good sign or no? The corridor turned right and then looped back left. Finally Polina discovered a passage which, for once, ran straight. Suddenly Polina stopped. She recognised the thing blocking the exit right away – a naked man.

Her first thought was that it was Tutyshkin; only when she edged closer did she realise it was, in fact, the Chekist officer Karnivsky, a knife in his throat and his uniform removed. Well, that was no shame – no angel would cry tears over the Chekist's grave. Next to him lay Starchenko.

Alyona gasped. "Who…"

"Starchenko. And the Chekist."

"But…"

"Stay there."

Polina reached down and examined the Chekists's wound. Did it mean that the Whites had been here or not? Polina started to make the sign of the evil eye, but then stopped - what was she, a peasant? Starchenko had been shot – presumably by Karnivsky – but no murder weapon could be found. But if Karnivsky had killed Starchenko, then who had killed Karnivsky? And was the murderer still around?

"Doctor Yevgrafovna – Zinaida – what do you think?"

The doctor glanced at the two bodies and then back at the large black square, like a space cut out from the world.

"So this is where Lepinov was murdered..." she said slowly.

"Well, yes, but Starchenko..."

"His body dropped to the bottom of the well."

Polina regarded her strangely. "Doctor Yevgrafovna, please..."

The doctor squeezed Polina's hand without looking. Alexei was somewhere behind them in the darkness, delirious and lost, half way between this world and the next. Had he killed the Red? Had he killed Lepinov? It didn't matter. What did another murder matter after all?

"Zinaida, please..."

Alexei had emerged from the tunnel disorientated and semi-conscious, whereupon he had somehow surprised Lepinov and Churkin: what the two of them were doing at the well, heaven knows. There was a struggle. At some point Lepinov was struck by Churkin's stick. But then? How did Lepinov wind up down the well? And why was Alexei's box atop his head?

"Zinaida, we can't stay here."

Did Churkin accidentally kill Lepinov and then take his life in remorse? But if so, why on earth would he place the Tranquilizer upon Lepinov's skull? And what then happened to Alexei? No, there was somebody else here, Yevgrafovna was sure of it, some darker power directing events.

"Zinaida, you must stay with us," said Polina, taking the doctor's hand. Outside a pale, ugly day was hauled out of the grey sky, the rain turning to sleet. Nadya paused. Smoke still rose from the remains of the Yellow House, and the sound of horses and men carrying on the wind.

"What do we do?" asked Nadya. "The soldiers are still out there. If they find us, then..."

"It will be fully light soon," said Polina. "We have to reach the village of women before then. The gloom will help us – who would search the woods in weather like this? We have to go before the soldiers sniff out our skirts. It's no more than a morning's journey. When we get to Chulm, we can ask the peasants for aid."

"The peasants?" said Alyona. "Why should they help us? If the Red's dead, that means that the Whites have already searched this place. The monastery's a better place to hide. The Cossacks won't stay for long."

"How do you know it was the Cossacks who killed them?" said Polina. Nadya peered out at the cold, grey wetness. Dirty snow covered the earth like plaster. "The killer may still be here, hiding the same as us. You want to bury yourself inside these tunnels? I'd rather take my chances in the woods. At least there you can feel the wind blowing on your bones."

Alyona glanced back at the passage and trembled. No, she did not want to be covered all the way up to her head.

"But the doctors," said Nadya, "Marya…"

"If they've any sense, they'll have fled too. Nadya, don't worry. When we get to Chulm, our heads will work better. Zinaida? Zinaida, what are you looking at? This way doctor, come".

The women made their way along an avenue of dead larch trees, crossing where stones formed a bridge over a deep bog. The mud here was awful: liquid on top, filth in the middle, harder muck down below. Above them the sky unfurled like a parchment, though whether auguring good or ill, 'twas impossible to say.

Instead of following the ridge back toward the Yellow House, the Graces, Alyona and the doctor made their way down a steep ditch toward the meadow. The women slipped and sunk, black mud trying to take hold of their ankles. What an awful place! Behind them the monastery lay collapsed like a fallen drunk.

When the women finally reached the birch wood, the land was

gloomy and silent. At first the trees were spread out like teeth on a pitch fork, but after a while they started to close rank, tall, grey birches, so close together the women had to form a chain. It was almost like being back inside the tunnels again – a labyrinth without end.

"Wait," hissed Alyona. "What's that thing?"

"Nothing," said Polina, "it's nothing."

"No, no," said Alyona. "Just there. I can see something, I swear."

"It's nothing. A bird, maybe."

"Not a bird. More like a man."

Polina shook her head. "You're seeing things. There is no man. Doctor, doctor, please keep up…"

In truth, Polina too sensed the presence of something following them, not 'over the hill and far away', but just around the bend, invisible and unknowable, like a needle without thread.

"There's something out there…"

"Alyona," said Nadya, "stop…"

"I can feel it."

"Alyona, please…"

Snow dripped on the trees like paint. It was cold and the women were badly dressed for a hike. Zinaida lost a shoe in the mud and Polina had to go back for it.

Suddenly everybody jumped; they could hear the sharp report of gunfire, somewhere back toward the House. Hadn't the Cossacks finished their killing yet? Then they heard three flat shots, like an execution. Nadya and Polina exchanged glances, but said nothing. What was there to say? After a while, a bird started singing, and the women rested by a clump of dandelions, nettles and chickweed. There was no sign of any path, never mind the post road. Chulm felt like the opposite end of the earth.

"I'm tired," complained Alyona. "I need to rest, to sleep."

"We must keep going," said Polina, "put some distance between us and the men."

"Polina, look at my shoes, look at my feet... we must rest, for the love of God."

"We can rest in Chulm."

"There is no Chulm. I need to rest here."

"This is nonsense."

"You go on. My feet have stopped."

Polina stared at Alyona with open loathing. It was only when she glanced around the clearing that she noticed Yevgrafovna was no longer with them.

"Zinaida? Doctor? Nadya, have you seen her?"

"She was here a moment ago..."

Polina marched up and down the dell yelling "Doctor! Doctor, where are you?"

"I swear Polina, she was right here..."

"Doctor, Doctor Yevgrafovna, can you hear me?"

While Nadya and Alyona looked on, Polina retraced her steps toward the trees.

"Doctor, where are you?"

The trees were still and dark. Blobs of wet snow slipped through their branches, like droppings. No birds, no animals. No doctor of psychiatry, either.

"Zinaida, we're over here!"

Polina plunged deeper into the forest, zig-zagging erratically from side to side. The leaves said autumn, but the sky said winter. Yevgrafovna was nowhere to be seen.

"Doctor, doctor – where are you?"

And then she saw her – still as a pillar, staring off into the far distance like a sailor searching for land.

"Zinaida, Zinaida," said Polina, panting. "Zinaida, where were you, what are you doing here? When I turned around you were gone. Zinaida, please, you must come back with us. *Milaya*, please, what is it?"

"I saw him," said Yevgrafovna. "Alexei. I saw him quite distinctly. He's still following me, Polina. I saw him amongst the trees."

"Doctor, please…"

Polina took her by the arm and caressed her back.

"I saw him and he saw me. He even raised an arm! He's still coming Polina. He's not done yet."

"Alexei? Yes, yes, yes. Now you come back with me, dear doctor – perhaps Alyona is right and we do need to stop, just for a little while."

As they turned Polina scanned the tree line and squinted: no guest, no captain. But she too could sense something watching, not here, but there, as close as the space between head and hat, as close as a blade and death.

"Doctor, I beg you, come…"

Zinaida smiled a thin smile, but it was bitter, bitter…

3

While the women walkd the tunnels, Marya and Aleshin spent the night huddled like kittens beneath the remains of an old dead tree. Marya dreamt about the baby, Aleshin about his mother. In the morning Marya had to get up to go and pass water. She returned covered in a light dusting of white.

"The rain is turning to snow," she said.

Aleshin nodded.

"Do you need to … go?"

"I went earlier."

"Did you?"

Aleshin said nothing.

"Doctor, Gregory, are you sick?"

"Sick? Whoever heard of a Russian getting sick?"

Marya gently touched Aleshin's shoulder, but he immediately turned away.

"Gregory, we have to get as far from the House as possible. The Whites will kill everyone. We must decide whether to head toward Chermavka, or the railway line. Chulm is too dangerous – the Cossacks will be there too. Gregory, are you listening? The Yellow House is gone. We need to make haste."

Aleshin shook his head. The Cossacks didn't seem real – more like something out of a dream. Besides, it was politically impossible that Denikin's forces could have advanced this far North: history was against them. The proletariat, the peasants and the party were united in the Revolutionary vanguard – plus, the roads were very poor. Most likely these so-called 'Cossacks' were no more than a gang of bandits and thieves. Both looted and killed – like all the forces of reaction.

Marya walked back to the stump and took Aleshin's hand. His hair stuck out in tufts, specks of mud spattering his glasses.

"Gregory, it's cold and wet and there are soldiers everywhere – we can't survive out here for long. Please Gregory, please … we need to think about ourselves now, about the baby…"

Aleshin looked at Marya and blinked. The nurse's features were crude and heavy, her skin the colour of sour cream. From her apron she produced a crust of bread made from rye flour and flax seed. He took it from her, read it as if a letter, and then handed it back.

"You eat it," he said. "For the baby…"

"Gregory, I…"

"You need to guard your strength. Here, let me help. " He held a broken branch over her like an umbrella.

"Nutrition is a very important factor – a Socialist child needs to be healthy and strong."

"I…"

"This child will be an important servant of the proletariat. We must do everything in our power to protect and nurture it in accordance with the building of a collectivist state."

"My angel," said, Marya, smiling.

The pair picked their way southwards between the trees, sheltering from the weather as best they could. The sleet fell in soft unpleasant lumps, the trees watching craftily. What did Aristotle call trees – men daydreaming? Well, perhaps. There was no frost yet; the leaves were wet and slippery rather than crisp. The smell of damp earth felt unbearably sad.

"Do you think it will be a boy or a girl?" asked Marya, seeking out Aleshin's hand.

"Hm?"

"Our baby – a boy or a girl?"

"A boy."

"A boy? Why yes, that's..."

"A little boy. I'll take him to the park for a balloon and ices."

"Oh yes! He would love that!"

"He'll look at the monkeys and the birds and then I'll put him on the carousel and he'll ride a horse called Sasha."

The doctor's expression was a little strange but no matter: for Marya it was pleasant to hear him talk about something other than the workers' indomitable will or the stout heart of the people. Yes, Gregory would be a good father: kind and strong and wise. Marya's own papa had been a drunkard, slow to talk but swift to turn to the whip. Aleshin would be like the village priest, a learned gentleman, filled with grace.

"Yes, yes, nutrition is an important factor, and ... Marya, Marya, are you crying?"

"No," she whispered, "just happy".

After a while they came upon a rough kind of path, cut logs laid over the worst of the mud. Aleshin held Marya up as she made her way across a trunk, her feet wobbling from side to side; Marya's shoes were made from saddle leather, their soles coming loose from the sides. Yes, Marya was a genuine representative of the toiling masses of the proletariat: whatever would his mother say when she saw her? And then he remembered – Mamoshka was dead and buried in the rich, black earth. The thought seemed as nonsensical as the Cossacks. Everything seemed to be slipping away from him now. He couldn't think what to do. Marya hopped down and kissed Aleshin on the lips.

"I want to make love to you," she whispered shyly, "I want to feel you…"

Still thinking of his mother, Aleshin looked at the nurse strangely. "Mm? Well, ah…"

"Oh not here," she laughed, "not now…"

The sleet was turning back to rain and Marya shivered.

"You're cold, you're wet. We must rest."

"Oh Gregory, I'm…"

"For the baby."

In truth, the doctor also felt close to collapse. He remembered how he'd felt in the forest after the ambush, and a fresh wave of despair rose up inside him. But he was with a woman now and women had always looked out for him – it was their nature, their meaning. To one side a crude shelter had been fashioned from branches and an old sack – a tramp's dwelling perhaps. He settled in beside Marya, then realised she seemed to be expecting something.

"I'm hungry," she said. "Do you think you could find some berries, something to eat?"

Aleshin looked out at the forest somewhat doubtfully.

"I need to rest a while … for the baby."

"What? Oh yes, of course…"

The doctor climbed to his feet and stumbled back out into the wet. Food? He had no idea. But he was to be a father, a parent… He paused. Wasn't the family a bourgeois idea to be discarded by the new age? Well, no matter. Socialism was the stage leading to Communism. The Red Dawn would come soon enough.

The doctor ran into the soldiers just the other side of a bog. One had just taken a dump and was clumsily hitching up his trousers, while another smoked a cheap *makhora* cigarette, wiping his boots on a tuft. When they saw Aleshin they grabbed their rifles and pointed. The doctor stopped dead in his tracks, hands in the air.

"Who the devil are you?" asked the one with the cigarette.

"Ah…"

The second soldier's trousers fell down and he hastily grabbed for his belt.

"Some kind of holiday-maker are you? Off for a stroll in the woods?"

The first soldier wore a beaver hat and broadcloth jacket lined with batting, while the second had a kind of long peasant cloak slung over an unidentifiable uniform. Were these Reds or Whites? From where Aleshin was standing it was impossible to say.

"You better talk, you dog!"

"I am a trained doctor" said Aleshin. "The institution was destroyed and I was forced to flee. Gentlemen, please, I promise you that my skills will come in handy … Comrades please help, I've been lost in the woods for days."

The second soldier was still struggling to keep his trousers up and cursed beneath his breath. Behind them Aleshin could see more soldiers approaching: Whites.

"My name is Gregory Nikolayevich Aleshin. I am a trained physician, employed by the Imperial state. Perhaps you have heard of my father? He was…"

One of the soldiers hit him hard with the butt of his rifle, breaking his glasses and nose.

"You alone?"

Aleshin made an indefinable noise.

"I said, you alone?"

"Uhlone?"

The soldier, a sergeant with bulging eyes and a bald, skull-like head, kicked him in the gut. "I can't be arsed dragging this bird all the way back to Sapezhnikov. Let's kill him here and now."

"What if he is a doctor? Ksyunin would…"

"Ksyunin, nothing. This place is full of Reds. One less would be no shame…"

The soldiers surrounded the doctor in a threatening circle. One had a long face and flayed nose, another sharp teeth and a long black tongue.

Marya, he thought – Marya could talk to them. Who wouldn't listen to a mother?

"N, nurse," he mumbled through bloodied lips. "A nurse…"

The soldiers looked at one another. "A woman?"

"Yes, yes, a woman… she's right this way."

A woman, thought Aleshin, a woman would save him – they always did.

"Oh ho," said the bald soldier, cheering up. "Got a woman hidden away have you, you dirty dog? Well, give us a bit, will you? Come on, you swine, show us what you've got."

Aleshin swallowed hard and looked back at the soldiers blankly. "I… I don't…"

"Come on lads, this sir has got a bitch! Maybe this trip wasn't a complete waste of time after all."

A woman, thought Aleshin. They always keep you safe.

One of the soldiers dragged Aleshin to his feet and started to push him toward the trees.

"You doctors, eh? Always got some skirt stashed away. Well, right O, Mister Doctor, where's this nursey of yours then?"

"Nurse? But…"

"Come on you shit … let somebody else have a bit, eh?"

Aleshin's head felt tremendously heavy, a strange fog before his eyes. Nothing about this was right. Sasha's tongue was as thick and black as steak.

"Nurse? No, no, no…"

Abruptly Aleshin lashed out at the bald soldier then threw himself at the White Guards. The sergeant knocked him down and stabbed him with his bayonet. Ho, why shoot? In this war, you never knew when you were going to run out of bullets. The blade went straight through Doctor Aleshin's heart: he was dead in an instant.

"Shit – how we going to find that Nursey now?" The sergeant looked around himself. "Over by those bushes – Zernov, Chaadaev, go see."

A few minutes later, the soldiers returned, empty handed.

"Nothing?"

"Nothing."

Aleshin's corpse was face down in the mud.

"What if he was a doctor?" asked the soldier with the cigarette. "He might have come in…"

"Who gives a shit?" said the captain. "Right, that's it back to camp – that sky says snow to me. Zernov, Chaadaev, fall in. Balls, look at the state of my boots! These woods will be the death of me, I swear."

4

Marya dug a hole and covered Aleshin's body as best she could; by the grave she left five stones in the shape of a cross. Inside her belly, the baby was very still: praying for its papa no doubt.

Eventually she set off in the general direction of Chermavka. Her boots were two clods of earth and the snow stuck to her lips.

Marya made it to the post road just before dusk. After about an hour of walking she heard movement and hid in a shallow, muddy ditch. An armoured car, pulling some kind of machine gun, had become stuck in the muck. A second truck – containing a bed of crates packed in straw, along with sacks, rope, and rusted metal pans – was jammed in behind it. From what she could see, these soldiers weren't Whites but Reds. She had heard many disparaging stories about the Bolshevik army – the Reds had no boots, the Reds had no guns, the Reds clapped sticks together to make the sound of gunfire – and was stunned to see so many soldiers coming down the road. There were even Reds on horseback – an idea as fanciful as rabbits riding wolves. A soldier in a brown hen's hat seemed to look straight at her. Marya froze. After a while, a band of soldiers dug the wheels out of the mud and the truck moved on.

Marya waited so long for the Bolsheviks to pass, that she finally fell asleep. It was the middle of the night when she awoke, and the nurse felt very, very cold. There was no light, no movement.

Of the Red army, only tracks and deep furrows remained. By the light of the moon, she grubbed around in the mud and found a husk of stale bread tossed aside from a wagon. A little further on, where the soldiers had paused, she found some potato peelings and hard seeds. It was like a little feast.

"Eat, eat, little baby," she said. "Who knows when we'll eat again."

Almost as soon as she'd finished, the moon slipped back behind the clouds and darkness rose up like a flood. It was too cold to sleep, yet too dark to walk. Instead Marya sang a lullaby and waited. The night was very long and she could see no stars. For a moment she thought she was falling asleep again, then realised it was Death she could feel pressing down instead.

'I'll be in Heaven before the morning,' she thought. 'Won't Gregory be surprised to see me?'

All of a sudden the baby started to kick and Marya's hands shot down to her belly. Something was tumbling and squirming in there, like a tiny fish swimming in a tiny pond. The movement scared her, and jolted her back to life. No, she couldn't let death take her: not with his seed growing somewhere inside her, just below her heart.

But where should she go? It was so dark and cold. There could be anything out there – wolves, bears, soldiers. Marya took two steps forward, holding her arms aloft like a sleepwalker. The main thing was to find some place where she could feel warm. Like a tiny mouse, she pushed her way into the undergrowth, searching out the densest patch of bracken. Among the weeds she could smell the sweetish odour of some kind of bloom: bog orchid, maybe. A bug tickled her ear and she heard some kind of cry. Yes, winter was just behind the door, but the black earth teemed with life, growth, hunger. Marya wrapped herself in Aleshin's coat and lay there as if in some kind of cocoon. To distract herself from the cold and the noises, she began to list all the boys' names she could think of: Gleb, Ivan, Boris, Arkady, Alexei. As soon as her little fish had a name, it all would be true. Never mind his patronymic: he had to have his own name, a name just for him. Everything depended on this. A name was a jug you could pour all of life into. Only those with a name had their lives inscribed in the Book of Life.

Kolya, Khristian, Evgeny, Ilya … there were as many names as there were blades of grass on the earth. Did all living things have a name – perhaps a secret name, unknown to man? She started naming the flowers in the bog, the pricks on the thistle … Semyon, Anton, Osip, Pavel … And the stars, did they have names too? But there were no stars. The darkness was solid and impassable, like a wall.

Marya's eyes closed, but then she felt the tiddler jump again, as if leaping from a fisherman's hand. Yes, there was life inside her, and life beyond her too. Mr and Mrs Beetle were still at work, collecting food and dragging it back to their home. Why, to a beetle this patch of earth would feel as huge as Russia, like half way around the world. Vasily Beetle, Sofya Beetle … rolling their load all the way from Saratov to Yaktursk, all the way to their three baby beetles, Maxim, Sergey, and Lena… Marya imagined Mr and Mrs Beetle rolling up the night into wee balls of black, then wheeling it across the span of Rus, leaving behind tiny splashes of light…

Yes, the night was long, but it too must pass. Marya buried herself in the coat, and slowly counted out the names: Anatoly, Valery, Dmitry, Yefim, Zakhar, Ignaty. After a while the sounds all started to blur into one another: Ignaty, Ifan, Leoneed, Nestor, Nester, Nestar. Names tumbled out of her but they no longer made any sense: suddenly Marya realised she was praying.

Her lamentations burst forth and floated up to heaven – and in this manner, Marya spent the night. When she opened her eyes again she saw that shapes had begun to appear around her, black turning to grey, trees rising up on all sides. It was an astonishing thing to see. Where once the earth had been nameless and empty, God now separated the darkness and the light, and there was evening and there was morning – the first day. A snipe cried out and somewhere beneath it, Mr and Mrs Beetle made off with the last dark marbles of night. Before long a row of poplars shuffled in from the right, sketchy and unfinished, with pencil-stroke branches and blobs of white paint. Between them Marya could see open country, the land green and white in the new dawn. O, to name such a thing! The snow hadn't frozen, but hadn't melted either; it looked like the first coat of paint before the workers came back to finish the job. Black trees, black earth, and the terrifying purity of snow: Marya stopped and prayed once more. The ground smelt rich and pungent, birds scampering from branch to branch, gossiping about berries and twigs and nuts. Marya climbed to her feet and the world opened up before her like a book. Foo, how could anyone hope to rule all this? The world was so big, such a thought was madness. Russia was as wide as the sky was high: only a lunatic would seek to paint the whole thing.

Marya wrapped the coat around her and returned to the road. Where else should she go? Inside her belly the future was knitting itself together with flesh and bone. In time her belly would be as big as Russia too: she placed one hand on Murmansk and one over Magadan. What business of it was hers if men slaughtered each other over this false Russia, the one found on all the maps? It was all a lie, sheer pretension. The real life grew within.

seventeen

1

Alyona, Nadya, Polina and Zinaida reached the village of women by nightfall. A group of peasants burning briars ran to tell the others, and the nurses were met by a band of women brandishing sticks and pitchforks. Only when it became clear there were no men amongst them, did the villagers allow them to enter. Ludmilla's murder had sown fear and distrust, but everyone knew that the policeman was to blame. Policeman? Yes, policeman. Dusya had led him away and then Dusya had disappeared too: most likely the Devil had taken her in his satchel as a treat.

In the meantime, the women had posted sentries at either end of the village, with orders to ring cow bells if they saw so much as a soldier's nose. Of course, the chances of the village making it through the war unmolested were slight – but a much greater problem was starvation. Everyone knew they didn't have enough food to see out the winter. If the village remained cut off, it was hard to see how the women of Chulm would make it through to spring.

Nevertheless the refugees from the Yellow House were fed and assigned to a dry hut of some fourteen women not too far from the *mir*. Dusya's shack was empty but nobody dared approach it: it was too far from the centre of the village and infested with imps and ghosts.

The news that the Yellow House had fallen and that Whites had arrived was, for the most part, greeted with indifference. Both bulls would trample the grass: one was as bad as the other. Just as the villagers had little time for news regarding the Whites, so too were the nurses bemused by news of Tutyshkin's activities. This was news? Polina had distrusted the so-called policeman from the start. His perfidy was no more surprising than the rain.

"If he killed this Ludmilla, then why not Petr – Lepinov too?" said Alyona.

"Maybe he was Sikorsky – and Aleshin was right," said Nadya.

"It's as I always said," said Polina. "Under those feathers was a wolf."

Of course in the greater scheme of things, the identity of the murderer meant less than last year's snow. It was no more than one murder committed amid a sea of murders, one more drop of rain in a deluge. The Yellow House, its guests, the remaining stocks of medicine – all was now gone. Would the nurses ever be able to use their training again? Not at Bezumiye, that much was certain. But one day the war would be over and whether Red or White, people would continue to get sick – even in Russia. What other choice did they have? The lame would stumble and the ailing would die. Everyone was a guest on this earth after all.

The only one who never spoke of the House was Zinaida. She ate little and stayed away from the other women as much as possible. Poor Zinaida! Her skin was pasty and her hair came out in clumps. At night the doctor burned with fever, biting her tongue and clawing at the air. But at least she no longer muttered Alexei's name or moaned fitfully about her experiments. Mostly she just lay on a horse-skin rug and slept.

The longer the refugees from the Yellow House stayed in Chulm, the worse the weather became. This was both a blessing and a curse: the early onset of winter was a catastrophe for any remaining crops, but also served to keep the Reds and the Whites from their door. In the meantime the temperature fell and the sleet turned to snow.

"Just look at it fall," lamented Alyona. "I'll be a Granny before I leave this place."

The Graces tended the ill while Alyona cooked and cleaned and pickled. Only the doctor seemed unable to move her carcass from the floor. Polina fussed and cajoled but to no avail; Yevgrafovna would not open her mouth for so much as a spoon. Once so full of opinions and positions, the doctor now seemed emptied of words. No thoughts, no arguments, no names: eyes that had burned with a steady intellectual fire now seemed little more than tiny black buttons, sewn tightly shut.

"Zinaida? Zinaida, you must eat."

No answer.

"Doctor Yevgrafovna, please … just look at your arms, my dove, there's nothing there."

The words seemed very far away, vague whispers in a foreign tongue. Polina's tone was familiar, but she could not name it.

Slowly, mysteriously, one day blurred into the next. No soldiers arrived – only snow. The outside world seemed to disappear.

One night – a full week after the escapees arrived at Chulm – the doctor was woken by a voice clearly and distinctly calling her name. The voice was gruff, male. Her first thought was that she was back at the Yellow House and Frumkin was yelling for her to help with a patient. Then she thought she was back in Moscow awaiting the results of the latest tests.

"Yes, yes, I'm coming," she snapped, absent-mindedly pulling a yellow scarf around her.

The doctor put on her shoes and made her way to the window. It was the middle of the night and snowing heavily. At first she could see nothing but the large, endless flakes, as if someone were trampling on Heaven's ceiling. Then she saw other, darker shapes: a fence, the out house, trees, Alexei.

The captain stood at the rear of the allotment, stationed beside the onions and the beets. One side of him was illuminated by a sentry's lanterns, the other eaten away by the night. He'd lost weight, his face strangely orange. Snow collected on his head like a cap.

"Alexei," Yevgrafovna whispered.

So it was true: her lover had followed her all the way to Chulm. True, one side of him was gone, and one of his arms had withered, but no matter: he had walked all this way, through the darkness and the snow, just to be by her side.

"Alexei," she said again, breathing harder.

Stepping over Nadya and Polina's sleeping bodies, Yevgrafovna pulled a fringed shawl around her and headed out of the door. It was terribly cold, like a slap across a cheek, the ground as hard as Plonsky's book on anatomy. Yevgrafovna took a step and her feet slid recklessly upon the ice. When she clung to a fence the wood felt like iron. How was she supposed to reach Alexei in a place like this? The sky had a hole in it, from whence somebody shook out the snow. A hole? No, a great black square, like a gash torn into the sky. The doctor looked up at it open-mouthed. A black canvas in a black frame: no wonder the night seemed so terrifying.

"Yes, yes," the doctor said. "I'm coming, I'm coming…"

Her cheeks flushed, Zinaida gingerly made her away across the allotment and toward the back gate. For some reason the allotment seemed much larger than she had imagined: it seemed to stretch on forever, like the steppe. Oh, how cold it was! Snow blew in her eyes and up her nose. Beyond was the darkness. It was as if an enormous black box had been placed on her head.

"Alexei," she called out. "Alexei, where are you?"

Zinaida pushed her way through the snow but the garden went on and on – like a document she would never finish reading. The trees, the fence, Alexei: all were still there, but very far away.

"Alexei," she cried. "Alexei, please…"

Snow blew cross-eyed across the night, zig-zagging without sense or purpose. And all the time the hole in the sky grew larger, a great black square, until it seemed almost to dwarf the heavens itself.

"Alexei, I can't see…"

A hole? No, not a hole. It was the thing itself, huge and black and annihilating.

Doctor Yevgrafovna's body was found the next morning, slumped in front of a tatty-looking scarecrow. The doctor had slipped on the ice and died of exposure. Her lips were blue, her skin as black as a slug. The ground was too hard to bury her, so Nadya and Polina wrapped up her body and carried it out to the woods. There they covered it with branches and frozen bracken. Nadya said she could feel something watching them, but Polina told her to hush. By the time they got back to the village both of the women were shaking. Alyona greeted them at the door holding a husk of bread.

"Whatever are we supposed to do in this dump?" Alyona lamented, chewing on the sour dough. "Life in the country is worse than being buried alive…"

2

On the 24th, the Bolshevik forces marched back into Voronezh, liberating the city from White rule. It was the beginning of the end for Denikin's men. Fighting at the railway junction at Kastornoe raged for another thirty days, but eventually it too fell to Trotsky's troops. By the onset of winter, Kursk was back in Red hands, Denikin's Whites pushed further and further South. And the Yellow House? There was no Yellow House – or at least, no one left to speak of it, which amounts to the same thing. The Cossack brigade who'd ransacked it was cut down four days later, attempting to cross the river near Stary Oskol. There were no survivors.

A Red unit investigated what remained of the sanatorium immediately after the Cossacks left. Amongst the bodies of patients and staff they found the remains of an enormous sea creature, inexplicably beached amid the burnt out shell of the dispensary. The monster – a great mound of rotting flesh – gave off a noxious stench permeating the entire estate, attracting an enormous quantity of foxes and wild dogs, which had to be driven away with sticks. Unsure what to do with such an unfathomable discovery, the Reds set fire to the thing with petrol, burning the putrid cadaver to a crisp (the officer in charge, Pirogov, was later arrested for a criminal waste of state resources and shot outside of Kursk.) Apart from the decomposing leviathan, little else of interest was to be found; whatever medicine or supplies there might have been had been taken away by the Whites, and everything else destroyed in the fire. Among the dead were several members of the Cheka; these were buried in a mass grave in the meadow by a wrecked car.

Thus the history of the Yellow House came to a close. The Reds themselves moved out soon after; they were needed at Kastornoe, where most of them would perish attempting to secure the long-blocked railway line. Aside from the court records of Pirogov's military tribunal, no account of the events at Bezumiye was ever logged. Pirigov's wild stories of an enormous whale were, of course, too ridiculous to be written down.

The Reds departed the Yellow House at mid day. It was a cold, crisp morning, the half-frozen mud gulping at the soldiers' boots as they passed. Their rations were low, but morale high: the Whites were fleeing south like whipped dogs.

As the unit travelled on along the post road, a figure emerged from the woods, his hands above his head, a red arm band shining over his leather coat.

"Stop!" yelled Pirogov. "Stop, who goes there?"

"A survivor," yelled a voice. "A member of the loyal progressive army of the proletariat."

"Survivor?"

"Yes, yes, all the others are gone..."

The figure turned out to be Konstantin Karnivsky, Chief Investigator for the Cheka in Davydovka. Karnivsky explained how he and his men had gone to investigate the Yellow House after reports that the House was a den of White spies. Attacked by Cossack forces near the House, the Cheka had been scattered. Some had made it to the House where they were shamefully murdered by the traitorous White Guard; Karnivsky himself had retreated through the forest to the ruins of an old estate. With only a single bullet remaining, there he had lain in wait, waiting for one good shot.

The Reds checked his papers, examined his uniform, and then handed him back his gun. Why not? The soldiers had seen enough action to know how chaotic and disorganised such conflict could be. The Chekist should lodge a full account with the authorities in Kastornoe; they would decide on the merits of his story. Karnivsky saluted and climbed on the back of a truck.

Unfortunately it wasn't long before the entire Red convoy became stuck on the road once more. After much cursing, it was agreed that the unit should halt and set up camp; the Whites had been driven far from here and no bandit would be stupid enough to attack the Red Army *en masse*.

And so it was that the fighting vanguard of the Revolution wound up in the woods near Chulm, eating a thin potato soup with a blob of runny millet.

Karnivsky had his head in a big bowl of *blondinka* when a stooped man with a long black moustache ambled over and held out a dirty hand.

"Konstantin? Konstantin Karnivsky? Turka told me you'd been found on the road. What the devil happened to you, Comrade?"

Karnivsky looked at the stranger rather hesitantly. "My men were attacked …a shoot out … it was perfectly awful, really…"

Comrade Moustache looked at the Chekist curiously. "I heard it was Cossacks working with the White Guard."

"That's right … bourgeois, um, recidivist …. fellows."

"But you escaped uninjured?"

"Foo – a few scratches."

"And your men?"

"All gone, I'm afraid. What can I say? Tears bring nobody back from the grave…"

The Red soldier, a large bulky fellow with a face that seemed hacked out of wood, nodded but stared at the Chekist uncertainly.

"Konstantin, are you alright? You look … ill."

"Ill? Yes, yes, I have seen too much…"

"Different … taller…"

"Ha Ha, yes indeed. Well, war does that to a man."

The old soldier nodded and re-arranged his cap. "Well, I'll let you rest Konstantin. We can talk later."

"Of course, of course. See you later … ah, Comrade."

"'Till later."

"Yes indeed."

After eating, Karnivsky went off to the woods to relieve himself. Foo, he would have to keep away from that moustache until they reached Kastornoe – who knew what might happen to the fellow otherwise?

Karnivsky took a piss and stared out at the audience of trees. Should he flee or should he remain? No, no, this was foolishness. He was a Chekist officer now, the scourge of the bourgeoisie: where else should he be except at the sabre's edge of the Revolution? His name was Konstantin Karnivsky. Without a name a man was lost.

Karnivsky put his manhood back in his britches and marched on. These trees were perfectly dreary: how was one to tell one from another? Instead he put his head down and walked on. Clomp, clomp, clomp: marching was what soldiers did, wasn't it? Being a soldier was tremendously exciting: a Chekist even more so. Sadly his boots failed to make the satisfying military sound he sought: the ground was too wet and boggy for that. Above his head the snow came down in lumps, the light squeezed out as if from a dirty rag. Where was he anyway? Karnivsky looked from tree to tree and suddenly realised he had no idea as to the way back to camp. A stab of fear went straight to his kidneys. What had happened? Had he somehow drifted away from all the others? He sensed that the cabin was somehow far away by now. Was he lost? The Chekist turned to follow his footprints in the snow, but for some reason they seemed to take him in a different direction entirely.

It was all very queer. After a few feet the boot prints were replaced by hooves as if he had somehow been turned into a horse. Karnivsky took out his pistol. Was this one of Dusya's tricks? But Dusya was dead, her body thrown in a bog. Her shade then? Foo, Karnivsky was a Chekist officer and did not believe in shades. He wore a leather coat and an officer's cap. His Red Star had five points. There were no spirits or demons. Marxist Leninism had done away with all of this.

"Dusya," he whispered. "Dusya, darling, is that you?"

Something was just ahead, obscured by the snow and the gloom. "Dusya?"

Karnivsky heard heavy breathing, a snort, and then a little grey horse trotted out from between the trees, her tail flicking evenly from side to side.

"Yana," said Karnivsky, looking into the horse's big dark eyes. "Yana, my angel, whatever are you doing here?"

The horse looked thoughtfully at the Chekist, taking in his uniform, coat and boots, and tossing her head from side to side. It was hard to tell whether she was pleased to see him or not.

"Yana, Yana my sweet ... it's me! I know, I know ... don't tell anyone."

Karnivsky took one step forward, Yana one step back.

"It's true, my heart! You and I are the last survivors of the Yellow House – everyone else is gone. How did you get out, old girl? I can't imagine the Cossacks let you hobble free..."

Yana shook her head as if bothered by flies. When she saw

Karnivsky's pistol, her big long tongue came out and tasted the air. She had no muzzle or saddle, indeed no sign of reins of any kind. Was it Yana? She leaned a little to the left, her leg a little lame. Her coat was wet and matted with briars and little husks. The little horse watched the man carefully, her eyes as deep and sad as a mother.

"Oh my darling, you can't imagine how wonderful it is to see you... I'm an officer now, can you imagine? ... What's the matter, old girl? There's no need to be afraid. Not even the Cheka hang horses."

Yana's breath came out in a big warm cloud, floating in the air like a ghost.

"Yana my sweet – there's no need to fear. The Red I stabbed – you think he was taking us outside for a picnic? Dusya too would have killed me given half the chance. Did you see how she brandished that knife?. The girl was a crazy one, Yana – you just had to look at her nails..."

Karnivsky advanced a little and the horse pulled back. Her eyes were two bottomless lakes, the edges ringed with rime.

"The Chekist, the witch ... just two deaths among thousands. And how many had these two killed, eh? In a war, murder sinks like a stone. The bitch was mad, clinked. That whole tale of demons and dead mothers ... sheer lunacy from start to finish. She deserved a dark house and a whip, more than any guest. Yana, my love, don't don't stamp your feet so – foo, what was this chit to you?"

Snow fell and the night pushed out the day. The little horse smelt of the forest and flatulence in equal parts.

"Yana, my darling, please."

The horse leaned to the left. Her little round belly shook as she struggled to support herself on her lame leg.

"Yana, what...?"

O, curse that horse! Her eyes were a hole you could drown in. Karnivsky lowered his open palm and held up his pistol instead.

"Ah, so it's about Petr is it? Well that's where you've got it all wrong. I wasn't Karnivsky then ... I was Sikorsky. Don't you see? Sikorsky's a murderer and that's what murderers do. Revolutions won't change that – nor doctors or sanatoriums or drugs. It all depends on one's name – Sikorsky kills, Tutyshkin investigates, Karnivsky judges – the name is everything. You need to have all three or it just doesn't work – even a horse can see that! What were Petr and Ludmilla? Evidence, clues. Sikorsky killed them just so Tutyshkin could stick his nose in. Everyone needs to play their role – killer, victim, judge. Not to have any name at all – that's the terrible thing, my darling."

Yana flicked her ears, her eyes as round as saucers.

"It was all just so dramatic, don't you see? As soon as I killed Petr, then Tutyshkin could go find the killer. And that was the exciting part: I could be both the murderer and the detective, like being the horse and the rider at the same time – um, no offence intended."

The little grey horse shook her head and started to turn away.

"Yana, Yana, where are you going? What is it, my darling? To be both Tutyshkin and Sikorsky: what actor wouldn't want to play both roles? It all depends on the name. One name kills, while another looks for the killer. Names are, are ... Yana, my darling, are you listening? Yana?"

The little grey horse trotted away from the clearing, back toward the wood.

Karnivsky's pistol shook.

"Comrade Horse," yelled Karnivsky. "I command you to stop."

Grisha snorted, pawed the ground, and then started to disappear, her shape turning back into a patch of forest.

"Yana! I command you!"

Karnivsky raised his pistol but the horse seemed to vanish, like a cloud.

"Yana, please..."

It was no use: Yana was gone. Would she blab? Not unless she wanted to wind up in town served as a Cracow sausage.

Karnivsky had looked deep into her eyes and she had looked into his. So what if she knew? Should Karnivsky be held responsible for Sikorsky's crimes? That would be like saying the judge should be held to account for the felony, or the doctor for the madness. One chose one's role and played it the best one could: anything else was crazy.

Karnivsky waited until he was certain the horse was gone and then holstered his pistol and slowly walked back in what he imagined was the direction of camp. Lost? A Chekist officer did not get lost! His name was Konstantin Karnivsky and he was an emissary of the All Russian Extraordinary Commission for Struggle against Counter Revolution and Sabotage. Let the *burzooi* tremble! He would strip such parasites of their furs, their jewels, their names. A Russian without a name was less than nothing - a mere straw in the wind. Little wonder the weak wept and the mad shook. The nameless disappeared into the void, but he would live forever.

Karnivsky smiled and wiped the wet snow from his eyes. On every side, the trees murmured swiftly, like the mysterious whispers of the mad.

Also published by Watermark Press

Carole Hailey
The Book of Jem

In the aftermath of catastrophic religious wars, God has been banned.

As snow begins to fall, a young woman – Jem – arrives in Underhill.
The isolated community offers her shelter, unwittingly unleashing events
that threaten their very existence.

Jem announces that she has been sent to Underhill by God to prepare the
villagers to fulfil a devastating purpose. Some believe she is a prophet and
defy the law to join her God's Threads religion. Others are certain she is lying.

With their fragile community beginning to fracture, Eileen, the first and
most devoted of the believers, decides to record the birth of this new religion
in her own Book of Jem.

As God's Threads gather for the apocalypse, the words Eileen has written will
determine the fate of Underhill and, ultimately, of Jem herself. But can Eileen
be trusted to tell the truth? And how can anyone know what to believe?

'**Bold storytelling, with the satirical force of Naomi Alderman's**
The Power **but its own claustrophobic sense of place.**'
FRANCIS SPUFFORD, author of *Golden Hill*